I0590132

FORGED HEARTS

THE COMPLETE SERIES

L. RENÉE RICHARD

ISBN: 979-8-9920441-3-3

Cover Design by: Designs By Charly
https://www.designsbycharlyy.com/

Interior Formatting by: Designs By Charly
https://www.designsbycharlyy.com/

Editing by: Editing Done Write
https://www.editingdonewrite.com/

L. RENÉE RICHARD

PLAYLIST

"Darkness at the Heart of My Love"—Ghost
"Nowhere to Go"—Bad Omens
"Heart Shaped Box"—Nirvana
"From the Pinnacle to the Pit"—Ghost
"Lonely Day"—System of a Down
"I Know How to Hex You"—Twin Temple
"Say it Ain't So"—Wheezer
"It's No Good"—Depeche Mode
"Never Gonna Give You Up"—Rick Astley
"Willow"—Taylor Swift
"Paint it Black"—Hidden Citizens
"Bad at Love"—Halsey
"Church Bells"—Carrie Underwood
"Hot in Herre"—Nelly
"Best of You"—The Foofighters
"Warning"—Morgan Wallen
"Voices in My Head"—Falling in Reverse
"Ghouls Night Out"—Misfits
"Kaiserion"—Ghost
"Square Hammer"—Ghost
"Still Into You"—Paramore

CONTENT WARNING

This story contains explicit sexual content and is recommended for those over eighteen. Profanity, assault, violence, and other topics may be triggering to sensitive readers. Please check my website for further information at L. Renée Richard.

When the summer dies
Severing the ties
I'm with you always, always
Will you walk the line?
My path serpentine
Remember always
That love is all you need
Tell me who you wanna be
And I will set you free.

-Ghost

BLACK WAVE

PROLOGUE

Sitting in my designated alphabetized seating, I barely pay attention to the valedictorian's speech. I hear words carried away in the stifling breeze, along with my hopes and dreams. At this point, that's precisely what they are. I vaguely hear about the promise of a brighter future because I now live in an all-encompassing eternal darkness.

That's right. I was once a cheerleader, a daughter, and a sister. I look to my side, expecting to see anything but an empty seat. The chair should have been occupied by Evie, my twin sister. I touch the tattoo we had inked on our birthday. Something special for us both, a reminder that we would forever be tied together in this life.

What once was a bright future was taken from us in what the police are calling a horrific, unfortunate accident. Now left alone, I am as dark as the man who tries to imprison me. He thinks he is all I have left in this world. Only his to toy with, to manipulate, to fear.

He may have taken everything from me, but he will regret the day he tried to kill my spirit. I will see him dead, if it's the last thing I do. It will mimic the already dead look in my eyes. I have to play the part, play along with the ruse.

BLACK WAVE

The commencement speeches come to a close. We toss our caps in the air in a final good-bye to our last year of high school. I walk away, not bothering to retrieve my cap from the ground.

A hand reaches for me and tugs me backward. Goose bumps on my arms rise in recognition of *his* touch—every nerve-ending screams in protest. I fight the urge to recoil or pull away. I instantly calm my features in a well-practiced act, until I turn around to meet his dark-colored eyes. Julian.

He looks down at me with a wicked grin. I can't believe I never saw it before.

"Emma. How are you holding up?"

The false concern in his voice unsettles me. An average person wouldn't detect this, but I know Julian.

I give him my best attempt at a smile. "Better than I thought on a day like this." I shrug, trying to downplay my tempestuous feelings.

He pulls me into a hug.

I feel the bile rise in my throat as I fight the revulsion his mere presence brings about. I lift my hands mechanically and return his embrace.

He kisses my forehead as any dotting boyfriend would in the public eye.

I sigh. "At least I have you." I get these words out in one forced breath, disguising each spoken word's bite.

My words appear to please him.

He stares down at me and grabs my chin more roughly than I anticipated, lifting it so I am forced to look straight up at his tall stature.

"You will always have me, Emma."

I swallow hard as I verbalize this known truth from my lips. "I know, Julian."

He grabs my arm and drags me to a black SUV with equally dark tinted windows. A man exits the driver's seat to open the back door for us. I get in without hesitation.

What can I do at this point? Not a damn thing.

He gets in after me, and we drive off. There is no one waiting for me. No one I'm leaving behind. I look out the window, seeing the greenery and scattering of bluebonnets along the roadside. I say a silent good-bye to my previous life.

I won't be coming back. Not now. That girl died along with her family that night. Yet, a stronger woman rose from those battered waves, breathing in a new life. The gale force winds gathered all my broken pieces and rearranged them into a stronger and more punishing life-force.

I am waiting on a black wave, biding my time. Until a powerful wave rises in the aftermath of a storm, unexpectedly leaving casualties in its wake, ensuring I will once again be free.

rises in the aftermath of a storm, unexpectedly leaving casualties in its wake, ensuring I will once again be free.

CHAPTER ONE

EMMA

ONE MONTH BEFORE GRADUATION...

I glance at the clock for the third time this hour in anticipation of hanging out with Evie. I never get a chance to see her anymore. In thirty minutes, I am officially off the clock for the rest of the day. She made us a special appointment for our birthday. She thinks I don't know what it is, but I have my suspicions. She's always been terrible at keeping secrets, while I am the master of secrecy. I've been racking them up like crippling debt over the past few months.

I have her present in my bag, and I can't wait to give it to her. Thinking about it makes me smile. I can't wait to see her face when she opens the gift. Another trip around the sun with my sister always by my side. Nineteen, to be exact, and I wouldn't have it any other way.

I am all grins when the door chimes alert me to the arrival of a customer. I turn around. "Hi, what can I..." I trail off mid-sentence as I stare into the blackest eyes. I try to keep the smile from leaving my face as I hide the disappointment at what his visit could only mean.

"Julian." I grab the cleaning rag to wipe the already sparkling counters. "I didn't expect to see you today." *He can't see the truth if he doesn't look into my eyes.*

Fear.

Shame.

Regret.

"Emma." He pauses just enough to make me hate the sound of my name. "Do I need a reason to see my girlfriend? I just thought I could show you how much you mean to me."

He moves closer to me, and I step back involuntarily. I look around, but there isn't anyone around. My shift is almost over, and then we are closed.

"I miss you, Emma. I won't see you for the rest of the day and I can't get my fill of you."

I move back out of sight from the people passing along the sidewalk, peering in through the windows. I turn to walk away, headed for the back hallway, but he moves quicker and always seems one step ahead. I feel a push at my back as he directs me to the supply room. I enter through the doorway and hear the click of the door closing behind me, but I don't turn around. I stand there frozen. He steps closer to me, and I feel the hard outline of his erection pressing into my back.

"Emma, you didn't think I would forget your birthday, did you?" His words are whispered in my ear, and then I feel his tongue lick from my ear down to my mouth.

I attempt a weak reply. "Julian, you don't have to plan anything. I know you are swamped today and have a business meeting later."

I would try anything to stop his attempt at whatever he wants to do to me now. I only hear his zipper being pulled down as a reply. He turns my head around midway to gain access to my mouth. He kisses me forcefully, biting my lip when I deny him entry into my mouth, drawing blood. He sucks my bottom lip and drives his tongue in. I hear him growl in frustration at the complexity of my multi-buttoned pants. Finally, he unbuttons them and forces them down my legs along with my panties. They pool at my ankles, restricting my movement.

He moves us forward by the shelves and pushes my head down to rest on one as he pushes himself inside me. He sets a punishing pace. He palms my breast greedily as I try to move slightly to steady myself.

"Guess what, Emma?" He slows his pace as he speaks softly into my ear.

I don't bother answering because he doesn't actually want me to. This is just a powerplay for him, allowing me to think I have any say in this.

"I'm going to let you come today because it's your birthday. How does that sound, love?"

"Oh god," is all I get out because, even though I don't love him, my traitorous body reacts to his commands, even the ones I want to control the most.

He reaches his hand around and rubs my clit in circles, gathering the moisture that is instinctually collecting from his languid assault on my body. *I can't believe I used to enjoy this with him. When did he change?* He pulls out almost all the way and slams back in, causing a wave of pleasure that shoots through my abdomen.

"No, no, no," I chant, and I can't help the orgasm that is starting to build from his ministrations.

He pinches my clit and thrusts in over and over until I am a quivering mess. As quickly as the orgasm comes, I am jerked around and simultaneously pushed onto the tiled floor.

"Open," is the only thing Julian says as he forces his cock down my throat. He fists my hair and fucks my mouth until I gag. I can tell when he is close to coming because his breathing has picked up. He forces his cock so far down my throat that I think I will puke. I don't have to endure this much longer as he comes shortly after, holding me to him. I feel it, but I don't taste his release until he pulls it out, along with the saliva dripping down my chin. I gasp for air and look up at him through blurry eyes.

He grabs my chin and holds my stare. "Happy Birthday, Emma. I'll be back tomorrow."

With that, he walks away, and I hear the door chiming, letting me know he has left. I pick myself up like always, vowing that tomorrow will be different. Maybe one day, I'll get away from him. I can't let this continue. I make my way to the employee bathroom and clean up. When I look more presentable, I return to the cafe entrance and see my sister sitting on one of the chairs, waiting for me. I stop in my tracks, immediately self-conscious of my appearance.

"Hey, Evie. I'm just finishing up here. We can leave in a minute." I flip the open sign on the door to closed, and as I walk back, I grab my stuff from the back.

Evie stops me and pulls me into a hug. "I saw Julian leave as I was coming in. He had a smug look, and I knew he had won something. Are you okay?"

I return the hug, trying to convey to her all the emotions I am feeling with just my body language. "I love you, Evie. I'll be okay." *Lie.* It isn't the truth, but what else can I say?

She pulls back from our embrace and holds me at arm's length, looking into my eyes. "You know that you can tell me anything, Emma, right? I'll be here to listen and help you with whatever you need. We can figure it out together. You are not alone."

I nod in acknowledgment and release her. "Let me grab my purse, and let's get out of here, shall we?"

Moments later, Evie and I walk arm-in-arm down the sidewalk. "So, you aren't going to give me a hint about the appointment you booked for us today?" I say jokingly because I am almost sure that we are having matching tattoos inked today. We have discussed doing this for years now. Since we got into high school, we thought this was a great way to show our twin bond on the outside too. Even though we have been adults for almost a year now, this is where the real road to adulthood starts: after graduation.

Sure enough, we stop outside of Dark Tide Tattoo Studio. "I knew it!" I shout while jumping up and down, holding onto Evie's arm. "I knew we were getting tattoos today."

Evie chuckles. "Yeah, you guessed it. Was I that obvious?"

"Well, we have only talked about this day for about four years now. It wasn't hard to guess. Are you ready to get this done?"

"Definitely."

I gather my sister's hand in mine, and we walk into the tattoo studio, ready to ink our souls together.

"Hi, ladies. Just fill out this form on the screen and let me know if you have any questions. I'll need your driver's license too." Lalo, the big biker who will tattoo us, disappears down the hall.

We are just about done signing the required documentation about informed consent that tells you what to expect afterward and the obvious that this is permanent, when Lalo returns, holding a sketch out to Evie.

"I know you showed me the Pinterest picture of the heart for you and your sister, but I modified it and made you something more original if you don't mind looking at it." Lalo hands Evie the sketch, and I move toward her to look at the results.

"Wow, this is beautiful," we chime in unison. I grab the sketch from Evie's grasp to study it further. The original twisted hearts theme is there, but it is in more detail, with our initials in the entwined hearts and our date of birth underneath. To say we like the sketch is an understatement.

Lalo claps his hands together. "Okay, ladies, who is going first? Follow me."

Knowing I might chicken out, I volunteer to get mine first.

"Let's print your aftercare instructions so you can take them home if you need to refer to proper hygiene." Lalo places the clear bandage over Evie's wrist and then leads us to the front of the studio to collect our paperwork. After settling our bill, we leave the studio feeling carefree, as all nineteen-year-old girls should.

We continue our walk downtown and I ask, "Evie, do you want to get any ice cream? I thought we could get some and exchange gifts at the park across the street?"

"I think that is a great idea. I want the usual mint chocolate chunk, please." She walks off to secure a table for two as I am left to order our ice cream. I get my usual bubble gum flavor and place them on the table with napkins and spoons.

Evie takes a massive scoop of hers and groans. "This is orgasmic."

I frown as this reminds me of Julian's gift a while ago. Evie stops midway to her mouth, withholding the next ice cream orgasm, and looks at me before placing the scoop down. "What's wrong, Emma? Is it the ice cream? I'd have that face, too, if I got *that* ice cream." She points at it as if its mere presence offends her. "The bubble gum in there is rock hard. You're going to crack a tooth, babe."

I look at her and attempt a weak laugh. Trying to change the subject, I reach into my bag and pull out her birthday present. I place it in front of her, and this time, my smile reaches my eyes. Seeing Evie happy, in turn, makes me happy. It heals my soul and rights everything wrong in my life right now. She picks up the gift and tugs at the strings holding the box. She removes the top and picks up another box in there.

"You are such a joker, Emma." She undoes the other box and stops when she sees what's inside. She looks at me, smiling with tears in her eyes. "I love it," she says in a hushed voice. She picks up the ring and slides it on her finger. "It's a perfect fit too."

I had it made at a local jeweler. Dave's castings provide quality work and create unique pieces for clients. He starts with the design, beginning with a wax mold. If you like it, then he will proceed with making the jewelry. Like our newly-inked tattoos, I had a twisted heart entwined together to remind us of our sisterly bond–and because she likes them so much.

Evie reaches into her bag, pulls out an envelope for me, and hands it over. "This is your gift, Emma." She clasps her hands together on the table, waiting for my reaction.

I look at it quizzically and then at her. "What is it?"

"Just open it, Emma." Evie shifts uncomfortably in her chair as she resumes eating her now liquid ice cream.

I pick up the envelope and pull out the sheet of paper. I read it aloud, "One month of Krav Maga classes?" This comes out as a question, and I stare at her for clarification.

Evie puts her ice cream aside and moves her hands up and down her pant legs, then places them in a contemplative gesture in front of her mouth.

"Emma, I am just going to come out and say it. I know that you are in an abusive relationship with Julian. I want you to be able to protect yourself. Remember, I know what it is like not to have control over oneself and feel vulnerable."

I wince at the recollection of Evie's trauma. It's hard for my sister to remember when she was almost assaulted in an alleyway. If not for the help of a Good Samaritan, the outcome could have been a lot different.

"I was only able to move on from that with the help of my therapist and the power I took back when I was able to defend myself."

I look at Evie, and I know this is our turning point. I have to tell her what has been happening with Julian and find a way to rid myself of his restraining persona. I *need* to break up with him once and for all.

Evie looks at me, hoping that this will be the day I confide in her and tell her what she already knows. The problem is that she has no idea what I have been through. I shift uncomfortably in my seat and look away. I hear Evie sigh.

I straighten my back. When I look back at her, it is with a new determination. "Evie, I need to tell you something, and need help."

CHAPTER TWO

EMMA

I sit there and tell Evie everything. I see her flinch when I tell her how I suffer at the hands of Julian and how I'm scared for my life. I'm afraid I can never be truly free of his firm hold on me. She listens without interruption. I purge myself until I deflate in a slump, feeling the weight on my shoulders lift. Finally, someone else knows what I have been going through, but is it enough? Can Evie help me escape Julian?

Evie speaks after what feels like an eternity, and I wait with bated breath to hear anything, any advice that she can give.

"I think we need to tell Mom and Dad, Emma." She sits up straighter and shifts closer to me. "I think this is a much bigger problem than we can handle alone." She pulls me in for a hug, and I hug her back, taking comfort in her love for me. She kisses the top of my head in a motherly gesture, and I almost lose myself in the tears that threaten to spill out of my misty eyes.

"I know. You are right. I hoped not to have to tell them and thought I could handle this alone, but I didn't see a way of making him forget about me. I think he is obsessed with me for some reason. It's not love, I know that, but I fear he won't let his favorite possession go, Evie."

I notice Evie's eyes widen, then narrow in anger. "Don't worry, Emma. We will find a way to fix this, but first, we must devise a plan to tell Mom and Dad. They need to know what we are dealing with. This way, you won't be blindsided by anything he may do to prevent you from leaving him."

I feel my sister's love for me, and I am so thankful that she is with me in this. "Okay, Evie. Let's do it. Let's tell Mom and Dad and remove this monster from my life. It might take some time, but I will be strong and leave him."

Evie stands and holds out her hand for me to take. I gladly do, as she helps me stand up in more ways than one. I hope I don't regret what I am about to do.

We take the long way home and chat about plans for our future. Seeing that most of my life revolves around Julian, I wasn't motivated to plan for this before. I feel a nudge on my shoulder. I see Evie looking at me expectantly, awaiting my response. She had asked me a question. "Sorry, repeat that, Evie?"

"I said, what do you want to go to school for, Emma? As a career?"

I smile at her and reply without hesitation. "A nurse. I want to be a nurse like Mom and help people. I will always have a job and could travel anytime I want to take a leave." I smile at her, seeing the same face looking back at me. It's uncanny how similar we look at times like this. Even for me. "What about you, Evie?"

"I want to help people too, but I'm unsure how. Maybe with therapy or just killing the bastards that hurt the ones I love."

I start laughing and hit her arm. "Stop that. You are ridiculous." I look over at her, but she isn't laughing. She looks like she is telling the truth and aspires to be some sort of vigilante. "Um, Evie, you are joking, right?"

She stares straight ahead and replies, "Mostly, but I would do it if I could. Take out the fuckers that cause pain and prey off weaker people. Who feed off of their insecurities and vulnerabilities. Scum of the earth that don't deserve to breathe the same air that we do."

"Woah, okay, Evie, this is getting dark. I would hate for anything to happen to you, and I don't think I could survive this world if you weren't in it. So enough talk about this stuff, okay?"

"Of course, Em. I am mostly joking, as if that would never happen. Maybe a therapist is more up my alley, huh?"

I nod in agreement. "Yep, I knew you weren't serious. You are about as harmless as a fly but with the potential to kick ass from all your self-defense classes. You are seriously one badass bitch." I look over at her and see her laughing. She snorts and pulls me closer, linking our arms as we walk the last block toward home.

Ultimately, we decided to wait another week to tell our parents about Julian. We want to plan how we will do it and the most appropriate time to do so. It will have to be when Julian isn't around, my parents are home, and we won't be interrupted.

I remember Julian mentioning that he will be out of town next weekend, and I decide to ask Mom and Dad if Evie and I can make a family dinner that night. This is when we will come clean, and with the help of my sister, I will tell our parents what has been happening to me and what Julian threatened me with to tie me to him.

Time flies by in a blur of last week's events. The final bell of the day rings and students rush out, anxious to leave the building. I take my time because I don't feel this way about leaving. I'd rather stay where I am if it means not seeing him. Julian will be waiting outside for me while he returns phone calls. He usually picks me up, and I know that since he is going out of town and won't see me for a while, he will want to have sex with me. The thought makes me recoil, but it's almost over, and then I will be free of him. Evie and I are planning to tell our parents tonight, and honestly, this has been the longest week of my life.

I have my yearbook in hand and tuck it into my bag along with some books for this week's upcoming finals. I zip up my bag and reluctantly leave through the school's front doors. I spot Julian's black SUV parked off to the side and make sure not to spark a conversation with anyone before I leave. I don't want him asking any questions about anyone I talk to. Most guys know I am with Julian and steer clear of me, showing that he is one scary motherfucker, and I am justified for having the thoughts I do.

As I approach the SUV, the driver steps out and opens the door for me, nodding in greeting. "Time to put on my game face," I mutter as I step in, and the door quickly closes behind me. I grab my seat belt, but my hand meets his. I let go of the seat belt as he tugs me closer and straps me into the middle seat closest to him. He puts his arm around my shoulders, smothering me with the bulk of his frame, and grabs my face and pulls me in for a kiss. I kiss him with as much enthusiasm as I can muster so I don't raise any suspicions.

He lets me go and stares into my eyes. "How was school, Emma?" he asks with such concern that I could almost think he might be interested in my day, but I know that he's really just trying to see if he can catch me in a lie or to reveal anything about my day that he doesn't already know about. I doubt there is much he doesn't know about my life. His dad runs this town, and his affluent family has so much reach and political affiliations that Julian is following in his father's footsteps.

"Good," I say in return. "I just have a few more finals to take, and then that's it. I can't believe I am graduating already," I say earnestly.

He nods and grunts, "Good, I am happy about that too. It seems like we are on the same page then."

I straighten in my seat. "Um, what page is that, Julian? I just want to be clear."

He studies me momentarily to see if I will say anything else. When he can see that I'm not offering any other information, he speaks again.

"Moving in with me. It seems like the logical step in our relationship."

I sit there dumbfounded because what do I say to that? No? How about a hell no? Instead, I stare at him, debating what to say next. I decide to just go for it. "What about college? I might want to go." I shift uncomfortably in my seat but try to remain confident.

He chuckles under his breath. "Maybe we could compromise, my little pet."

I look up at him and see in his eyes that he has no intention of compromising. It has always been his way only in this relationship. I mean dictatorship. "Okay, Julian."

He studies me to see if I will continue this conversation, but instead, he says, "You will move in with me after graduation."

This time, I can't hide the annoyance in his commands over my life. "What if I don't want to move in with you, Julian? I don't want to leave my sister." I immediately regret showing my emotions and love for my sister, even though he knows we are close. I have never expressed how much being away from her would hurt me.

He turns his body toward mine and grabs my face harshly. "Need I remind you what would happen to your parents' jobs if you disagree with my wishes? What about your sister? Do you want to continue a relationship with her, because I have been very accommodating with your love for your family. I believe in that, Emma. I, too, am a family man, and you are part of mine now."

I sink into myself and think before I speak this time. "Of course, Julian.

I am your family now, but please don't hurt my family."

"I won't hurt your family, Emma. You know that it doesn't have to be this way." He gently kisses my mouth and licks across my lips, demanding access.

I open my mouth, and he takes the kiss further. He unbuckles my seat belt and pulls me onto him, my skirt fanning above his trousers. I feel his erection pushing through the fabric of my panties. He lifts me, unfastening his belt and unzipping his pants. He pulls his cock out and fists it several times. He pushes my panties aside and lowers me before shoving his cock through my entrance swiftly.

I gasp at the intrusion of his dick. He fucks me in the back seat of his SUV with his driver hearing his grunts, not attempting to hide the fact that he is getting off. He brings me closer to kiss him, but when I turn my head, he bites my neck as he comes in a couple of jerky movements. He pulls me off him and again places me on the seat.

I go to grab the seat belt, and he stops me. I look up at him, and he smiles at me. "Are you forgetting something, Emma?"

I look at him and wrinkle my nose in confusion. "No," is all I can say.

He tsks at me. "You forgot to clean me off, Emma." He looks at his now semi-flaccid dick, and then, to be clear, he says, "With your mouth, Emma."

He grabs my head and pushes me down toward his cock. I sigh, resigned to the task, and gently hold his dick. I proceed to lick him up and clean up his mess. When satisfied with my job, he pulls my mouth off with a pop. My head rests back on the seat, and he buckles me back in. He pulls me in and kisses my forehead, appearing to care about me.

Soon enough, we are in front of my parents' house. The driver parks, and Julian reminds me that he will be gone again this weekend but will call me when he returns. The driver quickly opens the door. I can't meet his eyes, mortified by what I just did with him sitting in the front seat acting like he didn't hear Julian fuck me and how I provided his aftercare with my fucking mouth. Ugh. I jump out of the car and walk to the front door without looking back. I step through that door, determined to end this relationship with Julian, and know that things will never be the same after tonight.

CHAPTER THREE

EMMA

I pace the living room, waiting for Evie to get home. I grab my Airpods, and "Nowhere To Go" by Bad Omens plays. I walk back and forth, waiting for the door to swing open, showing the face of my salvation on the other end. In what seems like days, she walks through the front door as I run up to her—ripping the Airpods that I had been using as a distraction out of my ears. She hears my quick footsteps on the tiled floor and looks up, surprised I am running her way.

"Oh, Evie. I can't take it anymore." The tears I had been holding spring free and cascade down my cheeks.

"Shhh, Emma." She drops her bags on the floor with a thunk and strokes my head. She tries to whisper reassuring words of comfort, but there is no stopping the long-overdue tears that are free-flowing without abatement anytime soon. "It will be okay. I promise you, Emma."

"You don't know that, Evie. Please don't make promises you can't keep." I sniffle and try my best to stop the tears. Evie pulls me closer and moves the hair sticking to my drying tears away from my face.

"Emma, we will tell Mom and Dad when they get home. I can't watch you lose yourself to this guy. He's such an abusive piece of shit."

I snort and remark, "That's an understatement," as I try to sit up straighter on the couch.

"Come on. Let's clean you up before Mom and Dad get home from work. I have a feeling it's going to be a long night."

With that, we go upstairs. I change my clothes, wash my face, and brush my teeth, removing any reminder of Julian from my mouth. Evie and I sit and plan to bring this up to our parents. Ultimately, we decide on a straightforward approach to let them know the severity of my situation.

An hour has gone by, and I'm sitting across from Evie, who is sitting on the bed twirling the twisted heart ring I gave her, when the sound of the door opening and closing interrupts me from my thoughts.

Shortly after, I hear my mom's usual call of, "Evie. Emma. We're home. You girls there?" alerting us they are both home from work. The familiarity of it makes me smile, if only for a minute.

I quickly sit up ramrod straight in bed. I know it's showtime, but I am nervous about my parents' reaction to my situation. Will they blame me for allowing this? I blamed myself for not being strong enough to handle this situation alone.

Sensing my thoughts of impending doom, Evie extends her hand to comfort my racing mind as we walk downstairs together in a unified front. It's time for me to tell them about my relationship with Julian. I just hope they can help.

My mom starts crying. She doesn't even say anything, just starts bawling her eyes out, and that's when I know it's worse than I thought.

"Mom, are you okay?" I go to touch her shoulder, and she jumps up from her seat on the couch and wraps herself around me.

"I'm so sorry, Emma. I didn't realize you had been going through all this alone. I should have seen it. I should have known. I'm your mother. I should have protected you. With you now, and with E-vie then..." she cries, referring to the attempted sexual assault on my sister four years ago.

"Mom, you couldn't have prevented that attack and certainly didn't know about Julian." I am comforting her now, and the irony isn't lost on me. I've had months to process the situation, whereas she just learned about it today.

"I had the means to protect you girls, and I thought I was doing the right thing, but..." she trails off and looks at my dad, who doesn't appear in any better shape than her. Honestly, he seems worse, just sitting there looking utterly defeated.

Evie walks toward my mom. "What do you mean you had the resources to protect us, Mom?" I can't help but notice the look of annoyance on Evie's face, which is shocking, since she is always the voice of reason in this house, but something changed in her that night at the hospital–the worst night of her life. She left that hospital room determined never to be a victim again.

Mom looks over at my dad, and he nods. An unspoken permission is given as my mom begins telling us about her life growing up in Mexico, only a short distance from where we are now. I had suspicions, but Mom verifies everything I thought and remembered as a young girl visiting my family there.

I fondly remember spending time with my cousins and Uncle Andrés in Mexico. It seems like a lifetime ago. Because of my family's corrupt business dealings with the cartel in the small bordering towns of Matamoros, she kept us away from them. Despite the loss of contact, they were still her family. Although she moved to another country, she was only a few miles apart, separated by a literal wall. When I explained the situation to them, they were enraged at the monster that was Julian.

"Your grandfather was in the Mexican cartel. My brother, your Uncle Andrés, is now head of the organization." She pauses, twisting her hands around her lap and contemplating her next words.

She looked at Dad briefly. "Your father and I thought it best once you girls started to get older, teenagers specifically, to remove you from that life. We saw things starting to happen, and I just wanted something different for you. I met your father in college, and we married. I knew then that I had started separating from my family and needed to cut ties to deter you girls from the mafia life."

"What made you decide this? Is that why we've never gone back, Mom?"

She glances down at the necklace I still wear religiously around my neck. The one given to me as a present for my twelfth birthday—a promise for a future date. A date that never happened. I touch it instinctively, and it clicks.

I finish the sentence I know she is going to say. "You didn't want me to date Eduardo." I feel a stab of anger that hits me straight in the heart.

"I didn't want you to date Eduardo," she confirms aloud. "I knew that you would be involved in the cartel life forever, and that wasn't the life I wanted for you. I want you to have a normal life. One filled with a future where you aren't in danger. It seems I failed you, regardless of wanting something different for you both. Despite wanting to keep you girls away, my family is now the only one to help and keep you safe. To keep us safe."

"What happened to Eduardo, Mom?" I can't help but wonder at the boy who wasn't only my friend back then, but who had my heart too.

"I'm not too sure, Emma." She sighs but continues rubbing her hand down her face in frustration. "Last I heard, he had moved to Houston and owned a nightclub and a couple of other businesses there." She starts to pace.

"Well, it looks like he is a successful businessman then, huh?"

She scoffs. "Sure. Suppose you can call money laundering successful. Those businesses hide Eduardo's family's illegal activity, Emma. Don't be a fool."

I visibly flinch at her harsh words. Never has Mom used that tone with me, but since I've risked everyone's lives, this is the treatment I deserve. "You don't know that for sure, Mom. They could be legit." I feel protective of Eduardo. I try to make myself believe this. Believe in the boy who was so sweet and kind to me—the one who started to look at me differently that last year.

Evie stands and walks to my mom. "What about my assault? Did that have anything to do with the cartel?"

She speaks with a controlled tone, but her stance doesn't portray the sound of her voice. Her fists clenched at her side and the tic of her jaw tells of the rage buried deep inside her about being a victim that night—something she swore never to become again.

"I'm not sure," she says as she waves her hands back and forth through the air. "I do know that they are the ones who stopped the attack. The Good Samaritan that killed the man wasn't a random act of kindness by a stranger, if you can call it that. It was one of my brother's security details."

"Oh my god," we both say in unison, much like we commonly do, being twins. This time, we don't find it amusing as we usually do. "I knew it," Evie says. "It was too coincidental for a random Good Samaritan to shoot the killer and then leave without a statement." The fire in Evie's eyes ignites, fueling a rage that resides in her, one she rarely lets anyone see.

I nod in agreement. "If that is true, then do they know about Julian? Are they watching me, too?" I start to get a glimmer of hope that maybe the situation isn't that bad. Maybe there is hope after all, but my mom's following words kill that sentiment.

"No. I blamed them for the attack on Evie. I thought it was because of our ties to the Mexican cartel that you were targeted. I asked them to back off, and they did."

I slump in my chair, deflated at the thought that I'm alone. Evie clears her throat.

"What about Emma? Is Julian so invested in her because he knows about her ties to the cartel? I suspect his family is as corrupt as they come, and a union with them would be most beneficial in the political side of things."

I shake my head back and forth quickly. "No. That can't be right. Mom?" I look to her for confirmation, but I don't get that either.

"I have my suspicions that that is the case, too, Evie. I don't know, but he became so interested in Emma, and I just don't know anymore. The fact that I couldn't say anything about him being older because you were already eighteen when you started seeing him was bad enough.

"Before you can ask, no, there isn't a reason for you girls being held back a year. That was strictly a decision your dad and I made about your age and progression that year. You guys were held back in kindergarten. We needed child care, and you guys just started a little before you were supposed to. It was easier if we all went to school together, instead of me working different hours than your father."

Evie and I look at each other, relieved that there isn't anything else. We aren't missing any other information or truths in our lives that now seem to have been turned upside down with the revelation about our past.

My dad finally speaks, which shocks us briefly because he has stayed quiet, letting our mom talk this whole time without interruption. "I think it's time, honey, to call your brother."

He stands up and walks over to me and Evie.

"I am so sorry, girls. We thought we were doing the right thing for you. Sometimes, parents make mistakes. This was one of them. All we wanted to do was keep you girls safe, and we have failed miserably. We knew that when we married and decided to have a family we would have to make a choice. We chose wrong, but it was unforeseeable. We just hope you know we had your best interest at heart."

He takes us both in a strong embrace when he looks back at us, there are tears in his eyes. "Can you both forgive me? Forgive us?"

My resolve crumbles, and I hug him back, along with my sister. My mom comes in to join us, and we start to heal. Heal as a family whose life has been turned upside down with situations out of our control, but not anymore. We are going to take back control.

Mom looks up at us and grabs our chins softly. "I love you, girls. Never forget that. Now, I need to make a phone call."

With that, she walks away, and we stay in the living room, waiting for her to tell us what the next weeks bring.

CHAPTER FOUR

EMMA

ONE WEEK BEFORE GRADUATION...

We sit there waiting for what seems like an eternity for Mom to return from our parents' shared office space. She had undoubtedly been on the phone with her family, letting them know about the danger I put them in. It was hard to tell my parents all that Julian had threatened me with, how they would both lose their jobs, how his father would ensure that they wouldn't be able to secure employment in the surrounding areas outside of Brownsville. We would lose our home and friends, ruining us in any way possible. All because he wanted me.

I hear the door click shut to the office and my mother's footsteps heading our way. My dad, who was outside smoking a cigarette, which we hadn't seen him do since we were little kids, also returns when he sees my mom standing before us. He stands alongside us, and we wait for her to speak.

"I spoke to my brother, Andrés, and informed him of the situation," she begins. She rubs her temples to ward off the impending migraine she usually gets under anxiety-provoking circumstances.

I'd say that this predicament fits the bill. The frequent feeling of doom sets in with each passing second, sinking its claws into my skin as I patiently wait for her to elaborate. Sweat begins to run down my back, and I feel like I might pass out.

"He is going to come up with a plan. He is going to help us." She looks at my father, and he seems like he might cry.

He releases a sob of relief and covers his face momentarily. "That is such good news to hear."

"Agreed." Mom nods, running over to his side, where they embrace.

I fall to the couch and hold my head in my hands. I start to shake from the surge of catecholamines racing through my body in a flight-or-fight response, something I've grown accustomed to since Julian revealed his true colors months into our dating. Relief floods my system, knowing that if anyone can help me, it is someone stronger than Julian, someone more dangerous who happens to be on my side—my Uncle Andrés. Mom comes over to hug me, pulling me into her.

"I'm so sorry, sweet girl, that this happened to you. I wish you had confided in me sooner so I could have helped you." She looks over at Evie, who has still not said a word.

"Please continue acting like we don't know about this and continue the ruse. Pretend we have no idea what is happening, until Uncle Andrés comes up with a plan, and we can ensure you are safe–that we are all safe."

"Does this mean I will have to leave?" I shift back and forth on my feet, unsure of the future, and now I have no plans I know of. While other students my age are moving to go off to college, I am planning my escape from an abusive relationship. How did I get here? To this point, I have jeopardized everything and everyone I love.

"I don't know, but I'll have more to tell you this week. Uncle Andrés said to give him a couple of days to formulate a plan and get a hold of some people to move across the border, mobilize his security detail to help."

"Okay, so just act like nothing is up around him. I can do that." This week is the last week of finals before school ends anyway. We don't have much longer remaining before graduation. I can do it. I mentally prepare for what will seem like the most brutal week of my life, waiting in anticipation for my freedom.

The weekend passes by without a word from my uncle. I try not to think about when he will call, but it seems almost impossible when it's my life–my family's life–in his hands. I stay busy studying for finals, as does Evie. This Wednesday is our last final, and we finish high school. Graduation is Saturday, and I am anxious to get it over with. I hear a ding on my phone and check the text message.

Julian: I just returned from my business trip on my way over.

I look at the phone and frown. "Like I have a choice," I say out loud before typing my reply. With a snort, I promptly reply.

Emma: Okay. I'm here.

A few minutes later, Julian is pulling up out front. My parents and Evie are not home, and it's no surprise that Julian picked this time to stop by. It's almost as if he knows when they are here and when they are not. I hear a knock and go to answer the door.

He enters the house and looks around, scanning the living room. I answered his unasked question. "No one is home."

He smiles and pulls me in for a quick kiss. "Did you miss me, baby?"

I still my emotions, plastering on a fake smile as best I can. "Of course. You were gone all weekend."

"I like to hear that, Emma darling. I have plans for us this Friday before you graduate. I want to take you out to dinner with my parents. We are looking forward to your graduation."

"Oh." I look down and begin to fiddle nervously with my hands. Julian sees this and stills my hands for me. I gaze up at him, and he motions to move to the kitchen with his head.

"Why don't you get us a couple of waters? You look like you could use one, and I am thirsty anyway."

I go to the kitchen, looking over my shoulder. "Okay, I'll be right back then." I disappear and get us the water. When I return with our beverages, I find him walking toward the door.

"Julian? Where are you going? I thought you wanted water?" I say, extending my arms out, holding the two glasses.

He smirks at me and opens the door. "I need to go. Behave, Emma. Good luck with your finals, and I'll see you Friday."

With that, he leaves me in the living room holding the two glasses, wondering what the fuck that was about.

There is still time left in the two-hour allotted time frame when the school bell rings, alerting us that if we are finished, we can leave. I collect my things and exit the classroom for the last time as a student at this school. I'm curious if Evie is done, too.

Emma: Hey! All done. I'll be waiting for you near the car.

I leave the school, and the students hanging out by the doors look at me, giving me the sense they are talking about me. Luckily, I have other more important things to think about right now, so fuck them.

I walk to my car and place my bag in the back seat while waiting for Evie to text me back. Another thirty minutes go by before my phone begins to vibrate. Expecting it to be Evie, I look down and see that it is Julian.

Julian: How did it go? Does my special girl deserve a reward for all her hard work?

"I don't want anything from you," I say aloud, trying to be brave, knowing he can't hear me and I am safe from his cruelty.

Emma: I am all finished. Yes.

That is all I reply to his text message. I look up to see Evie walking my way. She is texting someone. I look at my phone and don't see a response to my message, so I know it isn't me she is talking to.

I run up to her and give her a big hug. "School's finished, sister. Finally. Aren't you excited?"

She hugs me back with less enthusiasm. She quickly puts her phone away and throws her bag into the car's back seat beside mine.

"Yes, but I am also unsure about what the future holds for us, you know? It's hard to get excited with so many unknowns."

I nod in agreement. "Yeah, but I am trying not to think about it. I am too scared. What if the plan doesn't work? Uncle Andrés hasn't told us about what is going on." I chew my nails pensively, praying that he can keep us safe.

She gives me a small smile. "I am sure it will all eventually work out. I just want you to know that I don't blame you for anything. I love you so much, Emma, and no matter what, I'll never leave you. Even if you think I am not around, a part of my soul will always be with you."

She brings my hand up to her mouth and kisses the inside of my wrist, where we got our matching tattoos.

My eyes water at the sentiment, and I promise the same to her in return. Evie makes me promise to be strong, take the gift certificate she gave me for my birthday and learn self-defense classes. "I promise, Evie. I will learn to defend myself."

She accepts this and places her arm around me. "Come on, let's go home, graduate."

We get into the car and drive out of the school parking lot for the last time before our graduation ceremony.

When we get home, our parents are already there waiting for us. All our schedules have been a bit off lately, with finals going on and ultimately finishing this week. Mom comes to us with a smile and what looks like good news.

"Uncle Andrés called. He plans to get us all out of here and away from Julian and his father's political stronghold."

"Really?" I do a little jump from excitement. "Mom, are we leaving? All of us?"

She nods eagerly. "Yes, we are all leaving together. We will go to Mexico and remain safe there under their protection. Julian can't get to you there, and he'll forget about you soon enough. You can even go to school there in Mexico if you'd like. If that is still your goal, they have nursing programs you can apply to."

"Yes, yes. That is amazing. When do we leave? What do you think, Evie?" I look her way, and she doesn't say anything, just shrugs. She's been acting weird today. I won't let her mood deter me from asking questions. "What's the plan, Mom?"

She looks over at my dad. "Well, Uncle Andrés is going to come for us after graduation. Then we all load up into a car and leave everything behind. Just disappear."

I let out a sigh, grabbing my hair in frustration. "I am supposed to go to dinner with Julian and his family Friday evening. Is this something I should still do?"

I look over to my mom and dad. They decide that, yes, I should continue to act what Julian considers to be normal. Okay. Then that is what I will do.

Julian mentioned that I should dress up since the restaurant that we are going to is a bit fancy. I apply my red lipstick like Julian likes and blot it with a napkin. I get a message from him when I pick my phone up to check the time.

Julian: I'm here.

Emma: Be right out.

I make sure not to take too long and kiss my parents. My sister isn't home, but my mom said she should be back any minute. A minute is something I don't have.

I grab my purse and shut the door behind me with a little pep, knowing this is almost done. Just one more day, and I'll be in Mexico after graduation.

CHAPTER FIVE

EMMA

I approach the SUV, and the driver opens the door for me. When I get in, I notice a girl I didn't know was in the car, too. The door shuts behind me, and I take my seat, looking at the scene before me, unsure of what is happening. The girl is kneeling in front of Julian. That's when I realize what is going on. His pants are around his hips, and he is thrusting into this girl's mouth. He doesn't even spare me a glance as he pushes this poor girl's mouth onto his cock, forcing her to take more of him. I hear her gag, and he sets a punishing pace fucking her face and using her like a random hole to fuck. I try to look away, but he grabs my chin.

"Look, Emma, look at how far she takes me in."

I hear the girl whimper as his movements become sporadic and his breathing picks up. This is his telltale sign that he is about to come. Another thrust, and he finishes, sending his load down her throat.

He pushes her off him, removes his handkerchief from his pocket, and cleans up before tucking himself back into his trousers. He tosses the used material to the girl kneeling on the SUV floor. She begins to wipe saliva, cum, and tears from her face. I look at the girl, not commenting on the situation but thankful that I didn't have to please him before I saw his parents tonight at dinner.

"Pull over," he says to the driver, and the SUV stops alongside an unfamiliar side street. "Get out." He looks at the girl and moves his head toward the door.

I looked at him because I initially thought he was talking to me. He looks at the woman and tilts his head toward the door again, indicating that her ride is over.

She protests, but the driver opens the door and removes her from the vehicle. She is unceremoniously discarded from the car like a piece of trash. I hear the door close, and the driver returns to the SUV and drives off, leaving the girl in who-knows-where Brownsville.

I look over to Julian, and he just slides his finger down my cheek in a gentle caress as if I didn't just witness my boyfriend getting head from a stranger in the SUV he picked me up in to go and have dinner with his parents. What a fucking head case.

"I didn't want to ruin your beautiful makeup tonight when we are having dinner with my parents. I did that for you, Emma. She means nothing to me, just like the woman I fucked yesterday on my business trip. I won't keep any of them, just you."

I want to rage and scream at him about how fucked up this all sounds, but what do I care. I will be out of this situation tomorrow, so with that, I will give my Academy Award-winning performance. He must believe me because he kisses me lightly on the lips and goes to lift my skirt. He moves his fingers up my legs and onto the slit on my pussy where he rubs his finger back and forth along the fabric.

"Take these off, Emma." I do and hold them in my lap. He takes them from me and puts them in his pocket.

I didn't even realize we had come to a stop. As the door opens, Julian helps me out of the SUV. He holds my hand as we walk into the restaurant. My only consolation is knowing my life will change forever when I leave here tonight.

We are dropped off in front of the swanky Argentinian steakhouse adjacent to the canals. Julian holds the door open and guides me to the hostess station with his hand on my lower back. The restaurant is busy, but when the hostess sees him, she smiles and greets him by name.

"Hello, Mr. Martinez." She blushes and tucks an imaginary strand of hair behind her ear.

I look over at her and laugh to myself. Yeah, I thought the same thing too. She just continues to stare, and I clear my throat. This makes her snap out of it as she looks my way.

"Right, sorry. I believe your parents are here, seated by the window overlooking the water. I'll take you to them. Right this way, Mr. Martinez."

"Perfect. My Emma loves looking at the water, don't you, love?"

I nod, acknowledging his comment. Keep it up for another day, I think to myself.

The hostess doesn't spare me a glance, and I enjoy the invisibility. She walks off, and we follow. I keep my head down while Julian drags me in my too-high heels. She stops at the table where his parents are seated and places two additional menus on the empty seats that belong to us before leaving. Julian pulls my chair out for me, and his mom beams with her delusional smile. His father looks at me dismissively as Julian sits across from him. I smile politely at his parents, waiting for this night to end.

The food looks fantastic, but I can't taste anything. I sit there and wonder when it will happen, constantly envisioning my new life and the happiness I long for away from this monster. I feel a squeeze in my hands. I look up and see Julian with an assessing stare.

"Are you okay, Emma? You look..." He stops, waving his hand around as if trying to find the correct word. "Preoccupied," he says and tilts his head to the side as if he can read further into my thoughts.

I look at him and then at his parents, who have similar expressions, except his father is staring at me with disgust.

I gulp, attempting to find my words under such scrutiny. "I apologize. I am just so excited to be finishing school and graduating tomorrow."

His mom smiles at me. His dad spares a glance at his son and picks up the rest of his drink, lifting his hand upward, indicating he needs another to the waiter passing by.

"Have you thought about what you will do after graduation, Emma?" His mother takes a long swig of her wine and winks at me.

I feel Julian squeeze my hand under the table, and I wince at the pain. "Um, no, not really." I look over at Julian and shrug. "The jury is still out, but I hope to have an idea soon."

His mother looks at her son. "Well, don't worry. I'm sure Julian will be happy to have you around more."

She beams up at her son, and he gives her his megawatt smile. "Maybe," she continues, "we will have a wedding soon? Hmm?"

I shift in my seat awkwardly. *Over my dead body.*

"Maybe, Mom." Julian grabs my hand and brings it to his lips. "You never know what can happen overnight."

I tense at his words, wondering what he means by that. I find that with Julian, there is always a hidden meaning to his words. My palms sweat as I think about just one more day, and this will all be over. I will be away from him.

"Emma?"

I hear his mom calling my name, and I shake away the thoughts that his words provoked. "Yes, Mrs. Martinez?"

"Are you okay, dear? You look pale all of a sudden."

His dad looks at his son, and I catch an upturn of his lip as he speaks. "Julian, maybe you should take Emma home, huh?"

I hear the rattling of ice cubes in Julian's drink as he finishes the last of his whisky. "I think that is a good idea, Dad. She has a big day tomorrow."

With that, he helps me to my feet, and we make our way out of the restaurant and to his car. The driver exits his door and holds the rear passenger door open, swiftly closing it behind Julian. We sit in silence that stretches out as we drive back to my house. Julian doesn't speak to me. I look out the window and count down the minutes to freedom. As we turn down the street that leads to my house, I notice a bunch of lights and a policeman who stops us mid-way. Julian's window rolls down as an officer puts his head near to speak with us.

"What's going on, officer?"

The officer acknowledges Julian and points his finger at the lights. "Sorry, Mr. Martinez, we can't let anyone down there. There's been an explosion, and we are actively trying to extinguish the fire."

I sit up and look where he's pointing, feeling dread. "What number did you say the house that caught fire is?" *Please, God, no. Please, no,* I chant to myself, hoping my greatest fear didn't come true.

"Oh, it's number 1322. The Taylor house," the officer states nonchalantly.

My stomach drops out as I realize he is talking about *my* house. I rip open the door—by some miracle, it is unlocked–and I run down the street.

"Wait, miss, stop. You can't go down there."

I hear the fading voice of the police officer as I throw my heels off and run toward my home. I stop, blending in with the surrounding crowd gathered around the chaos. My house is destroyed. My life is destroyed.

"Mom, Dad, Evie?" I scream out, my hand shaking, cradling my face. Julian catches up to me and grabs hold of me.

"Let's find out what happened, Emma." He holds me as he stops a firefighter coming out from around the back of the smoldering home. "Hey, can you tell me what happened? My girlfriend lives here." He points over at me, and the firefighter looks on with sympathy.

"I'm sorry, miss, but three people were in the house when the explosion occurred. They didn't survive."

I crumple to the ground, holding my face. A scream releases from my throat, but I can't control it. I can't control the sound that escapes me. I feel Julian's hands reach around and pick me up off the ground, and I move. He holds me against his chest as we return to the car. The door opens, and he places me inside the vehicle. I'm shaking from the shock. My mom. My dad. My sister. My everything. All gone.

I rock back and forth, willing myself to wake from this nightmare that is now my life. Julian hands me a drink.

"Here, Emma. Drink this. It will help calm your nerves."

I accept the drink and look at the liquid in the glass. Wishing I had died in the fire with my family, I drink the remaining contents, welcoming the burn that the amber liquid provides as it slides down my throat and into my stomach. Its warm and intoxicating effects suddenly make me feel sleepy. I drop the glass as it slowly slips through my fingers, which are now tingling. I look up at Julian to find him watching me. He pulls me closer to him.

"Sleep, Emma. When you wake up tomorrow, it will be a new day full of new beginnings." He whispers a lullaby into my ear.

To me, it is just the beginning of a nightmare. I go to respond but find that no words come out. I rest my head on his lap as he pulls me close, tangling his fingers in my hair. I try to stay awake, but it is futile.

"Evie," I try to call out. Her face is the last thing I envision as a black wave pulls me into the abyss.

CHAPTER SIX

EMMA

GRADUATION DAY...

I jolt awake. I try to stand but feel a wave of nausea and dizziness set in. Everything is black. I grab the bed I rose from to steady myself as sweat dampens my skin.

My eyes try to clear away the fog as I attempt to make out my surroundings. Slowly, things come into focus. I'm in a bed that I don't recognize. I feel myself start to hyperventilate.

I go to the door, but it doesn't open. I go to the window and pull back the drapes to see that it overlooks an expansive garden with decorative topiaries. I know this garden.

Then it hits me like a tsunami. My parents. Evie. The fire. No. No. No, it can't be. I thought it was a dream—a nightmare. I go to the door again and start to pound on it. I hear heavy footsteps make their way toward my door. I step back just in time to see it swing open.

"Emma, calm down. You are safe." Julian goes to approach me, and I can't hide my distaste for him this time. I pull back on reflex, and he notices my shift in demeanor. I've never done this before, but now I can't help it.

He steps back to assess me, like I'm a crazed woman escaping from a psychiatric lockdown unit depicted in movies.

"Emma, I suggest you calm down, or I will force you to miss your graduation today."

"My graduation?" I say slowly. I place my hand over my mouth to stifle my expression.

"Yes, Emma, your graduation. I have someone making your breakfast so you can eat something to shake off the residual effects of the sedative we had to give you."

"The drink." I look up at him to see him sneer.

I knew there was something off about the taste, and then I don't remember coming here or getting into the house, even less changing into these pajamas. Why does he have pajamas for me? That is freaking weird. I guess I should expect nothing less of this psychopath.

"Julian, I can't go to my graduation today. My fam..." I trail off, breaking out in a gut-wrenching sob that almost takes my breath away as I collapse onto the carpet.

Julian bends over to grab my chin and makes me look up at him. Anger radiates from his eyes.

"You can and you will, Emma. I am taking you, and we will go over to make funeral arrangements afterward for your parents." He stands again, grabbing me by one arm and lifting me.

"And my sister..." I touch the tattoos we got recently, and I feel my heart breaking. I go to speak, but he cuts me off. I look up at him and notice his expression changes only briefly. His mask is back in place.

"Don't worry about the money, Emma. I will take care of it. I will take care of everything for you from now on."

His penetrating stare makes me want to run as far away and as fast as possible, but I know it doesn't matter. If I run, he will chase me and bring me back. I don't want to be on the receiving end of his temper.

My uncle never did make it to us. Instead, they all died because of me. A wave of guilt crashes through me, attempting to consume me. My choices killed my family, and now I must live with that.

I finish my breakfast and decide to do as Julian says. He expects that, and

I won't disappoint him or else suffer the consequences. As I pull my chair back from the table, his mom enters the kitchen and sees me.

"Good morning, Emma. I hope you slept well."

My body goes stiff. *Is this lady for real?* This whole family is whacked. I decide on honesty.

"Actually, no, I didn't. You see, my family died in a fire last night." My fists clench at my side, and I fight the tears that threaten to fall.

She moves over to me. "Oh, Emma. Of course, you didn't sleep well. What was I thinking? Don't worry, dear, you are part of this family, and Julian will take care of everything." She taps my shoulder as she walks off.

I take some deep breaths to steady my heart's erratic beating that feels like it is shattering into a million tiny pieces. I envision my happy place, waves crashing on the beach, the smell of salt water, and a boy who held my hand–my heart.

I am pulled out of my trance when I hear voices in the hall. I make my way over to listen. I can hear Julian and his father talking in whispered tones.

"I take it you have everything under control, Julian. I don't want this to come back to bite us in the ass and screw up my re-election campaign. Even the smallest amount of questions can be detrimental to winning, despite me being the incumbent."

"Yes, Father. You have nothing to worry about. All bases are covered, and no one will ever find out about the details of the fire."

I cover my mouth before I let out a gasp. Fresh tears spring from my eyes, and I feel like I will throw up my breakfast. I hold it in to listen to the rest of the conversation but hear footsteps coming this way.

I pretend to be running from the kitchen and fall right into Julian. I brace myself against his chest as he grabs onto me to prevent me from falling back. "Julian," I say, burying my face into his chest to hide my expression.

He pulls me back and looks at me. "What's wrong, Emma?"

Let me think about that. *You killed my parents and sister, for starters, assfuck.*

"I'm just missing my family so much right now. Evie was supposed to graduate with me, and my parents won't be there." I don't realize how much I mean those words until they come out of my mouth. Even though he didn't directly commit the crime, he is responsible, somehow, for their deaths. Being with him last night, with his parents at the restaurant, gave him the perfect alibi for the perfect murder.

BLACK WAVE

Sitting in my designated alphabetized seating, I barely pay attention to the valedictorian's speech. I hear words carried away on the stifling breeze, along with my hopes and dreams. At this point, that's precisely what they are. I vaguely hear about the promise of a brighter future because I now live in eternal darkness—an all-encompassing blackness.

That's right. I was once a cheerleader, a daughter, and a sister. I look to my side, expecting to see anything but an empty seat. The chair should have been occupied by Evie, my twin sister. I touch the tattoo we had inked on our birthday. Something special for us both, reminding us that we would forever be tied together in this life.

We had a bright future, all taken from us in one horrific accident. That's what the police are calling it—an unfortunate accident.

Now left alone, I am as dark as the man who tries to imprison me. He thinks he is all I have left in this world. Only his to toy with, to manipulate, to fear him.

He may have taken everything from me, but he will regret the day he tried to kill my spirit. I will see him dead, if it's the last thing I do. It will mimic the already dead look in my eye. I just have to play the part, play along with the ruse.

The commencement speeches come to a close. We toss our caps in the air in a final good-bye to our last year of high school. I walk away, not bothering to retrieve my cap from the ground.

A hand reaches for me and tugs me back. Goose bumps on my arm rise in recognition of *his* touch—every nerve-ending screams in protest. I fight the urge to recoil or pull away and instantly calm my features in a well-practiced act, until I turn around to meet his jet-black eyes. Eyes that grasp onto your soul and whisper their sinister intentions through their penetrating stare—Julian.

He looks down at me with a wicked grin. I can't believe I never saw it before.

"Emma. How are you holding up?"

The false concern in his voice unsettles me. An average person wouldn't detect this, but I know Julian.

I give him my best attempt at a smile. "Better than I thought on a day like this." I shrug, trying to downplay my tempestuous feelings.

He pulls me into a hug.

I feel the bile rise in my throat as I fight the revulsion his mere presence brings about. I lift my hands mechanically and return his embrace.

He kisses my forehead, appearing as any dotting boyfriend would in the public eye.

I sigh. "At least I have you." I get these words out in one forced breath, disguising each spoken word's bite.

This seems to please him.

He stares down at me and grabs my chin more roughly than I anticipated, lifting it, his stature forcing me to look straight up.

"You will always have me, Emma."

I swallow hard as I verbalize this known truth from my lips. "I know, Julian."

He grabs my arm and drags me away to a black SUV with equally dark tinted windows. A man exits the driver's seat to open the back door for us. I get in without hesitation.

What can I do at this point? Not a damn thing.

He gets in after me, and we drive off. There is no one waiting for me. No one I'm leaving behind. I look out the window, seeing the greenery and scattering of bluebonnets along the roadside. I say a silent good-bye to my previous life.

I won't be coming back. Not now. That girl died along with her family that night. Yet a stronger woman rose from those battered waves, breathing in a newfound purpose. The gale force winds gathered all my broken pieces and rearranged them into a stronger and more punishing life-force.

I am waiting on a black wave, biding my time, until a powerful wave rises in the aftermath of a storm, unexpectedly leaving casualties in its wake, ensuring I will once again be free.

Julian arranged everything at the funeral home in preparation for tomorrow's services. There is a small service at the gravesite without the funeral mass or typical rosary the day before. I look down at where my family is buried together in a row. They now reside under a large and beautiful Mexican white oak tree. I'm glad the tree will provide shade for them and keep them cool. The thoughts swirling in my head aren't logical at the moment. I know how things sound, but I can't help the way my brain is working, trying to process that my parents are no longer alive to feel the Texas heat and my sister is no longer alive to… I don't get to finish that thought.

"Where will you stay, dear." Mrs. Mendoza, my English teacher, interrupts my pensive trance, sincerity and sadness lacing her question.

The rumor going around town is that his family feels terrible about my circumstances, and Julian foot the bill for my parents' and sister's burial services.

Before I can answer her question, Julian cuts in.

"She will stay with my family. She will be taken care of."

I close my mouth and fight back the frown forming on my lips. I always seem to be fighting my emotions around Julian.

Mrs. Mendoza looks at me, and as if reading my thoughts, she places a hand on my shoulder and pats it. "It will all work out, dear." She looks back at Julian, puts her head down, and hurries away.

This seemed to anger him, and he pursed his lips. Not everyone is susceptible to his charm. His grip on my waist tightens, and I bite my lip until I taste the bitter flavor of copper on my tongue.

I won't make a sound. I won't let him know that he is hurting me. Besides, he knows he is, and he likes it. There is nothing that surprises me about him now that I understand the complete depravity of this character.

I feel another person taking my hand in theirs. The firm grip wakes me from my trance. "I am sorry for your loss."

"Thank you." I must say this a hundred times more, or maybe it just feels that way. There is a large turnout, since my parents worked at the school. Many people still come over to speak with me and offer more of their condolences. They talk about my parents in the past tense, which doesn't seem real. Another half hour goes by, and I can finally see the end of the line. The last person approaches me; the face is familiar, but I can't recognize where I know them from.

"I'm sorry for your loss, ma'am," the stranger says. He leans over to hug me, but instead, I hear him whisper, "Be ready tonight, Emma." With that, he walks off without looking back.

I glance at Julian, who seems oblivious to my interaction with this man. Noticing that there isn't anyone around, he lets me say good-bye to my family at the gravesite for the last time before we walk back to the car.

It was a beautiful ceremony. Julian was the ever-attentive boyfriend in front of people, with a punishing hand that left bruises around the small of my back when no one was looking. Maybe they saw but looked the other way for fear of garnering his attention. Everyone expressed their condolences and praised Julian and his parents for their generosity.

As we drive off, the song "Heart Shaped Box" by Nirvana is playing on the radio. The smooth lyrics of Curt Cobain ring out as I touch the tattoo on my arm and think about how my heart will always be locked away in a heart-shaped box. I am in a lifeless, loveless, and abusive relationship. I just hope someone can hear my silent pleas to save me.

CHAPTER SEVEN

EMMA

I told Julian I wasn't hungry and asked to be excused from dinner. I was glad to be changed out of that horrible black dress. Donning a pair of leggings, a hoodie, and sneakers, I just want to spend time alone to mourn my family, although I would never tell him that. I enter my new prison and sit on the bed, moving my hand back and forth along the luxurious duvet. I think about the past year with so much regret.

I wish I could undo the day I met Julian. I wouldn't have waited on him and taken his coffee order. Hell, I would have called out sick and missed work that day. I was so smitten with this handsome, wealthy guy who seemed fixated on me. He kept showing up, and I was so excited when he asked me out.

I remember going home and telling my sister about this amazing and handsome older guy that I had gained the attention of. I was eighteen already and graduating that year, so why not? A million telltale signs about his behavior should have alerted me. Unfortunately, I didn't listen or heed the multitude of red flags. I was head over heels and over the moon about anything Julian.

I stopped seeing my friends one by one and only hung around with him. He stopped asking about what I wanted to do and even ordered off the menu for me in restaurants of his choosing. My opinions ceased to matter, and it was too late when I noticed what had happened.

Even when we had sex, I rarely got off. It was all about Julian. Sometimes, he would come home so angry and would push me on my knees to suck him off. I was forced to comply as he fisted my hair and I gagged on the punishing thrusts of his cock. The possessive side I found so hot was now abusive because it wasn't about love. It was only about control.

I think about my sister Evie. My twin sister was an artist. She saw the beauty in everything, except Julian. She knew he was inherently evil. I just wished I had heeded her warning.

Evie suffered her trauma when she was attacked at age fifteen. She was almost sexually assaulted, but someone had heard her muffled scream and struggle attempts. A Good Samaritan killed the men, and the cops arrived shortly after.

The Good Samaritan, my grandfather's private security detail, as we later found out, didn't stay when the cops arrived, but at that point, nothing could be done to make my sister talk. After she reclaimed her life through the help of therapy and self-defense classes, she became highly intuitive to people with ill intentions. She could almost sense their predatory nature and was always on guard, determined never to become another victim. Her last present to me was a gift certificate to Krav Maga classes. In memory of Evie, I promise myself that I will take those damn classes and become strong like she was.

The night of the fire that killed my parents and sister, Evie pleaded with me not to go out with Julian and his parents to the restaurant, not knowing how I had tried not to. It was only one more night, and then we would leave Texas. I go through scenarios in my head trying to answer questions that would yield different outcomes from the current one I am forced to live in. Would he have continued to threaten me by attacking my family's livelihood? Would having money and crooked political ties ensure those threats were carried out? Would my parents really have lost their jobs and my family be homeless? Whatever the outcome, I know he would do his best to ruin our lives. I had laid all my cards on the table when I finally came clean. They ultimately decided I was more important. I wish they thought I wasn't; maybe I would still have my parents and Evie around.

It's surreal how in just one day everything can change. They had planned to get us out of there and send me away. Julian must have found out. I also suspected that he had watched me. The tingling of the hairs on my neck was always the telltale sign he was nearby. It was almost as though I felt the evil close by. The sensation that your body warns you to move. That your life is in danger. The intuition that something is just not right.

That cost them their lives. I cost them their lives. The fire happened so fast, they were trapped inside, and it left their bodies unidentifiable. Now, penniless and familyless, I am utterly dependent on Julian, just how he wanted it.

Julian had told me in the car that the fire was being investigated. The preliminary report blamed the cause of the fire on faulty electrical wiring–the fire chief was paid to say that. I wouldn't put it past Julian's family to falsify a report.

I start to think about my mom's family and wonder when they will come and get me. He didn't count on my mom's estranged brother from Mexico coming to my rescue. Uncle Andrés is 'the Mexican cartel,' albeit a rival adversary. He took over from my grandfather. I can't even imagine Grandpops as a ruthless cartel leader. My mom left that life behind when she married my father, a teacher at the local high school. This is why Julian is unaware that her family is a problem for him and his plans.

I loved hearing stories about when my parents met in college in Denton, Texas. They both found jobs in Brownsville and worked together at the same high school. It wasn't a coincidence they could gain employment at the same facility. It is sometimes hard to retain teachers and staff nowadays. That was one of the motivating factors for relocating to the Valley, as the locals called it. My mom was a school nurse who sparked my initial interest in healthcare. That had been my career path–that is, until I had no path.

I lie back on the bed and extend my arms out. What was the turning point for my mother? I suppose hearing about how Julian threatened me made her see red. The mafia life never left her.

I haven't heard anything from Uncle Andrés, but I suspect I will hear from him soon, especially given the visitor I had at the cemetery. I know they were strategizing and didn't want to wait too long before moving to my rescue. That wouldn't surprise me. Time is of the essence. Perhaps Julian will underestimate him. That's what happens when you're an entitled, narcissistic prick, after all.

What does surprise me is the note I receive under my door, pulling me out of my memories. I get off the bed and bend down to retrieve it. It's my uncle. My heart rate kicks up, beating with anticipation. The note says, ***"I'm coming now."*** This time, I will be ready. I don't have anything to prepare. All I have is me along with my determination to be free. I don't have time to process this. Something flashes up ahead, and I blink as the realization sets in.

Seconds later, I hear a commotion from downstairs and loud footsteps approaching my door. The door flies open, and I see my cousin. "Come on, Emma. We have to hurry," I hear Adrian say.

"Well, if you're not a sight for sore eyes, Adrian."

"Cute, Emma, but we'll catch up later, huh?"

We get outside, hop onto an ATV, and rush out from the property. Adrian must know this area well because shortly after, we are dropping into a tunnel below. He reaches his hand back, grabs my wrist tightly, and pulls me forward.

"Hurry, Emma."

"I'm trying, Adrian." I trip on my Converse as we whip around the corner at max speed. I quickly regain my composure as he looks back at me.

"Almost there. Pick it up." His voice carries on the hot, sticky air.

My lungs are screaming for air, and my hair is plastered around my face, slicked with sweat. It must be one hundred-plus degrees down here. I can barely see in the dimly lit tunnel. Yet I trust my cousin completely. Besides, I would already be dead inside if it wasn't for him and my uncle risking their lives to get me out of Julian's imprisonment. I was constantly being watched and restricted in my outings now, more so since I was staying at his house; I barely had time to react before my family's plan was implemented.

I can't hear anyone following us, but that doesn't mean they have given up trying to find me. I doubt Julian will ever give up until one of us ceases to exist. As we speak, Julian is losing his shit at the thought of losing his favorite possession. That's exactly what I am to him—a possession. He is a spoiled sociopath with a narcissistic personality to boot. He is the eldest son of a revered politician and our city mayor. His family is as crooked as they come. His father seems to have several elected positions in town in his back pocket, as well as other influential organizations due to generous contributions which were only made to serve his agenda.

I see the light ahead, and my cousin's encouraging words pull me out of my memories. We come to an abrupt halt, dust kicking up around us. He grabs two bags and hands me one. I immediately fling it around my back, securing it around my waist. He racks back a Glock forty caliber and gives it to me. I take it from him and place it in my back pants waistband.

He knocks three times and opens the hatch-like door just as we hear the sound of a vehicle's ignition starting close by. He jumps out quickly, and his hand goes back down through the hatch to help me out of the tunnel. A van is idling as we haphazardly throw our items in through the back door.

"Come on, Emma," he says again, offering me his hand to push me in first.

I get in, barely situating myself, as he follows behind me.

Before we can think of closing the door, the vehicle lurches forward, and we take off through the brush into the night, leaving a trail of dust and caliche behind us.

I sit back and take some deep breaths to calm myself.

Adrian closes the doors and then spins around, facing me. He looks me up and down, quickly assessing for injuries. He doesn't realize that most of them can't be seen. That was Julian's MO. He'd leave bruises occasionally, but nothing screamed abuse, unlike the emotional ones he inflicted daily.

"You're all right, Emma."

It comes out more like a question. Adrian is eyeing me with skepticism. I won't show him any weakness.

"I'm good, Adrian."

I repeat this to myself as I am used to saying it. I move the backpack over and place it by my feet. Then I remove the Glock from my back waistband and put it on my leg facing the door.

All my training when I was younger comes back on instinct. The summers I spent with my family in Mexico were among my cousins, who were all taught survival tactics through playful scenarios. My dad was against us shooting guns when they wanted to start at such a young age. Prior to Evie's assault, we didn't continue with self-defense classes either.

Ultimately, keeping us away from the cartel life didn't help my mom. They all died in that fire. They left a life they wanted no part of and kept Evie and me away because they feared what it would do to us—put us in possible danger.

It didn't work out for any of us in the end, but maybe that is my fault. I'm the one who put us in danger. Is there really anyone else to blame? Could there be? Shaking my head at the thought of it being anyone else's fault but mine, I wipe the sweat off my brow with my sleeve. I gather up my long, blond hair and put it up in a high ponytail, finally getting it out of my face. I was never allowed to put my hair up with Julian. This act, albeit small, feels like a big FU in regaining my independence.

All these random thoughts go through my mind. I must have been singing one of my favorite songs, "From the Pinnacle to the Pit" by Ghost. Talk about fucking inspiration right there.

That's when I notice my cousin's eyes assessing me.

I stop singing and quickly feel awkward at the exchange. I look briefly at Adrian and glance around, avoiding a conversation now; however, he doesn't comment on what he sees, and I am thankful for the silence. When it becomes too much to bear, I feel the need to fill it. I rub my sweaty hand up and down my pant legs, rocking my gun back and forth.

"I am just glad that it is over," I say and peek over at Adrian when he doesn't respond.

He tilts his head as if trying to decipher if I am joking about our situation.

I hold his stare. "What is it?"

He shakes his head. "Oh, my sweet cousin. "This"—he lifts his hand with a dramatic flair—"is just the beginning."

CHAPTER EIGHT

EMMA

The lull of the rough terrain takes my mind off my cousin's words. I can't believe I didn't realize it. Julian will never stop trying to get me back. This is my life now. I just hope Uncle Andrés has a plan. I can't be retaken by him. I'd rather die.

In what seems like an eternity, the sound of brush swiping along the van's sides is no longer heard, nor is the feeling of being thrown about in the truck along the bumpy path. The van moves around a curve, and the road smoothes underneath the tires. We stop momentarily to hear an electric gate opening automatically as we proceed down a lengthy driveway. I might not be able to see where we are going, but I have been around rural Texas enough to know what the landscape looks like without having to see it.

The surrounding ranches have been owned by the same families for generations. Some were offered land grants when Texas was being settled and was still a part of Mexico. Although we are in a different country now,

I don't feel far from home. Maybe it's because I'm not.

There is no light leading the way. This is a private road that only people familiar with it know how to navigate. After driving another few minutes or so, we start to slow down. I hear the driver and another person speaking in Spanish. I wish I could look out, but the van boasts no view from back here.

I hear the sound of boots on the ground as the doors to the van open. I am staring at a man dressed in tactical gear. He surveys the back of the van and nods at Adrian. He closes the van door and taps it twice. The van continues through the iron gates, where we once again stop.

This time, when the door opens, I am helped out of the van by more armed men. I stand and immediately catalog my surroundings. The fountain in the middle of the circular drive is out of place. The easy fall of the water cascading down into the clear pool provides a displaced sense of tranquility.

Adrian jumps out of the van with our backpacks and throws one at me, returning my thoughts to the gravity of my situation. "Come on, cousin. Let's get you settled in."

I follow Adrian's steps to a spectacular Spanish colonial that boasts a beautiful balcony off the second floor with two considerably large additions. The stucco exterior and the clay-tiled roof have an earthy look that suits the desert-like climate of Mexico. The stucco exterior with cinder block framing provides a cooling element that helps insulate the house from the sun's relentless rays. It truly is breathtaking.

We open the grand doors and take in the expanse of saltillo tiles encompassing the entire home, sealed in a traditional, high-polished finish. So much careful attention was paid to every nook and cranny in this home, and it is apparent, even at first glance, the care someone took to make this a home. I should know because it isn't my first time in this house. Tia Cecilia died from cancer several years ago, but her memory still lingers in the home through her decor. Portraits on the walls tell a story of our family throughout the years—some I have missed out on because of my parents' choices.

I grab the necklace around my neck, a gift for my twelfth birthday, remembering my first love again—a wave in a circle with my birthstone, an emerald. As I touch it, I reflect on the boy who promised me a future. We were both young and still filled with the innocence of adolescence. The wave reminds me that I can change the course and fight any challenges in my life. My birthstone evokes themes of rebirth and renewal. Like the changing tides, the emerald is a reminder that as the flowers bloom in the spring, they are reborn again, new and perfect. He also stared into my eyes, the color of emeralds, and said the color was fitting. Goose bumps scatter around my neck and arms at the thoughts elicited about Eduardo, despite it being so many years ago.

Rubbing my arms back and forth, I shudder at the feeling of loss. Except this year, Evie won't be reborn. We won't celebrate a birthday together. Instead, this year reminds me of what was taken from me.

My twin.

My parents.

There isn't a day that I don't feel Evie with me. I thought that if she died, I would feel her absence, but it's as if she is still alive. She is protecting me, watching me.

I look up at the staircase that leads up to the bedrooms. I can hear children's voices—whispers of secrets between Evie and me as we slide down the banisters chased by Eduardo.

I always think about Eduardo, my first crush, and wonder what he is doing now. Is he still working for his family on the west coast of Mexico? When crime was at an all-time high within the cartel families, my mom decided to keep us away from her family out of an abundance of caution. But that wasn't the only reason. That was the last time I saw Eduardo. I guess he is in Houston now—a "business owner" of sorts.

He was a couple of years older than me, and I am sure my crush was all me. Still, I can't help but think that there could have been more if we had been around each other in our teenage years. Unfortunately, I never found out. I am sure he is married with many kids. I'm sure any woman would be happy to bear his children, if he grew into the man I suspect he did. Perhaps even an arranged marriage to benefit the organized crime families.

Our families were always together, especially our grandfathers, long-standing friends, or alliances formed between families. I didn't know the ins and outs of my grandfather and uncle's business, but I knew enough to understand that it wasn't strictly legal.

I knew much more than my parents suspected. Still, while I should have been frightened, I always felt safe and protected here. I knew that no one could ever hurt me because I was part of a well-connected family; nobody would dare to so much as attempt to harm a hair on my head without retribution from my uncle.

I felt the same way about Eduardo. I could see how he was so protective of me from a young age. I thought he was like an older brother I never had, but that year, on my twelfth birthday, I started to feel something different for him when he looked at me. When he gifted me that necklace, I had more confirmation of it. He promised me that we would go out on many dates one day. I laughed at the absurdity of that thought. He was going into high school soon, and the idea of him waiting for me was laughable.

"Welcome home, Mija."

I turn to the voice that startles me from my stroll down memory lane. "Tio," I answer back in greeting. I smile for the first time in months.

I make my way over to meet Uncle Andrés as he descends the stairs. He looks refined in his fitted trousers and dress shirt. The sleeves rolled up like he was busy working all day at the office. Despite his widow status, he never remarried, claiming he found his true love once, which was all he could ever hope for.

He pulls me into an embrace, and I hug him back. I feel him kiss the top of my head and breathe in his scent of whiskey and cigars. I hug him tighter and fight the tears threatening to fall.

He pulls me back to look at him face-to-face. "Emma, we will get revenge on the ones who took my sister and niece away from me. I will protect you, and know that you will always have family and a physical home here with us."

I melt at his words and seek comfort in them—this formidable force of a man who promises to seek vengeance. Just as I am going to ask how we are going to get revenge, he speaks up.

"Emma, first, get settled."

He lifts his hand, stopping any further argument from leaving my lips.

He shakes his head, expecting a protest from me about how I'm not tired.

"You have had enough excitement for today. We will get you settled in, and you need rest." He nods to my cousin. "Adrian, show Emma where her room is, please."

With that, he touches my shoulder, squeezing it gently. He begins to walk away as I stare at his back, but he stops to face me again. "Tomorrow, we will talk."

He must have noticed that I needed to hear those words. I relax and believe the conviction of his promises about seeking revenge. Footsteps slowly disappear around the corner and down the hall, where a door closes. The room is quiet as his men return to their protective posts, clearing the space.

I turn toward Adrian. I shrug, and he holds his hand out for me to take. "Come, cousin. I'll take you to your room now."

As my free hand trails along the wrought iron banister, we slowly walk up the winding staircase. The railing feels hard and cold under my touch. We continue up to the second floor and along the corridor to get to where I'm told is my room. Adrian pulls out a key from his pocket and opens the door. He turns and hands me the key.

"You're safe here, Emma, but this is the key that locks your room. It might make you feel safe..." he trails off. "Here."

He drops the cold metal key in my hand, and my fingers involuntarily clasps over the item meant to help me feel safe. The irony is not lost on me that I know how unsafe I truly am. I must rely on my uncle to protect me, praying that Julian doesn't find me. Or worse, make me return to his form of imprisonment. If he finds me this time, the punishment will be much worse.

Adrian opens the door to expose a splendidly furnished large bedroom decorated with soft feminine colors. He opens the double doors that lead to a veranda overlooking the property.

The warm breeze comes in, and I wince when I hear the sound of thunder. I walk in, following him out onto the veranda. I don't see anyone out there, but I know they are, just like the real threats that lurk in the dark, waiting for me to unknowingly walk into their trap.

The breeze picks up, and thunder and lightning erupt in the clouded sky, preventing the stars from shining through.

Adrian brings me back inside, closes the doors, and locks them behind him. He studies my face. I have no idea what he is looking for, but he won't find it there. I have learned to control my emotions and show people what I want them to see.

He smiles at me, and it isn't a happy one. It's filled with sadness and something far worse—pity.

He clears his throat.

"If you need something, please let us know, Emma. The bathroom has toiletries, and your closet is filled with suitable clothing."

He turns to leave, and I stop him.

"Adrian?"

He turns around, giving me his full attention. "Yeah, Em."

I bounce from foot to foot, feeling anxious about the uncertainty of my situation but grateful for the opportunity to be away from imminent danger. "Umm, thanks for everything."

He brings me in for a hug, kisses my forehead, and quickly releases me, turning to walk out the door.

I follow him and use the key he gave me to lock it. Once I hear the click, I slip out of my clothes and pull back the luxurious duvet. I turn the lights off and see lightning illuminating the night sky. I settle into bed as the heavens pour their tears down on me.

CHAPTER NINE

EMMA

I awaken to the sound of men talking outside in a familiar language. The morning light streams through the windows, and I can practically feel the morning dew steaming off the grass outside. We are well into summer here in Mexico, despite only being the end of May, and the temperature is hot. Hades hot. Luckily, I am in a climate-controlled house that camouflages the true feeling of summer.

I reluctantly get out of the most comfortable bed I have ever slept in and give myself a good stretch. My body feels unexpectedly well-rested. I open the closet doors and am immediately assaulted with a wardrobe for every occasion.

"Holy shit." I blow out a breath as I begin rummaging through the clothing, I settle on a pair of yoga pants, a mid-crop hoodie, and seamless undergarments, making my way toward a much-needed shower.

The bathroom is spacious, and the tiles feel cool under my bare feet. The colorful ceramic tiles in the shower are beautiful, and I ache to touch the bright-blue tile and trace the patterns I remember from when I was here last. The mosaic-looking tiles are a repeated theme throughout the house. The bright blues were a favorite of my aunt's.

I strip out of my clothes and turn the shower jets on. The steam fills the bathroom, and I immediately turn the temperature down, knowing it will feel good to be cool before I go outside to see my uncle. The scent of vanilla from the bath gel permeates the air, and I sigh in contentment.

After a most lavish shower, I dress quickly and put on a pair of Converse sneakers. I spread some tinted moisturizer on my face and apply minimal makeup. I won't need to do much today, since I am getting answers and learning about our revenge plan. Lastly, I put my hair into a messy bun and step out of my room, quickly locking the door behind me and pocketing the key for safekeeping.

I quickly take the steps to the lower level, fighting the sudden urge to slide down the banisters as I frequently did in my youth. I chuckle to myself, remembering all the suppressed memories of my time here. Resisting, I hop off the last step and walk toward the sounds of conversation coming from the back of the house. *Is my uncle still back there?*

I reach the kitchen and see many men outside on the hacienda-style courtyard terrace. I immediately notice that there is no female presence in sight.

Sure, I mumble to myself. It's not *a threatening vibe at all.*

It would feel *less* threatening if I'd at least recognized a few faces besides my uncle and cousin. I open the door to the covered patio, where a large spread of food covers the entirety of the table. The condensation drips from the carafes holding the breakfast beverages. The ceiling fans rotate, circulating the humid air that hangs in an oppressive blanket around us. It hasn't yet reached ninety degrees, a small blessing this morning. However, wait until noon.

"Sit and have some food, Mija." Uncle Andrés motions with his hand to the enormous food spread before us. I quickly take his advice, not needing to be told twice.

Adrian, reading my thoughts, smiles. "You didn't have to ask twice, huh, Dad? Some things don't change." Adrian chuckles at my vigor in stacking large quantities of fruit and Mexican confections on my plate.

I promptly sit on my chair and sprinkle a salt, lime, and chili mixture on my citrus fruits. Someone places a horchata on my right side, and I smile while beginning to eat. All my childhood foods are served, and I wonder if my uncle didn't plan this on purpose. Soon, someone clears their throat, and my bright-pink frosted cake is stilled midway to my mouth as I turn to the noise source.

"We should discuss what we must do about your situation, Emma." I hear my uncle talking, and I slowly place the cake back on my plate.

My uncle sees this and frowns at the action. I shake the crumbs off my napkin and pat the corners of my mouth, nodding in agreement.

"You're right, Tio."

I lift my glass of water, placing the condensation against my forehead. Gulping the entire glass of water, I set it on the table and face my body toward my uncle, giving him my full attention.

"Do you have a plan, or do you have any questions for me, Tio?"

He nods. "I have plenty, Emma. Though, why don't you start at the beginning."

And I do. I tell Tio how I met Julian and how he relentlessly pursued me, isolating me from all my friends until I was only with him. I tell him about confiding in my sister about everything I went through with Julian and the intervention of my parents and Evie, all leading up to the plan to run. It was supposed to all work, until it didn't, and they were killed.

"We didn't expect that either, Emma." Uncle Andrés stands from his chair and paces back and forth.

Adrian and I look at each other.

"How did it happen, Tio? I thought we were safe?"

He shakes his head. Regret and sadness are etched on his face before he conceals it.

"I suspect a listening device was hidden in your house, allowing him to hear about your plans. This gave him the heads-up he needed to eliminate the threat. I don't think he knew about us because my call was secure. He must have only heard one side, so he did not know who or what was said, only what your mother was saying. We never use names. She grew up in this life. She knew better."

I think about this and wonder if he bugged my house when we were dating and I initially trusted him in my home. Then it hits me. "When he asked for water, I went to the kitchen. When I returned with the water, he walked out the door, never drinking it. He was downstairs planting listening devices in my house." I shake my head and place my hand over my face. "How could I have not realized it?"

"We will never know now, Emma, since the evidence is non-existent. Everything was destroyed in that fire."

A tear escapes my eye, and I attempt to wipe it away quickly, but Uncle

Andrés and Adrian notice it, although they don't comment.

Keep it together, keep it together, I chant in my head, refusing to show weakness in front of my family.

This life doesn't allow for weakness, and I want to prove to my uncle that I can be strong and face whatever happens next. Except I am not strong. Evie was the strong one. I have to be strong like Evie, I think to myself.

"Does that mean I am safe for now, Uncle?" I take my thumb to bite my nail. It is a nervous tic I have had since I was a child.

Tio Andrés looks at me and nods. "For now, you are. It would be stupid for Julian to come across the border into my town and try to kidnap you. No one would be stupid enough to get involved and help him now."

I let out a breath I didn't know I was holding. "Well, at least that makes me feel a little better." I smile weakly at my uncle.

He frowns and then continues to tell me the truth. "You are safe for now, Emma, but not forever. Do I think he will forget about you and fixate on something or someone else? Not likely. His ego is bruised, and nothing is worse than a narcissist with a hurt ego. No, he will always be after you, but we must be smarter this time. Always be a step ahead."

"Uncle, that doesn't make me feel better." I run a hand over my face and chuckle nervously. "So what's the plan then?"

"We lay low for a while and let things settle." He shares a look with Adrian. I don't know what it means, but I don't like it.

"What's that look for, Tio?" I glance between them both, letting them know that I saw that awkward-as-fuck interaction and I want answers.

Uncle Andrés tugs at his goatee, rubbing the hairs between his fingers, contemplating his answer. I patiently wait, but I am starting to get nervous.

"What do you want to do with yourself now that you are done with high school?"

Well, that wasn't what I thought he would say at all. I laugh out loud because surely he must be joking, right? When I see that he isn't kidding, I stop and think about it.

"Before this happened, I wanted to attend college to be a nurse, like Mom, but I can't foresee that happening now. If I leave here, I must worry constantly about Julian and can't return home. He will find me and force himself on me. Besides, I don't have a home there anymore."

I hang my head down and hear the scraping of a chair before it topples over.

At my words, Uncle Andrés gets up abruptly with fists clenched at his side, walking over to me. "That motherfucker will never retake you and force himself on you against your will, you hear me? I will end his life, and consequences be damned, Emma."

I startle at the outburst but know that my uncle has a bad temper, and I am lucky never to have been on the receiving end of it. I am his beloved niece, after all. "So what do you suggest, Tio?"

He touches my cheek and kisses the top of my head. He motions to Adrian, and he walks over to his father. "I will find a way to make your wish come true. We will wait it out, find a way for you to get your degree, and ensure your safety." Just as quickly as he got up, he heads out of the patio with Adrian on his heels.

No one is around now, and I am left alone to my thoughts. *Did Uncle Andrés mean what he said?* I thought my college plans would be squashed now that I had this problem, but he seemed confident I could. Wow, to be a nurse was a dream, and now that my mom is gone, it would connect me with her to follow in her footsteps. *Would she be proud of me?*

I stand up, gather my pink frosted Mexican pastel and an empanada, and place them in a napkin for later. I see two men coming out of the brush toward the house, catching me off guard. *Will I ever get used to this life?* I understand why my mom kept us from it, but I can't help but think this would have been normal if I had continued to stay here over the summers.

I decide to go back to my room and rest up, think about what my uncle said and if it is possible. I take the key out of my pocket and unlock my door. I close the door, and the click echoes through the hallway. I lock up again and replace the key in my pocket. I put my pastels on the table by my bed and take off my sneakers.

My hoodie crop top hides my tattoo, and the bright red of the colors catches my eye. I lift my sleeve to expose the tattoo and trace the pattern. Evie saw one Marilyn Manson had and showed me something similar. It was corny as fuck, but we laughed, and it was so us because we were always together as one in utero and in this life. Just like the ones on our forearms, forged hearts as she had called them, we stuck together.

The irony is not lost on me that my family died in a fire that night. Evie once said what is forged in all of us can only be created through fire. When something bad happens and causes everything you once believed in and loved to burn, I'd like to think that our spirits rise with an unbreakable strength amid the flames. The newfound strength helps to heal you during these intense periods of pain you feel because you miss them so much.

Our pain becomes a black wave—unrelenting. You become grateful for the pain, welcoming it because at least it is an emotion that makes you feel something again when you were once incapable of feeling anything else. With that, you learn to free yourself from the life-sucking hold it has and everything else that has cut you to the bone.

Perhaps it will give us peace when we know that even in the darkest of nights, when we cannot see our way out of the pain, we can trust that the love we shared is forging something stronger in our hearts, healing us. Something that cannot be broken by anyone who tries to hurt us, no matter how desperately they may try to do so.

My sister. My best friend. The ache in my heart intensifies when I think about all that Julian took from me. I just hope that he can feel what it's like someday to lose it all, and I will watch him burn.

CHAPTER TEN

EMMA

The following month goes by in a blur. I made good on my promise to Evie about taking self-defense classes. It helps to keep my mind off things and allows me an outlet to fight the demons that threaten to consume any remaining goodness I have left in my heart.

"Lonely Day" by System of a Down filters in through the surround sound speakers in the gym. I say gym, but it is more of a training facility that most staff use to keep in tip-top shape. Given the nature of our job, fitness is a must. It has become my job, too, because I am becoming quickly acclimated to the mafia life. I love the family that I was kept away from. There is a fierce loyalty present in this type of environment, where you rely upon one another to keep you safe and are willing to sacrifice yourself to save your family at all costs. I realize that it was always there—engrained in every fiber of my being. The ease that I fell back into the life I grew up in and have now returned to was never really far away. It was always a rolling wave—the familiarity there breaks in a stable, unrelenting pattern.

The song finishes with the last line's screaming lyrics, and I realize that for the past month or two since Evie has been gone, I am finally allowing myself to feel the crippling guilt. I caused her death. Julian may have executed his plan, but that was why they died that night. It has taken some time to feel like I wish I didn't die in that fire with them.

After my workout, I decide to get on the treadmill and vent my anger. It is the healthiest way I can grieve. I've been depressed, and I didn't want to eat. I realize now that Evie wouldn't want that life for me—punishing myself. Her ordeal when she was almost assaulted showed me how strong she was. She begged me to become stronger, too. I chose to seek help instead of getting strong, and that backfired. I won't allow myself the same fate as before. When I meet Julian again, and I know that I will because he will never stop looking for me, I will be ready.

I see the door open in my periphery, and I stop the treadmill abruptly. I take out my AirPods and see my cousin walking toward me with a smile. "Looking good, cousin." Adrian comes over and peeks around on my treadmill mile count.

"I just started," I tell him to justify my one-and-a-half-mile log.

He chuckles and raises his hands in the air. "Hey, I believe you. No judgment here. I just came to tell you that my dad wants to talk to you in the courtyard."

I nod and grab the towel that is slung on the bar of the treadmill. I wipe the sweat off my face and around my neck and chest. I wipe down the equipment and stroll out of the gym, pleased with myself and the effort I am putting into getting stronger, not just in my body but also in my mind. I must have both faculties if I plan on fighting off Julian.

I walk to the courtyard and see Uncle Andrés sitting on the bench across from the water fountain. He has his legs crossed and a drink in his hand. I sit next to him and stare at the water cascading out of the fountain. The calming effects of the water dripping and cascading down the triple tiers make a bubbling sound in the otherwise quiet area. This is my favorite part of the house because it is enclosed and offers security in the hacienda-style home. I hear the rattle of his ice, and he brings the last of the liquid up to his mouth and tosses back the remaining amber fluid in his tumbler. I feel him look my way, and I turn to meet his stare. His lip quirks up.

"How has your training been?" He shakes his ice around, trying to loosen any drops of his whiskey.

I turn my body to face him. "Good. I could use more, but it has been a good therapy. An outlet to release some of my anger and try to ease the thoughts of my family's death that constantly plague my mind. It also keeps me busy, so what can I say."

He seems to think before he responds. "I'm glad to hear that. I thought it was about time to implement some of your plans."

Hearing this perks me up, and I stand abruptly. "You mean it's time to act and fight against Julian?"

He shakes his head. "No, Emma. It is too early, and they will be expecting it. I am talking about you returning to school and fulfilling some of your dreams of becoming a nurse."

I open my mouth to speak and then shut it. After a minute, I find my words. "You mean that? I can go to school to study nursing? College?" I am in shock because I thought that was just a dream. I didn't know I would be able to go to school.

"Well, not right away. I thought you could do your classes here, in Mexico, and then apply to nursing school in another town away from here. Maybe back across the border. He stands up and paces a bit. As he explains the plan, I can see the wheels turning in his head.

"Tio, I can't go back to Brownsville." My voice creeps up an octave as I become worried about being close to Julian again. I wipe the sweat that coats my forehead. I am not sweating from the workout at this point, but from the anxiety. He grabs ahold of his goatee, running his fingers up and down, as he usually does when he is deep in concentration. I don't know if he is aware that he even does it. I certainly am not going to bring it up.

"What do you think about Corpus Christi? It's not Brownsville. It's farther up the coast, and I think we could hide you, and Julian won't expect you to be there. You can go to a community college there. It has an outstanding nursing program, from what I hear. Just take everything here and apply to the associate degree program. It's up to you though."

I walk over to my uncle and embrace him. He chuckles and holds on to me, bringing a kiss to the top of my head. "So, is that a yes, Emma?"

"Thank you, Tio. I appreciate this more than you know. The chance at a degree that I can use to support myself later. That is a big yes."

He releases his embrace to regard me, and I can feel there is something he wants to say but doesn't continue. Instead, he nods and walks off. I look at his retreating form and wonder what it could have been that he wasn't saying. I try not to dwell on it and focus on the fact that I am going to college. I'll have a career. "*One step closer to being independent,*" I whisper to myself.

I lay back on the lounger and look up at the stars. It is so peaceful out here, and the stars are so bright. I used to do this often, but I wasn't alone. I remember one time I was out riding with Eduardo. We would take the truck. Since we weren't leaving the property, just riding through the acreage, avoiding the country roads, I sat close to him, feeling so carefree. My mom saw me and was upset about how I presented myself. It was no way for a lady to be acting. I thought nothing of it back then, taking off with a boy at night. The boy that was my friend until he wasn't. The man who never gave me my first kiss under a blanket of stars.

"Emma, you are hogging all the covers." He tugs at the blankets, and I hold on tight. I giggle when he tries to tickle me to let go.

"Eduardo, stop. I ate way too much. I think I could throw up," I stammer as he lets go to see the seriousness of my scrunched-up face.

"Okay, fine. Take the blankets, but just know you are a little thief, Emma."

I laugh and turn to face the boy who gets all my smiles. "Why do you always call me that?"

"Call you what?" he says with a smirk.

"Call me a little thief." He stares intently at me, so I blush, looking away and quickly changing the subject.

"It's so beautiful out here. I wish I could stay out all night and look up at the stars...with you." I say this last part in a whisper, but it doesn't get past Eduardo.

He grabs my hand, and I refuse to look at him. This moment feels different from the boy who would play football with us and push me down into the dirt face-first without remorse.

I swallow down the lump of anxiety in my throat. "It's so beautiful. I could get lost in this."

He runs his fingers up and down my forearm with the slightest contact. It feels like my skin is on fire from his touch, making my hands sweat.

"Me too, Emma. I wish I could stay like this forever, my little thief."

Suddenly, I am afraid we aren't talking about the stars anymore. When I can no longer resist, I turn and see Eduardo staring at me. I swallow down saliva that has lodged, forming a lump in my throat.

I see something cross my line of sight. "Look! A shooting star." I point with excitement at the streak across the sky. My giddiness is coming off in waves. I close my eyes and concentrate.

"What did you wish for Emma?"

Shaking my head out of the dream, I reflect on all my wishes. I would wish for a new bike when I was younger. Then, as I got older, I wished for an ATV to ride with my other cousins instead of riding with someone else.

That day, though, I wished for a boy I had crushed on to kiss me. Now, when I gaze at the stars, I wish for love. I know that my uncle and cousins love me, but it isn't the same. I miss my sister and my parents, but most of all, I miss being held and protected.

In Brownsville, the city lights obscured the stars, but out here… they are so brilliant and clear in the country. I see a shooting star and make a wish like I did back then. Maybe it's the little girl in me who used to look out at the colossal sky with hope and make a wish, but I wish on a star that someday I can find the fairy tale love that every little girl wishes for. Instead of Prince Charming, I want to wear the crown with that badass boyfriend who would give his life to protect his queen and would rather die than live without me.

CHAPTER ELEVEN

EDUARDO

She bobs her head up and down on my cock. Her red lipstick smudges all over her mouth and my dick. Her nickname is Cherry Pop. She always orders a rum and coke with cherries as her signature drink. That, along with the cherry-red lipstick, and you get the picture. The joke isn't lost on me that this is far from the first time Cherry was a virgin. Her saliva is pooling down her chin. I am almost about to come when she looks up at me with those big green eyes. *Fuck*. I shut my eyes and stop thrusting, pulling my cock out of her mouth as her teeth scrape the underside of it. I hiss in response. She immediately stands up and puts her hand on my chest.

"Eduardo, what's wrong, baby? You were about to come. I could feel it. Can I–"

I don't give her a second to finish her sentence as I turn her around facedown on my desk. I push her skirt and panties down as they remain stationary around her knees, restricting any further leg movement. I push my cock into her pussy without much warning. I mean, if she doesn't understand what is happening here, then she is dense.

Cherry grips the end of my desk and holds on for the ride. I lift her slightly by placing one arm under her hips. The position allows me to have a firm grip, keeping her in place. It also allows a better angle for me to fuck her. I fist her ponytail with the other hand and pull, causing her back to arch toward me. Cherry starts to groan, and I slow my thrusts, trying to get back to the feeling I had of almost coming before she looked at me. The familiar green eye color of a girl I've wanted to forget about—a girl I was told to forget about. If I did, she would be safe.

"Please, Eduardo, if you care about my daughter, you will forget about her. I don't want this life for her. You are going to start high school and meet girls your age. She's too young for you now anyway."

She looks at me, thinking I will say, sure, okay. I'll stay away from Emma. My little thief. "I'm sorry, Mrs. Ortiz, but I can't do that."

She quickly corrects me. Frowning, she replies, "It's Mrs. Taylor, Eduardo." I know this, but she tries to forget where she came from, and I quickly remind her that she is just like me, as much as Mrs. Ortiz-Taylor doesn't want to admit it—born into the same life. The same rules. The same mafia-style family.

"I figured you would say that." She looks me up and down disapprovingly and walks away.

When I returned the following summer to be close to Emma, she didn't return. Her uncle said that her parents broke ties with the family to give the girls what he quoted from her mother "A normal life." That was the last summer I saw Emma. My dad made me promise to respect the family's wishes, but the consequences be damned. My heart be damned. It wants what it wants, right?

High school came and went in a blur. I had my share of girls, but nothing in the form of a relationship. If I couldn't have the one girl I wanted, then I would go through it alone.

When I went to college, I moved to Houston, Texas. I was in a fraternity and made great friends who quickly became my frat brothers. Many of them I still talk to. I focused on the family businesses and, more importantly, made myself a name in the industry.

I own a few companies. One is a gym/fitness center, and the other is a nightclub—the one where I am supposed to blow my load into a bartender's red-lipped mouth. Instead, I had to turn her away from facing me because I was having flashbacks. Fucking triggers.

You know that saying you shouldn't eat where you shit? Well, I should take my advice, or it will come back to bite me in the ass.

I pick up my pace, and Cherry moans like a porn star. "Oh god, baby. Just like that. Harder. Faster."

I fight the urge not to roll my eyes and give the woman what she wants. Her breath turns into a high-pitched cry as her pussy quivers. My phone rings, and I stare at the name on the screen. Ramiro. Fabulous, what does my brother want now?

I pick up the phone mid-thrust, and the sound of skin slapping skin can be heard throughout the room. "Ram," I answer the call.

"Hey, dick," My brother responds. "What the..." he trails off.

Cherry's walls tighten around me, gripping my dick like a glove, and I come shortly after. Her breathing is all quick pants and then a moan in satisfaction as she falls on the desk with a grunt. She giggles.

"Baby, you fuck me so good."

I pull out of her and discard the condom in the trash. I pat her ass twice, letting her know the fun ride is over and please use the quickest exit line out the closest door. She stands still, looking over at me, and I move my head, tilting it toward the door. She gets the hint, tugs her panties upward, and pulls her skirt down. She goes to speak, but I cut her off, shaking my head. I point my finger at the door.

"Out, Cherry. Now." She nods and quickly exits. I hear my brother chuckle on the other line.

"You didn't have to pick up the phone, you know." He laughs into the receiver.

"Well, I knew you would just call back, so I was avoiding the hassle of having to hear the phone ring repeatedly."

"True, true," he quickly admits. "Cherry, huh?" His laugh intensifies.

I snort. "I know, right." He doesn't even have to comment further about the name. I've already heard it. "So, tell me, brother, what has you interrupting my nighttime club activities this late evening?"

He waits for a minute and clears his voice. His pause before speaking concerns me because my brother has no filter. The fact that he wants to choose his words has me quickly perking up with increasing paranoia.

"Ram, is everything okay? You sound serious." I worry because my brother is the biggest asshole to mostly everyone, except twin girls we both adored. Once upon a time, a long time ago. And, of course, our mother. "Is it Mom? Is Mom okay?" My voice rises as I try to calm the sound of panic rising in my throat. "Who do I have to kill?" I say in a low growl. It sounds like a joke, but I am far from joking.

He clears his throat. "I came upon some news today and reached out as soon as possible. I had to gather more details before I called you." His voice sounds different, sad even.

"Just spit it out already," I say, becoming more pissed off by the second. My anxiety skyrockets.

And he does. I just can't believe what he tells me. "Can you repeat that, Ram?"

"I talked to Dad today, and he informed me that the Ortiz family is mourning."

My stomach twists in knots. "Who died, Ram?"

"The Taylor Family," he says quickly, "but there was one survivor."

I wait for him to tell me what I pray is the one person I need to be okay. Please, God, I say in a silent prayer.

"Emma."

I let out a breath. "Emma is alive?" I ask quickly for confirmation. I grip the desk, hanging my head down. "Thank fuck. Thank fuck," I pant out in a whispered prayer to anyone who will listen. It is all I manage to get out before I can process the severity of the situation. "Tell me what you know."

We go back and forth on the phone, and Ram tells me that Emma's parents and sister, Evie, died in a house fire that destroyed everything. The house burned to the ground, with only one survivor. Emma was apparently out to dinner. She was spotted at a restaurant in town when the fire occurred. Talk about luck.

"What caused the fire, Ram?" I can hear his fingers drumming on the desk as he builds momentum—anticipation awaits his following words.

"That's just it, Eduardo. The fire chief reported it to be faulty wiring. It was an electrical fire, and it just spread too quickly. They were trapped inside and could not get out. They died of smoke inhalation before being rescued and passed out before being burned to ashes."

I cringe at the details of the accident. "They just couldn't get out? That seems all kinds of suspect if you ask me."

I can see Ram sitting at his desk thinking the same thing I am right now. Going through the scenario, it just doesn't add up. "The math isn't mathing."

"It was investigated though?" I need to know more details.

"Yep," he replies unconvincingly. "That's what they reported, but then the weird thing is that Emma just disappeared."

I sit up quickly upon hearing this. "What do you mean disappeared?" I try not to become upset because my brother is the messenger. Don't kill the messenger, right? But if I could reach into the phone and wring his fucking neck... He didn't do anything wrong. He didn't, but someone did.

"People are talking and saying that she is back in Mexico under the protection of her family, but no one has seen her.

I stand abruptly. "We have to find her!" I scream, slamming my fist against the desk. "We have to find Emma. We have to do something."

"Eduardo," he says, attempting to soothe me, "she doesn't want to be found. Her family doesn't want her to be found. Don't you get that?"

I run my hand down my face. "Emma's family is dead, Ram. How am I not supposed to worry about her." I feel my voice cracking.

"If you care about her, you will let her go, Eduardo." I can hear her mom speaking to me with determination. *"You will always be a part of this life. I want my daughter to have a normal life. One with school activities, prom, college, and a normal marriage with someone who helps her raise their kids. Someone who doesn't put a target on her back and put their family in danger. Risking their lives because of the life they were born into."*

I shake my head, not even trying to pretend that I will do this. "I'm sorry, Mrs. Taylor. I just can't let her go.

"I thought you might say that. But you see, you don't have a choice."

She leaves me there dumbfounded as she walks away, never to return to the house in Mexico again because I was dangerous. All because she thought I could get her killed.

The irony isn't lost on me that everything her mother tried to keep her away from was the one thing that could have saved her. I don't know what happened to get them killed, but it is clear that foul play was involved. I wouldn't be surprised to learn that the fire chief was paid off to falsify the report.

"Eduardo?" I hear Ram breaking through my thoughts as I try to make sense of this devastating news. "Are you still there? You are too quiet."

"Yeah, I'm still here. I'm just trying to wrap my head around the sequence of events. It seems fishy, but I don't know anything about it. I haven't talked to Emma in years, and now, how do I find her?"

I hear Ram let out a sigh on the other line. "We have to wait it out, brother. We wait and see what we can discover or hear from the families. If her uncle is protecting her, we will know sooner or later. That is, if they want us to know at all."

"Yeah, you're right." I agree with Ram because having him think I won't be a problem is best. I only want to find her and make sure she is okay.

"Besides," he continues, "you haven't even seen her in forever. You don't even know what she looks like anymore. How she is."

The truth is almost on the tip of my tongue, trying to break free and announce that I stalked her. Well, I stalked her socials and even saw her once through the window of a coffee shop. Emma had just started working there. She turned into such a beautiful woman. What had me smitten was her infectious laugh. She threw her head back and laughed animatedly with her hands, throwing them left and right to accentuate her point when telling a story or rehashing an event. So full of energy, so alive. "Thank god she is alive," I whisper.

"Eduardo? Are you still there?"

His words snap me out of my memories. "True, Ram." I clear my throat, wanting to end this conversation already. "Will you keep me posted on anything you hear?"

"Of course. Be safe, Eduardo." With that, he hangs up, and I do the same.

I am standing there unblinking at the oddity of the situation. I place my hand on my desk and lean over. My breathing picks up as the anger starts to seep over. I see a wet spot on some papers, probably from where Cherry came on my desk as I fucked her from behind. Because I couldn't look her in the eyes. Eyes that reminded me too much of the emerald-green ones I stared at once long ago and couldn't get enough of.

Anger rushes through me, and I hurl all the items off my desk. They fall and crash on the floor in a thunderous clatter. Any items initially missed from that first pass, I sweep off my desk until it is free of anything, and my mind remains full of everything that is Emma.

CHAPTER TWELVE

EMMA

PRESENT DAY...

After a few more minutes, my best friend Liv will be here to relieve me from this shift. I am looking forward to hanging out with the girls tonight. It's too bad that Liv has to work the night shift and won't be going out with us. We are all giving one last hurrah to spring break on Padre Island.

Liv and I graduated nursing school together and have been inseparable ever since. I didn't know anyone when I moved here, and she immediately brought me into her circle of besties. Immediately, they treated me like I was part of their gang of friends. I gathered that they all knew each other from grade school or at least high school and were a close-knit group.

Liv and I attended a recruitment event hosted by the hospital and decided to accept the positions immediately. We took a sign-on bonus after graduating, which helped since we had not been working while we were in school full-time. I took the offered day shift, and Liv took the much despised night shift. She is going to school to finish her baccalaureate degree in nursing and is already accepted into a nurse practitioner program, pending graduation in a couple of months. I am beyond proud of that girl. I'd be even prouder if she got her ass in here and relieved me from this god-awful shift.

I would like nothing more than to take a scorching-hot shower and scrape this pestilence off my body. I still smell that poor man's rotting toes in my nose. The stench was overwhelming, and I tried not to let him know that I wanted to gag right then and there. I shiver at the thought.

Dr. Hall, the never-ending flirt, throws his arm around my shoulders and pulls me toward the clock, pointing at it jokingly. I know he mostly means nothing by the action, and I have told him repeatedly that I was not interested in dating him. Dating a coworker or someone in a higher position of power is always a recipe for disaster. They hold all the authority over you, and I never want to be in that situation again.

I frown, and Dr. Hall seems to notice. "Are you okay, Emma? You seemed upset just a second ago."

I immediately school my features, and my mask falls back into place. I smile radiantly at Dr. Hall while simultaneously scooting out from his claustrophobia-inducing side shoulder hug.

"Of course I am. Do you see the clock?" Now that I am free from his restrictive hold, I point animatedly at it, waving my hands. "I am almost out of here, Ethan."

He smiles at my use of his first name when answering him. I knew he would like that, and it was a good distraction from asking pointed questions about my previous mood.

"If you'll excuse me, sir, I must finish some last-minute things before my shift relief person arrives." I see him eye me hungrily at my use of the word sir before nodding and walking away. I laugh to myself. Men are so predictable sometimes.

Walking to the medication dispenser, I see a tall girl nod at me. She heads my way with her long, wavy hair bouncing along her shoulders and honey-brown eyes holding back laughter.

"There you are, girl. I am here to relieve you. I witnessed that encounter with you and Dr. Hall, by the way." She bounces back and forth on her toes in a playful manner, much like the cat that caught the canary.

I give her the biggest smile because she just made my night. Ignoring her quest for more information about Ethan, I deflect. "Thank god you're here.

It's been hell today."

Liv attempts to stifle a laugh but fails miserably. "You say that every shift, Emma."

"I only say that because it's true," I counter. I carefully finish counting the narcotics in the bin before closing it. "I hope your night is better, but looking at the stacks of pending charts..." I trail off, giving her a sympathetic frown.

"Judging by the waiting room as I entered this place, I think I'm forever and eternally fucked tonight." Liv brings her hand to her temple with what I think is a weak attempt to ward off an impending headache.

I fling my arm around my best friend, but it is more like around her back because, damn, that girl is tall. "Well, let's hope nothing memorable happens." I release her side and push my remaining charts into her hands. Liv groans.

"Come on, Liv, I'll give you a report on my patients. Room ten has some pain meds ordered, and I'll give her those before I leave. Can you reassess her pain in a bit?" I walk away with a little skip in my step, knowing my shift is almost done for the evening. "I'll be back in a few minutes to give you a report on the rest of my patients. The sooner I do, the sooner I can get my drink tonight."

I finish my last remaining task and go to find Liv again. I am finishing my sign-out when I realize she is only half listening. I stop mid-sentence, scanning her eyes for clues as to why she is so distracted. If I had to gamble money on it, I bet it would be about her on-and-off-again boyfriend, Brodie. Now there's a douche canoe if I ever met one. But, hey? What can I do but support my friend in her bad decisions? I am certainly not one to advise about the best choices, considering all I lost because of it. I quickly shut that thought down; instead, I refocus on Liv.

"You know that we will all miss you tonight, right? It's the last time for a long time that we can get together."

"You have no idea how jealous I am right now, Em." I put both arms out and up toward her much taller stature and pull my girl in for a big embrace.

Liv reminds me that she will see us tomorrow and to take plenty of pics so it will seem like she is there with us. "Of course, you know I will. I expect to meet up with the whole gang tonight and will send you a ton of pics." I remind her about going straight to bed after her shift because I am only giving her a few hours of sleep before I pick her up for the last days of spring break on Padre Island. I grab my stuff by slinging my tote around my shoulder.

"I expect a large iced coffee and a greasy breakfast burrito when you pick me up."

That cracks me up because as much as Liv eats, the girl doesn't gain an ounce of weight. Ugh.

"Naturally," I retort. "Only the breakfast of champions for my bestie." I wave my hands over my head in a good-bye as I exit.

I spare one last glance at Liv to witness Dr. Hall's attention on her. He sends me a playful wink. I roll my eyes, turning my head toward the revolving door. I put on my sunglasses and take a cleansing breath of fresh, salty air before I head out into the Texas sun.

I place my scrubs in the sanitizing cycle of the washer and walk naked into the bathroom to take a scalding-hot shower. The hot water does wonders to wake my body up after working a grueling twelve-hour shift and rid my body of the emergency department germs. I sigh in contentment as I step onto my bedroom's fluffy faux fur rug. The apartment is cool, and the scent of lavender in the infuser provides a sense of calm energy as I scan the contents of my closet for an outfit to wear tonight. I hear my phone sound with an incoming text.

Ainsley and Val: Hey, girl. Running a bit later. See you in an hour.*Kissing emoji.

Emma: Alrighty.

I relax, knowing that I can count on the girls to never be here on time. I have a little longer to decompress. I make my way into the kitchen with a little skip in my step as I grab my favorite bottle of red and pour myself a glass of Freakshow wine.

I return to my closet and stare at the choices. I'm resolved to play some music. Walking over to my speaker, I hit my favorite song. Twin Temple's "I Know How to Hex You" blares out through the Bluetooth speaker. I sway back and forth to the rock and roll doo-wop sounds of Alexandra James's sultry voice.

I finish up my glass of wine and decide on a black romper with a fishnet-looking top. I braid each side of my hair and twist it back into a messy ponytail. I pair it with some black patent wedge loafers. I hate that my life has become shoes I could potentially run in, but better safe than sorry.

Looking down at the wedged heel, I wonder if maybe I should change into my Converse sneakers. Hm. What should I do? Fuck my life.

I resist the urge to channel my sensible side by pouring another glass of wine. As I place the glass on my bedside table out of sight, I notice the dark-purple lipstick residue lingers on the edge of it, and I go to the mirror to reapply more before I leave. I hear a knock at the door, and I quickly throw my lipstick in my purse before heading to answer it. I don't have to look to see who it is because Ainsley and Val are so loud.

I open the door with a flourish, and they come barging in. "Hey, Em!" they both say in unison, hugging me from each side. I lift my arms and gather them for a group hug, rocking each other back and forth.

"Are you ready to go?" Ainsley asks, releasing me as Val barrels toward the bathroom.

"Just gotta pee before we go," she yells, already shutting the door.

"I swear that girl has a squirrel bladder." Ainsley throws her hand over her forehead, shaking her head back and forth. She turns her attention to me. "You look nice."

She eyes my outfit, and I chuckle at her accusatory tone. They are both wearing flip-flops and tiny sundresses. It is the typical outfit here because it is so hot. I reserved that for my bathing suit at the beach. Of course, they just throw on little shorts and no shirt over their bikini top or wear it all day. Val comes back out, announcing she is ready, and that's all the motivation we need to have us heading for the door.

We all pile into the car and head out to The Surfboard Bar and Grill. This place is a hang-out that we frequent. It has good food, live music, dancing, and fabulous drinks. It is located on the water, so with luck, we will have a little breeze coming in or just some hot steam. One or the other, we will likely find out soon enough.

We pull into the bar parking lot, and by the looks of it, the place starts getting packed quickly. We notice a few cars belonging to our friends and look forward to seeing everyone. The music is loud on the outside deck, so we go there knowing that's where our friends will be. Sure enough, we see Zach, Brodie, and Crispin out here, along with Piper sandwiched in the middle. We move faster toward the tables and hug everyone in all our southern hospitality. Piper is throwing her hands up in the air along with her beer can, singing along to "Say It Ain't So" by Wheezer.

"I love this song!" she screams at us over the music. Piper returns her focus to the band.

"As if we couldn't guess that," I say jokingly, to no one in particular.

"R-ight." Brodie laughs at her dancing around. "She's not driving home tonight, is she, Zach?"

Zach shakes his head. "Definitely not."

We all laugh, knowing we are just getting started.

The night continues, as do the drinks. We take lots of shots, and I take pictures for Liv. I hope she knows that she is missed. One of the pictures is of our discarded shot glasses piled high on each other, resting on a napkin with the words, *I wish you were here,* written in Sharpie marker. Being a nurse requires always having a Sharpie marker in your possession.

I grab my clutch and excuse myself to go to the bathroom. When I turn the corner, I stop abruptly at what and who I see in front of me.

CHAPTER THIRTEEN

EMMA

I can't believe what I am seeing. That motherfucker. I quickly make a turn and head back around. I don't think he has seen me. I hurry back to our table toward Val and Ainsley. They are in a heated debate on whose turn it is to buy the next round. I tug on Val's sleeve, and she faces me.

"Emma, what do you think? Didn't I buy the last round?" She twists her lip up in a snarl at Ainsley. I throw my hands up at her face.

"Hey, Val! Focus. I need to show you something." I look at Ainsley and put my finger to my mouth to silence her from asking more questions. "Bring your phone and follow me," I say, dragging them by the hand to bear witness to the act. Their interest is now piqued, and they follow me eagerly. I slow down before we get to the corner, where I see that jerk. I halt, throwing my hand back and signaling them to stop. I turn around to face them.

"What is it, Emma?" they ask in unison.

I bring them in closer as if he can hear us around the corner, despite the loud music infiltrating through the open patio and the multitude of voices carrying over from the crowd gathered here tonight.

"I have just seen Brodie making out with some girl around this corner." I hear a gasp from Val as she puts her hand up to her mouth.

"No way!" She looks over to Ainsley, who looks back and forth at us, waiting to see if I am joking. I am, in fact, not joking.

"I swear, guys, it's him. I was so shocked. I headed to the bathrooms, rounded the corner, and he had some girl he was making out with and groping her against the wall for everyone to see."

"What should we do?' Ainsley asks.

Val shakes her head in question. "Should we confront him?"

I contemplate the best form of action at this point. "I think we need proof—proof to show Liv once and for all that he is a lying, cheating scumbag. If we just tell her, she may not believe it. I think we should video it, and then she can determine whether or not she wants to pursue this"—signaling air quotes—"relationship." This whole long-distance relationship is making her more unhappy due to the uncertainty of their situation. Are they together or not? From what I saw, I think not.

Val nods in agreement. She turns the corner with her video ready to record. I hold Aisley back because I don't want to draw any other attention to us, and I want to ensure we get this on tape for Liv. After only thirty seconds, but what seems like an hour, Val faces us with a look of disgust on her face.

"Come on, girls, I think I got enough footage. We need to watch this." She pulls us outside onto the deck that is a bit quieter and away from where the band is playing. We head outside, and she shows us her phone, hitting play. We all lean in to look at the scene on her recorded video.

The video zooms in on Brodie off in the corner by the bathrooms. He has a girl with long black hair pushed up against the wall. One of his hands is on her thigh as he holds her leg around his waist. She has a short black skirt with a purple halter top. Her breasts are smashed against his chest. They are grinding against each other to the music, and his face devours the side of her neck. Her head is thrown back in ecstasy, and his other hand is locked onto her very prominent, most-likely silicon, boob.

A guy begins to walk across the screen as we look away, not needing to see any more. Val shuts the video off. She sends the footage to Ainsley and me to have as copies in case one gets deleted.

"What should I do, guys?" Val whines and stomps her foot. "I can't send it to Liv. It will devastate her."

I agree with Val about this. "But I do think she should know about Brodie," I interject.

Ainsley volunteers to send it, and we don't have a problem letting her take the reins on that one. Ainsley types something out, her thumb hovering over the send button as she looks at us for confirmation. We both nod in agreement, and then she hits send.

After that, the girls and I fight off a bout of melancholy at having to disclose this information to Liv. We decide to call it a night and go home. We return to our table of friends, tell everyone good-bye, and plan to meet by the pier in our usual spot tomorrow. We don't see Brodie after that, and when we go to the bathroom before leaving, he is no longer there with that girl. Scandalous.

The drive home is somber. I turn on the music to fill the silence, and "It's No Good" by Depeche Mode sounds throughout the car. The girls drop me off at my place first, and they wait until I make it into my apartment and turn on the light in my bedroom before they pull out of the complex.

I drop my bag on the chair and take my shoes off. I undress and put on a tank and sleep shorts. I unbraid my hair, throwing it into a messy bun before I head to the bathroom to wash my face and brush my teeth. After completing my nighttime ritual, I dive into my cooling sheets and lavender-infused pillow.

I hear my phone chime, and I read the messages from Ainsley, Val, and Liv. She asks who that is with Brodie, but we don't know. I reply that I am so sorry and ask if she is okay. Liv replies that she isn't sure, but she needs to get back to work and will chat with us about it tomorrow.

I punch my pillow, attempting to make it more comfortable, but I know that it has little to do with my pillow and more to do with the thoughts that lay heavily on my mind. I close my eyes and dream of my best friend crying and I blame myself for causing her so much sadness.

Before I know it, morning is here, and Val and Ainsley have returned to pick me up. We are on our way to Liv's apartment before heading out to the beach, and as promised, I arrive with her requested breakfast items. The weather is punishingly hot, and the air is sticky with humidity, ruining the best of hair days. We park next to Liv's jeep and start loading things into the open back area.

When we get to the door, Liv answers, and we stare at each other, not saying a word. I feel responsible and reach out to her first. "Oh, sweetie, I am so sorry. Are you okay? I brought you breakfast."

Ainsley enters and hugs her, too, as Liv shakes her head and holds back the tears. "Are you going to confront him today?' Ainsley asks. "If you do, I think you should do it sooner than later." We all agree with Ainsley, knowing about his problems with alcohol and drugs, not to mention Brodie's decreased coping skills.

Val goes in for a hug next, adding her thoughts. "I think you should ignore him. You are way too classy to make a scene, Liv." Luckily, Liv is a classy girl, and there is no way it would happen, and she confirms as much.

"Come on, guys. Let's go have some fun." We all pile into Liv's jeep and soon head to the causeway. We spot our favorite mile marker and see that our small click of friends has indeed saved us a spot. Crispin is waving his hands in the air like air traffic control. I hear him call out to Rhett. He and Zach spring up from their chairs and begin maneuvering things out of the way to accommodate yet another vehicle in our circle.

I stick my fingers in my mouth and let out a whistle. "Come on, boys. It's not going to unload itself." They all laugh at my brazenness, and I know that, secretly, the guys love it. I flash them a pearly smile, and they laugh. I push my sunglasses up on the bridge of my nose and fan myself with my hand dramatically.

"Anything for you, doll," Crispin retorts.

"Now, that's the Texas hospitality we love," Liv and I say in unison. We both laugh, and I am glad I can help alleviate her somber mood. I head over to the guys as they pick me up from the ground and carry me around as if I weigh nothing.

"Your chariot, milady." Crispin places me in one of the lounge chairs, and I am not unhappy about it.

I let out a contented sigh. I place my finger to my chin and do my best pensive stare. "Now, if I just had a beverage," I say to no one in particular.

Crispin picks up the not-so-subtle cue, snapping his fingers. He laughs, shaking his head. "Coming right up," he says as he grabs me something to drink.

I see Liv looking at Brodie. I brace myself to run interference if need be, but when I think she will approach him, she turns around and goes to the water. She stares at the Gulf waves rolling on the shore, and my heart breaks for her. *"Cheaters are the worst,"* I say under my breath.

Just then, I hear footsteps approaching. I turn my head just in time to accept the beverage from Crispin.

"Here you go." He drops a cold beer on my leg and several ice cubes.

"Yikes!" I jump up, screeching. "That's cold. Oh my god, you did that on purpose." I'm flinging residual ice that hadn't melted on contact with my skin off my body as I plop myself back into the chair. Crispin chuckles and walks off.

I notice Liv looking intently at someone and walking past our cars. I walk a little over to where she is heading, and that is when I see a tall guy sitting in a chair with sunglasses on. He has his leg propped up and an air cast encasing his ankle. He gets up from the chair and begins walking toward Liv. *Interesting.*

I intercept Liv before she reaches him. I have so many questions. "Who's that guy?" I ask in more of a playful tone.

"That's the guy," Liv says as if I should know who "the guy" is.

"Who?" I ask because I don't know.

"His name is Dax, and he is 'the' guy."

I laugh. "Girl, you have some explaining to do." I touch her shoulder, encouraging her to move along. I witness this exchange, until suddenly, I feel like someone is watching me. I immediately become uneasy. I rub my arms back and forth as the hairs begin to rise.

Thoughts rush through my head—Did Julian find me? Am I in danger? I have had such a good time so far that I am waiting for the other shoe to drop. I have let down some of my guard. I swear that I felt this odd sensation at the club yesterday but chalked it up to the situation with Brodie. The cheating got to me. Despite their complicated history, I felt angry at his disregard for their long-time relationship.

With Julian, I wasn't too upset about him cheating on me behind my back, but he did it in front of me, too. How I saw Brodie with that girl—he didn't care about her friends being there, possibly witnessing his infidelity. I take some deep breaths to calm the anger I can feel rising within me.

When I am more relaxed, my skin starts to tingle again with that same awareness of being watched. This time, when I open my eyes and look around, scanning for a threat, nothing seems out of the ordinary.

I look toward Liv and Dax when I see a blond-haired guy of similar stature staring intently at me. At first, I figure he must be looking at someone else, and I glance around to see if that's true. Nope. His smile increases, and I hear him laugh across the lot.

Well, this day just became more interesting.

CHAPTER FOURTEEN

EMMA

Liv is talking with Dax, and his friends have also come over to chat with us. The guy who was staring at me came over to introduce himself, and I felt a sense of familiarity with him. I don't know what it is about him, but I am relaxed and at ease.

He puts his hand out. "Hi, I'm Jameson." He continues to hold my hand.

"I'm Emma." I look over to Liv and then back at Jameson. "How do you guys know Liv?" I pull my hand out of his grasp, and he frowns at the loss of contact. My lip pulls up at seeing how adorable he is when he pouts. His full lips puff out like a toddler who has to part with his favorite new toy.

"Liv didn't tell you?" He looks over at Liv and Dax, who are deep in conversation, much like long-lost friends catching up on the past ten years of not seeing each other.

"No, she didn't," I say reluctantly. "Although, she didn't have much time since she worked last night and…" I trail off, not wanting to discuss Liv's problems with a stranger. I don't feel that mentioning this is appropriate.

I don't have to because when I look back, I see Brodie has pulled Liv aside and they are now in a heated discussion. That girl from the bar is here and is laughing, walking away after saying something over her shoulder at Liv. Anger heats my face, and my fist clenches at my side. Jameson must notice because he touches my shoulder, and I tense at the feel of his hand there.

I see Liv walk away. "Excuse me, Jameson. I have to go check on my girl," I say over my shoulder as I walk off, intently focused on Liv right now.

The sadness is etched on her facial features when I reach her. I know she has uttered the words that should have been said years ago. She held out hope for some reason, but waiting for someone to change is nothing but a life full of misery and disappointment.

Liv walks back toward us, and I catch up with her. "I take it you talked to Brodie about last night, Liv?"

"Oh, yes," she sniffs, barely holding back her tears. "Brodie told her it was a mistake. I overheard their conversation. She also told me to enjoy her leftovers or something to that effect. I don't remember her exact words because I was trying to make my brain catch up with what was happening."

"Whoa," is all I manage to get out. "That's crazy, girl. What happened next?"

Liv shifts on her feet. "He told me he was 'drunk-impaired.'" She mockingly makes air quotes for emphasis.

I have to admit that I like this side of Liv. A side that finally makes me believe she has had enough of this shit relationship. I wish I could confide in her. I wish I could let my best friend know that I understand. But I can't. All I can do is be there for her. I feel like a fraud. I am a liar, but my selfishness has already put enough people in danger. I can't lose anyone else. I refuse to be responsible for someone else getting hurt or killed.

"Oh, using *that* excuse, is he?" I mutter the word '*asshole*' under my breath.

"R-ight, Emma!" Liv begins to raise her voice. "Like drinking and wrong choices are a medical condition of his."

I change the direction of this conversation. "Do you think you could ever trust him again?"

Before I even finish this sentence, Liv is shaking her head back and forth. "No. I told him it was over."

"Well, hell. What about this Dax guy? A spring break fling then?" I want to know all about this spectacular specimen of a man who seemed hot and heavy for Liv. His friend, Jameson, isn't bad looking either.

"I'm not sure," Liv replies, but she bites her lower lip, which she does when telling a little lie.

I chuckle. "Dax's friend is hot," I admit, and Liv laughs. "Come on, Liv. Let's get back to the party." I throw my arm around her shoulders and then remember how short I am. I scowl and curse in anger. Liv laughs, and I swear I see tears of laughter leaking from her eyes.

"Are you making fun of me?" I can't help but laugh along with her.

"Here." She throws her arm around my shoulders and tugs me closer. "How's this?" I hook my arm around her waist, once again annoyed with my short stature. "Perfect, jerk face. Let's go."

"Real mature, Emma," she taunts as we return to the beginnings of a bonfire.

Let the festivities begin.

Before we know it, the night is upon us, and the bonfire has increased in intensity. Even though my friends surround me, I can't shake the feeling that someone is still watching me. I thought it was Jameson, but I have been talking to him, and the feeling will not subside. It's not the feeling I had when I noticed Jameson earlier. The tingling of my skin was different. This feeling is the hair on my arms standing up and a tightening in my stomach. It reminds me of when you are at the amusement park ride, and you get to the top of the roller coaster, hovering there, waiting for your stomach to drop out at the quick descent into the abyss. That is what I feel, as if my stomach is on the precipice of dropping out.

I scan through the flames and don't notice anyone in particular. I look around and still don't see anyone. Unfortunately, I have to pee. I saw a skid-o-can farther back behind the sand dunes. I shift back and forth on my feet.

"Emma?" I hear a voice call my name. I must have zoned out because Jameson is looking at me strangely.

"Do you have to pee or something? You can't keep still?" There is amusement on his face. I know this is the perfect opportunity to get him to escort me to the portable bathroom on the beach.

I laugh, looking at him. "What gave it away?" I reply with a big smile.

"Oh, I don't know. It looks like you have ants in your pants."

"Ha! I hope not. What do you think about escorting me to the bathrooms? I need to pee, but I also don't like that it's so secluded over there and..." I gulp for effect. "Dark."

"I'd be happy to escort you." He reaches for my hand and swings it back and forth in a playful manner. "Come on. Let's go."

We walk hand-in-hand to the stalls, and I thank him before going in.

"Do you want me to wait here?" he asks. "I'll give you some privacy."

"Nope, no privacy needed," I reply before stepping in. "Can you wait here?"

"Of course." He smiles, and I close the door. After the longest pee of my life, I am thankful for the hand gel and somewhat cleanliness of the portable bathroom as the door loudly shuts behind me. Jameson grabs my hand again, and we return to the crowd of partygoers.

Before we cut through the sand dune, Jameson stops and faces me. He looks at me intently, and I feel this longing that I thought was dormant for so long. My breath hitches as he places his hands on my cheeks. I look up at him as he moves closer to me. He stares down at me with desire. I swallow in anticipation of what he is going to do next.

He picks me up, and my legs go to wrap around him. I feel his thick, long erection on my stomach, and I gasp when I feel his cock twitch at the contact. He looks at me, with one arm around my ass, holding me up, and the other arm crossing my back. I lick my lips, and he smirks, moving in. Our lips touch, and he kisses me passionately. I open my mouth for him and... Nothing. I feel absolutely nothing.

Jameson must sense me withdrawing from the contact because he stops and looks at me. I remove my legs from around his hips and place them firmly on the ground. He touches his lips and then gives me a questioning look.

Not wanting to make him feel bad about the awkwardness of that kiss because maybe he felt more than I did, I clear my throat. "Umm, we should get back to the group. They will wonder where I am soon." I look away from him and glance back toward the crowd that doesn't seem to be wondering where I ran off to at all.

"Sure. I'll walk you back." He retakes my hand, and I let him. When we are back in a place where we are visible, I release his hand and pretend to be fixing my hair into another messy bun that probably looks just like it does now. I hope no one saw us leave and then return like this.

I notice Liv talking with Dax, looking our way. I don't get to school my features because a scream penetrates the air and makes me look around. That's when I hear, "Help! Someone help!" I see Liv and Dax jump up and take off, and Jameson and I run toward the source of the screaming.

I see Dax crouched over Brodie, lying limp and unconscious on the sand. Liv is hysterical, and Jameson and I are just trying to help somehow. Dax seems to take charge and asks if anyone called an ambulance.

"I called an ambulance as soon as it happened," Ainsley reports.

"What's the ETA of the ambulance?" I hear Dax bark out.

We hear the faint sound of sirens approaching and know that help isn't far away. Soon, the paramedics are here and taking Brodie away on a backboard. He still hasn't woken up, and I think Liv is in shock. The girls go to get her jeep and pack everything up quickly. Dax announces he is taking her to the hospital, yet Liv still doesn't move. I see Dax stroking her face and telling her this isn't her fault.

I look over at Jameson; he is already preparing the truck. I hand him Liv's purse, and he takes it from me. He wants to say more to me, but now isn't the time. Everyone quickly loads up to follow the ambulance that left about five minutes ago. I jump in the jeep along with Ainsley, Val, and Piper.

The drive to the hospital is quick and silent. No one wants to comment about what transpired or our thoughts about Brodie's prognosis. We head into an emergency department similar to what we left not too long ago. Shortly after the CT scan revealed spinal cord compression, he underwent surgery. We all move to the surgical waiting room and await the results of Brodie's surgery.

When the surgeon asks for Liv and tells her that Brodie is asking for her, she goes through the operating room doors without looking back. Dax, Jameson, and his other two friends stand up. Dax looks utterly defeated as he wipes his hand over his face. Jameson says something to him and pats his shoulder. They make their way toward the staircase, and Dax looks at the doors as if he expects Liv to come back through any second. Jameson grabs his arm and leads him out. He takes a moment to look around, and his gaze lingers on me. He smiles sadly and then turns to walk out the door with his friends in tow.

CHAPTER FIFTEEN

EMMA

It's been eight weeks since the accident. The night at the beach where Brodie attempted to do a backflip, landed wrong, and the injury left him paralyzed. Liv has been there for Brodie through it all. From the night of the surgery to Brodie's rehab and moving to Houston. He will live with his father and have full-time nursing care. Liv didn't go to her graduation and has been a shell of herself since the night of the accident. She blames herself, and I understand, without a doubt, what that feels like. I try to get her to talk to me, to open up about her feelings. I feel like a fraud. Here I am, trying to get her to open up when I won't do the same thing I am preaching about.

I should be taking my own advice, but I can't tell her about my problems and how I feel the same way. Living with the crippling guilt daily is hard, just like putting on a mask of happiness. Where everyone thinks they have no care in the world. I'm just living in the moment and, currently, not feeling much of anything. I wish I could confide in Liv, but that would be selfish.

To tell her what happened with Julian would put her in danger. No, I have no one to talk to and no one to blame but myself for the loss of everyone I loved. I won't let him hurt anyone else just to ease my own conscience.

I finally get home after seeing Liv. She refused to let any of us stay with her, stating that she needed to be alone to process everything. After driving Liv's jeep back to her apartment and then Ubering home, I feel exhausted as the day's events weigh heavy on my mind.

I head to the shower to get the beach grit off my body. We tried to go to the beach, and it wasn't the same. The girl loved the beach, as did I, but it was too hard. We even went to a different mile marker to not have to be in the same area where the accident occurred. I hope that she can go back there one day. There were so many happy memories there, until there weren't. That one day changed it all for our small group of friends. I honestly just want to go to bed, but there is no way that I am getting sand all over the place.

I throw all my clothes in the hamper and jump into a cool shower. The tepid water feels good on my sensitive, sun-kissed skin. I don't bother with blow-drying my hair and decide on some mousse to hold in the light wave. I can almost see the sun setting on the horizon.

I close all the apartment's blinds, and the light-blocking window treatments are set to prevent the punishing rays from filling my bedroom until the sun sets around nine. I sigh in contentment as I pull the covers up to my head. I hear an incoming text message received on my phone as my mind shuts off. All my thoughts vanish, and I drift off into a deep sleep.

"Oh goodness," I mumble as I stretch out my limbs. I slept solidly last night. "What time is it?" I rub my hand over my face and twist my body to glance at my Alice in Wonderland clock on the bedside dresser. My uncle had it commissioned for me as a present when I graduated from nursing school. It was and continues to be one of my favorite books. I notice I slept the morning away, which is now reading noon on the rabbit's white-gloved hands. I lay in bed for a few minutes, staring at the ceiling and contemplating calling Liv to see how she is holding up, but then I think better of it.

I pick up my phone and see a text message from an unknown number. It is a video with a message underneath it.

Unknown number: 'Watch until the end.'

My finger hovers over the video as I hesitate to hit play. I'm sure it's nothing. Rick Astley's "Never Gonna Give You Up" will probably come on shortly after; I chuckle out loud. I click on the video, and a familiar scene appears on the screen. I see Val, Ainsley, and me around the corner of the bathroom while we recorded Brodie with that Alexis girl.

Someone was recording us. Mesmerized by the video from a couple of months ago, I continue to watch and remember the night we sent this to Liv. Instead of getting Rickrolled, I see a familiar face move across the screen. I can't believe what I am seeing.

"No. No. No," I chant. I drop my phone on the floor and sit on my bed, cradling my face with my hands. "Julian." I whisper his name as if conjuring an apparition. I pick up my phone and immediately dial my cousin Adrian.

He picks up after two rings. "Hey, prima. How—"

I cut him off before he can continue his salutations. "Adrian," I choke on a sob.

"Emma. What's the matter? What is it?"

"He's found me, Adrian. He was around when I was out one night. He was there." I walk in circles around my bedroom, biting on my nails. I feel light-headed, like I might pass out. "Oh, god. What am I going to do? He can't find me, please, Adrian."

"Em. I want you to take some deep breaths."

I do as he says and tell him about the video once I am calmer. "You know, Adrian, I felt like I was going crazy. I felt like I was being watched and thought it was just me being paranoid." I guess I had reason to be.

"What? When?" he asks, getting angrier with each question.

So I tell him about the times at the club and the beach. Even when I walked out of work, I felt someone was watching me. Luckily, security walked me out whenever I asked, claiming I was afraid after watching too many true crime shows and listening to podcasts on the way to work. Too bad I lived it.

"Where are you now?" he asks earnestly. "I want to ensure you are safe."

"I'm in my apartment. I am off today. Oh, Adrian, what do I do." I sink onto my knees on my bedroom floor.

He is talking to someone in the background—a woman. I hear a door close and a car starting sound shortly after. "Emma, I am on my way to my father's house. Stay put, and I will grab a bag and come to you. I should be there by tonight. Do not leave the house. Do you hear me? Do not leave the house."

I'm shaking my head, realizing he can't see me. Instead, I answer, "Okay.

I'll stay here and wait for you."

"Okay, I'll call you when I get close to town. Stay calm, prima." The line goes dead.

I sit up with my back against the bed and sob. I know that I am supposed to be strong, but I let myself have a false sense of security. And I almost had an everyday average life for a while, but that isn't in the cards for me. I will never have a normal life while Julian is alive. After I have plenty of time to feel sorry for myself, I start to get angry.

I ensure everything is locked and search all my belongings for anything that can be a potential bug or camera. When I feel that I have looked through everything satisfactorily, I sit on the couch and pull up social media feeds on my laptop. I no longer post on my account, but I decide to look for someone in particular. Someone I have put out of my memory for a long time.

I hit my Spotify playlist, and "Willow" by Taylor Swift plays on my Bluetooth speaker. I hesitate for a moment but then type in his name. *Eduardo Ruiz Houston Texas.* There are a few hits that are not him. Then, in one of the hits, I click on the profile.

Sure enough, I see the face of a boy who is now a man—and he is *all* man. I begin to Instagram stalk him. I see his club, and on the opening night he is so handsome in a suit. He was so stocky when he was little, but that stockiness turned to pure muscle. He is a vision standing in front of the club and inside under the lights all around, hitting him at different angles.

One picture in particular draws me in. I notice a tattoo curling up through his white shirt, escaping up onto his neck, but as mesmerizing as that is, that isn't what gets my attention. I enlarge the photo of his knuckles, where a word is tattooed across. I gasp when I see what it spells out. EMMA.

Oh, my. I stand up abruptly, and my laptop hits the carpet with a soft thunk. I grab my necklace and pace the small living room in my apartment, wearing a path back and forth. Taylor Swift continues with her song, the lyrics sounding out. Taylor Swift sings about wrecking plans and telling someone that he's her man. I think how true that is—the complexity that goes with loving someone.

I continue looking through social media post after post, until I hear my phone chime with an incoming message. It's Adrian.

"Oh, thank goodness," I say out loud because he is finally here. I must have been stalking him more than I thought, because the time flew by. I look out the window and see my cousin outside his truck, stretching as he slides out of the driver's seat.

I close the blinds and put away my computer. I hear a knock at the door, but I still check to ensure it's him. I look through the peephole and see Adrian smirking at me on the other side. I unlock the double bolts and let him in.

Adrian steps through and wraps me in a hug. He closes the door with his foot and locks it with one hand, not letting me go. I break down and cling to him like a lifeline. He holds me without saying anything and allows me to get out my emotions. After, I sniffle for what I hope is the last time.

He pushes me back. "Emma, it's going to be okay. I'm here to protect you, and we'll figure it out. My father is coming up with a plan as we speak. He told me to get here and he will call us tonight to let us know. Have you eaten?"

I shake my head no. "I could eat," I say, biting my lip.

His smile widens. "That's my cousin. Let's grab some food now that I am here, okay?"

"I'd like that." I put on my shoes, and we walk out of the house with an agenda.

We pull up to my favorite pizza place near my apartment, which is also close to my work, making it the perfect place for meeting up. They have a fantastic sourdough pizza crust with three hundred-plus microbrews on tap.

I walk through the door, and the bell jingles, letting the patrons and staff know about the incoming person, which so happens to be me and Adrian. I go to the table in the back, where I usually sit by myself with a book. This time, I have Adrian as my company.

Sumi immediately comes up to me and gives me a big hug. "Emma! I haven't seen you in a couple of months, girl. Where have you been?"

"I've been helping a friend through a rough time, and I've been otherwise working. I've missed you too, Sumi. Oh, this is my cousin Adrian."

She looks over at him and blushes. He puts his hand out for her to take, and she does but immediately pulls it back. The blush is now down into her neck and chest.

I save her from her embarrassment and order the usual. She takes one more look at Adrian and walks off. He chuckles when she leaves. I hit him on the shoulder. "Would you stop making my friends nervous? Geez, she was all flustered." I glance over at the bar and see her pouring us a beer. Poor Sumi. Maybe she should drink one.

For a while, I forget about my problems with Julian and enjoy the company of my family—what's left of it.

CHAPTER SIXTEEN

EDUARDO

At home, I finish reviewing contracts before it's time to leave for the gym. I stop by the kitchen area and make myself a latte to take with me on the road. The Breville state-of-the-art touchscreen espresso machine is top-notch, beckoning me to have a tasty caffeinated beverage despite not currently wanting one. Still, I'm glad I invested in this priceless piece of morning bliss machinery.

The latte infuses straight into a to-go mug. Picking it up along with my leather messenger bag, I close and lock the door behind me to leave my ultra-modern uptown apartment home near the Galleria. The exclusive penthouse level boasts terraces and a three-bedroom light-filled floor plan with a necessary wet bar and wine chiller. The twenty-four-hour concierge with a dedicated phone line is a game changer in my line of work, where I need security and a defensible location. I walk out to my garage with private access and enter my Bently SUV. I travel a short distance to my other business—my gym.

This morning, I had an early meeting with the contractors. The project helped with branching out with a legitimate business portfolio. It is all a front, but I do enjoy the non-criminal side. Sometimes, I forget the business I am involved in—my family's business and one I love more than I'd care to admit.

We opened this gym this past year, and it has done incredibly well. We place suggestion boxes at the entrance to improve our business and take the customers' suggestions to heart. Helena is the front desk person, but she is also my manager. I trust her implicitly, and she sorts through the comments, looking for improvements that we can add to the betterment of this establishment.

After much feedback from the members, we have decided to accommodate their request for a nutrition station and cafe. I can't deny that this gym would be almost perfect with that addition. I say almost perfect because I believe there is always room for improvement. Complacency is the death of any corporation; in my line of business, it could be the difference between life and death.

The gym is state-of-the-art with an indoor pool, sauna, indoor track, and all the standard gym working parts. Members will come to exercise in the morning before work and leave suggestions stating that it would be great to grab a protein shake, smoothie, or matcha before they go to work for the day. Bougie as fuck, but when you make this type of place in a prime location, the clientele demands a certain level of accommodations. I can charge up the ass for services, and they won't even flinch in paying for it.

In fact, they tell their friends about it, and more people sign up for the membership. We are almost at max capacity and will soon offer a waiting list spot only. Fuck. When there is a waiting list, it only fuels the consumer to desire a membership here more than ever. They feel that they are missing out, and we exploit that. I am in the profession to deliver on these requests. The more services and amenities, the more their fees increase, and so forth.

Equally important to the drinks is the need for lunch. Some patrons like to work out on their lunch break. Go figure. Now, that's dedication—something I can admire. After listening to my manager, Helena's, suggestions, I hired someone to rent the space from us. Businesses bid for the spot, and we have much interest, but we are looking for something hot and upcoming. It needs to be perfect. It's not the usual juice bar, vegan protein type of place.

We are holding interviews for the various small business owners vying for a chance to rent this space at one of the most popular gyms in the metro area. The lead runner-up is a small business specializing in poke bowls, superfruit bowls, smoothies, fresh pressed juices, coffee, and shots. It would meet the criteria that the gym members are looking for and the nutritional standards of serving members of a gym with high expectations such as ours. I also sample the goods and am impressed with the Hawaiian food flare. I order an ahi tuna poke bowl over white rice with avocado, cucumbers, carrots, edamame, and fresh ginger. They give me a twenty-ounce cold brew with Laird superfood brewed in-house. It is fucking amazing.

As I go over the space with another contractor and paperwork that requires my signature, I approach the front desk at the same time a woman approaches me. Initially, I notice that she has a body made for sin as I continue to peruse her voluptuous figure. She sees me appreciating her fine form and smiles seductively at me. She touches my arm with her long, pointed, manicured fingertips and trails it down my bicep and forearm. I raise my eyebrow in question to her bold moves as she leans in closer.

"I was wondering if you could show me where the locker rooms are." She looks down at my cock and then back up at my eyes.

I look her in the eye and run my tongue over my teeth. Contemplating the offer, I turn my head to the side. This isn't something unusual for me. She has noticed my appearance and probably my expensive watch and clothing. Gold-digging much?

Her breath hitches in anticipation of where this could go. I turn to look at the front desk. She follows the path my gaze has traveled, waiting for my next move. She probably expects me to tell Helena to cover for me so I can show her to the locker rooms.

"Helena?" The girl at the front desk looks up from her book as if she is guilty of doing something. "Would you mind showing this lady where the locker rooms are, please?" She puts her book down and walks our way. I stop her as she walks past me and whisper, "Maybe you should calm your reading down on the spicy romance books."

She snorts. "Yeah, that won't happen, Boss." Having quickly regained her regular coloring, she looks at the woman and walks past her. I don't give her another glance.

"Follow me."

The woman follows Helena but shoots a look back at me and shakes her head back and forth before following Helena to the locker room. I am willing to bet that she knows exactly where they are. Luckily for me, that is no concern of mine. There is only one person on my mind these days, and I hope to find her.

I go to my office and pull up my social media page. I advertise the gym and the updates on the food and cafe space. We have a comment right away about the excitement over the cafe. Then, I look to my club and post updates to the various DJs headlining on the upcoming weekends. This will surely fulfill the excitement recipe for any coming-of-age raver.

Influencers and elite society compete against other VIPs to gain entrance into my club. We spare no expense to provide a thrilling environment. It offers a rollercoaster of emotions, from excitement to fear of the unknown and endless pleasure. It's no secret that my club boasts endless drugs to satisfy every vice the patron desires. They only need to know the secret codes to access these substances and obtain access to a bathroom to partake in the ecstasy this atmosphere enables. As long as it is discrete, we don't care, which helps with the other side of my profession—the illegal one that is the backbone of our family's revenue.

After completing my work posts, I started to go the personal route. I don't post much on my personal page, but I keep it updated. I have a close group of friends from when I was in college and maintain good relationships with my frat brothers. We had so much fun then and stayed in touch. We get together quite often, but work prevents me from hanging out with them as much as I would like. I allow them access to my VIP area with exceptional bottle service whenever they want. It's a perk of being the boss. I can still work and then spend some time with them if they can come to party at my establishment. They also don't mind being granted access to one of the finest clubs in the city with VIP service.

I decide to pull up the social media for Emma and am not surprised when I see nothing recent. The last time she updated anything was a couple of years ago. It has pictures of her and her sister. I zoom in on the one picture of her and Evie. I almost stop breathing when I zoom in on the image and see Emma up close. It isn't her beauty that catches my breath, but the necklace around her neck. The chain that I gave her about a decade ago. She still wears it. The thrill that racks my body is intense, and my possessive side that has been fighting the urge to claim her rages. I knew it. I slam my fist on the table, and my laptop jumps. Fuck. Her mother kept me away, but I hadn't considered Emma's feelings.

Does she still think of me? Does she still want me? Is she waiting for me? These are all questions that I will get the answers to. She still wears my necklace, a telltale sign that she remembers me. Now, I just need to recreate our past and make her remember me in the present tense.

We are both of legal age now, and unfortunately, we never got to explore the possibility of more because of her parents. I respected their wishes, but I know they aren't around. She has no immediate family, and I'll find her, despite what her uncle wants, and I will protect her. I'll be the family she needs. If she will have me, that is. And if she won't, I'll have to convince her otherwise. I know I won't give up easily like I did last time, thinking I was doing the right thing. I am doing this for me and Emma—for our future.

Without considering it, I pick up the phone and call my brother, Ram. He finally picks up as I am about ready to hang up. "Hey, fucker, why did it take you so long?" I am annoyed, but the humor in my voice is still present.

"What the fuck, asshole? I was busy." I hear a woman in the background laugh as he discreetly tries telling his fiancée that it's me and he has to take the call.

"Is that Anna?" I say mostly to annoy him.

"Of course it's Anna," he growls into the phone. I hear my future sister-in-law's voice in the background and her telling me hi.

"Hello," I say into the phone.

"Yeah, just a second." I hear him kiss her, and the door closes. "Okay, I'm back."

"Wow," I mock. "Someone is pussy-whipped."

He laughs. "Damn straight. You're just jealous."

He isn't wrong, but I hate to admit that. I gather up the courage to ask him about what I called for. "Hey, I was hoping you could help me with something?" He doesn't comment; he just waits for more pieces of information. "So, I was looking through my social media stuff and came across Emma's profile."

He laughs at this. "Just fell into the profile, did you? Just stumbled across it, or did you type in her name and Insta-stalk her."

Not wanting to lie, I go with the truth. "I Insta-stalked her. What was more unsettling was that she was wearing my necklace in a picture. I gave her that about ten years ago."

"No shit," he says.

"No shit, brother," I echo his words. "I was wondering if maybe we could look for her. See where she is. I know her parents died in that sketchy-ass fire, but perhaps it is nearby?" He stays silent, but I know that he has listened to me and is absorbing it all, devising a plan.

"I think we could do that if that is what you want?"

I don't hesitate to reply. "That's most definitely what I want."

CHAPTER SEVENTEEN

EMMA

After consuming our weight in pizza and beer, I'm slightly buzzed as Adrian helps me back to my apartment. He brings his duffle bag and throws it on the couch. He begins to get out his toiletry bag and sleep pants.

"Hey. I'm going to use your bathroom for a second, okay? I'll be right back." He disappears into the bathroom, and I sit on the couch, twirling my hair, something I do out of habit when profoundly thinking about a problem.

Adrian emerges shortly after changing to get ready for bed. I stand and go to my room, returning with bedding for the couch. I hate that he has to sleep there after driving all this way. Soon, I'll be able to buy my house or become more settled, where I'll have a spare bedroom for guests.

I start to make up the couch with my bedding, and Adrian grabs a side of the fitted sheet and pulls it over the pillowed cushioned seats. I apologize to Adrian for the accommodations, but he just blows it off. He is too kind to comment about having to sleep on a sucky couch.

"So, cousin, what do you think of the plan?" He tugs on the last side of the sheet, and we drape the other top sheet and blanket, placing a couple of down pillows on top.

I actually love the plan because I have other feelings about it. Feelings I have yet to say aloud. Liv is also my best friend, and it seems like the right choice to help her. "I love it. Houston sounds like the right move." I instantly touch my necklace, and Adrian notices right away.

"Emma?" he asks. "Is there something more I should know about you wanting to go to Houston?" He motions with his chin, nodding at my necklace.

I look over at Adrian to see him frowning as he observes me, waiting for my reply.

I realize I'm still holding the necklace and drop it quickly. I cannot lie to my cousin. First, he would see right through it because we grew up together. Second, I find that I don't want to lie to him. I am at a time in my life when I have no one to confide in, and it scares me. I used to have my sister, and she is gone. I live with that realization every day, so I decide to be honest.

I sigh in resignation. "Maybe." It's all I can give him, and I shrug his concerns away.

His eyebrows shoot up into his hairline in a dramatic fashion, much like a cartoon character does when he hears shocking news. "Oh boy. This should be good. Should I sit down?" my cousin asks, but doesn't require an answer. He immediately plops onto the couch, grabbing one of the pillows and tucking one foot under his leg. He pats the seat next to him. "Sit and tell me all about it."

And I do. I start with me stalking Eduardo's social media. I bring my laptop over and show him everything I found about Eduardo and what he is doing.

"You know..." Adrian clears his throat, almost hesitant to bring this up, but continues despite his reservations. "He came looking for you the next summer back then. He expected to see you there, and when he couldn't find you, he had this look on his face. You had left, and we knew you weren't coming after your mom's speech about wanting to leave the restrictive confines of the mafia life."

He rolls his eyes. "She said it was both a blessing and a curse. She wanted to keep you guys away from growing up in that lifestyle. He told us she had approached him to leave you alone, but he said no. He stayed looking out the backfield with his hand in his pockets. Then, without another word, he turned around and walked out the front door. He didn't return the next day or the following summer."

I place my hand to my mouth. "I can't believe Mom told Eduardo all that, and he still came looking for me." I shake my head in disbelief.

Adrian clears his throat. "My dad spoke with him and told him that it was your parents' wish for you to have a life without corruption. He strongly requested that Eduardo not seek you out. If he cared for you, he would allow you to be free."

I don't know if it is just the topic or if I am sad about the friendship cut short and the potential for more. I think about all that could have been. I would have been promised to Eduardo. I would not have met Julian. I would be safe, happy, and have my family alive with me.

But that wouldn't be right, would it? My mom was the reason that this happened between Eduardo and me. I still would have been protected if we had my extended family. We were isolated and free, but there is something about being free. Sometimes, you make the wrong choices and suffer the consequences of your actions. Free will isn't really free.

I look at Adrian, and he gives me a sad face. "I have to go to work early tomorrow, but after work, I'll go to Liv and see how she is. I'll put my two-week notice in at work. I'll let her know that we are leaving for Houston together."

The following day, Adrian drives me to work. I told my nursing supervisor that I would be moving to Houston for family reasons, and I am officially putting in my two-week notice. It isn't untrue because I consider Liv my family, and she needs me too. I have my reasons for leaving, but no one can know about Julian. The corruption of his father's reach is an unknown factor to me. The fact that Julian has found me scares me. I escaped him for a while, but now he knows I'm in the States, so he has a better advantage.

My uncle wanted me to come back home, but I refused to. I can't leave Liv and don't want to live like that. Once I get to Houston and secure a location, Adrian will stick around until he can guarantee my safety. My uncle doesn't tell me if I have anyone around for security, and I don't want to make it apparent, so I don't. I thought I was safe, but maybe I never will be.

After the longest shift, I walk out with security to Adrian's truck. I wave to Todd and thank him. He smiles and returns to the ER doors.

Adrian looks over at me. "How was work? Did you put your notice in?" He pulls out of the parking lot.

"Hey, Adrian. Instead of going to my apartment, can you go by Liv's? I want to talk to her and tell her about the move."

He nods. "Where to?"

"Here." I pull it up on Apple Maps and connect it to his Bluetooth before answering his initial questions. "Today was good but long. I thought the nursing supervisor was literally going to cry after I told her I was putting my two-week notice in. One girl went out on maternity leave, and Liv and I are leaving, making the department down three nurses this month." I wave my hand around.

We pull up at Liv's apartment, and I see a light is on in her place. I look over at Adrian, and he gives me a reassuring smile. "Go, Emma. I'll be here waiting for you, cousin."

I smile at him affectionately. "How are you still single?" I open the door, and I hear him laughing.

"It's by choice, Em. Trust me, I have a variety of prospects."

"Yuck." I stick out my tongue at him playfully, much like when we were children. "I'll be right back." I go up to Liv's door and knock. "She better answer," I mutter under my breath.

After the third knock, I hear her approach the door and then the turning sound of her unlocking the double bolts. She opens the door, and I take in her appearance. She looks tired and sad. I push my way in, and she stands there for a second before closing the door and letting out a sigh.

Once Liv turns around, I rush in for a hug. "Hey, girl. How are you?"

She releases me without commenting and walks toward the table, retrieving the glass of wine she had been drinking before I arrived. "Did Brodie make it to Houston okay?" She takes a big gulf of wine.

"Thanks for thinking of me, and I don't know." She turns to look at me. "Did you want a glass?" She drains the rest of her glass and pours me one. She must see the concerned look in my eyes because she shakes her head. Her eyes are pleading *don't ask.*

"Just thought I'd come in and check on you after I got out of work." We sit at the table. "Have you heard from Dax?"

Liv stops mid-pour. "Not since the last text he sent the week after the accident." She doesn't comment further on this, but I know she didn't reply to his message.

"Liv, you know this isn't yours or Dax's fault, right? Brodie made those choices—to cheat on you, get drunk, and do a backflip drunk when he knew he shouldn't. You can't blame yourself for another person's bad choices. I won't let you. Those events were always his bad choices." Except I understand it—the guilt I feel. It was a wrong choice that caused my family's death. My bad decision. I was involved with a monster, and that relationship caused my life and everything I cared about to crumble.

Changing the subject, I look around the apartment. "How's the packing going?"

Liv also looks around at the chaos of her imminent move to Houston. "Slow."

She gets up to move another box, and before I can stop myself, I blurt out, "How would you like a roommate in Houston?" She stops mid-walk.

"What?" Liv stutters like she didn't hear me the first time, glancing back.

"You heard me. I was thinking about taking a travel assignment and just doing it. I figured now would be as good a time as any. And then we could stay together."

I look at her, waiting for a response, and see Liv's now turned in my direction, giving me her full attention. Her eyes brim with excitement, and for the first time in months, she smiles. "I would really like that," she stammers.

"Good." I stand up to embrace my friend. "I already called the recruiter for the travel agency in Houston and gave my two-week notice at the hospital today. It's a done deal. You're stuck with me again."

"Are you sure, Emma?" Liv looks nervously at me.

I don't want to give too much away, but I have learned there should always be some truth when omitting details. That way, the omission is believable, and the lie is easy to remember. So, I go for a partial truth. "I stayed here for too long and have to leave anyway." I laugh, which sounds bitter with resentment. "I was getting too comfortable." I wave my hand in my usual fashion and feel my lips pursing in discontent. I try to school my features, but it is too late.

Liv notices but doesn't comment. Her eyes squint, as if trying to see through the hidden meaning of my words.

"I'll call my job placement and make sure they can secure a place for two bedrooms. It shouldn't be a problem, and it will allow us to look for a place we can both like living in once we get there."

We say our good-byes and promise to chat later. I walk up to the truck, and Adrian unlocks the door. I jump in and almost miss the seat. I hear him stifle a laugh. "Not funny, asswipe." He full-on laughs now, not bothering to hide his amusement. I close the door and buckle up.

"You are just tiny with those little legs." He pulls the truck away, and we start the drive to my place.

"I don't have short legs. I told you I'm proportional." I shake my head and look out the window. "Anyway. I told Liv, and we are all set for the move. Now, we just need to get through these next two weeks before we leave."

CHAPTER EIGHTEEN

EDUARDO

ONE YEAR LATER...

I'm sitting in my office at eleven p.m., and the club is getting packed. This is when I do most of my work, choosing to stay away from the crowds and the patrons who try to access my club and, worse, the women who try to gain access to my heart. They are fucking deluded if they think that I could give them what they want. A first date, gifts, marriage. Fuck that. I have a business to run.

My father has been down my throat with the prospects of women who would make a suitable match for the son of a don. Many have tried and failed. They pretend they don't know who I am or don't see the money I have and want to get their gold-digging claws sunk in. I've seen it all. My dad wants heirs, and my mom wants me to find happiness in the comfort of a woman who will provide the stability my life probably needs, but a home isn't just having someone there waiting for you to satisfy the duties of the house. I want to look forward to coming home to someone. To see my kids in the likeliness of their mother, them greeting me and welcoming me to *our* home. I can't have that and have thought over and over about the fantasy of it all. I see my brother and how his eyes light up when he sees his fiancée. My hand rubs over the stubble on my face contemplating the possibility someday.

I'm pulled out of these daydreams when I get a call. I answer, pissed off from allowing myself to have these thoughts when I have work to do.

"Boss?" the voice of one of my bouncers calls. I know this can't be good if they are bothering me.

"Yes," I bellow into the phone. "What the fuck is it?" The door opens without anyone knocking.

I don't get the answer because Gustavo is holding his hand. I see the cloth covering it that is saturated in blood. A tiny drop falls to the floor and I growl. "Fuck."

I look at him up and down and signal him with my hand to come in.

"If you're calling to tell me about Gus, he is in my office, and I can see what has happened. Is there anything else I need to do about the situation?"

"No, Boss. It's been handled."

We hang up, and I turn my attention to my security detail.

"What the fuck happened?"

"That waitress Cherry is what fucking happened." He shakes his non-injured hand at me. "Her boyfriend came over here looking for you. She bragged to one of her friends about your 'attention' toward her. That fucker found out and came here to settle a score."

I scoff at this. "Cherry? Where is she?" I look at him, and my anger is barely contained at such a nuisance happening in my club and so early in the night at that.

"Escorted out with her boyfriend. She was hysterical about what happened, saying she loves you and for him to leave."

I bring my hand down my face. "Enough of this shit. Fire Cherry and ban them both from the premises."

"Already done, Boss."

"Good." I shake my head in agreement. "Now, on to more important things. Your hand? How is it? Do you need treatment?"

He nods his head yes.

"Okay then, I'll accompany you."

Gus tries to protest. "Boss, you don't have to do that. I know you are busy here. I can get one of the other security personnel to take me. I'll be fine." He starts to walk to the door.

"Gus, you are not just hired help. You're my friend. I've known you my whole life, and I said I will take you." I pat his shoulder as we walk out.

We walk into the emergency department, and it is a fucking zoo. As we walk to registration, someone is vomiting into a bucket. The clerk is kind, despite the craziness of this place on a Friday night. She looks at the blood dripping from his hand and frowns.

"He was stabbed, and the wound is deep," I tell her. "It hasn't stopped bleeding." She looks a little queasy, and I think that perhaps this isn't the best job for her, but I keep my thoughts to myself. "We might need some more..." I pause to look over at Gus. "Gauze, maybe?" He nods without saying anything, looking back at the lady.

She visibly gulps and nods. "I think maybe I'll put you in one of the rooms in the back, but let me get you to the triage nurse so they can look at you and make that determination. Just a second." She gets up and walks away.

As she does this, a lady in cuffs with a police escort falls back and hits her head on the floor. The 'thwack' that sounds across the room makes others gasp, and one child who witnessed the fall starts screaming. We stare at this clusterfuck and shake our heads.

"Yep, a fucking zoo," I comment aloud. Gus grunts in agreement.

Staff come out from behind the locked door and gather the woman in cuffs onto a backboard. One of the nurses yells at the officer to take the cuffs off. I have to admire these nurses. They have probably seen it all. It takes a special kind of person to have to deal with this level of shit on a daily basis. A couple of people place her on a stretcher and wheel her in through the doors, followed by the annoyed-looking police officer.

A man who must be the triage nurse tells me to come through a locked door displaying a green light as he holds his badge up to it, allowing us entry. We get up and proceed to follow him through the door. Once we get in there, he notices a trail of blood coming from the door to the chair he asked Gus to sit in.

"Fuck me," he mutters as he runs his hand through his hair. "Follow me," he mumbles in resignation. "No need to have you bleeding all over the place, and I need to unwrap that anyway."

"Fucking perfect," I say in agreement.

We follow the tall nurse into one of the bays that is big enough to fix a few stab wounds to the hand or other body parts tonight.

"I'll give this to the nurse assigned to this area"—he smiles maliciously as he continues speaking—"who'll be in soon. If you think you'll pass out, come get someone." He glances my way before leaving.

Gus nods also, but we know that won't happen. This isn't our first rodeo, and it's not as if he was shot in the chest. I think we are both remembering that time when only an inch over for the gunshot wound that went through his chest could have killed him. Luckily, the bullet happened to miss important structures and vessels. Otherwise, it would have been a very different scenario, and likely that we wouldn't be here today. Getting his hand stitched is nothing in comparison, but no one needs to know that.

About ten minutes later, the nurse comes into the trauma bay with what I assume is Gus's chart and, without looking at us, announces that her name is Emma, and she will be the nurse caring for him. She halts when she finally turns and looks in our direction. She looks right at me and drops the chart along with whatever she was going to say. One hand goes to cover her mouth as she gasps in shock, while I notice the other hand goes to the necklace I gave her a decade ago before she vanished from my life, but there she is, a vision from every dream I've had over the years made flesh and now standing before me.

Gus watches this exchange but doesn't comment. I stand and walk around the equipment to get to her. She stays where she is, and I look at her hand holding her necklace. I tower over her, and I realize how little she is. She looks up at me with those striking green eyes I have pictured in my mind over the years. The mental pictures that haunt my every thought and when I try to sleep at night stay with me in my dreams.

She sees me looking at her, holding my necklace. I break the silence. "Is that the necklace I gave you? You still wear it?"

She realizes she is holding it and lets it go. Her eyes are a little teary, and I instinctively want to keep her and wipe away the heartache about to spill from her eyes.

She swallows. "I never took it off. I've worn it since you gave it to me and held on to it when I never saw you again."

She looks down, and I grab her chin and raise it to look at me again. I always want her to look at me so I can get lost in those emerald-colored eyes. I need her to look at me so she can see the truth.

"I tried to return to you, but I had to honor our family's wishes—your family's wishes, too. I thought it was what you wanted. Had I known, I would have come to you sooner. I would have reached out to you after your high school graduation."

She steps back and turns around, not looking at me. I walk over and grab onto her, spinning her around. "What is it, Emma? Is there something wrong? I heard about your parents..." I let my words trail off.

She looks up at me. "Yes, but first, let's fix your friend here."

I don't like the redirection of this conversation, but I'll play along for now. "How do you know he is my friend, not my employee?" I want to know this girl's thoughts and how her mind works. She's all grown up now.

She laughs. A hint of humor touches her eyes as she looks at me and over at Gus, who still hasn't said a word, just staring at what I am sure is an amusing and conflicting exchange between Emma and me.

"Well," she continues, "if he was just your employee, then I bet you wouldn't be standing here personally seeing to his medical care." She raises an eyebrow, challenging me to deny it.

I laugh, and so does Gustavo at this. Gus finally pipes up. "She knows you, Boss. Is that good?" He looks at me in all seriousness.

I keep my focus on Emma only. "Yes, that's very good indeed." Emma blushes and turns her back toward us, gathering some supplies from the cabinet.

"All right." She looks at Gus. "Let's see what we've got here." She starts to unwrap his hand.

Gus pulls it back a little. "You're not queasy, are you, Emma? Of a little blood?"

I can't tell if he is testing her or seriously concerned after how the lady at the check-in desk reacted to his injury. He doesn't show much emotion, so it's hard to gauge his line of questioning. Emma just snorts.

"Please," she says. "I've seen it all my life." She must realize what she has said because she stops to look at me and then at Gus. Now, it's time for Gus to raise an eyebrow in question. She looks at me and smiles widely, displaying her perfectly straight white teeth. I can't help but return the smile. Gus watches the exchange.

"I think I'm getting the full picture now, Eduardo." He extends his hand for her to treat.

When she smiles at me like that, I imagine coming home from our line of work and seeing her welcoming me. I envision her pregnant with my child, her hand on her round belly, looking at me with that smile and a... future? Could that be in the cards for me after all? I'm unsure, but I know I'm not giving up on her again.

She unwraps the bandages and looks at the wound, frowning. "I need to clean this up to see what I'm looking at."

She puts Gus on a monitor and has him lie on the stretcher, which makes Gus grumpy, but he doesn't dare say a thing to her because he must sense that Emma is mine, and he won't disrespect her like that—friend or not. *Definitely not as an employee,* I think to myself. It dawns on me that I have now thought of Emma as mine for the first time in years.

After she cleans it up, she tells us that she'll be right back but needs to get the doctor to look at it. "Can you do it?" I ask her before she leaves.

She nods, then says, "I can't do it here because my license doesn't allow me to do this."

I smile at her. "Perfect," I announce and see Gus's recognition of my question dawning on him. Not only is Emma the perfect girl for me, but she can also help when I need to trust someone, and discretion is imperative. He nods in silent agreement.

She returns momentarily with a doctor in tow, and I frown because he seems too comfortable talking to my future wife. *Well,* I think to myself, *that escalated quickly.*

CHAPTER NINETEEN

EMMA

I despise doing the night shift, but one of my friends asked if I could please work it for her because she had a wedding to go to. Well, at least I have the day off tomorrow because I'll be sleeping most of it away. I make a mental note to set my alarm for noon to shop. Then I have light plans to meet up with some people from work. I'll have to get Liv to come out with me. I have a ton of preparation to get done for the girls' visit to Houston. They've always treated me like one of them, and I can't wait to see them.

As soon as I walk through the door of this place, there is one emergency situation after another, and it's only going to get worse after midnight. My parents used to remind me that nothing good ever happens after midnight, and as I look around this hellhole, I tend to agree with their assessment and stance on the issue. Nothing is good in this place.

I sigh in resignation as I take a much-needed sip of my coffee, looking around the forty-five-bed ER from the inner core nurses' area. The music in the nurses' station plays "Paint it Black" by Hidden Citizens. Rånya's chilling vocals just add to the vibe.

Everything that is harmful or evil seems to live in this place. The sounds of pain and crying combined with the sight of vomit and blood harden my emotions to when someone comes in mostly dead and we have to act quickly to save their life. I don't know how Liv did this god-forsaken shift all those years while attending school. This graveyard shift is a fitting name, and it royally sucks ass. I have a new appreciation for anyone who works the night shift because it is pure hell.

I'm pulled from my thoughts as the devil himself sets his gaze on me heading out of the triage room.

Lucifer, Satan, Beelzebub, or as we call him here at work, Brett, walks up to me with a purpose, and I fight the urge to roll my eyes at him. He is so condescending and full of himself. He thinks he is so good-looking, flexing his muscles. It just doesn't do it for me, which irks him to the max. Imagine a woman not throwing themselves at his feet—the horror.

"Em-ma," he calls my name using two-syllables, making me instantly annoyed. He brings his cupped hands forming a funnel appearance around his mouth back down after calling my name. He's such a jerk. He can't call me short, and he says my name like this because he thinks I am slow to hear things. You know, since I am short, the words have to travel down until I hear them. I get the meaning of his act; it's just not funny. I once tried to tell him that I knew I was short and could hear just fine. He smiled, knowing that he got to me, so he kept doing it every so often. To other people, it doesn't look like anything when he does things like this, but I know what he's implying. I decide not to react to his childish behavior. He knows how I feel when people call me short. Schooling my features to Lucifer, I smile brightly at him.

"Yes, Brett." I look up at him. He tries to stand too close to me as a means of intimidation. He doesn't realize I am thinking about punching him in the balls—one benefit of being vertically challenged.

As I look back up, I realize that I may not be throwing my best poker face on because he smirks at me. Ugh, he must be interpreting this all wrong. *I wasn't looking at your balls. I was thinking about punching you in the balls.* I shake my head to obliterate the appalling mental image from my mind.

"What is it, Brett?"

He hands me a chart. "Here. Your next patient is over in trauma bay four."

Brett is so smug, and I bet he thinks he is upsetting me by giving me a more complex patient, but it would take more than this to rile me up. I quickly glance over the chart and see his narrowed eyes focused on me.

"Is the knife or object still lodged in the wound?" I ask.

"No, it's not," he replies quickly.

"Pity," I say and give him a once-over before I walk toward bay four.

"Whatever," is all I hear as he walks back to triage.

I decide to get this over with and assess the damage to the hand wound. I step through the curtains into trauma bay four and announce myself like I do whenever I come into a room. Except this time, I am astonished. It's not the patient or their presenting trauma that makes me feel this way, but the man standing with the patient.

I instinctively grab my necklace and see when he notices what I am holding on to. The look in his eyes is cataclysmic. His nostrils flare with what I can sense as anger, although I don't feel it directed at me. Because when he looks back at me, his eyes soften.

"Is that the necklace I gave you?" He waits for my answer, and I want to deny it.

I am so overwhelmed by the feelings that come at me with the impetus of a tidal wave, making a flood of emotions pour over me. I know my eyes are beginning to water, and I can no longer look at him. It isn't just the thought of him leaving me but the realization that I don't have anyone in my corner anymore. Except for Uncle Andrés and my cousin Adrian. I am so grateful for everything they've done for me and how they stepped up to rescue me, putting themselves in danger. A potential danger I have seemed to cause everyone around me. Eduardo didn't abandon me but didn't come to find me either. I look down so he doesn't witness the barrage of conflicting emotions.

He raises my chin to look at him. I swallow, giving him the answer he already knows. "I never took it off. I've worn it since you gave it to me and held on to it even when I never saw you again."

He stares at me and I imagine he sees the sincerity displayed on my face. This time, he swallows before answering me. "I tried." Regret radiating from each spoken word. He stops and restarts with more conviction. "I tried to return to you, but I had to honor your family's wishes. My family's ultimata were clearly explained when your uncle called my father to ensure I didn't *bother* you." He says that word as if it sickens him. "I thought it was what you wanted. Had I known, I would have come to you sooner. I would have reached out to you after your high school graduation."

I know he can see the pain that crosses my face at the mention of my family and the sea of emotions that surge through me. He must sense that. I know he can still somehow read me like a book. I turn around so he doesn't see me. My guilt, my sadness, the mask that momentarily feels like it fell, exposing my truths, my secrets. Can he know? About Julian? I doubt it. If he did, he would have found me sooner, right? I have no idea. I bite my lip to stifle the cry that threatens to escape my lips.

He grabs my shoulders, spinning me around to face him. "What is it, Emma? Is something wrong? I heard about your parents..." his words trail off.

I look up at him. "Yes," I say, not wanting to have this conversation that should happen in private. Words that need to be spoken only where the chance of Julian not hearing is imperative. Am I being overly cautious? Yes, but I was wrong once and won't repeat that mistake. I continue, "But first, let's fix your friend here." He seems not to like or want the redirection of this conversation but doesn't push it along for now.

"Emma," he all but growls my name.

I touch his chest and look at him. "Later, Eduardo. This time, we will have our later, okay?" His eyes soften, and he grabs my hand.

"Okay, baby." He brings my hand to his lips, giving it a soft, wet kiss that makes me melt and my center throb. He releases my hand and steps away.

I now focus my attention on the actual bleeding patient. "Sorry about that, Gus." I laugh, but Gus still holds his bleeding hand, perplexed at our exchange.

I lay the patient, Gus, as Eduardo refers to him, onto the stretcher and attach him to our monitors. I just want to ensure his vital signs are stable and he hasn't lost too much blood. I doubt this type of man would admit to feeling faint because it would make him appear weak. Believe me, I know the type all too well. Like my whole life, to be exact.

Eduardo asks me if I can fix Gus, and I know what he is really asking. "Yes, but I can't here. My license doesn't allow me to do it." He smiles, and I leave to get the ER doctor working here tonight.

I return shortly with Dr. Hernandez in tow. He looks at the wound and asks if it was a knife wound. Gus nods, and Eduardo speaks for him.

"It was a fight at my club." He doesn't elaborate, and Dr. Hernandez waits for him to continue. When he doesn't, he looks over at Gus.

"Is that true?"

Gus nods but doesn't answer. I almost giggle at this exchange. Dr. Hernandez might think he is the top dog in this ER, but he doesn't understand the hierarchy in this room.

"Okay, then. Let's fix this. Emma, can you get some antibiotics? It says he has no allergies, so how about two grams of Ancef IM."

"Sure, no problems. Here is the suture tray and numbing medicine. I'll be right back." I step away, and Dr. Hernandez grabs my arm to stop me.

"I'm buying the staff food tonight. I couldn't find you earlier, so I ordered your usual order from the day shift. I hope that's okay?"

I look over to Eduardo, whose gaze is fixed on where Dr. Hernandez is still holding my arm. Eduardo's nostrils are flaring, and I see the tick in his jaw that lets me know he is very displeased at seeing another man touching me. Gus is tensed on the stretcher, anticipating a full-out loss of control on Eduardo's part, and is waiting to see what happens.

I remove my arm from his embrace, and Dr. Hernandez looks at me when I glance over at Eduardo, shaking my head at him. This seems to confuse him, and he looks back and forth at Eduardo and me, sensing a familiarity between us. Luckily for the good doctor, he isn't an idiot and picks up on social cues because he clears his throat and focuses back on Gus.

"That sounds perfect, Dr. Hernandez, thank you." I leave the room but turn back to see that Eduardo still fixates on me as I walk away. I mouth the word "behave" at him. He smiles brightly at me. As I walk off, I shake my head and hear Gus snort at the exchange.

I return with the antibiotic in a syringe and assist Dr. Hernandez where needed. Pretty soon, the wound is closed, and Dr. Hernandez stands. He gives Gus instructions about keeping the sutures clean and dry. I add some antibacterial ointment to the site and dress it.

"You'll need to get the sutures removed in ten days," he instructs.

Eduardo looks at me and tells the doctor they have that covered. I already know what that means, and I nod after Dr. Hernandez has turned around and walked out. "I need to give you this shot, Gus. Drop your pants," I say with a smirk, knowing how this will go. Eduardo stands, and the chair falls back, knocking over at the hastiness of his stance. Gus looks over at Eduardo.

"Oh, hell. Fuck that."

He walks over to me, and I can't help but wait for the reaction I provoked. "Over my dead body will you ever say that to any other man. Do you understand me, Emma?"

"Yes, sir," I mock him and wink.

His mouth twitches in delight. He steps closer into my space. He raises his hand to my cheek in a soft embrace and trails it down my neck, leaning forward to whisper in my ear, "You can call me that anytime, baby." His breath tickles and heats down my neck, and I shudder in response. He kisses the side of my mouth quickly, not hitting the area I want him to kiss. He pulls away. "Now, give Gus the shot in his arm, and we must be on our way."

I pull Gus's shirt down to expose his deltoid muscle and clean it with alcohol. "Are you sure you want it here? I could give it to you by injecting it into a leg muscle."

"For fuck's sake. Do you want to get me killed? I'll have to take my pants down."

I purse my lips. "Okay, if you insist." I give Gus the intramuscular injection, and he grimaces." I rub the spot. "It was too much medication for that muscle, but what do I know? I'm just a nurse." I place a *Frozen* princess bandage on it and pull his shirt up. "There. All done."

I hand them their discharge instructions.

"Okay, I'm going to need your information now, Emma."

I pretend to think this over. "Hmm, I guess I could do that." I write my number on the paper and hand it over to him.

"I need all the information, Emma." I must look puzzled because he points at the paper and hands it back. "Address too."

I blush but add it to the sheet and hand it back.

They start walking to the door. "What time do you leave here, and how are you getting home?"

"My shift ends at seven in the morning, and I drive here."

He nods. "Someone will be here to follow you home, and, Emma?"

"Yes?" I ask nervously.

"That will be the last time you drive to work alone. I'll be in touch this afternoon." With that, he walks away and leaves me here at a loss for words and, for the first time, a feeling of security.

CHAPTER TWENTY

EDUARDO

We leave the emergency department, and I can't think straight until I escape this cesspool of disease and pestilence. I am no germaphobe, but even I can appreciate the nastiness that coats every inch of that place. There is no way Emma is going to continue working there after we have kids. She'll bring that crap home. I shudder at the thought.

Gus and I walk together side by side, and patients and staff part for us, sensing the dangerous vibes we ooze from our pores. It's the confidence that comes with being the top dog, or maybe it's the amount of ink that adorns our bodies. Each tattoo represents or acknowledges our different memories or special moments in our lives.

Did Emma see the tattoo I had of her name on my knuckles? If she did, she didn't let on. I remember that day I got the tattoo. I had a tattoo completed of a tidal wave with a mermaid underneath. A mermaid that had a striking resemblance to Emma with her emerald-green eyes. She had my heart in her hand, like it had been pulled from my chest, and was weeping blood and tears.

I don't know what possessed me to do that vivid tattoo with an anatomical-looking heart covering where my actual heart resides–where it ceased to beat for anyone else. Maybe I was drunk, but it was true that Emma owned my ripped heart and held it in her hands.

We were more friends the day I was told I couldn't continue to see her. The feelings were there, but I was older than her. Geez, she was in junior high, and I was going to start high school. There is no way that I could pursue anything with her at that point. A couple of years at that age is like a decade in older years. I thought I had imagined it all and the feeling that might have made her seem much more of a goddess in my head, but after seeing her here today, I know that whatever feelings I had are real and never went away. If anything, they are stronger because she was always someone I confided in and trusted. I feel that is still true. She grew up and is even more beautiful than I would have thought.

She is short though, and that makes me chuckle. She always hated being so vertically challenged. Her sister, too, but I hadn't remembered her exact features. While their physical traits were similar, their personalities were vastly distinguishable. I had this fantasy in my mind that kept her there with us as little kids. Now? Well, now she is all woman. The curves of her body and the long blond hair that I itch to fist in my hand as I stare into those luminous green eyes and watch her mouth part, calling out my name as she comes. I'll kiss her, swallow all her cries, and lick away all her tears.

I wonder what all the tears she held back today were about. There is a story there. I sensed her sadness, but I don't know if it was about losing her family or if it was something else. I'll need to find out what has happened to her. Why was she left alone, and why did her parents die? It doesn't add up, but I want to make sure that she is safe, and until I can be reassured that my worries aren't justified, I will continue to keep her under my protection.

Gus remains silent as we walk to the car. He must sense that I am deep in my thoughts as he opens the door for me, despite his injured hand, and I get in. I start up the car, and he gets into the passenger seat. I turn to look at him.

"You didn't have to open my door, Gus. You're injured," I state the obvious, pointing to his hand.

He ignores this and gets to what he really wants to ask. "That's the woman from your tattoos?" He fixes his gaze on my knuckles and points to my chest.

I sigh. "Fuck. Yes, that's Emma." I rub my hands up and down my face, then reverse the car so we can finally leave.

He nods his head up and down and then drops it. He looks out the windows, deep in thought. I have my own issue instead of trying to determine what Gus is thinking.

I must return to the club and see what else has happened while away. Then, I need to consider digging into Emma's past to get a head start on what the woman is hiding from me. I sense there's quite a bit. I know just the person to unlock those secrets, too. Now, how much I want to piss off his fiancée is the real question because there is no way in hell that I will wait until tomorrow.

I enter the club, walk past my security, and enter my office. I shut the door and halt in my tracks when I see Cherry sitting in my chair. "What the actual fuck?"

Cherry startles at my anger toward her and immediately tries to soothe my temper. "Eduardo, baby. I am so sorry. We broke up, and he couldn't accept that I was in love with you. He came to try to win me back, but there is no one else but you."

I stare at her in utter shock because what the fuck is happening right now, and how did she get in here? She provocatively struts over to me and grabs my cock.

"Let me make it up to you, baby." She drops to her knees, undoing my zipper in one fluid movement. I immediately step away from her and zip my pants up.

"Are you out of your fucking mind," I snarl. I grab my phone and call Gus. "Send security in, Gus." I hang up. I look back at Cherry with venom that sprays forth from my mouth. I don't mince my words so that she understands I mean business when I say, "I *never* want to see you again in my club. Is that understood, Cherry?" She starts crying, but I continue reinforcing my point. "Use your words, Cherry. Say that you understand."

She nods and sobs out, "Yes, I understand."

"Good. You are not to return. If I so much as see you in my club again, you will regret it. Do I make myself clear?"

She nods just as two bouncers come barging in. I turn my anger on them.

"I thought I told you that she nor her boyfriend, ex-boyfriend, whatever the fuck he is, is not to be allowed in here ever again. So how is it that I returned from taking Gus to the ER after seeing *my* girlfriend there, and now walk into this." I point at Cherry to emphasize the 'this' point. "She is sitting in here alone on *my* chair in my office, huh?"

She gasps in shock, shaking her head back and forth. I can tell she wants to say something.

"Get her out of here!" I yell. "One more slip-up and I'll be finding and vetting new bouncers for my club."

They take a very tearful and shrieking Cherry Pop out of my office, and I slump in my chair. Fucking hell, what a night, and it's not over either.

I hit the phone number for my brother, Ram, and I know he'll pick up no matter what time it is. He answers, and I hear his fiancée ask who's calling. He tells her to go back to sleep, and I hear the sound of a door closing as he speaks.

"What the fuck do you want at this hour?" He is so grumpy at 3:00 in the morning.

"Please tell my future sister-in-law I'm sorry for the intrusion at this early hour, but I need to talk to you."

In hearing my sincerity, he speaks up. "What's up, brother? Everything okay?" Any anger he had at my phone call this early in the morning is quickly forgotten.

I run my hands through my hair. I swear I'm going to go bald like the old man. I'm beginning to understand how he lost his hair early in life.

"I had to take Gus to the emergency room tonight for a minor altercation at the club."

"Is he okay?" he asks.

"Yes, but that isn't why I called." I hesitate before I get the words out. "I found her." I wait for that statement to seep in.

"Found wh-o..." he trails off. "No way. Emma? You found Emma?" he asks for confirmation.

"Yeah. I did. Emma is working in the emergency department, Ram. It was such a coincidence seeing her there. Like it was meant to be, but something happened with her, and I need to find out what, and more importantly, I need to keep her safe. For me to do that, I need to understand what happened. Do you think I should talk to her uncle? Should I call him?"

Ram thinks this over. "Well, they weren't too keen on you wanting to pursue her, but honestly, I think it was her mom doing all that. Don't you? With her parents out of the picture, I think her uncle might be thankful to have you look after her."

That reassures me about what I have to do next. "I'll call Andrés, but first, can you find out what happened with her family in Brownsville? I need more information to see what is going on here. Is she in danger? A lot was weighing on her mind. I could sense it. I hope she will open up to me about it, but if not... then I intend to find out through any means necessary to keep her safe and protected."

"How is she?" he asks, sincerity pouring in every spoken word. We were all friends back then, when things were simpler.

"She's still short. I don't think she likes that, but I think it's cute as fuck." I laugh, trying to make light of the situation.

"You still care for her, don't you?" He waits for my answer, but it doesn't take long for me to reply.

"Of course. I've always loved Emma." Finally saying this out loud to another person feels good. It feels right. Now, I just have to tell her and hope that she feels the same way toward me. I don't think I can let her go a second time. I know I won't.

"I'll find out what you need. I'll be in touch, Eduardo. Be safe. Love you, bro."

He hangs up, and I ponder my choices while I sit at my desk. First things first. I call my main security detail, Philip, and have him come in.

A few moments later, Philip walks into my office. I will explain the reason why he is here. I need to make sure Emma is safe. He is her detail from now on, and I need him to keep me updated on her whereabouts and everything she does. I also ask him to order some red roses and deliver them to her address.

"I need you to give her access to the club at my office and put her name on the VIP list. Give her this card with the roses so she knows to come here." I hand him the access card for the club. He looks at me like I've lost my mind.

I know what it must look like. I have never cared for another woman in my life besides my mother, but Emma is not an ordinary woman. She's *my* woman, and there isn't anything I wouldn't do to protect what's mine.

CHAPTER TWENTY-ONE

EMMA

The girls are planning a visit to Houston. Val, Ainsley, and Piper are coming soon, and Liv and I look forward to the company. I send out a text to Liv.

Emma: I'm picking up some things for the girls' upcoming visit. Do you want to come?

Liv: YES

Emma: Well, that was easy. I thought I was going to have to bribe you. I know how much you hate shopping for clothes.

Liv doesn't reply, so I go about my business and rush home. Even though I am off, I promised my favorite people at work that I would meet them this evening. I got off early today. Well, early this morning, and I slept until noon. Remind me never to work another night shift. Hell, that was rough, but it turned out to be a very good thing, I think to myself as I touch the beautiful floral arrangement Eduardo sent, now sitting pretty on my table. Only day shifts for me. That work-life balance keeps my sanity, unlike my bestie, Liv, who continues to burn her candle at both ends. I laugh at that idiomatic expression.

My mom used that saying often, and I think of her every time I use it. It physically hurts my heart to think about it, but I refuse to make myself forget about them by not talking about them or taking the time to remember the good moments with my family. Maybe I am a glutton for punishment, but I miss my parents and Evie so much. I try to carry their memories with me as if they are still around. I probably need an appointment with a therapist, but what do I say when I am interviewed? "Yes, my family was kind of killed, but my psycho boyfriend tried to keep me in a locked house to rely on only him. His dad has political affiliations with the mafia, but my mom's parents are the mafia, too." Yeah, that won't go over well. Instead, I am trying my best to cope with the grief and guilt that occupy my daily life.

I get dressed quickly and am ready to meet my friends at the sports bar near the hospital. It is a place we frequent for some pre-clubbing drinks. It's kind of like tailgating before the main event. Happy hour is usually packed with people behaving worse around seven p.m. I grab my keys and admire the roses that occupy most of the kitchen table. They are so aromatic, and as I touch them, I sigh, remembering our encounter from the other night. Staring down at my key fob, I decide against driving there. Instead I open the app settling for an Uber, and place my key back on the table.

I glimpse at my phone. "Five minutes until they get here. Gotta love this city," I mutter as I close the door behind me.

I enter through the door and look for my friends. I go around a few people and head toward the other side of the bar, seeing the group sitting by the bar at a side table. As I walk over, I see a guy approaching me with purpose, and I stop mid-stride, worried about Julian, until I recognize him—Jameson. The guy that I met with Liv and Dax on Padre Island over a year ago. Geez, crazy. He pulls me into a hug as if we are long-lost friends.

"Oh my god. Who are you with? What are you doing?" I exclaim, throwing my hands in the air like I can't believe it.

Jameson points over to the table he was sitting at. "I'm here with the guys from the beach when we all last hung out, when..." He doesn't finish that sentence because we all remember what happened that night before the accident. "I honestly didn't think I'd ever see you again." He throws me a megawatt smile, and I can't help but smile in return. "Come on and say hi to everyone." He pulls me over to the table where his friends are engaged in conversation, until they all stop to look at us.

"Hey, everyone. Do you remember Emma?" He goes through the introductions, but I remain focused on Dax. He looks at me until recognition dawns on him, and it's as if the poor guy wants to ask a million questions. "Dax, you remember Emma, right? Liv's friend?" He pulls me in for a hug, and I laugh.

"Well, gentleman, what a warm reception I'm getting this evening."

Theo and Eric wave at me in unison, like they are waving to the Queen of England. Jerks. "Well, the whole gang's here tonight." I quickly turn my gaze back to Jameson, and we begin to catch up on everything we have been up to in the past year. I enjoy how easy it is to talk to him. I can see Dax from the corner of my eye sitting on the edge of his seat, radiating excitement at the possibility of asking me questions about Liv. Instead, he turns to me and asks if I want a drink.

I raise an eyebrow at him, calling bullshit, and he chuckles in response. "Sure, I'll take a gimlet." I hear them all laugh at me. "What?" I reply, shrugging, not getting the joke.

"A gimlet? Isn't that what older people drink?" He pats my arm in a placating fashion.

"First of all, shame on you, Jameson, for age discrimination and...well, I guess I am just an old soul too. Lastly, it also helps when it is later on in the night, and I just end up getting soda water and lime, and everyone thinks I have the fastest elimination process for alcohol consumption."

Jameson snorts. "All right, smarty pants. One gimlet is coming up." He steps away, and I can feel Dax staring at me. I look over at him.

"Will you just ask me already?" I laugh because he is so predictable. He looks like a love-sick popular jock in high school crushing on the nerdy booktrovert.

Then he spews a verbal vomit of questions all about Liv. "Finally," I laugh. "I was waiting for that." I proceed to catch him up quickly on how Liv has been and the guilt that eats her up on a daily basis, but how she perseveres, continuing to work and attend school. Jameson comes back with my drink, and I take a big swallow of the clean-tasting beverage.

"I moved to Houston for her, you know. She was a wreck. I worried about her and told her I was ready to make a new life for myself. Start a new adventure." I can see Jameson perk up at these words. Little does he know that there is another reason for my move. Despite Julian finding me, I am still trying to live my life, until he either catches up to me or I cease to exist. He once told me that if he couldn't have me, then no one would. I absolutely believe him. "Honestly, I couldn't let her come here by herself. She didn't even go to her graduation."

Dax rubs his hands down his face. "I tried to reach out to her."

"Yeah, she told me. She seems to have put all her focus into school and this per diem job we both work at the hospital."

This piques his interest, and he sits up straighter in his chair, but before he can ask, I hold my hand up, refusing to tell him anything more about Liv.

"I don't want to tell you anything more because you both need to talk first—"

"I saw Liv today," he interrupts. "I was with some woman from work. We, um, work together."

I believe Dax, but I am also not naive enough to think it was a platonic relationship. At least not initially. Before ending this discussion, I give him one last piece of advice. "If you want to make a go with our girl, you will have to try harder. She fell for you that weekend. And it scares her. And she is living with so much guilt that it is suffocating her. If you care about her, then don't stop trying."

I look for my friends, and I can see that they are giving me the 'what the fuck look.' I tilt my head up in acknowledgment. I say my good-byes and head over to my friends.

After a couple of drinks, I decide to message Liv.

> Emma: You will never believe who I ran into at our after-work sports bar! Jameson from Spring Break, and he wasn't alone.

I don't elaborate on who he wasn't alone with. I expect to hear right back from her, questioning what I mean and who else was there, if it wasn't blatantly obvious. Instead, I get radio silence, so I call Liv. She answers quickly; I know she's probably at home by now. Did I catch her before she threw on her comfy PJs, and I can't get her to come out?

"Hey, girlie! What's up?" I don't give her a chance to reply. "Get dressed and meet me out. I need to dance, and you're coming now."

I hear her laughing on the phone, so I hope she will agree. "Yeah, I guess I could. Where are we meeting?"

And that's all I need. I got Liv to come out. That in itself is not a small feat.

We talk about what we are wearing, and I tell her to wear something cute and sexy. Liv bursts out laughing. "Okay, so something low cut and short," she states jokingly. "Got it."

I scream-shout my excitement on the line. "Call me when you pull up. It's a big club, and I'll come out to get you." I hang up before she can say anything else, fist-pumping the air. "Yes!" I say to no one in particular.

Liv shares her ETA with me, and I see her pull up, look at the long-ass line, and get into line at the back.

No, no, I think to myself, that just won't do. I'm waving at Liv, screaming her name, laughing at her look of shock. I see her walk over to me at the front of the line, getting ugly looks from the girls waiting in the queue. I'm talking about death stares now. I immediately wrap her up in a hug.

"How did you get up here? The line is crazy!" she yells at me over the crowd's noise and loud city nightlife scene. The bouncer lifts the rope, and we walk through the club doors.

"Come on. Let's get a drink."

I drag Liv through the crowds, not letting go of her hand once. We walk toward the bar.

"Let's do some shots." I place myself against the bar to get the bartender's attention. He smiles widely.

Liv agrees, and I order two each. She tries to pay, but the bartender points to someone at the end of the bar.

"You ladies are all set."

We take our first shot, and he immediately pours us our second one. He pushes the next shots at us, and we look at each other, shrugging.

"So. How did you get us in here?" Liv asks. I take my last shot, suck on the lime, and discard it into the now-empty shot glass on the bar.

"I took care of the guy that owns this place. Well, no, not him, but an employee. I can't tell you much more because of patient confidentiality. I've probably said too much as it is. Blame it on the alcohol." I shrug in a sorry-not-sorry manner. "He told me to come here and put me on the VIP list." Liv takes her second shot, and I ask the bartender if this is from the owner. He raises his eyebrows at my question.

"No, it wasn't him," he says as he collects the glasses. "It was someone else," his words fading away as he leaves.

I should tell Liv.

"It was Jameson, then," I say quickly, not wanting to hide it from Liv any longer. I see the look on her face as she tries to place that name from her memory when it hits, and her eyes widen in surprise.

"I ran into him at a sports bar before calling you. Our favorite sports bar, and, Liv? He wasn't alone."

She stares at me and realizes who he wasn't alone with.

Without further questions, I point to the dance floor. Liv points to the roped-off area leading to a floor above us.

"That's the VIP section. I am not sure I have access to that area or if it is just to enter by skipping the entrance line. I was allowed entry into the club with this card, but I have no idea if my name is on *'that'* list." I tuck the card away and we stare at the darkened VIP area as Liv hits my shoulder, then points behind her.

"Come on. I don't plan on getting off the dance floor anyway," Liv says.

"I agree." I lead her to the dance floor, where the sound systems blare EDM, pop, and other mesmerizing dance music. As we start to dance, I shout by her ear, "I don't plan on getting off the dance floor either anytime soon."

CHAPTER TWENTY-TWO

EDUARDO

I have watched Emma's every movement since she entered my club, The Viceroy. Philip told me that she was outside. He delivered the roses and, obviously, the access card for the club. I am glad she didn't waste any time coming to me tonight. I didn't want to have to send for her. I see her walking around with a tall girl. Then return to the bar to take some shots. Tequila.

"Interesting choice," I mumble to myself.

That's not all that is interesting. I see Jameson, my frat brother, fixated at the end of the bar with his gaze set on Emma. He motions to the bartender to get the girls another shot and hands him a card to set up a tab. He is with a few guys, and they go to the VIP room. I'll visit him and see how he knows my little thief.

Jameson is standing with another guy, and they stare at the dance floor, pointing to someone. I zoom in on what has them transfixed and sit up, my spine rigid at the fact that they are pointing to Emma and her friend.

They go to the dance floor, and I see the guy Jameson was with, dancing alongside the tall brunette. He is standing behind her with his body gyrating with hers in sync to the music. When the song ends, she turns around appearing shocked to see him staring intently at her. Her face goes through a series of emotions until it softens and he leans in to kiss her. I see Emma's face up close on my surveillance monitors, and, much to my displeasure, I see Jameson looking at her.

"Oh, fuck no." I get up and call Philip to bring them up to the VIP area where I will meet them.

I am on my way to intercept her when one of my security people stops me in the back hall.

"Boss, I think there is something I should tell you about." He looks over at the bouncer with him.

"Yes, what is it." My patience wears thin because, while I want to know about the operation of my club, I am only thinking about what Jameson is doing with my girlfriend.

"We caught one of the bartenders stealing money." He shifts uncomfortably on his feet.

"How much?" I spit out. I look at both of them, trying to get them to hurry up and give me an answer.

"Not much, Boss, just a couple of hundred bucks, but it's the principle, right?"

I nod in agreement. "Get the money out of him, and if he doesn't have it, take it from him in flesh." I start to walk away, and they stare at me. I usually prefer a more hands-on approach when things like this arise, but now I can't be bothered to deal with a thieving employee when I have to get to my own little thief. Except she didn't steal money; she stole something far more valuable.

"Oh, yeah, and before you fire him, in case that wasn't obvious, bring him to my 'hospitality room' so I can see him personally." I open the door hard, banging it off the wall as I walk out of the office with a purpose—to find her.

I finally go up to the VIP section, where that tall girl accompanying Emma tonight sits on Jameson's friend's lap. Jameson is very close to My Emma. I see a brunette, sidled up next to Jameson, get up angrily as he refuses to acknowledge her. Emma seems amused, but I'm sure they see it differently. Only I know her genuine emotions. That is, if they haven't changed. That is something I'll need to re-familiarize myself with.

Jameson calls the waitstaff over as I approach the table. I have a big smile on my face for Emma.

"Emma," I say her name seductively so they get the meaning of my intrusion.

"Hey there, Eduardo," she replies playfully, her eyes alight with humor. "Thanks so much for letting us into the club and setting us up tonight. That was so..." She thinks of the word for a second. "Hospit-able of you."

I catch the play on words as I only reconnected with her at the hospital earlier today. My lips twitch in amusement. I see the group watching our dialogue and the playful banter between us that I thought we were being sneaky at concealing.

"Liv and I are having such a great time," she continues.

I see Jameson visibly tense. I give him a once-over, trying to determine how much of a threat my frat brother is and if I like him enough to let him leave here with all his teeth.

I turn my attention back to Emma. "I'll be in touch. I must attend to some business, but please enjoy yourself and let me know if you need anything." I feel their eyes on me, but the only eyes I care about belong to a green-eyed vixen who stole my heart long ago.

"So, you thought you could steal from me." I pick his head up to look at me. Well, from what he can see of me from two eyes that seem to be swelling shut as we have this conversation. "I never want to see you in this club again. You should be leaving here minus a limb, but I felt pretty generous this evening and I am in good spirits. I also don't want to get my hands dirty, so to speak. Consider today your lucky day."

I have the bouncers escort him out of my room, and after they leave, I trail behind, returning to the VIP section. It's almost closing time, and I notice that Emma is intoxicated. Jameson is hovering like a vulture, and my blood pressure rises.

"Este vato." He is fucking dead, brother or not.

He hands her a cup, trying to get her to drink water. I can't believe she got this drunk. She sways back and forth. Jameson clings to her, and I see fucking red. He may be trying to help her, but his intentions aren't strictly honorable.

I call Philip and have him get the car ready to take Emma and her friend home. It looks like her friend has other plans though, so I go up to Emma when I can't take it anymore.

"Philip is taking you home. Get rid of Jameson, Emma. The only name you are going to be screaming tonight is mine."

Her eyes dilate, and she whispers in my ear, "I'll hold you to that, babe."

I touch her cheek, feeling Jameson watching us.

She walks over to him, and he asks her questions, looking at me. I walk off, not needing to deal with this exchange. I know who will be with whom later tonight. I see Jameson at Emma's side as she sways a bit, and he holds her. Philip brings the car up to the door and gets in after her. I see her drive away without me for the last time.

I pull up in my black Porsche 911 turbo at Emma's apartment complex. I quickly get out and hit the lock on my key fob. Philip told me he dropped Emma off about thirty minutes ago and took a very dejected-looking Jameson home right after she closed the door in his face. He tried to enter her apartment, but my girl sent him away. I know she is alone, and I plan to take advantage of this alone time with her.

I take the steps two at a time and barely reach the landing when she opens the door. She stares at me while sipping something from her Stanley cup. Her face is washed free of makeup, and she wears a cropped tank and sleep shorts. I look her up and down in a slow perusal. I have never seen her look more beautiful. It's so similar to when we were younger, and I swear I feel like a kid again. I was pining for a girl I had to let go of. If I had known when I gave her that necklace for her birthday, all those years ago, that it would be the last time I would see her, I would have taken more time with her. That's the thing about good-bye. Sometimes, you're not lucky enough to have one. Emma knows this more than I do, and my heart pains at her having to endure that hardship and more all alone.

She smiles brightly at me, opens the door wide, and heads back inside. I trail behind her like a love-sick puppy. She places her drink on the table next to where the roses I sent her are standing on full display.

"Nice roses," I say with a smirk playing at the corner of my mouth.

"Oh, do you like them?" she asks, quirking an eyebrow upward. "My boyfriend got them for me. I hope that's not a problem for you?"

"Definitely not a problem for me. Maybe for Jameson though?" I ask in question as I move toward her.

"He was rather upset when I sent him home." She pretends to be upset about his departure, casting her eyes toward the ground, pursed lips.

I move in quickly, catching her off guard, and she squirms with delight as I wrap my hands around her waist and pull her to me. My fingers dig into her waist, and she fights the urge to laugh. She's always been ticklish.

"Just in case you were wondering, Emma…" I pause as I bring my mouth to her neck, trailing light kisses up to her ear. "I don't give a fuck about Jameson," I say harshly.

She shudders as my breath lays heavy on her ear. I kiss my way over to her cheek and pull back slightly as I reach her mouth. I stare at her. "You are fucking mine." I smash my lips to hers, and she opens her mouth to allow entry. I suck on her tongue and deepen the kiss.

"Where is your bedroom?" I take off my jacket and drape it over the chair. I undo the cufflinks on my dress shirt and unbutton it, taking it off and draping it along with where my jacket resides.

She just watches me, making me smile to see how I affect her. Her eyes widen when I go for my belt buckle, undoing it and my pants as they fall to the floor in a swoop, pooling around my ankles.

I step out of them, and my socks and shoes are all discarded on the floor. I stand in my boxers with my hard cock sticking out the top, my tip glistening. She is zoned in on it and involuntarily licks her lips. My cock twitches, and the mirth in her eyes says she saw it.

"If you keep looking at me like that, Emma, I will fuck you for our first time on this carpet."

She walks up to me. Her one hand touches my cock, rubbing the precum around the tip, making me hiss at the contact of her fingers. "Maybe later," she says. "Tonight, I want you to fuck me properly in a bed." She sticks her finger in her mouth and sucks my arousal from it.

That does it. I lift her up as if she weighs nothing. She wraps her legs around my waist as I walk through the door she pointed to as her bedroom.

"All night…" she trails off as she brings her lips to mine, and I lose myself in an all-consuming kiss.

CHAPTER TWENTY-THREE

EMMA

He carries me into the bedroom. His cock is hard against my center, and I grind into it, feeling the heat of our bodies and the wetness that pools between my legs. I have never been so turned on in my life. I thought teenage Eduardo was hot, but this is so much better. He is all man, and I haven't even had a proper look at his cock.

He places me carefully on the bed, like a fragile treasure he doesn't want to break. I look up at him hovering over me, mesmerized by the heat in his eyes that's directed at me. He's barely containing himself, and I relish in the knowledge that I can turn him on this much.

"Be a good girl and take your shirt off for me, baby," he purrs, and my core tingles in anticipation of speeding this process up, but he has no intention of getting to it. He is going excruciatingly slow, and it's starting to bother me. I need him to touch me, expose me, and make me his in the physical sense—the primal act of taking me and ravishing my body. I crave him, and it is driving me mad with lust.

I focus on him as I lift my tank top over my head and toss it to the floor, attempting to play his game. He pulls my bra down, making my boobs stick out over the top. He licks his finger and circles around one of my nipples, leaving wetness and goose bumps in its wake. He cups the other breast roughly with his hand, and I groan at the contact. He pushes me back on the bed and removes my sleeping shorts, finding I'm not wearing any panties. His nostrils flare, and he stares at my bare pussy. He looks at me with hooded eyes, and I arch my back up in response as if I am offering myself up to him—a silent permission to take me.

That must do the trick because his control snaps. I win. He drops to the ground, pulling me forward on the bed, and dives in to feast on my pussy. I cry out at the sudden intrusion. He is like an animal biting and sucking on my clit in tandem. I don't know what to feel. The pain mixed with the pleasure causes pressure to build rapidly. But whenever I feel an impending orgasm, he pulls back and then circles my clit slowly with his tongue, causing the tingles to subside.

I begin to whimper after he does this a couple of times, but then he adds a couple of fingers arching up toward my cervix while sucking on my clit until I feel it come on quickly, full force, and I cry out, my orgasm shattering throughout my body. He doesn't stop pumping in and out with his fingers until the pulsing starts to abate. He pulls his fingers out and licks them in front of me. I almost climax again. It's filthy and dirty, and I am so incredibly turned on by the sight of it.

I breathe in and out, my heart rate starting to slow down as if I've just run a marathon. My arm rests over my eyes and I suddenly feel spent. He stands and picks up my legs that have fallen open on the bed and rubs his warm, leaking cock up and through my folds, still slick from my arousal, to lubricate his shaft.

I lower my arm from my face and concentrate on his mouth, still wet with my juices. I look up into his eyes, and without breaking contact, he thrusts inside me, filling me completely. His hips are flush with mine, and he begins to move. He moves painstakingly slowly, and I almost can't take it. I meet each thrust with my own, and we have a rhythm that he decides to change up because he throws my legs over his shoulder and drives in hard. I cry out his name.

"Eduardo, fuck yes, harder, babe. Fuck me harder." I don't even know who I am right now.

The things coming out of my mouth should embarrass me, but this feels so good, so right that I can't stop the crudeness that leaves my lips. The porn star version of myself cries out so loudly that my neighbors will surely hear our lovemaking. The look I'll get from them… but I don't care. Nothing exists right now except the pounding of our hips and the thrust of his cock that hits my G-spot so deep that I start to orgasm again.

Eduardo's thrusts become more frantic as he starts to lose control. He is a beast, picking me up off the bed, knees bent, holding me close. He kisses me as he thrusts into me, pushing and pulling me onto his cock. My hips will be bruised from the tight grip he has on me.

I throw my head back, and he latches on to my boob, biting my nipple, and I swear I will climax again. He pounds relentlessly and pulls me into a searing kiss as if he is branding me. Finally, making me his. He sucks on my neck, leaving a bruise, crying out and throwing his head back. I look at him in the throes of passion. With his breath still labored, he brings his head back to look at me, and I smile at him.

He picks me up, still impaled on his cock, and the smile that graces his lips should be illegal. He leads us to my bathroom and starts the shower. He walks us in, and I feel him harden again. I look into his eyes, and he kisses me passionately as if he is making up for all the wasted years apart.

"About that all-night part?" he says as he leans me up against the wall and begins to move.

He comes into the bedroom with my Stanley Cup. "Here, baby, I want you to drink more water."

I take the cup from him and take a few more sips at his encouraging request. I know that I will be so thankful tomorrow, and after all the water and the ibuprofen I took before he got here, I should feel okay. Maybe that's wishful thinking because I know an imminent conversation we need to have will make me feel anything but okay.

"Emma," he says, and I sense that by the way he says my name, he wants to ask me something serious. I just wish it wasn't in the early morning hours before dawn.

"Yes." I look up at him and cup his cheek. I stare into his eyes and know that this will be the conversation I am not ready for, but it is necessary. If there is one person I can trust, it is him.

So I start at the beginning—with Julian. I see how his face hardens and the disgust that lingers in his features when I talk to him about the abuse I endured.

"Emma—" He halts his words, trying to remain calm. "Why the fuck didn't you say something sooner. Why did you let him treat you that way?"

"He threatened me and, more importantly, Eduardo, he threatened my parents. He told me there would be consequences if I tried to leave home. He would ensure my parents' careers were ruined, and we would lose our home and life as we knew it. I believed him because his dad is the mayor." He also is into some sketchy dealings, but I leave that part out for now. After hours of talking and crying, he holds me, and for once, I fall asleep without the fear of Julian.

CHAPTER TWENTY-FOUR

EDUARDO

Emma is sound asleep, and the thought of leaving her alone is agonizing. I get up and put my boxers on. I look for the rest of my clothes and realize that Emma, that little sex kitten, seduced me in the living room, and I left all of my clothes out there. I grab my watch from the bedside table and walk out to close the door to Emma's room behind me with a soft click.

I walk the short distance to the living room when I see Liv, Emma's roommate, drinking a glass of water. She was about to wave when she realized it wasn't who she thought it was. *Did she think it was Jameson? What the fuck?* I'm sure she will tell that guy she was with last night, whatever his name was—Jameson's friend—that I was here. I run a hand through my hair, giving her my best impression of an innocent look. Her eyes narrow, and I can tell she does not buy the innocent act. Oh, well, I tried.

"Hi?" Liv says in question. There is a reluctance to get near me. Maybe she senses danger when she looks at me. That wouldn't be wrong. Little does she know that I am not the real danger here. I am the closest thing to safety when it comes to Emma—and possibly her, since she is Emma's best friend.

I laugh at the thought. "Hi, Liv. I'll be out of your hair in a second," I tell her as I gather up my discarded items from last night's sexcapades.

"Just need to get dressed." I pick up my clothes, not bothering to change anywhere else. Fuck it. If she can't give a guy some privacy, she can see what a real man looks like. I grab my keys off the coffee table in the living room.

"I'll see you later. Have a good day." I throw her a wink before I walk out the front door. I just couldn't help myself. I almost laughed at her reaction.

After I leave Emma's apartment, I start to recall the truths she told me. I am reeling with anger. I know it took a lot for her to tell me about Julian, but I am glad she confided in me, and I vowed to protect her. I would keep her safe. The relief that flooded her face when I told her that shook me to my core. The fact that she had been out here alone, unprotected, killed me. I thought her uncle had someone following her, but I'll need more information.

I suspect she hid details that would anger me, but her parents and sister died. I couldn't say anything more after seeing the guilt surface in her expression after mentioning them. That she feels responsible for their deaths instead of blaming that monster she dated is ridiculous. When she also told me about overhearing a conversation between that scumbag and his father when she was imprisoned in their house right before her cousin came in to remove her from that place, it was suspicious as hell. I already suspected he had something to do with the fire that killed her family. After she overheard the conversation alluding to Julian's father having covered up the incident, it is obvious that there is more going on than just Julian's obsession with Emma, but it remains to be seen.

I won't let him anywhere near her. The only way I can do that is to provide her with twenty-four-seven security. I'll also need to tell my father and speak with her uncle about his plans so we can put forth a unified front. I won't have anything happen to her. Just the thought has me in a tailspin. If he found her in Padre Island, he would still be searching for her, and she probably won't escape him for long. I suspect he found her sooner than she realized, and he was about to execute another planned attempt at kidnapping her.

I get in the car and call Philip to meet me here. There is no way that I will allow her to be unguarded without me or someone looking after her. As I check my emails and catch up on returning messages, I notice Philip,

Emma's newly appointed security detail, pull up in the parking lot. I get out of the car and tell him what is at stake. After many assurances that he understands that Emma is not to leave his sight, I send a message to Emma before I leave the parking lot of her complex.

Eduardo: Philip is outside your apartment and is keeping watch on you. DO NOT go anywhere without him.

I'm waiting for her to text me back. The minutes tick by, and I begin to feel unsettled as the city lights pass by in a blur of colors through my window. I tap my fingers on the steering wheel, trying to calm the anxiety I have radiating through my body. No other person can unsettle me like this—only Emma. A text message alert displays on my car screen. I hit play, and a female voice speaks Emma's message.

Emma: Yes, sir.

I groan at the double entendre her comment insinuates. I speak into the car's voice assistant and send off a reply to her message.

Eduardo: Are you trying to make me wreck? Miss you already.

This time her answer comes without delay.

Emma: Please don't wreck.

Emma: Miss you more. Chat later?

Her sincerity makes me smile. I love how much she cares, and I don't miss the hidden meaning of her comment.

Eduardo: I'll never leave you again. More than chat later;)

Once those words enter the cyber air, I know truer words have never been said. I was forced to leave Emma, but nothing can come between us again. I snort aloud in the car for my use of a 'wink emoji.'

"What the fuck is wrong with me?" I utter to no one.

My brother would have a field day with these jokes at my expense. I have, for one, been busting his balls about his devotion to his fiancée. I'll have to do better when I see them, I suppose.

I pull into my parking spot and take the private elevator to my residence. My place has a separate key card for the keypad to get to my floor. It would be much easier to have Emma stay here. Then, I would not have to worry as much about her safety, not to mention the security system in my home is top-notch. That is a huge relief because I'll be able to keep an eye on her.

I just have to address her working schedule.

I don't care if she works. I fully support her independence, but not when a psychopath is stalking her. At least she has some safety measures in place there at the hospital. I'll just have to add to it. Contemplating how I will do all of this, I head to my office to make the calls that need to be made today.

"Eduardo. How are you, son?" I hear a door close as I suspect he is going to his office for a more private conversation. I rarely phone my father for a social call. I reserve those for my darling of a mother.

"Father, I need to talk with you about a girl."

I hear him getting out some glasses as if he thinks this is a call for celebration. He must think I am telling him about a marriage proposal or accidental pregnancy. Either of which would result in both, one way or the other. To be married with an heir. The click of ice confirms my suspicions.

"Continue. I can't wait—" He stops abruptly at the interruption.

"It's not simple." I know he can't possibly guess where I am going with this.

"Is she pregnant? Not a problem," he continues, as if it means nothing to him either way.

"Not yet, but it is someone you know." I clear my throat, contemplating how to give him all the news.

"Who is she, Eduardo? How do we know her?" I hear him take in a drink of alcohol as he blows a loud sigh into the phone.

"It's Emma." I pause for a bit when he doesn't speak. "It's always been Emma."

The glass, probably empty, hits the desk with a clunk. "What? Did I hear her parents died? The Ortiz family? What is going on, son?"

I told him what Emma told me, how we reunited in Houston, and how her safety was jeopardized. How I plan to take care of her, marry her.

"You can tell Mom the good news," I chide.

He snorts. "I hardly call this good news. Even telling your Catholic mother about an unplanned pregnancy is better than this." More ice clicks in a glass.

"Well, that is certainly a possibility now." I laugh so he knows I am mostly joking, but I wouldn't care if she gets pregnant with my child. That's the plan for later, anyway. I don't want to be the one to take away her choices though. She's had enough of that.

"I'm going to call her Uncle Andrés and see what he is doing to ensure her safety, and I hope I can count on you for support as your son and for your future daughter-in-law."

He sighs into the phone. "Of course, son. I just wish you hadn't picked the one woman you couldn't have. There are so many other options—"

"There are no other options," I growl. "And I wouldn't have to go through such a difficult time to be with the one person I love if it wasn't made this way. Things would have been so different if no one interfered. She'd be safe from so many unnecessary dangers."

"I'm sure you will discover that that isn't true, Eduardo, but I'll support you with anything you need. You can count on your family for that."

I hang up and can't help but reflect on the conversation with my father. What did he mean that it isn't true regarding unnecessary dangers? She wouldn't have met Julian if her mom hadn't stopped us from seeing each other. She would have been promised to me. That was always the plan, until it wasn't. Her parents would have been protected.

Alive.

I struggle to see how it could have turned out any different if she were mine.

I shower, hesitant to remove the imprint of Emma's smell on my skin. As I walk, I get a faint whiff of her scent and groan at the thought of last night. The anticipation of seeing her again is too much now. I must put her out of my mind if I intend to get any work done today.

I get out of the shower, needing to get to the gym and see how the new restaurant owners we selected for the space in our nourishment center are orchestrating, implementing the design, and advertising for their new customers. Before, they had a food truck-type establishment in the area, which would get them a guaranteed flow of customers who wouldn't hesitate to pay for a good product. This establishment is the type of place that could make them succeed and pin their name on the Houston middle- and upper-class demographic map. I, for one, am hooked and am glad to have a lovely family-run business in my gym catering to healthy food options for our patrons.

As I walk out the door, my phone rings, and I see it's my brother, Ram. I decide to make a coffee before leaving and prepare myself mentally for whatever he has to say. I am sure my father has already called him or, even worse, my mother.

I answer the phone without saying hello. It isn't needed because I already hear his voice coming through the phone.

"So, you told Dad that you are getting married?" I hear laughter coming out of the speaker along with a female voice.

"I am glad you are both laughing at my expense." I can't help but chuckle at his teasing. I had this coming.

"Let me ask this. Does Emma know she is getting married?" He starts laughing harder, a full belly laugh, wheezing as he tries to stop.

"Don't keel over without your inhaler," I reprimand him. "I'd hate to see you wheeze to death," I deadpan.

"Oh god, oh god. Okay, that was just too good to pass up. Mom called and told me the good news. Seriously though, does Emma know? Did you actually propose?"

I contemplate my words before I ask him. On the way home, I had thought about it but wasn't sure if it was a good idea. "Do you think I should ask her uncle for her hand in marriage?"

The line is quiet, and I swear I think Ram hung up or the line was disconnected. "You're serious, aren't you?" Ram's tone is quieter, and I hear a door close behind him.

"Yes. I have always loved Emma, and now…fuck, Ram. She is so alone, and I'm afraid something will happen to her. I left Philip with her as her protection when I am not there, but I didn't want to leave her side. I can't help but think about how things would have been different had we had the chance to be together."

Ram clears his throat. "I think you should call her uncle and see what's going on and get more details about this family. You know something is happening, and I bet it has more to do with Emma. Also, yes, you should ask her uncle for permission. I think he will be more than happy with the arrangement."

I nod and think about when I should call. "I guess I'll call sooner than later, bro. Thanks for the advice."

"Anytime, man." He hangs up, and the wave of uncertainty breaks, battering me with the fear that I could lose her again. I can't let that happen.

CHAPTER TWENTY-FIVE

EMMA

I finally get to spend a night with Liv. It seems like I never see her anymore. She has been spending all her time with her new hottie, Dax. I totally approve of that male specimen for her. I had to witness the emotional roller coaster of Brodie and Liv's relationship. After the accident, she seems to be coming more and more out of the personal guilt bubble she perpetually floats around in. The girl had a complicated history with that guy but also deserves happiness. The happiness that she currently has now with Dax.

I bite my lip. I understand how guilt can be all-consuming. I finally feel alive since reuniting with Eduardo. He has brought back so many happy memories from my childhood, and we frequently talk about everything we did when we were younger. Nostalgia is a bitch, and I welcome her with open arms. I wish those memories didn't have to end, where we had our separate lives without creating memories together, but we have this second chance to recreate new ones—our future together.

I heard back from the girls in Texas about our upcoming girls' trip, so I decide to text Liv.

> Emma: Hey! The girls are coming to visit. It's gonna be hella fun.

Not waiting for a reply, I take a quick shower, and then we can plan our attack on the town. I just have to run the details by Eduardo. He doesn't ask because he wants to control me. He asks because he wants to keep me safe, and I love that about him. He is so different from the men I grew up with.

I shower quickly, not bothering to wash my hair. It's almost coming out of my messy bun. I flip my hair back, and that's when I see a message written in the foggy condensation on the mirror.

I really hate condensation, I think to myself. *Liv is such a trickster.* I anticipate her shouting, *"Emma, the condensation...Ohr Nor."* It was our thing while working in the ER on Padre Island when we would place our iced coffees in the cubby. Every time we picked the plastic cups up, water would drip off the bottom, and we'd reenact our favorite Australian-based show.

When I get closer to the mirror, my pulse spikes. I start to feel faint, and I think I might pass out. I grip onto the counter, trying to prevent myself from hyperventilating. Once again, I look at the mirror in disbelief. Tears threaten to fall from my eyes, and my vision becomes blurry. I blink them back effectively, clearing my sight. I begin slowing my breathing down and chant in my head.

Breathe in.

Breathe out.

Don't run from me Emma

I can't look at the writing anymore. I wrap the towel tighter around my body and quickly leave the bathroom to call Eduardo. I almost crash into the door when I see someone in my room.

I jump back quickly. "Oh dear god, I didn't hear you come in." I laugh and look at her. "Did you just get home from work?"

Liv looks over at me, and I know she wants to ask me questions—the ones I have repeatedly been vague about. I see the concern in her stare, and that guts me. I want so badly to share my secrets with her, to lessen my burden by confiding in my best friend, but that would be selfish of me. I was selfish before, and the price was losing my family. Julian killed them. My sister, my best friend. I won't let that happen to Liv, and to protect her, I have to keep my secrets and somehow convey that she means the world to me. I look away.

"Let me get changed," I tell her and shut the door, effectively shutting her out, as well as the conversation. I hear the door to my room close, signaling Liv's departure. I immediately pick up my phone and call Eduardo.

It goes straight to voicemail. "Great. I guess I'll call Philip," I say aloud.

He answers on the second ring. "Is everything okay?" I hear his voice increase in intensity.

"Umm, yes. I tried to call Eduardo, and he wasn't answering. Do you know where he is?" The line is silent for a minute, and Philip clears his throat.

"Business." He doesn't elaborate. "Do you need anything? Are you upset about something? Did something happen?" I hear the urgency in his voice increase with each question. I hear the sound of the door unlocking, and I am afraid he will barge in at any moment. That would take a lot of explaining that I don't think I could do at this point, with Liv already witnessing my weird behavior.

"No, I'm okay," I say quickly before he scares Liv and bursts in, further adding to the many secrets I am hiding.

I can sense Liv getting close to asking me. The mental questions show through on her scrunched-up eyebrows or her narrowing eyes—suspicions I tend to downplay or use distraction techniques to prevent the onslaught of her questioning things I cannot speak to her about.

"Can you tell Eduardo I have to talk with him?" I wait, thinking about bothering him. "But it isn't urgent."

I hear him sigh, almost in relief. He must be returning to his car. "Of course, Emma. I'm just outside if you need anything, okay?" He declares reassuringly.

I nod, even though he can't see me. "Okay, Philip. Thanks."

I decided not to make a big deal of it or worry anyone. Liv is here with me, and Philip is outside. I'm safe. I repeat the words in my head until I believe them to be true. I'll tell Eduardo when he calls me—no need to panic. I change into my sleep attire and go to find Liv, but first, I need some wine.

I search for Liv and see her watching me from the kitchen. She grabs a wine glass from the shelf, pours a chardonnay, and caps it with a top that keeps it fresh. I can feel Liv staring and watching my every movement. She lifts the glass in my direction, and I give her a subtle nod indicating that I'll take a glass too. She is using Jedi mind trick nursing skills to assess me. I almost snort. My face will remain blank. I am the master of secrets.

"Here," she says, handing me a glass of wine. "You look like you need this." She probably thinks the wine will loosen my lips and get me talking, but I hate to disappoint her if that is her objective. Maybe she thinks I need one, and I think the worst about my best friend's intentions. I have become the most distrusting person ever. She sits next to me, pulling her feet underneath her.

"How was your day?" I ask, taking a big pull from my wine glass. And back to those distraction techniques I am so good at.

"Good," Liv comments. "I saw Dax there," she states excitedly, and I can't help but smile. She loves talking about Dax. Seeing her happy again makes me happy.

"No way!" We sit on the couch with our wine glasses in hand. "Tell me everything." I grab her leg and squeal, genuinely excited to hear about Liv and her new man.

She tells me about her insecurities with her boyfriend but is happy they are together. He made it official that they were an item, and I'm sure it will spread throughout the hospital rumor mill.

Thinking I hear my phone ring, I run to my room, shouting that I will be right back. When I get there, it is just a group chat from work, and I roll my eyes. I throw my hair back up in a messy bun and walk out to rejoin Liv. I see that she has put on some music and is dancing to Halsey's "Bad at Love."

"That's my girl," I call out as I join her in screaming lyrics into a wine glass. We laugh hysterically, and I don't remember feeling so carefree. We fall onto the couch, and another song ends as we sip our wine.

Liv looks over to me and says, "So, will you tell me why I came home and saw Eduardo practically naked in his boxers, pulling up his pants in front of me before he left?"

I wince at the thought of her witnessing my man pull his pants up, but I can't help but put the visual in my head. Liv is watching me, expecting an answer, and I feel like a shit friend for constantly dodging a response to her questions, so instead, I go for honesty, or what little I can provide.

"I sent Jameson home, and Eduardo came over after he left. I didn't plan on anything happening between us, but it did, and that's all there is to it."

Liv looks at me in shock that I opened up to her. A slow smile spreads across her face, and I almost laugh at how much I needed this girl talk with her.

"How did you meet him?" She sits up straighter, hungry for information.

"And here it begins, the never-ending questions." I roll my eyes playfully.

She smacks my leg with her hand. "Oh, you are not getting out of this one, Ems."

"Long story short, an employee of his was injured at the club, and I guess that was what brought him in. The triage nurse, the one I call Satan, took him into the trauma bay and handed me the chart. I entered the room to introduce myself and placed him on the monitors. I called the doctor—"

"Trauma bay?" Liv interjects, eyebrows raised in question.

I pause before speaking, taking another drink of my wine, not wanting to have this conversation. "Stab wound to the hand." I bite my lip, not wanting to elaborate.

"What?" Liv practically screams. "Stab wound to the hand?" She flicks her hand at me.

I try to downplay it as much as possible because it really was nothing life-threatening. "Oh, it was nothing. It needed some stitches and didn't hit anything important in the way of vessels. Weirdly, it looked more bloody than the wound was. Lucky, actually. You know how some things are more vascular, and the bleeding looks worse?" I pause, deciding how much I want to say. I'm sure it wasn't just his blood, but that's not for her to know.

Liv looks at me. "The hand is more vascular?" she asks, tilting her head sideways, questioning my medical knowledge.

"Whatever, let me finish the story." She puts her hand up, signaling for me to continue. "Eduardo showed up, said something to his employee, and sat in a chair, staring at me while I worked."

"And he sent you flowers?" She smiles at me, and I almost sigh.

"Yes, he did. Weren't they beautiful?" I gaze adoringly at the wilting floral arrangement.

"Definitely." Liv wants to say more but doesn't, instead opting out for a change. "So when are the girls coming?" she asks excitedly.

I immediately perk up at this. "In a few weeks!" I am vibrating with excited energy at this point.

"Well, we will have to plan a great outing for them and show them the town," Liv states, happy to be spending time with me. I nod in acknowledgment but become weary.

Liv grabs my hand. Her touch reassures me without prying for more information.

"We also have to go shopping for outfits," I tell her.

"Sounds like a good time, Emma, but I don't have much money to go shopping," Liv states matter-of-factly.

I grab Liv's hands, holding both in an embrace. I feel so many emotions flow through me as I hold onto her hands. The friend who had always been there for me. Who introduced me to her friends and made me feel welcome from day one.

"Don't worry about it, Liv, I got you, my boo," I say. "I got you covered, girl."

She nods. I feel sadness radiating off her, but also for myself. I swallow the lump forming in my throat.

Don't go.

I want to tell you everything.

If only it wouldn't get you killed.

Like my family.

Liv gets up from the couch, letting go of my hand. She tells me she has some things to do. I sit there and think about everything that Liv and I said, as well as the unspoken words. We both are in newish relationships, and I am terrified. I am so terrified of royally screwing it up.

I go back to my room and wait for Eduardo to call me. I decide to take one of my romance novels and begin reading about fated mates. I love this stuff. I read for an hour and feel my eyes become heavy with sleep. I tuck my Kindle under my pillow and prepare for a restless night when my phone rings.

I check the number and notice that Eduardo is calling. I answer the phone in earnest.

CHAPTER TWENTY-SIX

EDUARDO

I have to work tonight at the club as a few things require my attention. I didn't want to tell Emma, but I am meeting someone who may have information about Julian and the Martinez family. It's the perfect time for the meeting, since she isn't here with me, electing to spend some quality time with her friend, Liv. Although it won't be a late night, I miss having her here with me. The club is also a primary source of my income, as much as the other dealings that occur here, supplying a better compensation for my family's overall business endeavors.

Seth, one of my father's business associates, was in attendance. He seemed to remember the name of Julian's father and said he would do some digging around for me. I asked him to use discretion; he knew he owed me a favor. That's the thing about this business. We all have our secrets that we want to keep. The one thing our organization hates is associates who talk.

At the close of the meeting, he vowed to stay in touch, and I felt a small amount of relief in knowing that we might find out what really happened to her parents and sister and why Emma is still being pursued. All along, I've suspected there is more to the story than just Julian wanting Emma for himself.

My phone rings, tearing me away from my thoughts. I go upstairs to my office from the basement's back stairwell, where we usually conduct business. This area has a room for complete privacy and is soundproofed. It's also where we keep people who need questioning. I look down at my screen and see that it's Philip calling.

"Yes, Philip." I enter the office and loosen my tie.

"Boss, I'm sorry to bother you, but Emma was trying to reach you. She called me and sounded...off. I asked if she needed anything and was on my way up when she said no, but for you to call her."

My pulse quickens. "Have you seen anything? You are there at her apartment, correct?" I pour myself a drink and let the cool amber liquid settle me. He reassures me he is there and hasn't seen anything that appears suspicious. Liv is there with her, and she is fine. So why do I feel unsettled?

"Thanks. I'll call her now." I hang up and immediately call Emma. Fuck, I knew that I should have just brought her here. I hate that she is alone at night. Either she comes here with me or—

"Eduardo?" She sounds out of breath, and I am on alert.

"Baby, is everything okay? What's wrong?" I suddenly feel that there is most definitely something very, very wrong.

"Umm," she hesitates. "I'm okay. Liv is here, and Philip is outside, but..."

"Emma, spit it out," I almost yell into the phone, trying not to scream at her. It isn't her. It's my fear of losing her again. I'm scared that something might happen. I grab my keys and head out the door. "I'm going to get you. Stay there and pack a bag. No, better yet, pack a suitcase."

She's quiet on the other line for a minute, and I think she hung up. I look at the phone, and she is still there.

That's when I hear her say, "Okay, hurry." And I fucking do.

I speed all the way over there and think of all the ways to gut this prick slowly and painfully. I hate the number he did on Emma and is still trying to get to her. If he touches a hair on her head, he's dead. Honestly, he's dead anyway once I find him. I'm raging when I pull into her apartment complex parking lot. What was I thinking even allowing her to stay here? Without me?

I jump out of the car and see Philip run over to me.

"Is something wrong, Boss?" The concern in Philip's voice is palpable, and I look over to him.

"Emma called and sounded off, almost scared just like you said. I didn't give her time to explain and she told me to hurry. I'm going in to get her and bring her home with me." I almost say *where she belongs*, but I don't.

"Wait there, and then follow us to the penthouse," I bark as I race away, taking two steps at a time to Emma's door. I knock lightly and text her that I'm outside. She opens the door, slowly stepping away. I walk in and close the door behind me. I look her up and down, and she jumps into my arms.

"It's okay, baby. What is it?"

She breaks away and looks at me. "I have to show you." She grabs my hand and leads me into her room. I'm confused as hell and wonder what she is doing.

When we reach her room, she closes the door behind me. She saunters into the bathroom, almost hesitating, then starts the shower. She closes the door and returns to stand in front of me. Now, I am confused. I'm sure my bafflement is visible on my face. Where is she going with this? She looks at me, biting her lip. I arch an eyebrow at her and wait, not uttering a word. She clears her throat and averts her eyes.

"I came home and was looking forward to hanging out with Liv." She pauses and still hasn't made eye contact with me as she recounts the events. "I took a shower, and I..." She trails off, and her breathing is labored, as if what she is about to say pains her.

"What is it, Emma?" I am freaking out inside and don't want to scare her by yelling. "You can tell me. I'll fix it."

She lets out a small gasp, almost a cry, shaking her head back and forth. I am on high alert, not liking where this conversation is going. I want to shake her, make her tell me because I am freaking out. She looks me in the eye and says the words that are my undoing.

"Eduardo, he found me."

I see red. My nostrils flare, and I try to hide my anger. "What do you mean he found you?" I spit out. "Baby?"

She doesn't say anything. Instead, she grabs my hand and leads me into the steamy bathroom. She looks at me and then points to the mirror.

That's when I see it.

Don't run from me Emma.

I stare at it. My breathing is labored. I get my phone and make a call.

"Philip, we have a crisis here. Emma is in danger. We are going to my place. Have extra security sent. She won't be back here alone and definitely not to sleep. We will be out after she packs up her things."

I turn to her and pull her into a smothering hug. "Baby, I won't let him have you."

I think to myself and repeat it in my head, *You are mine.*

Mine to love.

Mine to protect.

"Now, let's get out of here."

I help Emma pack a bag for now so we can get the fuck out of here. She leaves Liv a note to tell her that I came over and persuaded her to stay at my place. She left the message in plain sight and wrote in a playful tone, so Liv thinks nothing of it. Little does she know the chaos brewing surrounding Emma's life.

We drive to my house in record time and enter my secure complex. I knew I should have brought Emma over here and insisted she stay with me, but I was trying to be considerate of her feelings and independence. I knew she was staying with Liv and came to Houston to help her deal with some issues. I also know that her reasons weren't entirely selfless. She was scared of Julian and tried hiding from him after saying he found her in Padre Island.

After I get her settled in my room, I leave her to ensure everyone knows that Emma is my number-one priority and she is to be watched at all times. I added another person to her security detail along with Philip to ensure she is protected with another set of fresh, watchful eyes. I also told them that if she wants to get a hold of me, she is to be immediately put through. If I am in a meeting, interrupt. I don't know how to make it any clearer.

I can't imagine if something had happened and she couldn't reach me. In fact, that is what happened. She had tried to contact me but couldn't. What if it was more serious? What if he was there? I shiver at the thought of her being helpless and taken from me. I won't let it happen. Maybe I can put a tracking device on her. We will get something for her tomorrow—a necklace or bracelet to let us know where she is, just in case. That will at least make me feel a little better when I don't have my own eyes on her.

I need to talk with Emma, so I return to our room and find her sitting on the bed. Her legs are crossed, and her head is in her hand. I close the door behind me and see her head swing up. Her emerald-green eyes are fixed on me. I immediately go over and sit on the bed next to her. I pick her up and sit her on my lap. She holds on to me and places her arms around my neck. Her scent envelopes me, and I kiss her head, saying soothing words I didn't think I was capable of. My life doesn't allow for this kind of talk, but with Emma, I find myself saying everything I've ever wanted to tell her.

Words I've thought about saying to her if I was given a second chance.

Words I would have said to her if this wasn't our second chance, but if we had stayed together all this time.

She leans into me and raises her head to look up at me. I bring my lips down to hers and kiss her passionately. I want to convey all my love to her, along with all my insecurities and fears. I try to tell her I can't lose her again, but I don't. Instead, I kiss her, letting my body show her what she means to me. I break the kiss reluctantly.

"Emma, we need to talk, and I want you to listen." She nods, and I am expecting more of a fight, but I guess when you have been hiding and fearing for your life, you have to explore all options.

I tell her about the addition to her necklace we will get soon. She agrees, and nothing will seem amiss since she already wears this necklace. I want to buy her something unique; this isn't exactly how I envisioned this going. At least it will serve a purpose and keep her safe.

The next piece of jewelry will be an engagement ring. That could be an option. If I marry her, then everyone will know she is mine. She will be safer, except this guy is unhinged. It will bring her into the spotlight, and she doesn't want that either. When I give her a ring, I want it to be because we want to be married, not for her to be forced into a marriage of convenience with me. I don't think she would see it as that, but that's how it would seem. She has had so many choices taken from her that I want her to choose me.

"Emma, I will have you stay here. We also need to figure out something with your work schedule. Do you want to continue to work?" I ask her because I don't want to take that choice away from her.

"Yes," she replies. "Do you think it's okay and safe for me to continue working at the hospital?"

I want to answer no, but I can't have her at the club with me all night. In the daylight, she is safer. Monsters come out to play at night. That is what Julian is—a monster.

"What if we change your shift to nights? Would that work? I would know where you are for those few days, and I can have extra security around for you without drawing suspicions. I pick you up from work, and you sleep at our place. We will be spending a lot of quality time together."

I smile at her and bring her hand up to my lips. I lightly press an open-mouthed kiss to her hand and bring her finger into my mouth. I suck on her finger and lightly bite her. She pulls her hand back and laughs.

"I like the plan," she says. "But right now, I'd like to not think about the plan." She smiles mischievously at me.

I stand up and shrug off my jacket. "I agree. No more talking in general. Just you screaming my name." I lunge at her and bury my mouth in her neck. She shrieks with laughter, and a wave of happiness washes over me at hearing that sound. A sound I hope to hear for years to come.

CHAPTER TWENTY-SEVEN

EMMA

"Hey, sis, are you ready to go?" Evie jumps up on top of the counter with excitement.

I swat her ass with my cleaning rag. "Get off the counter. We have customers." I place my hand on my hip, and she laughs.

Evie looks around at the only customer in the corner of the cafe with Airpods on, typing away on a computer. She snorts. "Nice mom impression, Em. And you have, like, one customer. For real though. I'm starved, and I'm thinking…" She pauses as if there is anything to think about. "Street tacos?" She says this like it's a question, but we both know that she has her sights set on the Me Muero Por Los Tacos food truck. It literally translates to I'm dying for tacos. This spot, located across from the park, has become one of our favorite places to eat and is super inexpensive. The truck is run by a young couple who have quite the following. In the summer, they also go to the beach and do fruit cups, paletas, and liquadas. My mouth waters at the thought of the frozen sweetness on a hot Texan day.

"Hmm." I give my most pensive look, staring out into the vast emptiness of the cafe. The traffic from lunch ended as quickly as it started. "I suppose we could do street tacos." As I say this, my treacherous thoughts quickly go to craving some elote. Their street corn covered in crema and spices is orgasmic.

We hear the door's chime, alerting us to another person entering the store. We avert our gaze to see Jackson walking in, interrupting our heated debate about elote versus their spiced potato wedges.

He throws his bag behind the counter. "Ladies, looking ravishing as usual." He gives us a wink, and that causes Evie to laugh. He looks her way and eye fucks her slowly, and bites his lip to stifle a moan. I almost laugh at his playboy act. We all know Jackson is a fun guy. You just have to realize that there isn't more to him. If you are looking for a romp in the sack with nothing meaningful, then he's your guy. Many girls have tried to get him to commit, but he is upfront with them all. If they think they can change him, they will be sorely disappointed with the outcome.

Of course, Evie isn't falling for his womanizing tactics. She rolls her eyes. "Still not going out with you, Jackson." She looks him up and down, clearly not liking what she sees.

"Eves." He clutches his chest and band T-shirt with his hand. "You wound me with your cruelty." His hair falls into his face, and he brushes it back. I have seen this move hit its mark with the ladies, and I can't say that he doesn't have rizz. The boy is extraordinarily charming, and he knows it.

"Please," she counters, "that's why I saw you come out of the dressing room with Katrina wiping her mouth at The Naked Contessa boutique." She arches an eyebrow, begging him to deny it.

The look in his eye says he enjoyed that encounter very much. "You are too much, Eves, but it's time for me to clock in and for you guys to have some fun." He waggles his eyebrows as he walks off.

"That guy is a piece of work," Evie mutters.

I laugh. "I think you like him, Evie. I see the way you look at him. He is kind of hot." She doesn't deny it.

"Em, I don't mind sharing. I just don't want to share my men." She smirks and jumps off the counter. "You know what I mean?" She isn't looking at me but at Jackson, who stands there with his mouth open. He quickly closes it as I look between the two of them.

"I have no idea what that means." I toss the cleaning rag over the counter and grab my bag as Jackson rounds the corner. He recovers from whatever that expression was that flashed on his face, getting straight into work mode.

"Have a great day, ladies." He gives us a little wave but doesn't look back at us as Evie and I exit the shop. Weird.

We walk arm-in-arm laughing about what we did today. "Let's cut through here," Evie says. "I'm so hungry I could chew my arm off."

We cut through the alley instead of walking around the blocks to get to the food truck, electing to take a more direct route. We are so enveloped in our conversation as we reach the end of one alley to enter the next one that we don't notice them until we come face-to-face with two men. We recognize both, and I'm immediately frozen in place. I open my mouth to speak, but nothing comes out.

I feel a tug at my arm and hear my sister speak up. "What do you want, Julian?" He takes his gaze off me, and I feel as though I can breathe again, if only momentarily.

"This doesn't concern you, Evie. This is between Emma and me." He steps closer to me while maintaining eye contact with my sister.

"Of course, it concerns me," she counters. "Emma is my sister. My twin sister," she states defensively. Julian just snorts.

"Well, even that can be changed, Evie." He nods at his driver, urging Marcus forward. Marcus grabs Evie's hand and tries to drag her away from me.

"Marcus, what are you doing?" I turn to try to help my sister.

Julian grabs my arm. "Do not say another man's name in my presence ever again. Do you understand me, Emma?" His fingers are digging into my arm and will surely leave bruises. I try my best to pretend he isn't hurting me, but I know he will just hurt me more until I make a sound alerting him that I am in pain. I let out a small whimper, and he disengages his grip slightly. He must feel that the hurt isn't enough if I am not showing I am hurting.

"Emma," Evie cries out. "Are you okay?" She tries to push Marcus away, but he is just too big for her to fight off.

"Shut her up," Julian barks at Marcus. He covers Evie's mouth.

"Ouch!" I hear Marucs say and yell expletives at Evie in Spanish. "You stupid bitch." I hear Marcus shout "fuck" as I hear the sound of a hit. I look to see Evie slumped over on the ground as Marcus bends over, holding his crotch. Evie is lying on the ground, a bruise already showing on her face.

"Well, look at what you've done now, Emma." He growls in anger at me. "You made Marcus have to hurt your sister."

"Fucking bitch bit me and kicked me in the balls," he snarls as he tries to stand upright.

Julian pays no attention to his hurt driver. "You'll have to make that up to me, won't you, sweetheart?" he says sweetly, as if he almost cares about me while he continues stroking my cheek. I want to throw up as the tears come rushing out and down my face. He holds me close, stroking my hair. "Shh, it's okay, honey, I'll make it better." I shake in his embrace. "Leave the sister there, Marcus. Let's go." He pulls me along.

"No, Julian, stop." I try to escape from his hold. "We can't leave her there, Julian, please," I beg, yet he keeps moving. I look back at my sister slumped over on the floor. I break away from him and run over to Evie, dropping down by her side. I notice that she is still breathing. Julian picks me up, dragging me away. I see the SUV parked around the corner as he drags me to it.

"No, Julian, please, stop. We can't leave Evie. Evie!" I cry out. "Stop."

But he doesn't stop. He never will stop.

I feel someone shaking me. "Don't touch me!" I scream, and then I feel someone holding me. I cry out and try to escape. I open up my eyes, but I only see darkness. I feel someone stroking my head.

"Shh, baby. It's me, Eduardo. It's okay. I've got you. It's just a dream. You're safe."

I stifle a cry at his words. "I'm safe," I repeat.

He kisses my head, and my breathing starts to regulate from the fight-or-flight response I felt upon awakening from the nightmare. I'm sweating, but I also feel cold. Goose bumps gather along my body as I fight the twitches that threaten to take over.

Eduardo starts to rock me back and forth in a soothing manner, all the while whispering softly in my ear, repeatedly verbalizing that I am safe, that he loves me.

I grow stiff in his arms. I turn to him, and the soft moonlight illuminates his tan features. He is looking at me lovingly.

"You love me?" I ask in question.

He sighs, kissing my cheek. "Of course, I love you, Emma. I was given a second chance with you. I just regret that I didn't fight harder for you—for us. I thought I was doing what was right. I should have been there to protect you all along."

I look into his chocolate-brown eyes and see the truth there—the sincerity.

Hearing him say this is my undoing. All the emotions I have held back come bursting in a tsunami of tears. I cry for my family and mourn their death. I realize that I haven't let myself miss them since they passed away. My sister. My best friend. Eduardo holds me through it all, rubbing my back until there are no more tears to cry. Until all I have left are some hiccups.

I get the sleeve of his hoodie that he placed on me when we got to his house and bring it up to my nose. His smell—whisky and leather—lingers on it and reminds me of home. A home I had when I was younger around my family. When Eduardo was around wearing a leather jacket that made him devilishly handsome. A jacket he placed on me when we went outside, sneaking out to look at the stars.

I bring the sleeve over my hand and wipe away the tears that have crested and lay fallen, pooling along the neckline in their aftermath. The taste of my salty tears lingers, and I wipe the evidence away. Eduardo rises toward me, kisses my tear-stained face, and places soft, open-mouthed kisses all over. He holds my face in his hands and stares into my green eyes.

"Emma, I promise I will find this guy and end his life. I never want you to feel unsafe again, and I promise to keep you safe for as long as I walk this earth. You are my everything." He trails a finger down my cheek, and I shiver in the wake of his sensual touch.

My body is alight; he is the match, burning me from the inside out. I can no longer deny that we were always meant to be. Call it kismet. I know for sure that I am safe with him. While I can no longer help my family, I will make sure to help myself and seek the revenge my family should and will have.

I look him in the eyes. "You'll help me kill him?" I touch his face and keep my hand on his cheek.

He holds onto my hand. "Yes, baby. I will be there when you end his life. I want to witness you rise in a giant wave of destruction, taking out anyone who stands in your wake. Whoever stands in the way of getting your revenge. You are strong. You withstood so much and emerged stronger, a punishing force that will prevail. I promise you."

My chest rises and falls at his encouraging words.

He thinks I am strong.

He believes in me.

I will get my revenge.

I repeatedly tell myself this until I believe these unspoken words to be true. It's as if he has my heart in his hand and is physically mending the broken pieces together with a needle and sutures.

Friedrich Nietzsche once said, *"What doesn't kill you makes you stronger."* Songs were even written about it. My heart withstood the worst heartbreaks and suffering; through it all, I am reborn, resilient, and strong.

CHAPTER TWENTY-EIGHT

EDUARDO

I got Emma to change her schedule to night shifts, and I feel better knowing that she is in a somewhat secure building with video surveillance and many people who would notice her absence should it ever occur. I can tell she doesn't like the shift as much, but after several weeks, she has developed a routine. Even the nurse she calls Satan has backed off. All he needed was a little persuasion.

I laugh at how he almost pissed his pants when I confronted him. Serves him right. She is working peacefully, free of that dickwad's insulting behavior, and is able to be part of the much-needed ER team. Not to mention that she is also well-liked there. She has a fantastic personality, and she is hot. I hate that people ask her out or flirt with her, because it comes up when I get updates about her throughout the night. Luckily, I know that she is committed to me and that trust is something I have with her. We have history and a long-standing friendship, which are the makings of a strong future. A future that we will be able to have now.

I hate the way things happened. She was forced to leave Brownsville, but I may have never had the chance to reunite with her if not for Julian's actions against her family and her meeting Liv in school. He is still after her, and that thought frightens me more than I care to admit. I have never had a weak spot, but now I do. I can be exploited, and they know I will do everything in my power to make sure she is safe and keep her with me always. Not from just Julian, but from the countless criminals that come into my life through our various business ventures. Enemies who wouldn't care about using my girlfriend or, later on, my wife and kids to get what they want. I'd like to let them know what that means to hurt what's mine.

My heart.

My life.

My future wife.

The thought brings a smile to my face.

"Eduardo? Did you hear what I said?" Helena has this shit-eating grin on her face.

"What, Helena?" I try my best to use an intimidating voice on her, but she isn't buying it.

"Well, well, well. What has Eddie all preoccupied this morning?" she sings-songs, and my teeth grind at admitting that I was daydreaming about Emma. A beautiful short, blond-haired goddess I left this morning in my bed to sleep off her work night.

I recall her coming home. She places her bag on the foyer floor and walked into the house, removing her hair from her bun. She runs her hand through her hair and massages her scalp with her long fingers. I stand there in the kitchen, enthralled, sipping my Americano, having very impure thoughts about my girlfriend.

As if sensing these thoughts, she looks up at me and smiles the most sensual smile as she saunters over to me. I put my coffee down, and the lust that coats every pore of my body leaks my scent of arousal. She sits across from me at the counter and licks her lips. I stop the groan that threatens to escape my lips as I look her over. "How was your night?" I ask. I always want to ask her about her work night.

She sighs. "Busy. I am glad it's over with." She yawns, and my heart melts.

"Are you tired, baby?"

She looks at me and gives me a slight nod. "I want to go to sleep, but I'm just so wired from our last patient. There was an accident, the patients almost died, and we barely saved their lives. It's such a good feeling, but the adrenaline rush, mixed in with the fatigue, just makes me jittery and tired at the same time. It's like I had three espresso martini shots right before bed, ya, know?"

I shake my head, understanding the feeling. Maybe it applies to terminating a life instead of saving one, but the feeling is still the same.

"I understand, baby. I think I can help you to relax." I walk toward her, relinquishing my firm grasp on my coffee.

"Eduardo, I am covered in gross hospital cooties." She tries to scoot away, but I hold her in place.

"Emma, you aren't even wearing the scrubs anymore."

"Well, that's because we change into some at work and back into our clothes before we leave. Most people do. Oh, except for Satan."

I snort because she won't let the grudge go. "I still need a shower, Eduardo. I don't want to make you late." Her expression is sincere. "I know you are busy, and I take up a lot of your time."

"Emma, don't ever feel that way. You come first, and I run my own businesses. That is the perk of being the top dog." I laugh, and she visibly calms. "Now, let me take care of you."

I pull down her joggers and panties, inching her bottom off the barstool. They hang around her ankles, touching the floor, and I quickly remove them and her Converse sneakers. I drop to my knees and look at her above me. I kiss her foot and move myself upward, leaving a trail of kisses on her calf as I hook one leg over my shoulder. I make my way to her center, blowing a stream of air onto her core. I feel her shiver, and I look into her eyes as I make my way to part her folds.

A groan escapes me as I see her glistening pink pussy spread out for me. Her scent that is purely Emma, fills the air, and I swipe my tongue along her center, eliciting a moan from her. She slumps down a bit, trying to bring her center to me, and I hold her down with one hand splayed across her abdomen.

With her folds parted, I fuck her with my tongue. I suck on her clit and pump my fingers in and out of her cunt while curling them upward, flicking them upward to find the spot that makes her cry out. I remove my fingers and use both hands to bring her forward as I bury my face in her pussy. I hold her in place while I suck on her clit and she screams my name, holding my head in place as her body convulses.

She starts to giggle and tries backing away, but I continue to lap at her, cleaning up every bit of her cum. Her arms fall to the side, and I stand up, seeing her eye me from her slouched position. I wipe my mouth and chin. The wetness coats the back of my hand. She gives one slow exhale. I smile knowing I succeed in relaxing her.

"Now, how do you feel? Do you think you can go to sleep."

She doesn't even speak, just nods.

"Good," I say as I pick her up, guiding her to the shower. I place her on the expansive bathroom counter and start the shower. "I`ll be at the gym. I'll call you after lunch?" I ask, and she continues to nod. "I see I have rendered you speechless," I say jokingly, rubbing at my jaw and licking my lips that still very much taste

like my sweet Emma's pretty pussy. She strips and laughs, watching my pants tent in the process.

"Love you," she says as she gets into the spray of the water.

"Love you too," I say as I take my hard-on and reluctantly leave.

I'm pulled away from my thought of Emma to the sound of laughter. "Eddie?" Helena shakes her head. "Someone sure is smitten." She waves at a customer coming in.

"Don't fucking call me Eddie," I say, rubbing my hand across my face. I get a faint scent of Emma and smile.

"I would have thought you would say, don't call me smitten," she counters, and I shrug. "I knew it. Good for you," she replies, sincerity lacing her words. "You need a good woman in your life."

"Well, I have one, so you don't need to worry about that anymore."

Her smile widens. "About time."

I look over at the cafe, noticing a line forming at the counter. "How's the cafe doing, Helena? Have you noticed a lot of activity there?"

She looks at me, knowing I changed the subject, but not commenting on it. "Besides today?" She gestures over to the cafe, waving her hand about. "Yes, actually, there has been quite a lot."

"That's good to hear. I am glad for us but also delighted for the owners. They are hard-working and might just need this opportunity to get their name out in this area. Their food is fantastic and fits our location perfectly. I already overheard one of our gym customers asking about catering an event at their workplace, and that makes me happy to hear. They have the potential to branch out." Just as I begin to ask Helena another question, I see a familiar face sitting at a table with a woman who is not Emma's friend, Liv.

"Excuse me, Helena, I have to chat with someone."

"Oh, boy," Helena counters. "That's never good." She turns around to help a customer coming up to the counter.

I chuckle, not disagreeing. I turn to walk toward Jameson's friend, Dax. Now, to see what this is about.

I observe Dax and this girl for a bit to pick up a feel for the vibe. Their body language suggests an awkward conversation. Dax is mimicking a defensive stance, and it appears he would wish to be anywhere than here at this moment.

I reach their table and notice that the attractive woman is angry. Well, that's interesting. "How's it going? Dax, right?" I extend my hand in what I hope is a non-threatening way.

He takes my hand, shaking it in a firm grip. I expected his hands to be soft, but surprisingly, they are calloused. Maybe from surfing?

"Eduardo, good to see you."

So he does remember my name.

"Thanks again for your generosity at the club the other night."

I nod, shifting my gaze between him and the woman currently giving him daggers. His body would be dismembered all over my gym floor, if her looks could kill.

"Eduardo, this is Tatiana, one of my work colleagues."

She purses her lips, and I know exactly what this is about. Meeting in a public place. This is the 'I am seeing someone else' type of discussion. This woman is beautiful but probably a complete psycho.

I turn to her and see her dainty, manicured hand extend to me. I, in turn, embrace it. Amusement lingers in my eyes at this awkward-as-fuck exchange. Dax is exuding major anxiety at this situation. No doubt, he thinks I will tell Emma all about it, and in turn, she will tell Liv. I have to think about that for a bit. "Good to make your acquaintance Tatiana."

Dax eyes me up and down, noticing my slacks and button-down shirt. I know what he is silently implying. What am I doing here? He watches me with suspicion, which is fucking ironic since I'm not the one here with another woman.

"So...you don't look like you were exercising here? What brings you over? Looking for a membership?"

I laugh at this comment because the guy is clueless. I shake my head. "No, I don't need one since I own this gym." I wave my hand, extending it to the gym in an exaggerated performance.

I see the shock and questions that run through Dax's mind. He swallows, and I give him a menacing smile. I see the recognition on his face that alerts him to the fact that I am a dangerous man. Good, I think to myself. He should be afraid. If he does anything to upset Emma, I'll have his balls. If that means making her friend Liv unhappy, and it just so happens to make Emma worry about her further, then I will take that personally. I may be a mafia guy, but my parents loved each other, and I hate a fucking cheater.

"I had no idea," he says, looking between Tatiana and me.

"Yeah," I admit. "I have my hands in a little bit of everything, I guess you could say." Changing the course of this conversation, I say, "Emma was telling me about the gala. Are you guys going?"

I hear Tatiana snort—a very unladylike snort at that. I smirk, knowing precisely what I am doing, getting the hoped-for response. I look at Dax, the mirth dancing in my eyes. He scowls, knowing and understanding setting in. Tatiana must have thought I was referring to her when I asked if 'they' are going. Dax knows I am referring to Liv.

"Well," she replies sluggishly, "I thought I was going, but it appears that I am out of a date," she retorts, practically snarling like a rabid dog at Dax.

The guy has the decency to look remorseful. I look over at the girl who is now out of a date. She is attractive, no doubt, and well put together. Any man would be happy to have her as a companion to that function. No doubt she would be dressed to the nines. Tatiana perks up at my perusal, but it is not what she presumes.

I scrutinize people, assessing, judging, and calculating to see if they are a threat to anyone I care about, which happens to be Emma. I don't want any retaliation that could affect my little thief. Emma would be very upset if Tatiania is resentful toward Dax and takes it out on Liv, since they all work at the same hospital. They both have had some terrible things happen in their past, and as for my Emma, well, some are beyond that.

"Well, that's a shame. A beautiful woman like you shouldn't be waiting on anyone that doesn't put you first." She seems to perk up, eyes alight. "Unfortunately, I am already promised to another or I would take you." I give her a sincere smile and a good-bye handshake, hoping she can be someone's everything one day and stop taking the offered scraps.

"It was nice talking to you, Dax. I thought you should know that the girls will show up at the club for a girl's night. If you understand my meaning, I have everything set to ensure they are well taken care of." He nods appreciatively. I ask anyway just to confirm. "You work that night, right?"

He runs his hand through his hair. "Yep, Liv mentioned it briefly but didn't go into details, but I know I work. I appreciate that, Eduardo." His expression softens at the mention of his woman, Liv.

I wave it off dismissively as I walk away from the clusterfuck of this conversation. I chuckle to myself. Poor guy almost shit himself watching me, and the look on his face when I told him I dabbled in a bit of this and that. Fucking priceless, I laugh to myself. Now I have to wait until noon to call Emma.

CHAPTER TWENTY-NINE

EMMA

Eduardo and I fall into a pattern of domesticity. I almost forgot that I have an unhinged stalker after me. He vows to keep me safe, and I feel the safest I have ever been. Since the day Julian revealed his true colors, I haven't been familiar with having someone care about me like this. Not since my family was alive.

It's not that I don't appreciate everything Uncle Andrés did for me, risking his life and that of his men to break me out of Julian's stronghold. Now, I have someone I talk to every day. We eat dinner together when I am off, and if I have to work at night, we have breakfast before he leaves for the gym, and I sleep after working a night shift in the ER while he is off working. It's, umm, nice? Normal? I have a family again.

I try not to let the memories of my past taint my day. After all, it is my day off, and I want to see Liv. We had been making plans with the girls coming up from Corpus Christ to visit us, and it's finally here. Eduardo encourages me to have fun with them, but I have to have security with me at all times. I honestly don't fight it. I feel better knowing that I have someone watching out for me where I can let my guard down a bit.

I sent a group text to Emma, Val, and Ainsley, letting them know I was going to the apartment Liv and I shared. We are all meeting there, and the girl should be making record time on the interstate if I know my besties and their problem with adhering to the speed limit on the open Texas highway.

I pull up to the apartment with Philip by my side. "I don't see anyone around." I look in the parking lot as Philip drives us around once again.

"I'll walk you up and check things out. If everything looks clear, I'll wait in the car to ensure you are okay." He looks over at me, and I smile.

"Thank you, Philip. I appreciate that." I haven't returned to this place since I saw the writing on the wall. Literally. I shudder at the thought of him being around my belongings. Did he touch my things, place anything there to allow him to watch me?

When Eduardo and a few of his men went to gather most of my essentials, they checked the room extensively and couldn't find anything, but it still wouldn't surprise me if there were. Julian is very resourceful, and that thought is the nightmare my dreams are made of.

While waiting, I make a cup of coffee and get my laptop out of my bag. I glance down at my watch and wonder what is taking so long. "They should have been here by now," I mumble under my breath as I search for articles in the Brownsville newspapers about anything related to Julian. I'm reading an article about Julian's father being re-elected when the door swings open. A very green-looking Liv walks in with the assistance of Ainsley and Val. I jump out of my chair.

"Liv, what's wrong?" I immediately think the worst. Did Julian do something to her?

She looks up at me, and some vomit is on the side of her mouth. I grab a rag and head over to wipe it away. "Hey, girls, make yourself at home. I should have something for vomiting." They look at each other, worried about schooling their features, but they bring their bags to the living room and sit on the couch, looking over at us.

Liv tries to downplay things as usual. "I have been exhausted from school and work in clinicals. I felt super dizzy today and must be dehydrated because I haven't been drinking enough water." She looks around at us, seeing if we are buying the lies that she is selling.

I narrow my eyes at her, and she continues.

"You know how it is?"

I shake my head. "I think I have some medication to help with that.

Come on, let's get you cleaned up and find something to wear." I grab a water bottle from the fridge and hold her hand, leading her to her bedroom.

Once we get into Liv's bedroom, I close the door and turn around, hands on my hip. The annoyance is displayed in my features. "What the fuck, Liv?"

She looks like I slapped her. Okay, that may be too harsh. Her eyes narrow back at me.

"I could ask you the same. What the fuck is up with you, Emma?" she retorts as we stand there, not allowing any secrets we may have to be spoken between us.

"Are you pregnant?" I grab her boob and twist it.

"Ouch." She grabs her boob, rubbing it. "What are we, twelve-year-old boys?" She is angry with me but is hiding it or in denial. The vomiting, the dizziness, the missed periods perhaps?

"You need to take a pregnancy test." She nods in agreement, and I get her some medication from her drawer where she keeps her headache and anti-nausea medicines in a bag for emergencies.

"I have an upcoming appointment with Planned Parenthood to refill my birth control," she says, rubbing her forehead.

I go over to her. "You know I love you to the moon and back, right?" She returns the embrace.

She has tears in her eyes when I pull away. Let her keep her secrets. I can't disclose mine and wouldn't want to put her in any more danger than I would have if I had continued to live here.

Opting for a change of conversation, I clear my throat. "Let's get ready, shall we?" I turn on Carrie Underwood's "Church Bells," and we laugh at the crazy memories. It was a favorite song we frequently played on the old-fashioned jukebox in this dive bar during our nursing school years.

"For old time's sake," I say, hitting play on my phone, and the girls laugh. Soon, we are all dressed and ready for a much-needed night out.

We elect for an Uber, or at least that is what the girls think. Instead, Philip drives us to the club. The club is packed, and the girls are excited. My besties are wrapped up in short dresses and mini skirts, ready to break hearts.

I lead them to the front of the line, smiling at the bouncer. He nods at me and opens the rope, allowing us entry. By this time, everyone knows me or is made aware of who I am. I turn around to make sure everyone makes it through and grab onto Liv to keep her close to me. Yes, I am hovering like a mother hen, but she is my best friend, my ride-or-die.

We go to the VIP section and walk up the stairs single file. The bouncer at the entry to our VIP area stays with us, standing by our table. He is replaced by another person, allowing access into this secluded space. A nervous-looking waitress comes over to take our order.

"I really missed you guys," Val and Ainsley say in unison, exchanging excited squeals at the opportunity of having us all here together again.

The petite waitress comes back with our bottle service. The security guard comes over, and before she can pour us anything, he stops her and they exchange a look. She stops what she is doing as he picks up the tray's contents and makes himself a drink. The girls watch with curiosity, and he takes a large swig and nods at her. She continues to pour us drinks and leaves after we all have one in our hands.

I don't know how to make this seem normal, but I try to take their concern away from that weird exchange. "I guess he is making sure it isn't diluted." I shrug. "I think that has been happening. Call it quality control." The girls seem to buy it and pick up their drinks. I see them looking at someone, and I turn to see what has gathered their attention.

My man is walking this way, looking dangerously handsome. His tattoos are visible past his sleeves and reaching up toward his neck. The one I had my tongue over earlier today.

The girls thank him for letting us skip the line, but his attention is always on me. He leans over to tell the security guard something, and the security guard tenses. He nods and looks over at me. I squint my eyes, wondering what he said. Before I can ask, Eduardo leans over and kisses the top of my head.

"Behave," he says with a playful wink. He walks away to the other bouncer at the stairs and looks back at our table. He pats the guy on the shoulder and leaves the area through the back stairs.

Needing a distraction from my worry, I pick up the liquor and pour us some shots. "Come on, girls, let's take some shots and go dance."

We dance for a couple of songs, and when "It's Getting Hot in Here" by Nelly comes on, the girls scream in excitement.

"Yay, who doesn't like a little 2000 throwback!" I laugh, throwing my hands in the air and my head back. I am feeling the temperature rise as more people pack into the small space to dance around us.

I see security around us, and they are talking into their headset. The sight makes me nervous, and I look around apprehensively. I see one motion over to the other side of the dance floor with his hand, and I am on high alert, no longer feeling so carefree.

A big, muscular guy comes over wearing a tight-fitted Henly shirt with tattoos in similar places to Eduardo, but it isn't Eduardo, and I don't like how he looks at me. He starts to grind against me, and a small commotion occurs on the dance floor. I see security approaching us and tapping the guy on the shoulder. A very pissed-off Eduardo tells the guy something in his ear while looking at me. I look over at the guy, and he nods, recognition of his misstep clearly visible in his facial expression.

Eduardo grabs my hand to lead me off the dance floor. I was starting to get creeped out anyway, and I am relieved that he has me in his embrace. I look back to see if the girls are following me and notice Liv. She is leaning over a barstool, and I run over to her, yanking my hand away from Eduardo. This shocks him, and he follows me, waving security over.

"Pick her up and take her to my office." Eduardo has security over in seconds as they take a now very passed-out Liv upstairs.

I grab a cool compress and place it over her forehead, and she stirs. "There you are, Liv." I am thankful she is coming to, but I am no less scared of what happened to her. "You made us all so worried."

She tries to sit up but seems to think better of it, placing one foot on the floor to steady herself, I assume to stop the vertigo. I hear Eduardo talking on his phone, saying to let him in and to bring him up around the back to his office. Moments later, a distraught Dax comes in to scoop Liv up in an embrace. When she has difficulty standing, Eduardo offers to help him to get her into his car.

Eduardo comes back in, and the girls and I are still trying to figure out what to do. I decide to make the most of the time with them, and we return to the VIP area with our hearts a little less intact, missing the girl who completes our circle of friends.

CHAPTER THIRTY

EDUARDO

I had to get on the phone and call Dax to tell him about his girlfriend lying passed out on the sofa in my office. People pass out occasionally in my club, but no one has ever been brought up here. Emma had hovered over her best friend, clearly upset. She doesn't need any more shit in her life. I understand her concern for her friend, but I am more concerned with the fact that someone was touching my girlfriend and, even worse, the thought that he was used as a distraction for someone to get to her. If Liv hadn't passed out, Julian could have gotten to her. After they left and Emma returned to salvage the rest of the night with her friends, I had to confirm whether we needed to be worried now.

I had let my staff and security know in a meeting before the girls got to the club that there was a person of interest, a man who posed a threat to my girlfriend. I showed them the picture and made everyone aware that if, for any reason, questions or suspicions came up, or worse, if this person was near Emma, I was to be notified immediately. No call was to be taken lightly and no question considered stupid.

I was glad we had the insight to have this meeting beforehand because I received a call from someone who met the criteria for such an occurrence. That put everyone on high alert, and we thought we had the person in our sights when the incident with the guy getting handsy with Emma happened, and then Liv passing out added to the debacle, making us lose sight of him in the crowd where he later vanished.

I sit in my office watching Emma on surveillance, surrounded by her friends, some discreet and some not-so-discreet security in the area, all watching. I doubt anything will happen now, but I won't take any chances, and the thought of her going back out there with her friends was hard to let her do. I have the face magnified on my security monitor and a few men around me. I ask for Philip to be brought in as well. He walks in, shutting the door behind him.

"Boss, you wanted to see me?" Philip, my most trusted friend and Emma's personal security detail, stands before my desk, looking around the cluster of men in my office. I motion for him to come around to my side of the desk so that he may get a better look at the face I will show him.

"Philip, have you seen this man?"

He takes a look, leaning in closer, and lets out a breath slowly. He nods. "Yeah, I have. I've seen him a couple of times. I thought it was a coincidence..." Philip trails off.

I stand from my chair abruptly and it topples over. One of my men comes in to right it.

"You thought it was a coincidence?" The anger in my voice rises steadily, as does the anger radiating throughout my body. Repeating his words slowly, I say, "A...couple...of...times?" My fists are clenched, and I try to calm my anger. "Where? When?" I pace the room, walking back and forth to give myself a purpose other than punching my most trusted security personnel—dare I say, friend.

Philip goes to sit on the couch, placing his head in his hands. Looking up at me, he rubs his hand over his face, steepling his hands together under his chin. Philip stands and begins pacing just as I had been. He stops and turns toward me. "I know I saw him in the coffee place by the hospital that Emma likes to go to. He was on his computer with headphones on. Not the Airpods, but like Beats or something like that."

He looks away as if trying to remember more. "I noticed him..." He pauses and looks back at me. "In the hospital waiting room." He has the decency to flinch as he continues to fear my unexpected outbursts. "He was reading a book, and I thought he was just a patient. Maybe he lived around the area. Now, I know it wasn't, Boss. I am so sorry."

I stand, staring at Philip with barely controlled anger overtaking my body. My nostrils are flaring as I try to unclench my fists. "Men, leave us now."

The guys look at one another and then at Philip with a sad look—a look that says good-bye, nice knowing you.

Philip stares at me and pays no one else a second glance. Once the door closes, I go to lock it. I sit at my desk and motion for him to sit.

"So now that that show is done, I have a job for you." I smirk at him, and he lifts his eyebrow in confusion.

"I don't understand. When you texted me with 'impromptu acting needed,' I tried, but I have no idea what you are getting at. You already knew the times I spotted Julian when I told you, but somehow, you made me look incompetent, and I want to know why?"

"Oh, yes. I like the extra commentary about the Beats, not Airpods." I wave my hand around my ear. "Very believable, by the way."

He throws his arm out in a theatrical half-bow. "Of course, but what's the plan? I know you have one, and for some reason, I think I am in fake trouble?" He poses this like it's a question.

"Yes, I think there is someone giving information to Julian. He seems to know when Emma will be somewhere and about her party tonight with the girls. I will let everyone think that you will be punished and appoint someone else to be around Emma as a driver. You will still watch her, but without anyone else knowing. No one will be allowed to see you."

He shakes his head, seeming to follow the plan. "So, are you going to kill me? Is that how everyone else will believe I am no longer around as Emma's security detail?"

I look at him, nodding in confirmation. "Well, fake kill you, but yeah." I let that sink in a bit

He grabs his chin, pondering the idea a bit. "Ok, so what next?"

"I will call the guys in and have them escort you to the basement. You'll be held there, and I will let you out through the back door. I'll need to call my computer geek to come over and help me scrub the video, in case anyone else sees it, but I'm not too happy with him these days." I roll my eyes. Philip snorts.

He stands abruptly. "I have an idea that may work, but you must hear me out."

I narrow my eyes in suspicion. "Spit it out already. I know I'm not going to like it."

He laughs harder. "Oh, you will hate it, but it might work, Eduardo."

He proceeds to tell me the plan, and I abso-fucking-lutely hate it. I can't deny it's good though, and it might just work. I make the phone call reluctantly, all while Philip gives me mock words of encouragement. I should kill him after this, if he weren't such a good friend. He's lucky I don't have many friends, and I am currently not accepting any applications to fill his spot. It's too hard to make friends at our age. The fact that we were once all friends in college surprises the hell out of me.

An hour later, Jameson is at the door, and a very suspicious Eli eyes Philip up and down with disgust. I look at Eli, and he nods, closing the door behind him. I see his retreating form on the camera outside my office and look at Jameson. He eyes me with concern and mistrust.

"Jameson, good to see you, brother. I am glad that you were able to get here so soon. Like I said earlier, it's important." He sits forward in his chair.

"You mentioned important and Emma's name in the same sentence, which is why I am here so fast," he clarifies, and it makes me furious as fuck, but I have to think about what's more important—Emma.

My Emma, I almost growl in my possessiveness over the girl I have loved first and only.

"Right," I say in what is probably a sarcastic rebuttal. Jameson visibly straightens and stares at me. I get up from behind my desk that I was initially sitting at and move over to the front, feeling more relaxed with my feet crossed, extended out in front of me. My arms are pulled back on my desk. I want to get in his face and for him to understand what I am doing and what needs to be done to keep Emma safe.

"Jameson, I called you here because I know that you care about Emma, and I need your help. What I am about to disclose to you is to stay between us in this room and no one else. It is about her safety, and I can't jeopardize that." He sits up, looking at me and then Philip. Concern etches his features, and I reluctantly wait for his acknowledgment.

"I understand," he says. "What can I do to help? Is she in trouble?"

I pause because I don't want to tell him, but I have to do it to keep her safe, even if he may be in love with her. Believe me, man, I know the feeling. "I don't know the history between you two..." I pause to see if he will elaborate, but he doesn't. That fucker. "Yeah, well, I have known Emma for most of my life." He seems confused about this, and I tell him about our families being business associates and up to a point about us reconnecting. I explain the abusive relationship with Julian, minus the details and how we think he and his family are responsible for her parents' and twin sister's death.

He looks up. "Twin sister?"

I shake my head. "Yes, she had a twin sister named Evie, who was her best friend. She misses her terribly and blames herself for their deaths."

He stands up and looks as furious as I feel. "This guy is still after her? He was here tonight?"

I nod in confirmation. "I need your help looking at the security feed to see if I missed anything, and I also need you to wipe it a little bit." He looks at me, confused. "Well, since you installed it, you know more about it than anyone else would, right? You are the super geek of the bunch?" I laugh when I say this because it has always been a joke about how brilliant the guy is. There are worse things to be called and known for—like a mafia criminal. I shrug as I think this through.

"Why do you need it wiped?"

I look over to Philip and then at Jameson. "Philip here has to die, and I don't want there to be evidence."

Philip snorts, and Jameson seems to want to be anywhere but here. "You're fucking joking, right?"

"Mostly," I say, trying to rile Jameson up. He may be a tough guy, but he isn't a killer and surely not a part of this life. I decide to put him out of his misery. "I need it to look like I killed Philip, but he will stay hidden and keep an eye on Emma—from the shadows. With everyone thinking he is dead, that will give us the upper hand so that he can go unnoticed. People won't suspect he is secretly watching out for the person giving Julian information if he is thought to be dead. We need to find that out before he gets to Emma."

Jameson looks over at Philip and then at me.

"Okay. I'm in."

After Philip is presumed dead and the surveillance feed is wiped, I invite Jameson back up to my office for another chat. This one is between us. "I want to know what happened between you and Emma. I know that you have feelings for her." I leave it there and wait for him to tell me what I have had suspicions about. If he slept with her, I don't know if I could contain my rage, but it was before we reconnected. I had meaningless sex, too, and... I can't even think about it anymore. It just kills me inside.

He is looking at me and blows out a long breath. "Nothing." He stops trying to decide how this will go if he tells me something I don't want to hear. I have been known for having a bad temper and losing it. "We met on Padre Island while on Spring Break. That's when Dax met Liv. He was a patient in the ER and met up at that beach the next day. We shared a moment, and then that was it. I was hoping for more, but then we came here, and she saw you. I don't know."

My breathing has increased, and I can't get the idea or unthink that he fucked my girlfriend, future wife, and future mother of my children. I just can't let it go, and I have to know.

"A moment?" He shakes his head yes.

"Did you fuck my girlfriend?" I come out and say it, laced with the most controlled anger I can muster.

He looks at me and shakes his head. "No," he says quietly. "We had an awkward kiss, and that's it. I think Dax and Liv thought there was more between us, and I wanted there to be, but now she is with you."

"Awkward kiss?" I ask, waiting for more details. He rubs the back of his neck.

"Yes, awkward as fuck. It felt like I was kissing my fucking sister, despite being super attracted to her." I snort. "I can't explain it, but I feel super protective of her, too."

"Okay, sister fucker."

He laughs, and that breaks the ice a little. "You have nothing to worry about. I care about Emma, but if she is happy with you, I just want her to be happy." He shrugs noncommittally.

I get up and pat him on the back. "I'm glad to hear that. Now, I need your help with a tracker for Emma."

CHAPTER THIRTY-ONE

EDUARDO

I get Eli to drive us home and drop the girls off at Liv's and Emma's old apartment. The girls say their good-byes, and I drag a reluctant Emma back to my place. I help her tiredly walk to the bedroom, where she quickly washes her face and gets into her pajamas. She gives me a quick peck on the lips and dives on top of the bed. Before I can tell her good night, I hear her soft snores. I kiss the top of her head, pulling the covers over her body. Now, it's time to make a long overdue call.

I turn the light on in my home office and stare at the phone for what seems like an eternity. "Here goes nothing."

"Hello," the familiar voice picks up the phone.

I cringe at the same voice that told me to stop seeing Emma. If I loved her, I would let her go.

I haven't heard this voice in about a decade, but anger bursts through me at the memory of our last exchange. Things went differently then, when he told me I should respect Emma's parents' decision. I went looking for

Emma the following summer, but her mother held true to her word in not returning with the girls to her brother's house.

"Andrés? This is Eduardo Ruiz." I let that sink in for a bit and wait to see what he will say in the introduction.

"Eduardo." He pauses in what I am sure is confusion mixed with what I hope is also some regret, but I highly doubt it. Andrés Ortiz doesn't feel bad about his decisions or have regrets.

"To what do I owe the pleasure of this call?" He's curt but not unpleasant.

I know we have the same goal in mind–to keep Emma safe, or at least that's what I remind myself when proceeding with this exchange.

"I am calling about Emma. I just wanted you to know that we have reconnected, and I am keeping her safe."

I hear Adrian, her cousin, in the background.

"I'm putting you on speaker, Eduardo. Adrian, my son, is here."

I respect the disclosure, but it isn't needed. I'm not the same kid I was back then, and I won't be walking away, no matter the cost.

"Hello, Adrian," I say in greeting, which he reciprocates.

"Gentlemen, it has come to my attention that Emma is in danger. I have moved her in with me after a scare at her apartment." I hear a chair topple over.

"What the fuck happened?" Adrian is upset. Not knowing about another issue with Julian before this conversation looks equally bad since they are supposed to have someone watching Emma; however, their piss-poor job is ridiculous.

"Julian Martinez is a dead man. I am currently gathering information about his family and should have some idea what their obsession with Emma is. He was in her apartment and left her a message in the bathroom mirror. He is fucking with her, and I am not at the liberty of him toying with my girlfriend." I hear a series of expletives leave Andrés's mouth.

"What do you mean your girlfriend, Eduardo?" He isn't very gracious in concealing his feelings about Emma and me rekindling our courtship.

"Is that all you got out of that?" I applaud his reaction. At least I am keeping her safe, unlike these fuckwads. Instead, I continue as if this doesn't phase me.

"Well, that is also the reason for my call. I appreciate that you have been helping Emma, but I feel I can assist and be there for her. I know her parents are not around and—"

"Let me guess," he interrupts. "Do you think you can date Emma now that her parents aren't around to prevent you from being together? Eduardo,

I was never against it, but…" He seems to rethink what he was going to say. "How does Emma feel about it?"

"That is part of the reason I am calling. We have been given a second chance, and I never want to lose her again. As her next of kin, I'm calling you as a courtesy, and as her next of kin, to ask for her hand in marriage officially." I hear a drink being poured, and I understand the sentiment. "Is that a celebratory drink I hear you pouring?"

He sighs, and when I think I will have to marry her without their approval, he finally acquiesces. "I know that you love her and will keep her safe. My niece has lost so much. If you can bring her joy and provide a home, then you have my blessing."

Adrian verbally agrees in the background.

"I appreciate your approval. I will keep you posted on what our sources find out. I will also update you on our wedding announcements when I propose to Emma. That is, if she accepts it, of course."

I hear Adrian scoff as if he has moved closer to the speaker. "I will keep you posted as well."

Andrés counters, "I, for one, haven't been able to find out anything. You, being on the other side in the US, might be more successful."

We hang up on a consensus. I feel more relaxed knowing that Emma is mine and I only need her to agree to my marriage proposal. Now to think of how to get the girl.

Julian seems to slip away and hasn't been seen in a few months, but that doesn't mean he isn't plotting or planning to abduct Emma. Emma questioned where Philip was, and I told her he had a family emergency to take care of. Everyone else thinks he is dead, but I won't tell her the same story. She won't discover what I said to other people because my men wouldn't dare tell Emma I killed her bodyguard because of a mistake. I've had her watched at work, so I know Julian hasn't shown up again in the waiting room or at the coffee shop she likes to frequent.

Today, I have a surprise for my girl. I spent the whole day at the gym tying up loose ends when Helena started talking about a concert she was going to buy tickets for. The girl is always going to some heavy metal venue, and I only half listen, but when she mentioned her Ghost concert tickets, I perked right up.

"Excuse me, what band?" I ask, but this time, I listen thoroughly to her ramblings.

"Oh, so n-ow you are paying attention to me?" she snorts, typing data into the patient account on the computer.

"Sorry, but this band you mentioned is… Ghost? Are they the ones who wear the masks, and the lead singer dresses up as a satanic pope?" I look at her with exaggerated interest.

"Yes." She narrows her eyes on me. "He doesn't just dress up. It's part of the lore," she replies, annoyed at my lack of Ghost band knowledge. "Why do you ask?"

I can tell she thinks I'm going to make fun of her, but I'm asking because Emma loves that band so much. She is obsessed with the Ghouls and even wears little bracelets made of beads with letters spelling out 'little sunshine.'

"Emma loves that band, and I want to take her to the concert." Obsessed might not even cut it with the way she sings all the songs and has the two little stuffed dolls of the lead singer. The little doll is creepy as fuck too.

"Hmm." She seems hesitant to give me more information. "Well, I doubt there are more pit tickets, but you can at least get her some VIP experience tickets to the ritual."

"The ritual?"

She just shakes her head. "Never mind." There are still a bunch of options. "There." She starts typing into the computer screen. "Here are the seats left. See? Take a look for yourself," she says as she turns the screen my way.

Ultimately, I purchase two VIP tickets that allow us early access to the venue, a better parking option up close, and free merch. I think she'll like it. Needing reassurance, I decide to ask a fan. I really do want to make her happy.

"Do you think she'll like it, Helena?"

I see her tilt her head to look at me, and what she sees makes her eyes soften and she smiles. "I think she is going to love it. I bet she will be super excited to go." She gives me a little side hug. "You did good, Boss." She squeezes my shoulders once more and walks off.

I feel good about the surprise and hope my plan to keep her safe won't backfire.

I finish at the gym and walk out the door a little earlier to pick up Emma at our home. She works later tonight, and we now have a routine going. I never thought I'd be a guy who likes the mundane routine of domesticity, but I do. I might be enjoying it a little too much. Maybe it is just because it is with Emma.

I pick her up and we head through the Starbies drive thru line per Emma's request. I order her an iced matcha latte, and espresso for me. As we pull out into traffic, I hear her favorite band play on Spotify and laugh when she asks about attending the concert. Little does she know that she'll be getting the full VIP experience soon.

I hate to admit that I always like having her with me, and dropping her off at work is always hard. Seeing her walk away through the doors and the possibility that it could be the last time I ever see her again guts me. This threat with Julian has to stop, and I won't let these thoughts take up space in my head any longer. I am becoming that clingy motherfucker that everyone laughs about. I laugh, thinking about the time during our family's last Christmas conversation when Jasmine, my future sister-in-law, explained her favorite romance trope–omegaverse–to us. The alpha obsessed with his omega.

I have a little skip in my step thinking about Emma and how she will lose her shit, and I can't wait to tell her about it. I place my messenger bag on the table, along with the food she wanted to get before work tonight, when I hear her phone ring. She sees who is calling and answers it, talking with Liv on speakerphone.

"Hey, girl, how are you feeling?"

She has her back to me and hasn't noticed that I am standing there listening. I would usually go about my business, but something has me standing there. Her bubbly demeanor radiates sparkles and rainbows down the line. And I am captivated by it. This is the happy woman I always wanted to see.

"I am feeling better. This is just my first obstetrician appointment."

Emma rubs at her temples, and I imagine her trying to ward off an impending headache.

"So, it's true then, Liv? You're pregnant?"

I nod, even though I'm not part of this conversation, but after the way she acted at the club, it was pretty apparent that was the case.

Her words echo back Emma's. "I am pregnant with Dax's baby." She lets that sink in before replying to Liv's answer.

"Are you happy, Liv?" She looks sad, and I watch her wanting to come over and hug her. Tell her she isn't alone, and I will always hold her when she needs me to, for better or worse.

Liv answers with more conviction, and I believe her when she says that she is indeed happy about the news and about her and Dax starting a family.

She continues, "I know it's weird to say, but I feel I was destined to be his since I met him. The way he makes me feel and the way he touches me. It seems familiar, like I was already his, and he was mine."

Emma stays silent for a moment and then breathes before speaking. She grabs at the necklace I gave her, and my heart stops. "Yeah, I understand that. Sometimes, you can't fight who you end up with. Sometimes, it's just the way things are meant to be."

They end the call, and Emma turns around, releasing a slew of expletives as she clutches her chest. "You scared the crap out of me, babe." She walks over to me and kisses me on the lips. Before she can let go, I pull her in with my hand firmly planted on her ass as I let her feel the effect she has on me. My cock is rock-hard, but that will have to wait.

"I have a surprise for you," I say as I pepper kisses lightly down her neck.

"I hate to break it to you, babe, but your monster cock is no surprise." She laughs, her eyes alight with humor as she grabs my dick.

I laugh and grab her hand. "You keep grabbing me like that and the surprise I got you will have to wait."

She removes her hand reluctantly. "So the surprise isn't you feeding me your cock?" She raises her eyebrows, and I groan.

Now she has me all worked up. Maybe we could fuck, and then I'll give her her present. I decide on the latter and take my phone out of my pocket. She eyes me suspiciously, and I can't help the smile that forms on my lips, despite trying to remain stoic. I can see her getting agitated that I am on my phone and pushing her hand away from my cock. She thinks I am blowing her off as if I would prefer anything on my phone than to her touching me.

I forward her the proof of purchase for the "Imperium" VIP experience Ghost concert tickets. Her phone dings with an incoming message, and she opens it eyeing me suspiciously as I place my phone back in my pocket. Her eyes widen, and I can tell she is looking at the tickets, and a smile that melts my dark heart begins to blossom on her face. She looks over at me and unexpectedly throws herself into my arms, but I catch her. I'll always catch her.

"Now let me thank that cock of yours," she says.

I kiss her, and she drops to her knees. The look in her eyes is something I will remember until my dying days.

CHAPTER THIRTY-TWO

EMMA

I am getting dressed when Eduardo comes in. It's a bit cooler today, and even though the holidays are right around the corner, Texas doesn't have many temperature changes, but when it does get colder? Holy mother, it's cold.

I put on some leggings and my favorite hoodie by my favorite band. I scream internally. I still can't believe I will see Ghost in concert soon. I have been riding that high all week. I wish it were sooner, but what's a few months, right?

"Hey, baby." He bends over to kiss me quickly, breaking me from my Ghost-lust-filled trance.

"Hey yourself," I say, looking up at him like he hung the moon and stars. The same moon and stars that we gazed at together when we were younger, making plans when we thought we had a future. All the time in the world, but we both learned how precious those moments are and how they can all be taken away in the blink of an eye.

"I got you a present," he states matter-of-factly.

I stop applying my mascara and look over at him. An involuntary smile pulls from my lips, and I swear he blushes.

"Eduardo? Did my big bad, mafia boyfriend just blush?" I question playfully, and he grabs the back of his neck, rubbing at an imaginary spot.

He shakes his head and looks at me. Amusement lines his face, and I love that look on him. It's as if I am staring at the boyish Eduardo who first stole my heart, except he is no longer a boy. He is all man. My man. He sits on the edge of the bed, and I drop down to my hands and knees, crawling to him. His pupils dilate, and his breathing picks up.

"Emma? What are you doing?" he asks. I go up to his legs and plant my hands over his thick, muscular thighs, rubbing my way up to his cock.

"I already had this present this morning, but do you want to give it to me again? In my mouth this time?" I lick my lips for added effect and wish I hadn't put my mascara on yet since it will probably run down my face in another minute, but I think that is his favorite look on me. Thinking about this makes me smile.

He holds my hand on his cock. "Emma, as much as I'd like your mouth on my cock, I do actually have a present for you." He pulls out a wrapped package, and my heart melts at seeing the vulnerability in his eyes. I squeal at the thought of getting a present. It has been a while since anyone bought me a gift, and I love that he put some thought into it. He puts his hand up to my cheek and strokes it gently.

"If you still want to suck my cock in thanks after you open your present, well, I won't turn the offer down," he counters.

I laugh, shaking my head. "You got it, baby." I wink and lean over to kiss his cock through his pants. I see it jump in response to my affection, and I chuckle.

"Goddamn tease," he says playfully as he readjusts himself.

I get up and sit on the edge of our bed, holding the box in my hand.

"Go on. Open it, babe," he encourages.

I look at him and nod with a smile that spreads from ear to ear. I unwrap the gift to see a velvet box. I place the golden wrapping paper off to the side and open the box carefully. It's an earring, bracelet, and matching pendant set—a starburst earring in white gold with emeralds and diamonds. The pendant matches the earrings, and I am in awe.

"This..." I swallow, trying not to cry. "Is so beautiful, Eduardo. Thank you." I veer around to hug him, and he pulls me into his arms just a few inches away from his face.

"The stars remind me of us, gazing up at the stars. I remember you saying how they look like diamonds in the sky. The green reminds me of the color of your eyes. It's your name that falls from my lips when I see a shooting star, making a wish. It's your name forever on my lips." He gives me a kiss that is soft and lingering. It lets me feel all the emotions we convey and all the ones we don't say. How time is precious, and this time is ours. He pulls away.

"One more thing." He clears his throat. "I had a tracker put into the necklace." He points at the large pendant. "I didn't want to mess with your pendant I gave you when we were kids, but I thought you could wear both on your necklace. Or put that one on the bracelet.

I look over at him. "How romantic," I deadpan.

Eduardo looks at me. "Emma, I just want to keep you safe."

"I know. I was only kidding. But honestly, thank you, Eduardo. I love it."

"Here, let me help you put it on. I put on the earrings, the bracelet, and the necklace."

"It is perfect." I touch the pendant, knowing that it is my lifeline to Eduardo.

"There is a button on it. If you depress the star, it will send an SOS to my phone and my security team with your location. The device will let us track you, in case that is ever needed. I hope we never need it, Emma, but I am unwilling to risk the chance."

I nod in agreement. I'm sad that this happy moment has turned into talking about my safety once again. I can't wait for the day that this is a distant memory. To live life in peace without fear of someone trying to kidnap me. When you are married to a mafioso, things like this are always possible, but I trust Eduardo to keep me and our future children safe.

I speak the words that we are both thinking, but always afraid to voice aloud. "Do you think we will always have to worry like this?"

He cocks his head to the side, trying to read my expression. "About danger?" he asks. I nod once. He rubs his chin.

"I'm not going to lie to you, Emma. Our life together may always have the potential for danger, but I vow to keep you safe. Always." He grips my chin for me to look at him.

"What about our kids?" I counter.

His lips twitch. "Definitely. But first, I need you to marry me." His playful expression is gone, and now all I see is determination.

I place my hand up to his face and stroke his cheek. "Well, love," I say, placing a chaste kiss on his lips, "I guess you are going to have to ask me first to find out my answer."

He grabs my face and kisses me. His mouth desperately seeks possession over me, and I open for him. He fucks my mouth like he fucks my pussy, dominant and commanding. I feel all the emotions that Eduardo places into it: protection, adoration, control, dominance, and most of all, love. I feel it to the tips of my toes. I could never be loved like this again. If living a life of danger with him is all I could ever have, then I'll take my chances in this life. The life that my parents tried to keep me from.

He lifts me into bed and places me on the pillow at the head of the bed. He straddles my body with both of us clothed. He places my gifts on the bedside table and returns his gaze to me. He lifts my arms in the air and removes my dress over my head, discarding it on the floor. He stares at my breasts, kneading them through the soft lace bra. He shoves the bra down, pushing my tits out, then tweaks the nipples with his fingers, making them pebble in anticipation of his mouth on them. He looks at me longingly, his gaze roaming the entirety of my body down to my thong, soaked with my desire. He leans over and buries his face in my drenched panties, inhaling deeply.

I feel the wetness leaking around the pantyline seam. Eduardo notices this and licks at the side of my panties, pushing back the material, moaning as he buries his face in the scent of my underwear, rubbing his face in it as if I'm marking him with my scent. It is filthy and erotic, and I am so undeniably wet for him.

He rips them off my body and throws the torn material to the floor. He begins to unbuckle his pants to free himself of their confines. Pushing his pants down, he drags them past his ankles and kicks them off with his boxers. His dick is beautiful, long, thick, leaking precum beading at the tip. I lick my lips, wanting to taste him, intentionally leaning forward to catch the moisture with my tongue. Eduardo leans forward and drags the end of his penis along my lips, coating them in his arousal. I dart my tongue out and flick it over his cock, feeling it twitch and harden further, with my tongue tracing a figure-eight pattern over the tip. I lap and suck, causing him to groan.

This must snap whatever restraint Eduardo has because he parts my lips with his finger and holds my mouth open as he thrusts his cock inside. I feel him hiss as his cock scrapes my teeth. He grabs my head, lifting it up as he straddles my chest. He hangs one arm over the headboard as leverage and starts to thrust in and out. His moans become louder as he fucks my face. I love seeing him come undone, and he moans and grunts in approval, calling me his fucking star. He shoves his cock so far down my throat that I think I'm going to gag, and he holds me there, shuddering. He pumps in and out deeply with small movements, holding me down on his cock. I think he is about to come, but he pulls out abruptly, cursing.

"Fuck, Emma. You take my cock so well." He lifts me up. "Come on, baby. On all fours."

I quickly get up and lean over with my face down on the bed and ass up in the air. He kneads my ass, parting the cheeks as he bends over, licking from my clit to my ass. I almost come on the spot. He slides his cock through my wet pussy lips and lines himself up. He thrust in in one push, all the way to the hilt. He grabs my hair, picking me up from the bed with my back arched up, taking every inch of his long girth. He sets a punishing pace, and it has my toes curling in just a minute's time.

He sits me up, and I am upright on his cock, straddling him reverse cowgirl. He bounces me up and down on his cock forcefully, the curve hitting my cervix with each thrust. He pinches my nipple hard with each hit. The sounds echo with the slap of our bodies as the scent of sex permeates the air in our bedroom. He licks up my neck, whispering filthy words in my ear as he sucks my earlobe into his mouth.

"I'm coming, Eduardo," I announce. "Keep going. That feels so good," I cry out as my orgasm hits, and my walls clamp down on him.

He keeps going through the spasm, pushing me forward, placing me back on the pillow, face down, and holding my ass up in the air. He lets go and entwines our hands, pushing me farther into the pillow. His balls slap my ass, and the sound of wetness fills the room as he fucks me.

After a few more thrusts, he comes with a loud "Fucking feels so good" as his hot cum shoots into me. He lays across my back, still holding my hands down as I slump flat onto the bed, totally spent.

He pulls out of me, grabbing my fingers forcefully. He pulls me over so that I am now laying chest down on top of him as he runs his fingers through my long hair. He holds me close, telling me how much he loves me. How I am his, and he is mine. Then he asks, "So what do you say, Emma?"

I look over at the questions lingering in his eyes. He brings my hand up to his mouth and kisses me.

"About what, Eduardo?" I ask as I rub my fingers across his lips.

He nods his chin at my finger, and that's when I see the massive rock on my hand. I sit straight up and look at it. He sits up and joins me.

"Will you marry me, Emma?"

CHAPTER THIRTY-THREE

EMMA

"Will you marry me, Emma?" He looks at me, waiting for my answer. I stare at the sizable emerald-cut solitaire occupying a large portion of my finger in disbelief. I don't think I have ever been this excited in my life, but I still haven't answered. My heart races, and I feel like I may throw up. I frown. I feel a hand caress my cheek, and I look up to his face. Tears begin to fall when I realize I don't have anyone to walk me down the aisle or give me away.

As if sensing my thoughts, Eduardo clears his throat. "I hope you don't mind, but I reached out to your uncle and asked him for your hand in marriage. It wasn't exactly permission because anyone who tries to tell me this time that I can't have you or attempts to tell us we can't be together can get fucked." He wipes my tears with his finger. "He said he would give you away," Eduardo says in almost a whisper, "if you'll have me."

I place my hand on his cheek. "Yes. I would love to be your wife. The answer is always yes."

He looks at me with a fierce protectiveness. "Not just my wife, Emma. My partner in this life and the next. My everything."

I kiss him, showing how much I love him. We stare at each other, and I wonder how things would have been if we would have stayed together. I am so scared of what the future holds because of the uncertainty of Julian, my stalker. I won't entertain bringing a child into this world as long as he is alive.

He shocks me with the next question. "How would you feel about us visiting with your family for Christmas in Mexico?"

I look up at him, blinking. "Umm, like next month?"

He laughs. "Yes, next month. We will have a quiet Thanksgiving here. I know you have to work that night, and we can't do much, but you have the week of Christmas off, right? I remember you telling me this because Liv's getting married?"

I can't help but laugh. "Well, she doesn't know she is getting married yet. I mean, they just got engaged, but with the baby coming, Dax wanted to whisk her away for the holidays somewhere tropical, and he was going to have the venue all ready for them. He knows she will say yes while they are there."

I was confident she would be okay with it when he asked me about it. I told him I would like to get her something because I know her mom probably couldn't afford it. I had to be all stealth-like in claiming that I had to get her measurements for the gala dress in case we needed it altered. I mean, of course, we would need to do this. As her belly grew, so would the need for the dresses to accommodate the increased girth of pregnancy, but we could always get another. I got her a beautiful dress for her wedding and some Christian Louboutin shoes with blue embellishments. Her something blue. I can't wait to hear all about it. I can't wait to share the news with her.

Shaking myself from these memories, I blink and smile up at Eduardo. "Yes, let's go." I squeal a little in my excitement, and Eduardo kisses my forehead.

"Perfect," he says as he rolls over. I look at my ring again and smile.

Realizing he is getting up, I ask, "Where are you going?"

He looks back at me. "To make the arrangements, of course." He smiles and leaves me in the room, and I fall back onto the bed.

I can't remember when I have been this happy. I haven't seen my family in a while, and I miss my uncle and cousin terribly, not to mention the rest of the bunch. It will be good to see everyone and have a Christmas with family after all these years.

I am pulled from my thoughts when my phone rings. I retrieve it from my pocketbook and see that Liv is calling. "Hey, girl? What's up?" I can't wait to tell her my news, but I hear her sniffle. Immediately thinking something is wrong with the baby, I straighten my body, preparing for the worst. "Liv, what the hell happened? Is the baby okay?"

She stammers out, "Yes, it's..."

I release the tension and figure it must be Brodie.

"What did the fucker do now, Liv. I swear he is asking for it." I feel for the guy after everything he has been through, but he is still selfish as fuck.

"I told him about the pregnancy and moving in with Dax. He saw my engagement ring, and it was just too much. He told me to get out and he needed time to process everything. He doesn't want to talk to me." She is crying, and I am not there to console her.

"Do you need me to go over, Liv? I can be there soon," I tell her, already packing up to go over.

"No, Dax will be home soon, and I just wanted to talk to my best friend. You are the only one I tell everything to. My ride or die, right?"

I shake my head back and forth. The guilt of this being a one-way street is too much sometimes. "Right, Liv. Your ride or die forever. I love you, honey. Are you sure about not needing me to go over?" I hesitate and look at myself in the mirror. The fraud and lies I tell myself daily stare back at me, and I hate what I see.

Liv continues. "He said he needed time through the holidays to be alone and not talk to me." She blows her nose, and it sounds so squeaky.

"Honey, you are making yourself sick. Think about the baby. You need to take care of yourself, okay? This is good. Maybe he just needs time. You've always been there for him. You sacrificed your own happiness long enough."

She blows out a breath on the phone. "You're right," she relents and blows out a long, audible breath through the phone as she stops crying.

"Of course I'm right, Liv." I hope she takes my advice. I worry about the girl. Dax is so good for her, and I just hope she takes this time to enjoy herself away from the mindfuck that is Brodie.

We hang up, and I sit on my chair at the vanity looking at myself in the mirror. Eduardo walks in and sees me upset.

"What's wrong, baby? When I left you a few moments ago, you were happy. Did you change your mind about marrying me?" I see the joke Eduardo is making. I think there is some uncertainty swimming in there.

"Of course, I haven't changed my mind about you. You are the one constant thing in my life, and I will never feel anything other than wanting to spend the rest of my life with you."

He smiles at me and kisses me. "Okay, so what's this about then?" he asks. The concern on his face overwhelms me. I have someone in my corner, and I love that he is here.

"It's Liv." I hesitate. "Her usual Brodie drama."

He whistles. "Still?"

"Yep," I reply. "He found out about the baby, Dax's proposing, and her moving in with him and said that he needs to be alone and have time to process everything. Liv is upset because he doesn't want to speak with her, and maybe after the holidays, they can talk about everything then." I get it all out and blow upward, causing my hair to rise off my forehead. "That guy is selfish as fuck."

Eduardo rubs his chin, thinking it over. "I understand that I don't know the full story, only what you've told me, but, Emma..." He pauses, thinking about how to formulate his response, and I can tell that I'm not going to like or agree with what he says. "The guy is in a wheelchair, and he lost his girl, friends, and life as he knows it. He doesn't even have a family who cares about him. He needs to talk to someone about it all."

I think about what Eduardo said and realize that Liv is the only constant in his life, and now he is losing that, too. Sure, he cheated on her, and no one likes a cheater, but he has more than suffered.

Laying my head in my hands, I groan. "Ugh, I hate when you're right, Eduardo."

"I know, babe. It's going to happen more than you care to admit. I just see things from a different perspective. I love that you are fiercely protective of your friends." He ruffles my hair like a little kid. "Now come on, I want to show you what I booked for us."

With that, he leads me to his office, and I stop thinking about Liv and how our friendship seems one-sided. I'm doing this to protect her, I tell myself. I say it so much that I start to believe my lies.

Eduardo and I went all out for Thanksgiving. We had it catered for us. After it was all set up, the caterers left us to eat alone. We had no one over, and we spent a quiet day alone until I had to go to work, which meant I couldn't even have any wine with our early dinner. Adulting is so hard sometimes, but I am looking forward to spending the holidays with my family in Mexico and maybe reliving some childhood memories.

I thought it would be an excellent idea to go shopping with Liv and both of us could get some things for our trip together. Dax finally asked her if they could get away for the holidays. He told her about going to the Caribbean for Christmas, and I couldn't agree more. She has her mind on Brodie, and the fact that they are not talking lays heavy on her mind. She's worried about him. She's worried about his mental health. The guy has a lot going on, and few people who were in this corner championed him through this rough time in his life that changed everything he once knew. We can all see how depressed he is, and he needs to fix that. I hope that he gets the help he needs.

I can't tell her I already knew about her island trip and that Dax intends to marry her there. He wants to be married when the baby is born. It was a romantic gesture, sweeping her away and getting married. If I thought that Liv would have said no, I would have told the guy no or that she isn't ready, but she loves him so much, and this is their second chance. I know how important second chances are too.

When he asked me if I wanted to contribute anything to Liv's special day, I was glad to be able to. Since we can't be there, I want her to have something special, something that will remind her of me for the rest of her life. She is the one person in my life I can count on. Even though I feel I can't tell her everything. It's because I care about her so much that I can never tell her, but I can show her. I can show her my support and happiness about her special day by giving her the dress and something blue for tradition.

Dax asked her mother for her hand in marriage, and I contacted her to let her know that I would happily buy her dress for her. I think her mother was relieved about that, and she could maybe not pick up so many shifts to help Liv.

We haven't spent much time together. Liv moved in with Dax, and I knew Eduardo would spend time with me at my old apartment, but since Julian left that message, I feel safe and less violated staying at his place. Seeing my reflection in that mirror reminds me he could get to me anytime, and I am still very much in danger.

Liv and I decided to meet up to do some shopping in the River Oaks District in Houston. Eli parks my car in the garage, and I can't wait to meet Liv. We will shop and then eat at my favorite French cafe on the corner. It boasts beautiful outdoor covered seating and is a perfect spot for a late lunch. Not to mention, their drinks are superb. I could go for Chanel No. 6 martinis as well.

I walk up ahead, and I know Eli is following. I miss Philip so much, but he had a family emergency that couldn't be helped. When I asked Eli if Philip would return soon, his eyes narrowed, and he said "doubtful." Whatever that means. It isn't my business, I guess. I try not to ask too many questions. I know it's a waste of time, and I won't get a straight answer anyway.

I round the corner and see Liv walking toward me. I run a bit to reach her sooner and hug her tightly. I put my hand on her expanding belly. "Hey, beautiful, Auntie is here."

Liv laughs. "Best auntie ever," she agrees. "Come on, let's do this."

We walk up the sidewalk arm in arm and find a store we both want to enter. The lady in the boutique greets us and asks us to let her know if we need anything. I see the moment she catches our engagement rings, and her smile beams a bit brighter.

Right, I think to myself. She knows we have money to spend.

Liv is shuffling through the racks. "I feel bad about using Dax's credit card to buy stuff," she says in a whiny voice.

"Yeah, sounds rough," I deadpan. "I wouldn't. He wants you to have some nice things for the trip, and let's face it, Liv, you need some clothes you can wear in a few months, so let's get to it. Chop. Chop." I mimic clapping my hands with each word. She side-eyes me and grumbles something intelligible.

We both try on some outfits, and the salesperson rings us up gleefully. I bought a bit too much and saw her look at my ring again. I wonder if Liv will notice. I planned on telling her that night when she called me crying, but she was so upset about Brodie that I thought it wasn't the right time. I wanted to see her in person to tell her my good news anyway, hence the reservations at the French cafe.

As we are walking out, I see a woman walk in with oversized black Chanel sunglasses covering most of her face. She looks expensively dressed and wearing a plaid wool-blend beret. After all that, that's not what stands out. It is her glossy red lipstick that matches her unnaturally red hair. She stops and looks me up and down. Her lips turn upward in disgust.

"Do you have a problem?" I question the woman.

She turns to me and scoffs. "No, I just don't know what they see in you." She turns and walks off. I'm left there stunned.

"What the fuck," I hear Liv say, and I look at her.

"You heard that, right?" I ask to make sure I didn't get it wrong.

She looks at me, confused as well. "Yep. What was that about?" Liv asks.

I shrug. "I have no idea, but let's get out of here before I get arrested."

Liv snorts, and we walk out hand in hand, mostly Liv pulling me out of the store reluctantly.

CHAPTER THIRTY-FOUR

EMMA

We round the corner of the restaurant where we have our upcoming reservations. I approach the lady at the hostess station who seems busy looking at her computer screen. "Hi," I tell the woman, trying to get her attention. She doesn't look up. "We have reservations for two under Emma Taylor, please."

The hostess notices me, smiles, and looks through her list. "Sorry, but we don't have a reservation under Emma Taylor," she replies, sounding sad but not actually being sad about saying it.

I put my finger to my chin, wondering if the reservation could be under another name. I look at Liv, shrugging. "Eduardo made the reservations, and I have no idea what he put the name under."

Liv shrugs as well, offering up some suggestions. "Did he put them under another name or his name, maybe?"

I think about it. It seems logical. The hostess looks annoyed as we go back and forth with it, trying to figure it out.

"Are you sure he made it here?" she asks, and I nod a yes.

"I know it is. I asked him, and he said he did it. "Is it under Emma Ortiz Taylor or no Taylor at the end?"

She looks again. I see a frown cross her lips as she looks back at me and my ring finger. The one that currently houses my engagement ring. Liv still hasn't seen it. I hide it a little because I want to tell Liv about it over lunch.

Liv goes on. "Do you think he put it under his name, Emma? Under Eduardo Ruiz?"

This makes the girl cough as we both look over at her. "Are you married to Eduardo Ruiz? The one who owns the gym uptown and the nightclub?"

I look at her without answering. My eyes narrow, and I am about to speak when Liv interjects.

"Is it under Emma Ruiz?"

The lady looks at the reservation and then at us, nodding. "Ladies, let me show you to your table." She turns abruptly without looking back to see if we are following.

Liv mouths, "What the fuck."

I just shrug, shaking my head and trying to catch up to the hostess. Liv isn't usually one to make a scene, and I don't want to have this conversation about it here. I can guarantee that Eduardo and I will have this conversation when I get home.

Why would he do that, and why here?

Did it have something to do with the hostess out there?

So many questions, and I better get the answers. I feel the jealousy and redness creeping up my neck as my cheeks begin to flush.

We sit at the table where she places down two menus, telling us to enjoy our lunch, and leaves without another glance our way. We sit, and a waiter comes up to us right away. It gives me the opportunity to cool off. My anger subsides for that moment.

"Good afternoon, ladies. Have you been here before?" We both nod, and he smiles. "Okay then, can I get you something to drink?" He looks at us patiently.

I already know I want a French martini, and the one here comes with champagne. I need it now. "I'll have the Channel No. 6 martini, please," I say before Liv gets in a word.

She just shakes her head, laughing silently.

"Of course, and for you, miss?" He looks Liv's way, and she just shrugs.

"Sparkling water with a lemon twist, please."

"Great, I'll be right back with those. In the meantime, here are some lunch specials for today and a special dessert made by the pastry chef." He hands us the daily menu on a sheet of paper and walks away.

Liv immediately dives in with the inquisition. "Okay, what was up with that hostess? Why would she ask that?"

I shake my head, also feeling perplexed. "It beats me, but it is clear that she slept with Eduardo or wanted to. Maybe they were…dating?" I look up at Liv, grabbing my necklace without thinking, tugging at it. I take a swig of my nasty table water, waiting for the fluorinated taste to hit, but it doesn't. "Thank god. I thought it was going to taste like pool water."

Liv laughs. "We are at a nice restaurant, Emma. I doubt it tastes like pool water here. Now, tell me why you think that." Liv must sense when I am trying to change the subject. She's had years of this with me and is well practiced, so she is familiar with my tactics and plays along.

"I know, I forgot, but I always prepare myself for that first sip, you know?"

She laughs. The waiter comes over with our drinks, and we place our orders. The martini couldn't have come sooner. I also order another martini with my food, since I know I will need more alcohol to deal with this amount of shit in my life.

Liv places her hand on her belly. "I look forward to a drink when this little one is born." She keeps her hand on her stomach, now displaying a progressing pregnancy.

Soon, there will be a baby, and I long for the day I can have a family with Eduardo.

"Are you happy, Liv?" I look at my friend, and I can see when she looks at me that she is in love and happy, whereas that look wasn't there before.

"The happiest I have ever been. I thought I loved Brodie and he was it for me, but I realized we were just comfortable with each other. We didn't have the connection that Dax and I have. I just wish things could have been different and the accident never would have happened."

I grab her hands from across the table. She has made such progress in therapy and talking to someone about the guilt that she carries.

"Liv, you know that isn't any of your fault. He made a terrible choice that had terrible consequences. Sometimes, people make mistakes that cause harm to other people they love, and it can't be undone. We think, what could we have done differently? If I didn't do this, then this wouldn't have happened. But it did, and all we can do is try to move on. Learn from it and try to forgive. Otherwise, the guilt will kill you."

She squeezes my hand and smiles. That is when she sees my ring. "What the heck is that, Emma?" She points at my engagement ring.

I smirk. "Took you long enough," I say, wiggling my finger at her. "That's why I asked you here for lunch. I knew you wouldn't notice, and I was trying my damnedest to hide it from you, but now it seems like the time to flaunt it."

She touches it and brings her hands to her face. Liv exits her chair and walks over to me, leaning down to hug me. She rocks us back and forth. "I am so happy for you, Emma. Please tell me all the details."

She moves back to her side of the table, and I tell her the clean version of how Eduardo proposed and that we don't have plans for the wedding to take place anytime soon. I ask about her wedding plans, and she says the same. No plans yet, but maybe before the baby is born. I smile, knowing that she will be married by the end of the year, which is only a few short weeks from now.

"What do you make of that woman out front?"

I shake my head. I knew she wouldn't forget about that. "The hostess? I assume that she knows Eduardo. A lot of women do. He is a very wealthy and successful man, but he's all mine. We have our past, Liv, but that's not important. What's important is that he chose me, and we are moving forward. We can't change anything we did, but I am his, and he is mine." I want to tell her more. I want to say to her he has been mine for as long as I can remember. He was always supposed to be mine.

Our food comes, and we order a crème brûlée. It has a dark berry gel with orange crystals served with lemon gelato. Liv orders the mille-feuille with fresh red berries. Delicious is the only word I can use to describe the food. I am so full right now and am so glad that we went shopping first on an empty stomach. I might not have been able to fit into anything, but I didn't want to feel this stuffed. We signal the waiter over, and he asks if we need anything else.

"I'll pay this, Liv." Before she can protest, the server holds his hand up.

"The bill has been paid for, and the gratuity as well. Thank you, ladies, for coming to dine with us and for your generosity." He pulls our chairs out for us, and we stand, perplexed as we leave the dining area.

We are passing the hostess station in front, and Liv looks into her purse for her keys before we go outside the restaurant—typical thing for living in a big city. Always have your keys ready with panic button mode, or as my mom taught me, use your keys as a weapon, intertwining them in your fingers to punch or stab an eye. I internally laugh, remembering when she taught my sister and me that technique. It scared us for a couple of days, but we recognized the importance of it.

"Liv, we can give you a ride to your car. In fact, I insist." She shakes her head.

"Emma, you have done enough. Eduardo paid for that whole meal, didn't he?"

I hear the hostess from earlier snort. I turn around and look at her, remembering we have an audience.

"Do you have something to say? If you do, then I suggest you say it."

She looks at me like I'm beneath her. Little does the hostess know who I am and who my family is. Eduardo and I are the same. I may not have been in this life all along, but I was born into it, and my uncle is too, also passed down from my grandfather, of course.

"What do you have that I don't have?"

I look at her, walking up slowly to her station. She senses the danger, backing up a little, and maybe I am dangerous. I have a dangerous family and a dangerous fiancé.

"I have his heart," I say, lifting my flashing diamond to her face, "and his ring, if you count material items. I have many material items if you want to get technical. Even before him." With that, we leave, and I don't bother further acknowledging someone like that.

We give Liv a ride to her car, and I am fuming over the audacity of those two women—first the red-haired one and then the one at the restaurant. I am sure that Eduardo slept his way through the greater Houston area, but I just wish I didn't have to deal with his conquests breathing down my neck.

Eli helps me with my bags, carrying them into the apartment, and I thank him for his help. It feels odd that Liv and I both live with our fiancés and still have an apartment of which we still continue to pay for the lease. The lease contract is not up until next year. We didn't expect to both be engaged. I am sure that if you asked us last year where we saw ourselves now, it would not have consisted of Liv being engaged and expecting a baby and me engaged as well. It is strange how things work out sometimes. Eduardo wanted me to keep the lease contract so if there is more activity with Julian, they could catch him there instead of at our home. We are still trying to track his whereabouts, but he remains untraceable.

I am putting my stuff away when Eduardo comes in looking scrumptious in his workout gear. He came straight from work at his gym today. As I take him in, I am glad to be off tonight. He looks at me with his deep-brown eyes and tousled hair. Curls just hanging a little over his right eye. He walks toward me and gives me a hug and kiss. He places his chin on top of my head.

"Did you have a good day out shopping with Liv?" He pulls back to look at me, and I tuck a piece of hair behind my ear. He searches my eyes, and I look away, stepping back.

"Yes. We did."

He cocks an eyebrow at me. "Why am I sensing a 'but' here, Emma?"

"*But,*" I begin again with emphasis on the 'but' mimicking him, "I was verbally harassed by two women today when Liv and I were out."

He moves in closer. "What do you mean harassed?"

And I begin to explain. "Well, the waitress was shocked at the restaurant when she saw my engagement ring. Thanks for making the reservation under 'Emma Ruiz,' by the way." I say that with supreme sarcasm to ensure he understands further questioning is coming from that separate topic. "She said, and I quote, '*What do you have that I don't have?*'" I spare a glance at him, and he looks furious.

"Well, you have had me, Emma, from day one. We lost each other once, but I swear I will make it up to you."

I hug him, and I never want to let go. "The other girl was equally psycho. She all but bit me like a rabid dog. I had no idea who she was, but she knew me."

I see his head tilt to the side. "What do you mean she knew you? What did she look like?" I feel his fingers tense protectively around my shoulders.

I attempt to remember. "I'm not sure because her face was hidden behind a large pair of sunglasses, but she had an unnatural shade of red-colored hair and red glossy lipstick to match. Definitely well-off."

I feel Eduardo stiffen in my embrace, and I look up at him. "What's wrong, Eduardo? Do you know who that is?"

CHAPTER THIRTY-FIVE

EDUARDO

I walk to my soundproofed office and quickly call Philip. I know Emma will have questions, but I need to check this out first. It never occurred to me that Cherry could pose a threat to Emma, but I have a suspicion, and my intuition is rarely wrong. There can be no mistakes regarding Emma's safety. Philip picks up on his usual second ring.

"Hey, Boss, what's up?" I clear my throat.

"Philip, we have a problem I need you to check out. Remember that server, Cherry, from the club?"

He scoffs into the phone. "Yeah, the girl you hooked up with?"

I cringe at the memory. I must tell Emma, but I don't want her to know that. She knows I slept with women, but I don't want them to come to light. It looks like I am a little late for that, but I want her to know that there has been no one since that last night with Cherry in my office. Since I found out about her, I went for what I truly wanted. Her, just her.

"Eduardo, are you still there?"

I stop myself from having these thoughts. "Yes, unfortunately, that's her. Emma was shopping today with Liv and ran into Cherry at River Oaks. She was dressed in expensive clothing and shopping at high-end stores."

"Interesting." That is all Philip says.

"She also said that Cherry confronted her, saying 'I don't know what 'they' see in you' to Emma in the store." That makes the hair on the back of my neck rise. This must also trigger something in Philip because he immediately confirms my exact thoughts.

"What do you mean she said 'they see in you'?" he asks.

"I honestly don't know, but it is an odd choice of words. Also, Cherry was a server with a loser boyfriend. He could barely keep a job, so she picked up extra shifts. I assume it was also to be close to me. When I met her, she was money-hungry and broke. Her boyfriend was a bit possessive and held a job, but not by any means rich." Replaying Philip's and my questions in my head, the intrusive thoughts resurface that this could be something more.

I blow out a breath and brace myself for the words leaving my mouth. "Do you think when he said 'they' that she meant me and..." I pause, not even wanting to speak his name and have my suspicions confirmed.

"Julian?" Philip finishes my thoughts for me. "Yeah, Boss. It's very possible. You said Emma relayed the fact that she was dressed in designer clothes and shopping at luxury stores. He must be. Possibly even buying her off, or worse, leading her on as if he wants Cherry. That girl screamed for attention and was drawn to rich, powerful men. She must not realize how dangerous Julian is."

"Do you think that she is the one giving Julian information? Maybe she still has access to the club? Do we know for sure that she isn't around there anymore? Maybe, somehow, she is still able to or is helping Julian to track Emma's movement?" Each question makes me want to vomit. My involvement with Cherry could cause Emma harm. I am starting to sweat. If I am responsible for Julian getting to Emma, I don't think I could live with that. I won't let him have her. I start to pace the room, thinking of a way to stop this once and for all.

"Philip, I need you to be vigilant and see if you can track Cherry's movements. See what she is up to. Maybe through her, we can finally find out where Julian is hiding." I don't know where to begin. My thoughts are muddled as I try to make sense of this fucked-up situation. We are leaving in a little more than a week to Mexico to see her uncle and spend our first Christmas together there with her family. I will think of a plan by then and let the family know. Perhaps together, we can devise something to end this once and for all.

I end the call with Philip, and he promises to stay hidden and see what he can find out about Cherry and Julian. If anyone can, I know that Philip will pull through. He is trustworthy and someone I can call a true friend. With Jameson helping, we can track him down sooner.

I need to go and discuss this with Emma before she jumps to conclusions about Cherry. I am sure she has figured it out, but I don't want to have to tell her about my suspicions that Cherry, my previous hook-up, is the one telling Julian about my girl's movements. That would only scare her and not help the situation.

I leave my office and mutter under my breath, *"Well, here goes nothing."*

I find Emma curled up on the couch with a glass of wine and her Kindle. She has her hair in a messy bun, fuzzy socks, and wait, are those glasses?

"Since when do you wear glasses?"

She quirks her head to the side, assessing me. I am sure she can sense the stalling.

"They are blue light glasses to prevent a headache." She doesn't say anything else. Just stares at me.

"What are you reading?" I ask her, further stalling the conversation about Cherry.

"Mafia romance, of course. What else?" She shrugs. She is still watching me.

I would laugh if I didn't know she grew up in the mafia life, but I know she did, making this much more amusing. She is using the same techniques against me, and I wonder if she even knows what that is—using silence, not answering, allowing the other person to feel uncomfortable so that they need to fill the silence and end up giving themselves away. This girl? She could wait forever, just watching me. Since this is my Emma, I stare right back at her.

She lifts an eyebrow at me. "Cut the crap, Eduardo. Who were the women?"

I start to hesitate and then sigh. She waits patiently for my response. Knowing she won't like what I have to say, I sigh again, rubbing my hand over the stubble on my face. Still, she waits, just looking at me, devoid of emotion. She has learned to school her features, and I hate that she has to do this with me. I want to be the only one who always sees her genuine, unabashed emotions. I look up at her and can't help but wince. I know that she has shut down, and it guts me. How many times has my girl had to do this before?

I inch closer to Emma and gently hold onto her face, stroking her cheek. Still, she doesn't change her expression.

"The woman from the restaurant is a customer at the gym. She hit on me before when applying for a gym membership. I can't remember the exact details, but she was agitated when I pawned her off to someone else to show her the 'locker room.' I knew her intentions and I wasn't interested. It might have even been Helena who had shown her around, but I'm not sure at this point.

"I remember she listed that place of employment as a hostess on her application when I was punching the demographic information into the computer. I remember that scenario because I was afraid she would come back and tell me something at a later time. I looked over her account just in case, and it stuck out. When I made the reservation, I don't think she realized I was the one who called to place it for you, but I thought it would send a big FU to her. She came in again recently, and I told her I was engaged. I thought that was the end of it. That is nothing compared to what I have to tell you." I get up off the chair and pace around. Emma continues to sit and just looks at me.

"The other girl was a waitress at my club. Her name is Cherry." At this, Emma snorts, and I see the anger begin in her eyes as she slows her breathing. "I hooked up with her a few times." I wait and look for Emma's reaction, and she sits there, fists clenched at her sides. I will myself to continue. "One time, her boyfriend came to start shit at my club and found out she had been cheating on him. I, of course, had no idea, nor did I care because I was not interested in a relationship with her. It was something we did at work only."

Emma stood up at this. "So you fucked her in your office or some shady part of the club." She starts to walk off, and I run to her. I grab her hand and spin her around.

"Emma. This all happened before you, and I swear it would not have happened if we were together. I stopped hooking up with her when I learned your parents had passed away."

She looks up at me, trying to control tears that threaten to fall.

"When was the last time you were with her, Eduardo?"

I cringe at the memory and don't want to tell Emma, but I won't lie. "Cherry and I were together that night when Ram called to tell me." I look at her and grab her tight, burying my head in her neck and breathing in her scent. She smells like my bath soap. The one she uses because she loves it so much—to remind her of me. "Look, Emma, I love you, and once I learned what happened to your parents, I haven't been with anyone else since, even after all those months from when Cherry and I were last together until I saw you in the ER that night."

I feel her tremble against me. "Does she still work there?" I shake my head and push her back to look at me.

"I fired her even before I reconnected with you again. Like I said, her boyfriend caused a scene, and she came in proclaiming how she told him she was in love with me, and he couldn't handle that. I didn't even know she had a boyfriend, Emma." I look up at her and place kisses along her face. "I told her I didn't feel the same, and she could no longer work there, especially with the scene her boyfriend–or ex-boyfriend–caused."

I kiss her on her lips, pressing hard, trying to convey how much I love her. How much I want only her. "Emma, if you see this woman again, I want you to tell me, okay? I want to make sure she isn't a threat to you."

Emma doesn't seem to get it because she says, "I'm not scared of her, Eduardo. She can't hurt me."

I almost tell her about what I think is her involvement with Julian, but I don't want to alarm her, so I keep these thoughts to myself. At least until I know for sure that Philip has confirmed such things to be truly accurate. Until then, it's all just speculation, and it would cause her to worry unnecessarily.

"I know, baby. You're a badass. My badass." I pick her up, and she wraps her legs around my waist. Her mask is slipping. Her eyes warm to me, and I am so fucking sorry that I wasn't with her then, but this is our time, and I don't want to concentrate on what could have been—just us moving forward.

I walk her over to the couch and drop her down. I look down at her, pull her glasses off her face, and the hair ties out of her hair. Her long blond hair falls along her shoulders. I pull back, breathless from her beauty. I tug off her pants, panties, and socks in one go. Her band hoodie still covers too much of her body, so I lift it over her head and leave it on with her arms still in the sleeves. She isn't wearing a bra underneath it; her full breasts hang deliciously on her bare body. I pull my joggers down and let them drop, showing my commando status.

Emma's eyes flare. "You went commando at work?" She seems to get upset at this.

"They have a built-in liner," I tell her, and she laughs. She laughs so hard that she twists sideways and is now snorting. Her breasts are heaving up and down as her body convulses with laughter. I move down and start to tickle her.

"What's so goddamn funny, Emma?" I am still tickling her and trying not to laugh at myself. She's wheezing, trying to stop laughing at my expense.

"Are those Lululemon lined joggers?" She is now in a fit of tears.

"I'll give you my Lululemon right here," I say, grabbing her sex. I drop to my knees and throw her legs over my shoulders, twisting her onto her back again. I drive in to nip and lick at her pussy, which effectively shuts her up. Her restricted arm goes over her face, and she moans. I twist my tongue into her pussy and begin to fuck her with it. She squeezes her legs around my neck, trying to bring me closer. I hold onto her thighs.

I drop her legs, standing up, and drag her to the side of the couch with her legs hanging off the arm's end. I wipe my mouth and bend over, licking circles around each nipple as she arches her chest to allow me better access. I suck on one nipple and hear the pop as I release it from my mouth. I drag her legs over my shoulders, lining up my cock with her dripping pussy and sinking in. I hold her one leg over my shoulder and the other I have wrapped around my waist. I drive into her, and the sound of our coupling fills the room along with the sounds of sex.

I grab her hip and plunge in over and over. My ball sack slapping her ass, and I lean over. My teeth are biting and marking her beautiful, unblemished flesh. With each mark, she moans, and I feel she is close to orgasm. She arches into me, and I smile, loving how this woman loses all control. Her lips fall open, and I lower myself, licking up her neck and fucking her mouth with my tongue like my cock is fucking her pussy. I am so horny now that I know I will not last long. I feel her walls clench around me, locking my dick in a vice grip as Emma screams out my name.

I stand up and bring her hip toward me as I fuck her hard. I come shortly after with my head thrown back. I throw myself over on the couch, and I hear Emma make a barely audible sound.

"Oof." She tries to push me off. I wiggle around and get her on top of me, bringing her up to my body to kiss her.

"Can you taste yourself on my tongue, Emma?" She sucks on my tongue, and I swear I will come again. "My dirty little thief." I kiss down her neck and suck. I am leaving yet another mark on her body. She swats at me.

"Those better go away before we go to Mexico and see my uncle and cousins," she says playfully, moving her hair to one side.

"Oh, please. You think they don't know we have sex? Are we going to be in separate rooms there too?" I ask playfully, but they better not do that to us. We are engaged, for fuck's sake.

She laughs. "I don't think so, but we might need to get everything in before we go. In case we don't have sex while we are there. It will feel weird to have sex in my uncle's house," she says poutily. I slap her on the ass and she yelps.

"Maybe I'll take that sweet ass of yours there at your uncle's house, huh, baby?" I laugh, and she shudders. "You'd like that, wouldn't you, sweetheart?" I kiss her neck and travel up until I kiss her on the mouth. I move us to get up. "Come on, let's go shower and grab something to eat. I want to hear all about the good parts of your shopping trip." I lift her, and we head to the bedroom. I feel a little better but can't help feeling like a rogue wave lurks in the heavy seas, waiting to uproot our lives any moment.

CHAPTER THIRTY-SIX

EMMA

"I know, Adrian." I roll my eyes as Eduardo looks at me in amusement. "I am so excited to see you, too."

"How long is your layover? I wanted to make sure I wasn't late to pick you up."

I hand the airline worker my phone so that she can scan my boarding pass. "We are just boarding the plane and will be there soon." Eduardo takes my bag from my hand so that I can finish up my conversation with Adrian.

"I hate that you guys had such a long layover and couldn't drive."

I pause, knowing the reason why we couldn't drive, and try to put Julian out of my mind, so that I may enjoy the holidays without him taking up space in my head.

"I know it sucks. We have to travel through Dallas and then fly from Dallas to Mexico. It is so stupid. One would think the international airport here could give us a direct flight. At least it was less than an hour's flight up to Dallas," I agree with him, and Eduardo rolls his hands in a circle, subtly telling me through hand gestures that I need to 'wrap up' the phone call as we take our seats on the plane.

"Yep, see you soon. Tell Tio I love him and will see him soon too. Bye." I hang up without allowing Adrian to reply and look at Eduardo, who is smiling at me.

"What?" I ask, and he gives me a bigger smile.

"Nothing. It's just cute watching you interact with your cousin. He seems so possessive of you. He cares." He shrugs.

"Yes, and I can't wait to see the rest of my cousins too. Are you ready for the Spanish Inquisition?"

He laughs. "Hm. I'm not sure. Do you mean unifying our families or using brutal methods to cause widespread suffering?"

He arches his eyebrows up in question.

I, on the other hand, bend over laughing. Wiping the tears from my eyes, he looks at me with his chocolate-brown eyes, humor alight in his smile. It causes the dimple that is usually hidden to make a guest appearance, and my heart melts. This is how it should always be between us. The way we fit so perfectly together—the ease of our relationship. One day, it will always be like this. I lean over and give him a chaste kiss.

"It might be a little of both. Are you up for the challenge?" I hold my hand on his cheek, and his smile displays his beautiful white teeth, showing me the tiniest of gaps that I have been fixated on since we were kids.

I remember a conversation about it when he said he would get braces to close the slight gap on his front teeth all the way, and I told him not to because I loved it so much. It was quirky and unique. He smiled bashfully at me and looked away. I kept staring at him, wondering what he was thinking of at that time. I loved him then when I didn't understand the concept at such a young age.

"Of course, baby. I wouldn't expect anything less."

My phone vibrates, pulling me away from our conversation. I notice a message from my online chat group. I've been chatting with other fans of my favorite band that are also going to the concert in a few months. Excitement builds as we all wait for the day to get here; some talk about what they are wearing, making me think about what I will wear. I want to find a blue sequined jacket to put over my tank top. While thinking about that, I can feel Eduardo looking at me.

"Who are you chatting with?" Concern is etched on his face.

"Oh." I look at him and show him my phone. "Just some people who are also attending the concert we are going to. The fan page is an excellent way to meet other people and sometimes meet up at the shows."

Eduardo raises his eyebrows at me. He disapproves of this as I notice he stiffens in his seat. I immediately feel uncomfortable and remind myself that he isn't Julian.

"Are you sure it's safe, Emma? I mean, you don't know these people, do you?" He looks down at my phone and then back up at me. I know he only wants to keep me safe. He only uses controlling behavior with me when it is in the bedroom, and there is not a complaint from me on that front.

"Well, no, but that doesn't mean it's unsafe. It's just a band fan page where we all talk about band stuff—nothing else or really personal information is given. The band has a huge fan base, and everyone here only talks about the band or gives info about the playlist for the band. Things like that." I can see the concern in his eyes. I lean in to give him a small kiss on the lips. "I won't give out information about myself. Don't worry." He brings me close to him and nuzzles into my neck.

"I love you, Emma, and just want to keep you safe. I know I say that a lot, but it's true." He always reminds me of this. It's as if he is trying to make me understand. He says the very words I repeat to myself when I become paranoid about being controlled by another person. Julian controlled me and everything I did.

I lay my head on his shoulder, breathing in the comforting smells of his body wash. The same body wash I used in the shower to have his scent with me all day.

"I know, babe. I promise. It's okay."

We are interrupted from our moment when the airline staff call out on the speaker that we will be boarding soon with a direct flight to Tamaulipas, Mexico. We get up and stretch to board the plane after the three-hour layover for a small flight over the border. We contemplated driving, but then we would have to drive through or around Brownsville. I vowed never to return, so here we are, taking the long way around to see my family in Mexico, a few miles over the Texas border.

I pull my backpack over my shoulders and follow Eduardo to board first. He extends his hand and holds onto me as we board the plane. We have the second row in first class, so only two seats exist. I place my bag underneath the seat and have my Kindle out so I can read on the plane. The flight is short, with the duration being a little under two hours. I figure it's just enough time to get through the rest of my book. Who doesn't love a good dark romance book, right?

I buckle my seat belt and begin to watch other people board the plane.

I love watching people, imagining what their lives are like. I wonder what people think when they see me or what they think of Eduardo and me. Do they know who we are? Do they know what I want to do, especially to the man who took so much from me? The girl who pretends always to be so happy but is dying on the inside. Maybe one day I can genuinely be happy, and I hope it's soon.

The flight takes off, and I start to chew on a Twizzler. It's one of my favorite candies, and I get a ton of crap for it too. Eduardo said it tastes like wax, and he'd rather not waste time eating it. I pop the rest in my mouth and open up my Kindle. Eduardo laces our fingers together, and my eyes start to get heavy. I yawn, and Eduardo kisses my head as I lay it on his shoulder.

"Why don't you take a nap, Emma? By the time you open your eyes, we'll be there." I nod in agreement and decide to take his advice. As soon as I relax into his shoulder, he wraps his arm around me, pulling me close to him in a solid embrace.

I must have fallen asleep because I hear a commotion on the plane and feel someone shaking me.

"Baby, it's time to get off the plane."

I open my eyes and see everyone standing. I immediately wipe my mouth, self-conscious that I am drooling. Eduardo catches that and smiles. He tilts his head to the side, indicating for me to look at his shoulder, and then I am mortified.

"Oh my god, no!" I bring my hand up to my face, and he chuckles.

"I couldn't bear to wake you up. You even snored a little. It was cute." He smiles at me, and I cover my face, throwing my Kindle in my bag.

"Now I know you love me because that is not sexy at all." I shake my head and he grabs his bag. His brown eyes sear into me with lust.

"You are sexy as fuck." He reaches around my neck and kisses me hard. I pull away and hit his arm. I hear a girl giggle and I look over at her. She smiles at us with hearts in her eyes as she picks up her Colleen Hoover book, tucking it under her arm.

Not exactly my type of romance book, but hey, to each his own.

"Stop, just stop." I pull away and we both laugh at my expense and join the people walking off the plane.

We walk straight out of the terminal without going to baggage claim. Eduardo and I will get everything we need and keep it at the house. I still have clothing there from when I lived with my uncle, and Eduardo said he'll grab a couple of items if he needs anything else. Everything he has is in a carry-on. It's a personal trip, not business, so he doesn't need anything fancy.

I'm on my phone and smiling when we see Adrian pull up to get us in front of the door leading into the airport departure and arrival area. He puts the car in park and jumps out, much to the airport security's displeasure.

"Prima." He picks me up and kisses me on the cheek. God, I've missed him. He clasps hands with Eduardo and does a one-sided hug. He opens my door to the back, and I jump in as he and Eduardo get into the truck.

He looks in his rearview mirror before pulling out into the airport traffic. It's a small airport but has a lot of traffic and security. Now and then, security increases depending on the amount of crime in the area. I would say that now would be one of the high crime times, especially with increased travel between families around the holidays.

We make the twenty-minute ride to my uncle's house, and as we pull in, I am glad to be back home. I consider this my only real home filled with so many great memories. Our voices echo through the house as Adrian closes the door. Soon, I hear Uncle Andrés come in through the house from the kitchen.

"Mija, how are you?" He kisses the top of my head and hugs me tightly.

"Tio, I am good." I motion with my hand for Eduardo to grab onto and bring him closer. He wraps his left arm around my waist.

"Andrés." He puts his hand out to shake hands with my uncle. "It's been a long time."

I listen to his words, but there isn't anything inhospitable about it—nothing that expresses contempt.

"Yes, it sure has, Eduardo, but I am glad you are here now." He looks at me and claps his hands together.

"Well, Emma, you guys go freshen up from your trip, and our family will be coming over this evening for a party. They are all looking forward to seeing you and catching up. Your cousins will be over to set the band up, and we will start the barbeque pit in about an hour. Please help yourself to anything that you'd like. This is your home, Emma." He squeezes my arm and walks away.

I lead Eduardo up to my room. Since they didn't specify if we would sleep in different rooms, I will let that go for now. I open the doors to the balcony, allowing the light breeze in. It's cool, and I love this time of year. I can wear my hoodie right now and be comfortable. I look out at the landscape and enjoy the view.

Eduardo comes over to me and hugs me from behind, bringing me into him. He wraps his arms around me and nuzzles into my neck. I sigh in contentment. How often did I wish he was with me when I was alone in the house after my parents died? I look back at him and see him looking out through the trees.

"What are you thinking about?"

He looks at me and waits before saying what he is thinking. The breeze blows my hair back a little, and I shiver despite it being warm for this time of year.

"I'm thinking maybe before we leave here, we can take the truck, lay in the bed like we used to, and look up at the stars." He smiles at me, and I swoon seeing the dimple pop just a little, reminding me of the innocent boy from my childhood.

"That sounds so romantic." I feel him nod.

"Yes, and then I can do all the naughty things my pubescent body wanted to do to you back then." He pulls away before I can smack him. "You are such a mood killer."

He laughs and starts to remove his clothes. "Eduardo? What are you doing?" my voice raises a few octaves. "We are at my uncle's house and it's daytime. Everyone is walking around."

He rifles through his bag. "Um, I'm getting some new clothes to shower the airport off my body?"

My face flushes. "Oh, yeah, that's a good idea." I go to grab a new outfit from my closet.

"Are you joining me?" He stops at the door. I can tell he wants to laugh.

"Go!" I point at the door as he chuckles, closing the door behind him. I hear the sound of voices carrying through the courtyard, some of them familiar. I jump off the bed and head downstairs to see the rest of my family.

CHAPTER THIRTY-SEVEN

EDUARDO

I leave the shower and enter an empty room, absent my fiancèe. Her scent still lingers, and I inhale deeply. I wasn't kidding about taking her to look at the stars like we did when we were younger, lying in the back of the pickup truck. I was inexperienced, and Emma was too young. Now, none of that is true, and I can't wait to do all the things we should have done together.

I see my erection start to tent the towel that is still wrapped around my waist. Even just thinking about her makes me hard. I'm going to need another cold shower if I continue to think about her. I dress quickly, throw my bag into her closet, and venture out looking for Emma. I head downstairs, following the sound of a party gathering in the courtyard.

I don't have to go far when I hear her laugh echoing through the inner patio. Her voice carries on the dusty air. Before I can seek out Emma, I see Andrés leaving his office. He looks behind me to see if Emma is around.

"Eduardo, before you go out there, I'd like a word with you." He holds the door open, and I walk into his office, which is full of Emma's family and some members of his security team. I also noticed that this isn't a request but an order, and I hate how he throws that in my face.

It is a bit intimidating being at the mercy of Emma's family without anyone here to have my back, but I know they won't do anything to me. They want to be sure Julian is taken care of as much as I do, and lucky for them, I am the man to get the job done. Besides, it would be poor form to take me out here. They know I love Emma fiercely and will not rest until she is safe and Julian is found. We have history. Our families have a history. Andrés sits behind his desk and motions for me to sit next to Adrian as the rest of his men stand around.

"Do you want a drink?" He already poured me one, or maybe it was for himself, but I don't ask.

"Please." I extend my hand and he nods. He advances toward me, handing me the drink, and I thank him for it. He sits in the chair behind his desk, and I wait to hear what he has to say. I can feel them all staring at me, but my focus remains on Andrés.

He clears his throat. "It has come to my attention that one of your girlfriends may be helping Julian to track down and spy on Emma?" I don't miss the tick in his jaw. I stare at him and wait for him to finish. "Explain."

This line of questioning makes my heart speed with anger. I have to control my breathing to remain calm because of this motherfucker. To say that Cherry was my girlfriend and make it seem like I have multiple girlfriends, or worse, insinuating that I am cheating on Emma, is ridiculous.

"First, just to clarify, Cherry was a waitress at my club. She was never my girlfriend. She may have wanted a relationship, but I never gave her that impression. Her boyfriend came into my club and caused an upset with the staff. He caused a fight and had to be thrown out. When I found out that Cherry was the cause of it, announcing to her boyfriend that she loved me and chose me, I set her straight and fired her with pay to leave the premises." I take a drink and down the contents of my glass, letting the alcohol soothe the anger spreading across my face.

"I was never with that girl after, nor have I seen her. I reconnected with Emma and have been with her every day after that day. I am engaged to her. I love her and will protect her until my dying day." I look at Andrés and Adrian as I say this so that they understand that I am not playing around nor entertaining any other women in my life.

I go on to tell them what happened with Emma at the boutique in uptown Houston, as well as my suspicions that Cherry may be helping

Julian with gaining information.

"Cherry wasn't wealthy but has recently come into some money. She has a fancy apartment and dresses in designer clothes. She went from begging for a shift to not working? Something is fishy, but what concerns me is that she mentioned to Emma that she, and I quote, didn't see what *'they'* saw in her."

Andrés sits up in his chair and looks over to Sergio who is already on the phone. "Do you have the address of this place?"

I nod and write it on a piece of paper for him. He looks at it and hands it over to Sergio.

"Another thing." I pause, and Adrian sits up and leans over to me. I'm glaring already, and I haven't even said anything. "I'd like to keep this between us, but as you know, Philip is a good friend and was Emma's security detail."

Adrian snorts. "So you killed him. Yeah, some friend."

I look at him, lift my lip in a half smile, and shrug. "You heard that too? Well then, my plan worked better than I thought."

Adrian cocks his eyebrow upward and looks at his father. "So Philip isn't dead?"

I shake my head. "No, he is very much alive. I never told Emma he was dead. I just made it look like I killed him for allowing Julian to get near Emma. We knew he was close, and Philip did tell me. Jameson, my frat buddy who does my security system for the club, came over and wiped the cameras when Philip was led into the basement. Obviously, there weren't any cameras in there, so he was escorted out, and the cameras were wiped clean of any evidence. He has been helping me to track Julian and see if anyone from the club is letting Cherry in to help Julian stalk Emma. She could have been taken one night at the club, and I think it's someone close by working at my club or someone who has access to it. Either way, we will find out soon and end that."

Adrian looks toward his father. Andrés rubs at his beard in concentration. I don't know what he is thinking, but I am sure he has something to contribute to helping us find Julian. He stands up, walking across the room to look out the window. I already know that he is looking at Emma down in the courtyard. "We haven't been able to track him following Emma. He has been with his family or showing up at sponsored events, but never anything suspicious. Then, he is gone on business, but there is nothing that we can find or use against him."

I nod in agreement because I have had the same findings. "We have seen him on camera twice, and he was in Emma's apartment. I have a feeling his patience is running out." They are all looking at me.

"Why do you say that?" Adrian's fists clench at his side.

"Well, he was always just watching her. Now he is coming at her. He has been close to taking her in her place. That is why she is always with me or has someone with her. Philip is finding out some more information and should have something more concrete this week. That's why my men think he is dead, and Emma doesn't think that because the men would never admit that to her."

After another drink and a consensus about coordinating information, we decide to step out and join the festivities. Although this took much longer than expected, it was needed. I would rather speak about him at the beginning of the trip than at the end. It's best to clear the air and get it out of the way.

I see Emma outside, and she is drinking a Corona with her cousin, laughing and carefree. I wish I could see her like this all the time. She picks up her cousin's son, and I walk over to her. She swings him side to side on her hip, talking to him and kissing his puffy cheeks. The boy is laughing as she blows kissy noises on his neck. He grabs her hair and laughs. I wrap my arm around her and snuggle into her neck.

"God, you look good carrying a baby," I tell her, and she laughs.

"Oh no, we are not having a baby anytime soon." She eyes me, but I see her joking with me.

"Are you sure? We could start tonight under the stars," I tell her because I am mostly kidding, but if she says yes, I would definitely put a baby in her, even if the timing isn't exactly right. With Emma, anytime is the perfect time for me.

"I'd like that, Eduardo." She kisses me on the lips, and I bite her bottom lip, sucking it into my mouth. She pulls away and hands her cousin her baby, and I take her hand, staring down at her.

"As much as I'd love to carry your baby, Eduardo, I think maybe we should wait. Maybe until..." She trails off, and I know that she is worried about Julian. I grab her face and turn it back to me.

"Soon, babe," I promise. I kiss her forehead, and her cousin's band starts to play.

They're pretty decent. I chuckle as Emma starts singing "The Best of You" by the Foo Fighters. The barbecue pit starts to smoke, and the scent of meat cooking mixes with the earthy smells of mesquite wood burning permeate the air. I take a deep breath in, and my mouth begins to water.

Emma looks at me and laughs.

"Did you miss Tio's brisket?" She leans into me, and I am salivating at the thought.

"Most definitely, yes. The man can cook some brisket." The song changes into "Warning" by Morgan Wallen. She leads me out onto the makeshift dance floor in the inner courtyard. I feel all eyes on us, but I don't care. I only see her. We hear her cousin whistle, and I chuckle.

"Was that the dinner bell?" She kisses me.

"Not soon enough. I'm starving. You?"

She looks at me. "Yes."

I bring her in and kiss her. "Then after dinner we will take that drive out to look at the stars, and I'll eat my dessert."

She swats my arm. "Come on, let's eat."

I follow her through the crowd gathered tonight and enjoy the time with my future wife and family.

The trip was over sooner than I would have liked, and we had to return to reality. Emma was sad to say good-bye to her family. The safety she felt there was soon missed, and the anxiety of returning to Houston is palpable. I give her a reassuring squeeze as Eli picks us up from the Houston airport, and we drive home. She looks out the window in contemplative silence.

"What are you thinking about?" I want to know what bothers her.

She looks over at me, smiles dimly, and then returns her gaze out the window. "I'm just worried that I might not be able to enjoy the holidays with my family anymore. I never thought I wouldn't have my parents or sister. They were taken from me one night, and I never got a chance to say good-bye. What if I don't see them again? What if that was the last holiday with them too?"

I grab her hand and bring it to my lips, giving her hand a light kiss. "I promise it won't happen. You will have us. Always."

"Don't make promises you can't keep. Evie would say the same thing, and look at what happened to her. She learned to defend herself and encouraged me to do the same thing, and look at what happened. She promised that she would never leave me."

The city whizzes by. The holiday decorations are still up, and I wonder where that fucker is hiding. Is he back already watching her? Watching us? Soon. Soon, I'll have him and make him suffer. Emma will get her revenge and be free of the blackness that shrouds her.

CHAPTER THIRTY-EIGHT

EMMA

Eduardo made me stay away from Liv for her safety as well as mine, and it seems like I haven't seen my best friend in forever. I found out Liv is having a boy and is so happy. I wish we could go shopping for baby clothes, but I understand she is in danger just hanging out with me. Learning that Julian is closer than we thought puts things into perspective. Liv is pregnant and if anything happened to her, I wouldn't be able to live with myself. I don't know what I would do if anyone else got hurt because of me.

I think about my parents and my sister, whom I miss daily. There isn't a time that goes by that I don't wish my sister was helping me plan a wedding. I see her everywhere and in certain things that I hear. Sometimes, I can even hear her talking to me through different people.

Occasionally, I pretend that one of my online friends is her, and we are excited to see each other at the Ghost concert. I know it's not healthy, but I am beyond caring about that. I want to see her so bad that I imagine her across the street looking at me just to look again, and she's gone. That's what happens when your guilt consumes you. You think you must suffer and can't forgive yourself for what happened.

After returning from Mexico and promising my family to be careful, I promised Liv I would go to the gala. This is the first time since our shopping trip that I will see her. I picked up the dress from the seamstress last week and know it will fit. I asked Dax to give me some guesstimates from her wedding dress, and I came up with something that would allow for expansion. If it is tighter, that's okay because it will still look gorgeous on Liv's tall stature and lithe body.

My knees are bouncing up and down as we round the corner to my old apartment that I shared with Liv. Eduardo agreed that if I took Eli, I could return there for a couple of hours to visit with Liv and give her the dress.

I carry the long material folded over my arm by the hanger and knock on the door before entering. I still have the key because we still have a lease. Eduardo doesn't want Julian to think I never go here, but I feel unsure since I know he has been here. When he wrote not to run from him in the mirror, I did not want to return here ever again. I feel like my personal space, my sanctuary, was violated. Did he touch my things? Go through my drawers? It's contaminated with pestilence, and I can't stay here without feeling the sense of dread creep into my subconscious, alerting me to the fact that he could get to me.

"Honey, I'm home!" I shout as I walk through the door, shutting it with my foot as I throw my tote on the table and place the dress over the sofa. I hear Liv shuffle out of the room. She's in her robe, and when she sees me, she begins to run over.

Meeting her halfway, I go over and hug her, rocking her back and forth like I never want to let her go. "Oh, Liv. I miss you so much, bestie." I pull back so I can take a look at her. "Are you even pregnant under that robe?" She releases it, and I see the baby bump. "Oh-my-god. Look at you! You are so cute."

Liv blushes and holds her belly, turning to the side so I can see her baby bump profile. "Thanks, Em. I don't look super big, do I?" She is almost self-conscious about it, and I laugh.

"Please. You are pregnant, not big. If I were pregnant, I'd be much bigger because I am so short."

Liv looks at me. "Are you...?"

I have my hand up to stop that line of questioning right away. "Nope, we are not."

Liv just smiles. "Okay. Maybe not yet."

I laugh and swat her arm. "Maybe in the future we can hang out with our kids. Right now, that is a big no for me."

Liv laughs at my quick response to no babies. "Okay, show me the dress."

I reach over and hand it to her. "Okay, Liv. Let's see how it looks."

She grabs the material, feeling the softness of the fabric moving freely through her fingers. She does a little squeal. I sigh, feeling content in this moment and knowing it won't last long.

"I'm going to pour myself some wine to see this. I know you still have some around, right?"

Liv laughs. "You know me so well." She points to the living room. "Yes, on the wine rack that sits on the dining room table."

I see my favorite wine sitting at the top of the rack with a duck on it. "Oh, yes. My favorite duckie cabbie." I open the bottle like a pro and pour myself a solid eleven ounces of wine. I sigh, welcoming the complement as the fruity overtones of blackberry, cherry, and plum assault my taste buds. I fight the urge to smack my lips. Liv just stares at me.

"I'm so envious of you right now." She looks at me and smiles. "Do you have to look like you are enjoying that wine so much?"

"I feel so much better now. Perfect. And yes, I do. You go show me how stunning you look in that dress."

Liv runs out of the room into her bedroom with the dress. I swear the girl is practically glowing. I am the one jealous of her. She looks happy now. I thought I'd never see that look on her again. It is long overdue.

While I am waiting for her, I decide to go to my old room and look around. I go to the bathroom, and when I stop to wash my hands, I stare at the mirror. Julian was standing right there when he wrote that message to me. My breathing picks up, and I think I am having a panic attack. I breathe in for a few seconds, hold it, and then blow out, repeating the process until I feel calmer.

"Fuck, I need more wine." I walk out to the dining room and top off my wine though it wasn't empty. My hands are shaking, and Liv is standing in the hall looking at me when I look up. I try my best to school my features, but I am afraid she's already seen it. My mask slipped, and all I can do is deflect and redirect her questions. That is, if they even come. She knows, after all these years, my secrets stay hidden.

When I look at her in that dress, I smile genuinely.

"Look at you!" I go over, almost skipping with giddiness at seeing my friend so radiant. "Liv, you look ravishing in this dress. Dax is going to rip this off of you after the gala."

She squares her shoulders to look at me, pointing her finger and wiggling it in my direction.

"Ha, that's where you are wrong, Emma. He'll throw the back of this dress over my head and take me from behind up against this wall instead."

I almost spit out my wine, but unfortunately, when I try to prevent that, I snort it out my nose instead. Choking, I sputter. And that's what I get for pouring so much wine in this glass.

"Why, Liv, you little minx." I manage to sputter that out in between clearing my nostrils of the wine in a coughing fit. "Now," I wheeze, finally managing to stop coughing, "that is the funniest thing I have heard. Where is my shy friend I once knew?"

We both chuckle, and I look around, noticing that Dax isn't here. "Where's Dax?"

Liv shrugs. "Oh, he went to pick up his altered tux and should be back soon. Nothing like waiting until the last minute." She starts to ask something but stops.

"Um, so how are things with Eduardo?" She pauses, and I know that she thinks I will not answer her. It reminds me of how much of a shit friend I am. I'm about to answer when she spins the question, shocking me. "You seemed happy with Jameson, and then you met Eduardo…" She trails off, not finishing the sentence. I just stare at her. Liv notices my hesitation and continues breaking the awkward silence. "I never did thank him for helping me that night when I found out I was pregnant. Fainting. Passing out at his club was not one of my finer moments."

I go over and place a hand on her arm. "Oh, Liv. Don't even worry about that. I pause, wondering if I should continue. "Yeah, I liked Jameson, but it wasn't there. When I met Eduardo… I don't know. He makes me feel." I leave it at that because that's precisely what it is. He makes me feel. After years of being numb when my parents died and I lost my sister, I didn't think I would ever recover.

My best friend died that night. A big part of me died that night.

The remaining part of me wished I would have died too, alongside them in the fire. I feel like I live in this earth-bound prison where I must watch over my shoulder and risk being captured by Julian—a worse fate than death.

Liv watches me and tries to finish my sentence. "Happy?" she asks.

I rub my lip back and forth, trying to explain without giving away too much of my story. I look over at her and hope that this at least answers her question.

"Even better. He makes me feel safe."

She looks at me in confusion. "Safe?" she questions.

I smile sadly at her and drain the entire contents of my glass. I grab my keys, effectively stopping the conversation before it even begins. "I better go. Still have to get a quick bite to eat before seeing you guys at the gala."

Defeat shines in Liv's eyes, but I can't let her know. I can't let anyone else know.

"Sure, Emma. I'll see you there. We are sitting at the same table, right?"

I start toward the door and hug her before I leave. "Of course. I'll let Eduardo know."

I sit with Eli in the car, feeling unsure about my future. Will I always have to deal with Julian? Will I ever be truly free? We drive through uptown, and I look around at people in shops and walking with friends on the sidewalks. I see a couple jogging toward a park, and I feel empty. I want that life. A normal life, but I'll never have that. In some way or another, I will always have to watch my back, but wouldn't it be nice to be rid of him finally?

My fists clench. I want him to suffer. I want him to die. I don't think I have ever really thought about it like this. I do know one thing for sure: he will pay for what he did to me and my family. I won't rest until he is gone from this earth, but not until he feels what it is like to lose it all.

I grab my Airpods and turn on Spotify. I recently played and hit "Voices in My Head" by Falling in Reverse. The song is my anthem, my battle cry. I tear myself down, and I feel all the guilt consuming me. The struggle I think about every day is that I don't have my sister.

I wonder what we will do today as I ride alone in this car. Oh, wait, not alone, but with a driver hired to keep me safe. My inner voice tells me I am to blame, but self-doubt takes over when confronted with whether or not I can continue. My sole mission is to take back my life. To break free from the confines of self-doubt I have, and it overtakes me like waves in the sea. The wind picks up, and I am tossed around with no life preserver. If I die, I will die trying. If I drown, I'll do so trying until I'm buried at sea.

CHAPTER THIRTY-NINE

EDUARDO

"What the fuck do you mean? I'll be right there. I want you to take him to the basement," I spit into the phone as I rush to go down to the nightclub.

Philip discovered that one of the bartenders was helping Cherry acquire information about me and Emma. I haul ass to the club and park sideways in the back alley, running into the building and up to my office. Jameson knocks on the door a few minutes later.

"Come in!" I shout as he walks into my office. I am pulling up the feed as he towers above the security monitors on my desk.

"May I?" he asks, and I stand from my chair and push the seat over to him. He hits a few buttons and pulls up a feed that has Gage, our long-time bartender, walking in the hallway, with Cherry leading him over to a back storage room where we keep many expensive liquors, candied Luxardo and Maraschino cherries, and various other nonperishable items. Jameson enhances the sound on the computer as I hover over him, watching the scene unfold.

"What do you have for me, baby?" She stalks toward him, and he smiles widely. She drops to her knees, unbuckles his jeans, and unzips his fly. They fall to the floor with a loud clunk as his heavy metal belt hits the tiled floor. She looks up at him, licking her lips, and he steps closer to her as she grabs his ass, digging her fingernails into his flesh as he hisses and his cock bobs. She rubs her cheek up and down his cock and looks expectantly at him. "I want to make you feel so good, and then I want you to take me any way you want, but you have to tell me what I want to know first." She turns her face sideways, licking up the underside of his shaft and sucking on the tip as she releases him, stops, and looks back up at him expectantly.

"I heard him talking about a concert he was taking her to. It was her favorite band." He stops talking as Cherry grabs his cock hard and takes it into her mouth all the way back into her throat. Gage holds onto the shelf and knocks a bottle off, hitting the floor and spilling contents all over.

"Fuck, that was a five hundred dollar bottle of Johnny Walker Blue Label. Son of a bitch."

Cherry stops and looks at the mess, frowning. She continues to look at the spilled contents while lapping at the tip of his cock. "Hm," she purrs. "Tell me more so you can bend me over and fuck me already."

He grabs her head and pushes her onto his cock again. She takes it willingly. "Let me fuck your mouth for a minute first." He backs her up to the wall and places his hand above her. She grabs his ass hard as he pounds into her mouth, stilling each time as he hits the back of her throat. Her head goes back, and he groans. She hollows out her cheeks, and he bucks forward and comes down her throat. She continues to lap at him, licking him clean as he rubs her cheek affectionately.

"You suck my cock so good, Cherry." She pulls herself up, licking her lips, and lifts her dress, showing that she isn't wearing any panties, and then pushes her tits out the front of her already low-cut dress. She grabs her tits, shoving them upward, and Gage eyes them greedily.

"Tell me more," she moans, flicking her nipples back and forth.

Gage tells her everything she wants to hear. He dives into her boobs, kneading and licking. He turns her around, and a couple more bottles fall off the shelf.

"Motherfucker!" I scream out at the monitor.

He turns her around and pushes her down on the shelf. He sticks a finger in her ass and then another, scissoring it back and forth. He takes his stiff cock and presses it against her ass and thrusts forward. I watch about another thirty seconds of him fucking her ass, until I am sure there isn't anything else said about Emma.

I get up, and Jameson follows me into the basement. Eli is still guarding Emma, so I have another few men there waiting on me. I see Gage there chained to the wall, and I walk in, hitting him in the face. I punch him over and over, until Jameson holds me back.

"Um, you might want to ask him questions before you knock him out." He grabs my arms, halting any further action.

I stand there, attempting to control my ragged breaths. "Tell me everything," I speak to him in a low growl. I smell the scent of urine and realize he pissed himself. "Alejandro, come over here." Al walks up and waits for me to give my order. I am walking out the door. "Make him speak. I have to take Emma to a function tonight. Too bad you won't be relaying information to Cherry anymore."

Al punches Gage in the ribs, and I know he's broken a couple. I look at Jameson, and he nods. I know he'll keep me posted. He is determined, just as I am determined to ensure Emma is safe.

I hear Emma enter through the door as I speak with Philip on the phone. After returning from our trip from Mexico, we have been actively trying to keep tabs on Cherry. I believe that she will lead us to Julian if we are patient enough. Patience has not always been my biggest virtue.

After extensive investigation, Philip discovered that Cherry seems to have come into some money and now lives a life of luxury in a spacious apartment in the Uptown section of Houston, nearer than we'd like. He wants to tell me more, and I know that he has been working hard to find out if there is any correlation between Cherry's newfound wealth and Julian's retaining new information to help him stalk Emma.

When I see the haunted look in Emma's eyes, I can't concentrate on anything else Philip needs to tell me. "Hey, can I call you later?" I interrupt.

"Sure, Boss, I'll keep digging and keep you posted. No worries," he says, and I end the call.

I stand up from the island barstool and drain the rest of my whiskey from the glass. I approach Emma as she puts her purse on the foyer table.

"Hey, baby. How was your day?" I bring her into me, and she softens, releasing the tension she held onto from the emotional weight bearing down on her shoulders.

"Exhausting." She lets out a long breath and pulls back from me. "I feel like such a shit friend to Liv," she says, hiding her eyes from me.

I pull her hand away from her face and tuck a loose strand of hair that fell from her messy bun behind her ear. "And why is that?" I look at her and wait for her to explain.

"She knows that I hide things from her, and every time I change the subject or deflect, I see the hurt it causes her. I want to tell her everything, but I'm scared. The last time I did that, I caused the people I love to suffer. I never want to burden anyone with that again. I'd rather be buried with my secrets."

"Emma, let me carry that burden for you. You are my partner in this life, and you no longer have to go through this alone. I am here." I hold her face in my palms and kiss her. I want to show her how much I love her in that kiss, and I understand just how much she loves me. I can feel it, and I hope she knows what I say is true. I grab her hand and lead her to the bedroom.

"Here, let me run you a bath and you can relax before the gala. You'll see your friend, and we can hang out with her and Dax."

She seems to perk up at this. "Maybe that's all we need is one good night out." She discards her clothes and walks into the bath, and I can't help but watch her as she steps into the tub.

I palm my cock through my pants and try to halt the erection tenting them. She sees that and calls me over. I lean down and kiss her.

"Later, I'll worship you. Now, you relax while I finish up on a call with Eli about security for the gala." She pouts and I laugh. "You can choke on my cock later, baby." I wink at her as I walk out.

After talking with Philip again and then Eli, I have an idea how tonight will go. We suspect Julian might be at the gala and will be watching to see if anything is suspicious. Eli understands that he is to be around in case things get out of hand and is to follow Emma everywhere. With two people on Emma, one that doesn't know about the other, I feel better about being in a crowd with eyes on her.

I walk into the room and see Emma putting on the jewelry I gave her. She wears her engagement ring and her necklace that she never goes without, as well as the tracker I had Jameson get for her. She is wearing a green dress that matches the color of her eyes. Her hair is plaited in a loosely curled braid wrapped around to the side that lands over her right chest. Pieces of hair fall from the plait at various stages, and it looks simple yet classy. She steps into her six-inch stilettos and is considerably taller than her regular five foot two inches, or at least that's what she claims her height to be. I walk to her and pick up her braid, twisting the loose pieces of the end in my finger.

"I like this," I tell her and flick it back and forth. "I think it will be fun to use later." My eyes find hers, and she smiles mischievously. She licks her lip and reaches up to gently kiss my lips. I bend, allowing her to pepper light kisses down my neck. She looks back at me and then my shirt.

"Oops, I think I got a little lipstick on your white shirt," she says sincerely.

My lip curls up in a smirk. "You don't have to mark your territory, Emma. I've been yours forever." I grab her hand and lead her out of the room before I destroy her pretty hair and makeup.

We enter the gala, which is busy with patrons begging to display their wealth and social status in the community. It's the same with all the galas. Even though this is for a good cause, they still have to be wined and dined before contributing to the community or overpaying for a silent auction item bid.

I know many people from the gym, my club, and other non-legal endeavors are here. There are a surprising number of politicians from the local area as well. They use the opportunity to network as much as possible.

I mingle, and I introduce Emma as my fiancée. She is engaging and charismatic. I hate that she gets the attention of men, and I certainly don't want her getting the attention of some of the men I see here tonight.

I receive a message from Philip saying he needed to check something suspicious, and my heart accelerates as I look around for Eli. I spot him, and he is watching us. I tip my head to the side in Emma's direction, and he nods. I want her watched now more than ever.

I see Emma looking around, no doubt to find Liv. We haven't seen her or Dax, but I am sure they must mingle and play the part just as much, since this is Dax's mother's charity.

We hear someone take the mic and see Dax's mother, Isabella, attempting to get everyone's attention. We go to our table as other people do the same thing. Just as we walk to the table, we see Liv and Dax approach from the opposite direction. Liv hurries over to Emma and hugs her.

"Geez, Liv, you'd think I didn't see you a few hours ago." She laughs, separating herself and taking a seat next to me.

I shake Dax's hand as he takes his place next to Liv. We all settle into our assigned seats, and soon, dinner is served. The silent auction follows, and we bid on a bougie charcuterie basket with a bottle of Emma's favorite wine, Caymus. When Liv's phone rings, Emma tells me she must go to the bathroom before her bladder bursts. Emma is scrutinizing Liv saying something to Dax. Liv looks at her phone, answering it as she walks off. Emma follows her, telling me she'll be right back. I send a message to Eli to let him know Emma is on the move. He makes eye contact with me and walks over to her as she disappears around the corner, following Liv. Dax is frowning and shaking his head, looking in the direction Liv went.

CHAPTER FORTY

EMMA

"I'll be right there, Liv." I head into the bathroom and quickly relieve my bladder from the extension and stretch of too much water and wine with dinner. I rush back out, looking for Liv. She looked so upset, and I know that whoever called her had terrible news. I thought I heard her say Melissa, Brodie's nurse, so that can only mean that it has to do with Brodie once again.

I am pondering all the things that could have gone wrong when I run straight into a man. I step away, muttering my apologies, and he says it's not a problem when I look up and stare into the eyes that have brought me so much agony. Eyes like his psycho son.

"Mr. Martinez," I gasp, and his eyes narrow, quickly scanning the area. He doesn't have time to act because I rush out the door searching for Liv, heading toward an outside door. I see him walk toward me as I push past it, and he hesitates. I can't worry about that. Eduardo and Eli are here somewhere; I'm safe. For once, that is the furthest thing from my mind because I can only concentrate on getting to my friend. The look on her face as she left the table concerned me.

I spot her and then see Liv drop the phone and slump to the floor.

"Liv!" I shout at her, but she doesn't respond. She doesn't even look my way.

I pick up the phone and hear Melissa crying from the other end of the line. Melissa replays the story about Brodie being rushed to the hospital on the brink of death.

"Oh god, no." I throw my head back, and the tears come to my eyes. I hang up and drop down to Liv, trying to shake her. She isn't listening. It is as if she has checked out of her body and completely shut down. After all the girl has gone through with the Brodie situation, I would, too. Why did this have to happen when things are starting to go so well?

Dax flies through the door along with Eli. I give him all the information. Dax moves, picking up Liv, and I follow them outside with Eli on my tail when a black SUV pulls around the corner. Eduardo jumps out, scanning me for any injuries. I shake my head at him, but I can't stop the look he gives me, as if he knows what happened before Liv fell onto the ground. We all drive to the hospital that Brodie was taken to not long ago.

The next few hours are the worst with how history is repeating itself, except this time, it is the end. The doctor comes in and gives us the news. Brodie didn't survive the infection that wreaked havoc on his system. Just like that, another life was lost.

I see a broken person in Liv. Broken attracts broken. I understand her and her damaged parts that are so similar to mine. Misery loves company and all that, and boy, have we both had our fair share of it. Just when they had rekindled their friendship, Brodie was no longer depressed and angry. When he began accepting his disability, this happened. It's ironic how life is sometimes. Just when you think things are better, the other shoe drops and kicks you in your ass. Eduardo holds onto me as we sit by Liv. My hand is on her shoulder as she sobs into Dax's chest.

We step out of the SUV to hear thunder cracking across the sky. It is fitting that there should be a storm approaching. It's as if the angels are weeping along with us. I am devastated for Liv. With her pregnancy, I worry about all the stress she is under. She is a shell of her former self. The priest talks about the Kingdom of God, a long speech about His son returning to be united with Him. There are a lot of people here who made the trip. I know it makes the family happy to see that their son was so well-liked by many people. He had an impact on all our lives at one point or another.

I walk to the car and see Liv alone after everyone has left, still holding on to her single rose. It's as if she doesn't want to throw it in the grave because that will be it.

The final good-bye.

She releases it, and my lips part as I see the agony on her face. She looks up at the sky as if she is talking to God. I am wracked with sobs, watching and not being able to help her. As much as I claim to want to take back my life, I haven't. Liv has faced all the obstacles thrown at her. I am afraid that this is all too much. I can't seem even to help my friend as she goes through the loss of Brodie. I haven't even told Eduardo about seeing Julian's father, Mr. Martinez, at the gala. There just hasn't been the right time, or at least that's what I tell myself. The truth is, I'm numb. I don't care.

I see Dax pick up Liv and bring her toward the car as Eduardo goes around the side to open the door for him. I witness Dax rubbing a circle with his thumb around the top of her hand, and I look away, feeling as if I am invading a private moment. I look out the window as the rain slides down against it, finding it ironic as it mimics my tears on my cheek.

We get home, and I drop my bag on the foyer table, exhausted from today's events. I kick my shoes off as I fall onto the couch. I sit there cradling my head in my hands. Eduardo comes over and starts to rub my back.

"Baby? Do you want a drink?"

I nod as he saunters over to the bar and pours us both a couple of fingers of an amber liquid. I don't ask questions, but take it as he places it into my hands while taking a seat beside me. I sit back, and he picks my feet up, placing them in his lap, and then begins rubbing them, causing me to release a moan. He stares at me, assessing the likelihood of a complete breakdown as I down the whiskey in one long pull. He takes the glass from me and places both of them on the table next to the sofa. He pulls me onto his lap, and I curl into his body as I sob.

"Baby, what's wrong? Are you okay?"

"No, I'm not. I feel so bad for Liv. I couldn't help my family, I couldn't help Liv, and I certainly can't help myself." I ugly cry into Eduardo's chest as I pull at his shirt, wiping my tears and snot away.

"Shh," he soothes. "Let it all out, Em. It's okay."

He holds me like this for what feels like hours. When I have no more tears to cry, I pull away and wipe my eyes. I shake with a sob, but no more tears fall. "Am I officially broken? No more tears to cry, and I am gutted."

Eduardo takes my hands, making me look at him.

"Emma, you are not broken. You are so strong. Resilient. What you have been through would have made weaker people crumple. You are still standing despite everything you've lost. You've always been there for Liv, and I am here to be there for you, to pick you up. I am here to make you believe in your strength and will always be there to catch you if you fall. But you are still standing, and he hasn't won."

I stand up and pace the room. "For how long, Eduardo? How long do I have to fear for my life and hope he doesn't take me or hurt someone I love?" I look at him, hoping he understands how much I feel for him. He is my world. I pause, closing my eyes as I shudder at the thought of seeing Julian's father. The way he looked at me. There is more to the story than him wanting me with Julian. The contempt he held for me was scarier than Julian's ill-treatment. I open my eyes and look at him.

"At the gala, I saw Julian's father. He knows where I am, my friends, and who I am with." I say it all and get it off my chest. "I can't help but worry that he will hurt you all."

Eduardo stiffens. "What! Why didn't you tell me? Emma, it's been a week. He could have come at you or us. I can't prepare for him if you don't tell me. I can't keep you safe if I don't have all the information. You can't hide things like that from me."

I look at him, and he looks away. I don't know why he did that, but it makes me cautious. Is there something he isn't telling me? Should I be worried?

"Fuck." He pulls on his hair and walks to his office. "Stay there. I have to make a call." I hear him on the phone, and he looks at me, shutting the door. Not caring about staying put, I walk to my bedroom and strip out of my wet funeral clothing. I put on a robe and let the hot water from the shower billow in the air. The steam rises in waves.

I stand under the hot water as I hear the door open. I see Eduardo through the frosted glass drop his clothes on the bathroom floor before he enters the shower behind me. He holds me under the hot spray, trying to stop my body from shivering. He pumps some shampoo into his hands and lathers my hair, rubbing his fingers through my scalp. I tilt my head back at how good his fingers feel massaging my scalp. He rinses off the shampoo and repeats the same actions with the conditioner, making sure to detangle my hair with his fingers as he washes it out while his strokes remain gentle and soothing. He washes my body with his shower gel, rubbing the suds over every inch in a languid caress. His hands don't linger as they usually do when we share a shower because this act isn't about sex. It's about showing how he cares for and wants to take care of me, even when I'm at my most vulnerable and cannot.

I worried him when I told him about Mr. Martinez, and he lashed out in anger. I should have told him, but my safety wasn't a priority then. He rinses me and steps out after washing the soap from his body too. He has a big fluffy towel and dries me off, slipping an oversized T-shirt over my head. We walk back to the bedroom and lie in bed. He covers me and gets into bed with me, spooning me with his body pressed against my back. Even though I can feel the hard line of his erection on my back, he doesn't try to make a move to fuck me. He just holds me and rubs his hands in a circle around my stomach while the other runs through my hair, rubbing my forehead with each pass of his thumb.

"Eduardo," I moan as he moves up and down my neck with light kisses. He nibbles on my ear, and I feel a pull from my core. I want more. I always want more from him.

"Please, Eduardo. Make me feel something."

He turns me around and looks into my eyes. "Emma, you are the most important thing in my life. You need to fight and take back your life. Only then will you be truly free. You have to continue to fight, Emma."

He gets on top of me, moving my legs apart with his knee. He positions himself with his cock lined up with my entrance. He stares down at me, hovering his body over mine. He kisses me and thrusts into me with one hard pass. He pulls my lower lip in his mouth as he balances his body on his forearms while continuing to move fluidly in and out. He buries his face in my neck and sucks on my skin, marking me all over, reminding me I am his. His thrusts become harder, as he leans into me a little more, repeatedly hitting my cervix with a delicious pounding, causing my climax to build rapidly.

I can hear my wetness and the sound of our skin smacking together. He takes my nipple into his mouth, lapping at the tender bud. His thrusts are unrelenting. I come with a gasp, shouting his name as my inner walls spasm with my climax. He comes on a groan as he spills into me. He kisses me softly on the lips. My breathing starts to regulate as I come down from my high, and my vision that blackened with my orgasm subsides as I open my eyes to bring me back into my reality.

I see Eduardo looking at me intently. "Fight, Emma. Fight for us."

His words empower me. He makes me feel again, but now I feel too much. I'll take it. It's better than not feeling anything. It means that I am alive and he hasn't won. The wave of emotions consumes me, and my rage for Julian will overpower the worst storms.

CHAPTER FORTY-ONE

EDUARDO

Things have improved over the past months. Liv has turned the corner, and she and Emma are closer than ever. After the funeral, Liv broke down, and Emma was in a constant state of worry for her mental and maternal health. All that stress wasn't healthy for the baby. Dax was always by her side, and Emma was gone a lot to stay with her when Dax couldn't. At least I knew where she was, and Eli was always close behind me.

We are sitting at the breakfast island having Mexican sweet bread and coffee—a definite Mexican food staple. We have some time to kill before the concert, and Emma could hardly sleep last night. She couldn't believe the day was actually here. I had to feel her moving back and forth all night. She even got up to pee at least a couple of times. I couldn't take it anymore, and I pulled her into me, spooning my arm over her. I held her until her breathing evened out and she finally allowed me to pass out too around two-thirty in the morning.

I look over at her and see her doing her crossword puzzle. Without looking at me she says, "I wonder when Philip is coming back."

She distracts me from my thoughts as I was looking at her and thinking about other things. She looks over at me, but I honestly have no idea how to broach that subject.

"No idea, babe. He just said maybe soon after things clear up." I shrug because my words aren't exactly untrue. She doesn't ask for further details. It's pointless. I won't give anything else away. The less she knows the better. I had people watching her, and I just hope that is enough.

"Okay, I was just curious," she continues, not really done with this conversation, "but I don't want to pry if Philip has problems with his family. I understand the need for privacy sometimes."

I reach over and squeeze her hand, returning my focus back to my computer screen on my laptop. We sit there in comfortable silence, and I think about the concert tonight, wondering if something could happen. Could tonight be the night he tries to take her?

Julian hasn't reappeared, but we are waiting for what he could do next. We also haven't heard anything from Julian's father, but I'll bet that he called his son right after he saw Emma. She mentioned that he looked at her with anger all the times he was in her sight. It was as if her presence disgusted him, and I don't understand why that is. There has to be more to the story, and I told her uncle and cousin that a few times during our visit in Mexico over the holidays.

We know Julian is in Houston, and after following Cherry, she hasn't led us to anything we consider noteworthy. After her informant at the club was placed in the ground, her well of information dried up, and she no longer had access to that source.

I had an emergency meeting with the staff and told them she was not allowed in this club. If I found out she was back in there, it would cause immediate termination or worse. When they asked about Gage, the bartender that was fucking Cherry and telling her information about me and Emma, I let them know that he wouldn't be around to cause further problems as he is no longer working at the club. I left it at that and let them come to their own conclusions about Gage's whereabouts.

Jameson and I have become closer, and I trust him to help me with Emma. I feel better that she has a button to hit in an emergency—the starburst pendant. Emma gets up from the stool and tells me she is going to start to get ready.

"Are you sure? We still have a lot of time until we leave for the concert," I inform her, but she just smiles at me.

"I have to do my makeup and costume. It might take a while." She looks at me and smiles mischievously.

"Should I be scared, baby?" I wonder what she has up her sleeves, and by the look in her eye, I can tell that she is planning something epic.

"You should always be scared, baby." She leans over and bites my lip.

"What the...?" I touch my lip, but she didn't break the skin. She smiles and winks at me, and then slowly turns around, walking off, leaving me now very turned on. I think I have met my match.

I pick up my coffee and decide to make another, but this time with a little bit of alcohol in it. I move the stool she'd been sitting on over and throw my feet up on it and relax, knowing that Emma will be in there for a while getting ready for tonight. I can make my plans with the extra security I have for us tonight without her knowing. I smile to myself as I look at our bedroom door. I am more than curious to see what she has up her sleeve tonight.

I get ready for the concert in the spare bedroom. I don't want to take away from Emma getting ready in our master bedroom. When I walked in there it was total destruction. There was makeup everywhere and I was assaulted with a hit of hairspray to the face as I approached her from behind. At least she didn't hit me in the eye. She swears that this stuff is all natural and cruelty free, but I bet it fucking hurts to get in your eye. I've been sitting on the couch answering emails from work, until I finally hear the sound of the bedroom door shut.

She walks out of the room dressed in black fitted, ripped jeans with an Eponymous Tour Ghost concert shirt. Her hair is pulled back with two inverted French braids that wrap around in a wild ponytail. Her long blond hair hits mid back, and her face is painted with ghoulish makeup. She is wearing platform black Doc Martens boots. The look is completed with a bright-blue sequined blazer she spoke about getting specifically for this concert to match Papa, the lead singer. She is a sight to behold, even in her ghoulish attire.

She sees me and smiles. Her black matte lipstick makes her teeth look even whiter and her smile wicked. I have a fitted black shirt, jeans, and boots. Nothing special. This is about Emma. It's her night, and she has been looking forward to it since I bought the tickets. She grabs her phone and a clear plastic bag that most concerts only allow into the venue. I realize that I have been staring at her when she clears her throat. I stand and put my phone away mid message as I take her arm, and we walk out of the apartment through the front lobby.

CHAPTER FORTY-TWO

EMMA

Eli is there with the car, and we are soon on our way to the event. The concert is about thirty miles north of Houston, so we have a small drive ahead of us. Eli messes with the radio and hits the Spotify app.

"What do you guys want to listen to on the ride to the concert?" Eli drags his finger through the recently played section of the app.

"Oh, I made a playlist. Here, put this on." I connect my phone, and "Ghouls Night Out" by the Misfits starts to play through the car speakers. Old-school Glenn Danzig's vocals begin with the three standard power chords infamous in punk rock music—the powerful simplicity of the genre is refreshing. I also made a concert song playlist for the event tonight with every song the band planned on singing, starting with Ghost's first song, "Kaisarion."

We drive and get most of the playlist, and I sing to every song. I feel Eduardo staring at me, and I catch Eli looking in the rearview mirror, catching glimpses of him suppressing a laugh. I don't have the best voice, but I don't give a damn. This is the best music ever. When we get there, Eli comes to open the door, and Eduardo grabs my hand, helping me out. We start walking toward the venue, and I see everyone dressed in decorative attire. Eduardo looks around and then smiles down at me.

"Looks like you've found your tribe here. You should probably hit the port-a-potty before we get in there."

We go through the line, get our merch, and walk it back to the car. I don't want to lose my signed poster. We are allowed early entry and walk in to look through some of their stations in the VIP lounge. It has displays of the band and pictures. A little food spread is laid out for us, but I am too excited to eat. A lady walks in and lets us know that we will be lining up for those who have pit tickets, and my smile drops. It isn't that I am not appreciative of the chance to be here, but what I wouldn't do for pit tickets. Eduardo looks over at me.

"Let's lineup so you get a good spot."

I look over at him in shock. "What did you say?" I blink at him several times because I couldn't have heard right.

He smiles at me expectantly. "I had Helena give us her pit tickets, baby. We need to line up for the pit."

I fling myself into his arms. "Oh my god. I love you so much more right now. Let's go."

We follow the lady as she climbs on an ATV. We walk and are lined up for the concert pit entrance at the front. Once we get in there, you don't leave, so I am ready for this.

We await the beginning act, and I take my phone out and check my online chats. Her name is Genevieve, and she is in the States for the concert. I am so excited to meet her after finally chatting with this girl. She lives in New Zealand now, but was originally from Texas and still has family here. That's the great thing about online friends. You have so much in common and would have typically never met if it wasn't for modern technology.

Eduardo peers over and sees me chatting. He frowns, and I see the way he looks at me. Always so protective. He assumes everything is a threat to take me out.

The opening act was fabulous, and now it's time for the main attraction. I think I am going to burst with happiness. The Ghouls and Ghoulettes come out first on stage, and then we are blessed by Papa Emeritus IV.

Eduardo looks over at him and then at me, screaming his name, and he shakes his head.

"It's part of the lore, Eduardo. Just go with it. It's going to be amazing." And it is. Before I know it, the concert finishes with "Square Hammer," and I am losing my mind. I have gone through a series of emotions in the past couple of hours. Anticipation, excitement, happiness, and sadness that it is over all too soon.

The ghouls are out front in their masks, tossing picks, and I see Eduardo jump up in the air. He keeps his arms in as he lands back on his feet, slightly swaying. I look at him, and he holds out the contents of what is in his hand. I scream and grab it.

"A fucking pick. Yes!" I run in place and squeal with excitement. I throw myself at him and kiss him. "This is so much better than my mummy dust cash I got earlier that shot out of the cannons."

He shakes his head as tears break the corner of his eyes. He is now wheezing.

"Are you laughing at me, honey?" I poke him in the chest, and he just shakes his head, trying to control the onslaught of laughter that threatens to continue at my expense. He stops and kisses me.

"I love you Emma. Come on. Let's get out of here. I have to pee so bad."

We walk out slowly through the crowds of people, and I walk into the women's bathroom as Eduardo does the same into the men's bathroom next door. He said he will be right there when I get out. I agreed to wait for him. I see the line of people, but it goes by quickly, carefully managed by bathroom attendants.

I go to the sink to wash my hands, and a girl is putting on red lipstick in the mirror. I immediately recognize her from the other time I was shopping with Liv. I look away, and she continues to stare at me. I decide to confront her.

"What are you looking at?" I meet her eyes defiantly. She looks at me with disgust.

"Me? My name is Cherry, and I was Eduardo's girlfriend before you came along and stole him from me, so you know what? I took your boyfriend to see how you like it."

I look at her with confusion. "You were never Eduardo's girlfriend."

"Oh, honey, I know you can't keep up with the sexual needs of a man like that. The way I sucked him off or the way he bent me over his desk at work, pounding into me as I screamed his name. Hm. He doesn't love you."

The anger inside me explodes at the thought of Eduardo doing anything with that girl. "Oh, he doesn't love me, huh? Is that why he wants to marry me?" I know it is a poor excuse to flaunt my ring, but I shove it right in her face, and it contorts with anger.

"I don't care anymore because now I have Julian, so you can have Eduardo."

I look at her, and she must get the reaction she wants. "You're lying," I tell her, stepping back looking around for the man who still hunts me.

"Oh no, I am perfectly serious right now." She walks closer to me.

"Cherry, you need to get away from him. He will hurt you," I plead with her, pointing at her to listen to reason. "That guy is sick." I am no longer angry with Cherry but concerned for her life, but she doesn't seem to care. She only sees me as a threat to her happiness. I grasp the top of my head, unsure of how to make her see it.

"You don't understand, Emma. He is obsessed with you, and we can't be fully together if you continue to be in the picture."

I step back again, scared when I see that crazed look in her eye, and suddenly begin to feel faint. "Stop, please just stop." I look around. I need to find Eduardo. I turn around to leave and find him when I hear a commotion outside. A fight has broken out, and that's when I feel the sharp object behind my back.

"Follow me, Emma, if you know what's good for you."

The fight is a huge distraction, and I don't see Eduardo. Cherry walks me out the side doors and out of the pavilion. We walk across the street and down an alley with an empty building. Everything is so much more amplified at night. The shadows seem to come out of everywhere, posing a threat. My sense of dread increases as Cherry brings me into an old warehouse that is in various stages of remodeling. My boots echo in the open room.

Cherry lights a candle that sits there as if she prepared for this whole thing. My mind fills with every twisted scenario, and my need to escape takes over. I see that she has a knife. I step backward and trip over a cord lying on the floor. She takes this as an opportunity to come at me. She gets on top of me, lays the knife by my head, and starts to choke me. She pins me down, straddling me with her arm around my throat.

She may be bigger, but I am stronger. I often think back to Adrian and me in the gym, and survival instincts kick in. I grab ahold of her hands, locking them against me. This causes her to become unsteady and unable to stabilize her arms upward. I twist my body, and we fall sideways. Now, I am on top of her and punch her in the face. Blood pours from her nose, and I hear her cry out. I jump off her and pick up the knife.

I see her trying to get up, holding her nose. I step back, holding onto the knife, and then I see her smile. Blood is staining her teeth, and she looks unhinged. She looks behind me, and that's when I see him—Julian. He is here, and he has finally found me. I hit the emergency star on my bracelet. I just hope it's not too late.

CHAPTER FORTY-THREE

EDUARDO

I leave the bathroom to wait for Emma, but she hasn't come out of the bathroom yet. The lines were long to get in there, but they went by quickly, and I knew I'd beat her out before she finished. I see two guys throwing insults back and forth to one another right where I am standing, and I find it fucking annoying as hell. I just want to get Emma and get out of here. I am starting to feel uneasy, and I need to find her and attach her to me ASAP.

Expectantly, blows start flying between the two guys, and I let out a frustrated sigh. A large crowd forms and people start pushing each other. One guy is drunk and is extremely obnoxious. The other has a black eye that is starting to form.

I make my way out of the commotion and look toward the bathroom. I see another girl that was close to Emma in line walk by me, and I know Emma is finished but now is nowhere to be found. I whirl around, looking for her, and hit a call to Eli. He answers on the first ring.

"Hey, Boss, are you guys headed out soon?"

My stomach drops. "Emma isn't with you? I've lost her."

"Oh, fuck," is all I get from Eli.

"Call Jameson and bring him down here. He said he would be close by in case we needed him." I look to see where Emma is on the GPS tracker and notice that she is in the area. I see the star moving toward a few buildings down the street. I run out of the pavilion and jump into Eli's car.

"Here. Look, Emma isn't far from here. We have to get to her." I see my phone ringing, and it says it's Jameson calling on the illuminated screen.

"Jameson," I answer, out of breath. "Where are you? Someone has Emma. I just know it."

"I'm at this restaurant down the street. I got stood up tonight. I'm on my way. I see her in this warehouse not far from here. Do you see it?"

I look at the star shape on my screen, nodding. "Yeah, I see her. We're on our way." Just then, we all get an SOS from the location Emma is at.

"Oh shit. Emma is in trouble." I just hope we aren't too late.

We speed to the location of the building that the SOS came from. We scan the area, and nothing looks out of the ordinary. The building is dark. I see Jameson running over from across the street, and a few of my men are walking around the park across the street, ready to intervene if necessary. Eli, Jameson, and I walk into the building, trying to be as discreet as possible. I have my gun, as does Eli, and we give one to Jameson should the situation arise for him to need it. Better to be safe than sorry.

The door is open, and we walk into almost blackness. Except, I catch sight of golden hair that shines brighter than any light. A beacon calls out from the dark of night, guiding a ship into the safety of storming waves at sea. A light shines, and I see Cherry. Her face is messed up, and I look at Emma, who is unhurt from what I can tell. She is tied to a supporting column in the middle of the room. Cherry's eyes are bruised over, and it appears her nose may be broken. I take pride in my girl; she let her have it. I wonder what caused such an exchange. Emma locks eyes with me, and Julian steps in from the corner with his gun pointed at me.

"Drop your weapons and kick them forward."

We all lower our guns and drop them, as he says. Cherry has a knife to Emma's neck, and Julian has our firearms. Emma is still staring at me. Julian steps in front of my line of sight, blocking Emma.

"Don't fucking even look at her. She's mine and for my eyes only. You remember that."

My jaw ticks, and I could murder that asshole if I knew that Emma wouldn't get hurt.

Cherry's head snaps over to Julian. Her knife leaves Emma's neck and falls at her side. She looks hurt by his words. She moves toward him, and we watch, anticipating what will happen. If she pushes him, we could get to Emma or take him down. There are three of us.

"What do you mean she's yours?" The feral, unhinged look in her eyes is scary even for me to witness, and I see Emma cringe inwardly. Cherry snaps her sights on Emma. She is defenseless as Cherry lunges for her.

"I'll fucking kill that bitch. She can't have you too. I did everything for you, Julian." She goes to attack Emma, and my girl braces for it, but Julian intercepts her and pushes Cherry onto the floor.

"No one else hurts Emma. She is only mine to hurt." The spit flies from his mouth, and he is indeed the monster Emma described him as. Cherry lies on the floor and attempts to get up. Julian walks forward to her and points his gun at her.

"I can see you are going to be a problem. I was hoping we could have some fun together, but I don't think it will work out anymore, Cherry." With that, he lifts his gun and shoots her twice in the chest.

She lands backward as red appears on the ground, pouring out from her chest wounds, making the red of her shirt even darker. She places a hand on her chest as blood comes out of her mouth in a cough that sprays blood all over the floor. Julian lifts his gun once more and shoots her in the head. Three bullets and Cherry is gone.

I stare at her dead body. Her eyes have fixed, locked on something she no longer sees. I know that she is gone. I look over at Julian, who has already lost interest in Cherry, if she ever held any interest for that man. He walks over to Emma and stands off to her side.

"I think this has gone on long enough, Emma, don't you? Why don't you tell Eduardo who you really love." He looks over at Emma expectantly. I lunge forward, praying that I can get to him, but he sees me from the corner of his eyes. He lifts his gun at Emma.

"I wouldn't do that if I were you, Eduardo." He tsks. "If you claim to love her as much as you say, it would be in your best interest not to move any closer." He moves closer to us and kicks the weapons out of the way. I look over at Jameson and Eli. We all have the same pained expression of anger and sadness in our eyes.

"Say it, Emma!" he screams at her, and she looks him in the eyes, not backing down.

"I'll never say that to you, Julian," she says low enough, but its effects are crushing to Julian. His eyes narrow, and he lifts his gun to her. Emma locks eyes with me and mouths *'I love you always.'*

EPILOGUE

EMMA

I know my time has run out. Julian has found me, and it's over. I can't say that I don't have so many regrets in my life. I can never make amends for all the lives lost at my expense. Eduardo has been the best at keeping me safe, at least up until now, but it was always going to come to this. This moment when it all changes.

I hope that he doesn't blame himself for this. It was bound to happen, and now it's over. I can't control many things, but I can manage this. If I am gone, I won't be a burden to anyone anymore. My family is all gone, and I know Eduardo might be sad for a long while, but eventually, he will move on and have the chance to be happy.

I glance over at Cherry and stare at her vacant eyes. She was so alive just a moment ago; now she is dead on the floor because she became involved with Julian.

"I think this has gone on long enough, Emma, don't you? Why don't you tell Eduardo who you really love." I hear him say this, and I just continue to stare at him. He will wait a long time if he seriously thinks I will ever say that to him. I look over to Eduardo and mouth, *'I love you always.'*

This enrages Julian, and he lifts his gun and points it right at me. I can no longer look at Eduardo and see his sad eyes looking back at me. I close my eyes, accepting my fate, and think of all the times we had recently. I see all the time spent with my sister and my family in Mexico. I see all the times spent by Eduardo and me under the stars. The time he gave me my necklace. When he proposed and worshiped my body. I smile and accept my death. I hear Julian say good-bye to me, and Eduardo screams, "No!" I hear the trigger fire, and then nothing.

I hear a loud thunk, and I open my eyes to see Julian on the floor beside me. Eduardo is running over to me, and Jameson is looking over at someone with his mouth hanging open as if he is seeing a ghost. Eduardo is rubbing my arms up and down and is holding me tight.

"Oh, my Emma." He is kissing me over and over and has a firm hold on me, getting me out of the chair and lifting me into his arms. I follow Jameson's line of sight, and if Eduardo wasn't holding on to me, I'd pass out.

She walks over to me with a smile on her face. Her hair is cut short and slicked back, but it's her—Evie, my twin sister.

"She's alive." I sob, and Eduardo holds me up.

He looks over and shakes his head. "You were always one for dramatics, Evie."

"Good to see you too, future brother-in-law." She hugs Eduardo and then grabs on to me.

"Sis, I've missed you so much." She hugs me, and we both cry. I am wracked with sobs, but it sounds odd because I am also laughing. I suppose these are tears of happiness. I swear, sometimes I don't understand myself. Eduardo walks over to Jameson, and he is staring at Evie.

"Close your mouth, James. You're drooling on the floor. It's not a good look."

I watch the exchange. He looks at me and goes to say something but stops.

"That's Emma's twin sister, huh?" he says aloud.

"Boy, you're a fast learner, aren't you?" Eduardo mocks.

"Fuck off. She's hot. I think I'm in love." He grabs his face and rubs his hands repeatedly as if trying to wake himself from a dream. In walks Philip, and Eli groans.

"What the fuck? Is everybody coming back from the dead?" Eduardo gives him a look and shakes his head.

"Too soon?" Eli says, and Eduardo snorts.

"Yeah, a bit, but I get it. It's ironic as fuck." Eduardo walks over to me and my sister.

"I'm just glad that it is all over," Eduardo says on an exhale as he hugs me from the side and brings me into a tight embrace. I feel Evie look over at me and smile. I return it and then look over to my future husband.

"Oh, Eduardo, I have a feeling that this is just the beginning," I say, remembering the words Adrian said to me not so long ago.

"Fuck, I was hoping you wouldn't say that." Evie looks over at me, winking.

"That was one sweet chokehold release that you got out of, if I do say so myself, Emma." Her eyes go wide, as do mine.

"You saw that?"

Evie nods and laughs. "Fucking epic, girlie."

"So what now, Evie?" She looks over at us and then grabs the back of her neck.

"We have a lot to talk about."

Emma snorts. "That's an understatement. I mean, what happens n-o-w?" Evie stares at me with a look that promises to wreak havoc. It's the look she would give me when we knew we would get into trouble. She takes one of her black-gloved hands and extends it to me in an invitation.

"Well, Emma, now that you are free, tell me who you wanna be."

TWISTED TIDES

PROLOGUE

Emma sits tied to a chair. Her hands are restrained while Julian presides above her. A maniacal look in his eye shows the depravity residing in his soul, ready to unleash his fury at any further attempt to take his prized possession from him.

Emma thinks her time has run out, but I've been watching from afar, waiting and biding my time. My heart twisted, grieving at seeing her alone and at his mercy, unable to intervene all this time.

My sister thinks I died in that fire, but it was necessary to save her life. I was so close to her that night as I watched our life as we once knew it go up in flames. Julian had carried her away and placed her unconscious body into an SUV. Now, all of our family secrets and twisted lies will come to light.

Despite Emma hiding from Julian with the protection of our Uncle Andrés, Cousin Adrian, and Eduardo, Julian has managed to locate her. No amount of skillful planning could have prepared her for this exact situation.

Eduardo has been the best at keeping her safe until now, but it was always going to come to this. I hope that he doesn't blame himself, but it's obvious by the anguish on his face that he's waging an internal war, which excites Julian, who wears a sadistic smile. Eduardo's need to keep her safe, concurrent with feeling helpless and having no weapon to use against Julian, could be a recipe for disaster, but it was unavoidable, and now they all think it's over.

This moment is the pivotal point in our family's story. The defining moment when everything you hold dear is tested, and you can only hope to walk away with no more casualties—your body, mind, and soul intact.

I can sense her emotions. I have always been able to, and now, in this moment, it's increased exponentially. Emma feels if she is gone, she won't be a burden to anyone any longer. Eduardo might be sad for a while, but eventually, he will move on and have the chance to be happy.

She'd rather die than see him hurt, but doesn't she realize that there will be no getting over her? She is the light in our crazy darkness—our beacon of hope in a storm that wages destruction on our family.

We would do anything for her.

Who knew that it would be Cherry, that crazy bitch, to hand her over to Julian, thinking that once Emma was gone, they could be together. Julian has found her, and now it's over. She sits, restrained to a chair, entirely at his mercy, and Cherry lies dead on the cold cement floor.

Unfortunately, Julian has no merciful tendencies.

Emma spares a glance at Cherry. Her vacant stare is fixed on something she no longer sees. Blood speckles Cherry's face from her final breath. Now, her lifeless body, slowly growing cold, is lying in a pool of her own blood, showing how quickly we can be taken from this world.

A shudder runs through Emma as she tries to control her emotions and refrain from showing Julian weakness. I bet she wonders if she will have the same fate.

"I think this has gone on long enough, Emma, don't you? Why don't you tell Eduardo who you really love!" Julian bellows triumphantly, his voice echoing in the ample, empty space of the warehouse. He's delusional.

Eduardo makes a final attempt to get to Emma, but Julian already has his weapon pointed at my sister. He tsks as he kicks their firearms from their reach. Eduardo pales, shaking as he restrains himself from lunging toward Emma.

No, she is strong. I can't help but smile as she rolls her shoulders back, preparing to face her death head-on. She accepts her fate. She closes her eyes, and that's when I know this has gone on long enough.

This moment changes everything. I can't control much, but I can manage this.

I nod, willing this exchange to be over. Mateo catches on. His weapon is ready to fire at the right moment.

Mateo is by my side, as he has always been these days. I can't say that I don't have regrets in my life. Seeing her this way almost breaks the protective barriers around my heart, which have been carefully crafted into place throughout the years. I can never make amends for all the lives lost at our expense. I can see the same thoughts reflect on her face. However, I can try to punish those who hurt us and continue to be a threat to us.

Julian waits for her reply, getting angrier by the second at her continued silence. I narrow my eyes at his demand. She opens her jade-green eyes that match my own and stares at him sans emotion.

Emma juts her chin out at him in a last attempt at defiance. I smile, knowing she is still brave, despite the circumstances. Emma will make him wait a long time if he seriously thinks she will ever say those words to him.

She refocuses her gaze at Eduardo one last time. I bear witness to what she believes are her final words to him as she mouths, '*I love you always.*'

My smile widens. *Yes, that's my girl.* I internally fist pump the air. I can't help but be proud. A final 'FU' to the man who made her life miserable for months.

Julian's face contorts in rage as he lifts his gun and points it right at her. She can no longer look at Eduardo and see his sadness looking back at her with tears in his eyes. She finally closes her eyes one last time.

I see her smile and imagine she is thinking of all the time spent with our family in Mexico. All the times she spent with Eduardo under the stars. The time he gave her the necklace. When he proposed and worshiped her body.

And it's the exact moment she accepts her death.

"Good-bye, Emma," I hear Julian say.

Eduardo screams, "No!"

I hear the gun fire, and then…

CHAPTER ONE

EVIE

"BODIES" BY DROWNING POOL

A loud *'thud'* echoes through the open room. I step out of the shadows that have been my home, shielding me from the living. Upon hearing the noise, Emma opens her eyes to see Julian on the floor beside her. Her eyes widen in shock as Eduardo runs over to her, and Jameson, their friend, looks over at me with his mouth hanging open as if he is seeing a ghost. I stare back at him, gauging his intentions before shifting my vision to my sister.

"Oh, my Emma." Eduardo kisses her over and over. With a firm hold, he lifts her out of the chair and into his arms. Eduardo pushes her away from him to assess her for injuries as he rubs Emma's arms up and down, then he pulls her close against his body just as quickly, holding her tight as if she'll be abducted again.

I see her follow Jameson's line of sight, and if Eduardo wasn't holding on to her, she'd probably pass out. Jameson hasn't stopped staring at me, and I can feel him willing me to return his stare. Instead, I need to focus on what's important right now—my sister.

I walk over to her with a smile that matches hers. I can see her take in the physical changes to my appearance: my hair is cut short and slicked back, but it's still me—Evie, her twin sister.

"She's alive," Emma sobs, and Eduardo holds her up, equally as shocked.

"You're alive?" he asks somewhat rhetorically. He looks over and shakes his head. "You were always one for dramatics, Evie."

"Good to see you too, future brother-in-law." I chuckle and hug Eduardo, and then Emma grabs on to me, almost pulling me down with the unexpected sheer weight of her body as she clings to me as if I will suddenly disappear into thin air, like a ghost. She wouldn't be wrong. That's what I have been all this time.

"Sis, I've missed you so much." I hold on to her. She hugs me, and we begin to cry. I can't help the emotion that comes over me. I've held it in for so long that it now pours out against my will.

Her body shakes, wracked in sobs, but it sounds odd because we are also laughing.

"I suppose these are what you call tears of happiness." I laugh as we rock back and forth in a tight embrace.

"Yes," she laughs. "I swear, sometimes I don't understand us, Eves."

Eduardo shakes his head, leaving us to chat. He walks over to Jameson, who is staring at me. "Close your mouth, James. You're drooling on the floor. It's not a good look."

From what I can tell, Jameson doesn't respond.

I wonder if he recognizes me. He must. I turn my head back to watch the exchange. Continuing to stare, Jameson goes to say something but stops.

"That's Emma's twin sister, huh?" he asks.

I curl my lip up in a half-smirk.

"Boy, you're a fast learner, aren't you?" Eduardo mocks. He slaps Jameson on the shoulder.

"Fuck off. She's hot. I think I'm in love."

I smile full-on now, conveying with my eyes what's to come.

Jameson scrubs his hands repeatedly over his face as if trying to wake himself from a dream.

Still holding on to my sister, I bring her around to give my full attention to Jameson. I give him my signature pouty, red-lipped smile. "Sorry, I missed our date by the way."

Jameson's mouth opens then closes. I smile wickedly, and then I see the moment it clicks. His sight is firmly set on my lips. "That was you. It's always been you."

I nod once. Our stare-off is interrupted when Philip walks in.

Eli groans.

"What the fuck? Is everybody coming back from the dead?" Eduardo shakes his head in disbelief, dropping it in defeat.

"Too soon?" Eli says, and Eduardo snorts.

"Yeah, a bit, but I get it. It's ironic as fuck." Eduardo walks over to Emma and me, hooking his arm around my sister and bringing her in for a side hug.

"I'm just glad that it's all over," Eduardo says on an exhale as he kisses the top of Emma's head, increasing the tightness of his embrace as if he is afraid to let her go.

I smile as I watch them. Emma returns the smile and seems to understand my thoughts as twins sometimes do. She then looks up at her future husband.

"Oh, Eduardo, I have a feeling that this is just the beginning," she says, echoing similar words spoken to her not long ago.

"Fuck, I was hoping you wouldn't say that, Emma."

I wink at her. "That was one sweet chokehold release that you got out of, if I do say so myself, Emma." Her eyes go wide, and mine mimic my twin's expression.

"You saw that?" She jumps happily.

I nod and laugh. "Fucking epic, girlie. I guess you took my advice about the self-defense classes?"

Emma tosses her head back, laughing. "You could say that. So what now, Evie?"

I grab the back of my neck, wondering how to approach this topic. As if reading my mind, Mateo emerges from the shadows I stood in what seems like a lifetime ago.

"We have a lot to talk about." Mateo takes his place beside me as they look between us, and Jameson visibly winces. I'm reluctant to look away. The need to soothe and care for him overwhelms my senses. My hand twitches to reach for him.

Emma snorts, distracting me from the emotions I was almost ready to act on. "That's an understatement. I mean, what happens n-o-w?" She raises her hand above her head in an exaggerated motion that makes my heart weep at the familiarity. I stare at her with a look that promises to wreak havoc—the same look she would give me when we knew we would get into trouble.

I extend one of my black-gloved hands to Emma in an invitation, and she quickly takes it. "Well, Emma, now that you are free, tell me who you wanna be."

"Let's finish this, Evie."

I give her a nod, and that's all that is needed. I've waited for this moment, and the time is finally here. My body almost hums with the excitement of what's to come.

I grew up in a web of twisted lies, deception, and secrets. From a young age, I knew these truths were buried in our family. The hushed words that stopped altogether when I entered a room. My emotions rage beneath the surface, a swirling rise of battered waves against my black, vengeful beating heart.

My sister remains holding my hand; an unspoken solidarity thrums in our veins. I couldn't be happier at her newfound strength. She brings a sense of calm to my thunderous emotional turmoil, battling against my unruffled, carefully constructed exterior. These feelings always attempt to overtake me as I fight for control, which I need in all aspects of my life—what I eat, how I act, and how I fuck. It's the only way I know how to live now.

I look at Jameson with the need to release this pent-up anger and frustration. Who would have thought this handsome man would be precisely the person who could soothe my aching heart?

I refocus on my sister, nod once, and extend my hand toward Mateo. I don't look at anyone around us as he looks at Emma and smiles. He then extends his hand toward her. I hear Eduardo rush over to stand behind Emma.

Jameson mimics Eduardo's movements without realizing it, and I feel his warmth behind me. His body heat calms me, and my body leans closer without my permission. I take a few deep breaths to bring a meditative mind as my feelings attempt to surge out of control. Breathe the air in and blow it out. I can almost hear my therapist's voice as I count to ten the way she taught me all those years ago. Now, I have Jameson, my anchor in my sea of self-destruction.

Emma's eyes scan me assessingly, clearly not entirely understanding what is happening. I smile and nod reassuringly, silently conveying that it's okay—I'm okay with this. She trusts me explicitly and looks at Mateo, staring into his eyes—what some people call the portal into the soul—in an attempt to gain clarity. The moment it clicks, her expression softens and she takes his hand.

My family is now complete.

The short-lived moment of unity ends when I hear Eduardo growl behind Emma, staring at their joined hands. We all burst out laughing, breaking the gravity of the situation, and Mateo can't help but join in. Eduardo is so ridiculous when it comes to Emma.

"God, can you calm down? We are having a moment here. You know, even when we were younger, you had to help her off the ATV or out of the truck. No one else could even attempt to help her or you would go off on them. It was always so obvious, Eddie." I stomp my boot on the cement flooring, hearing the echo sound off.

He breaks his gaze from Emma, sparing me a glance. "You know I hate when you call me that, Evie." His voice is full of warning, but his face is dueling with putting up a show and embracing the familiarity of our beautiful memories when life was simpler. I'm sure that's partly why our parents acted the way they did, although their reasons were faulty.

Mateo steps toward Eduardo as he visibly stiffens in a protective stance around Emma. He extends his hand. "It's good to finally meet you. I'm Mateo, their brother."

I hear the words leave his mouth, and tears threaten to fall. He's never been able to say these words aloud or introduce himself as our brother. That was taken from him, this simple act of belonging.

Jameson places a hand on my hip, giving it a slight squeeze. To hear Mateo say this truth out loud... Well, let's just say that it is everything. One suppressed truth finally coming out. There are so many more left to go. I give a contemplative sigh.

I turn toward the sound of sniffles. Emma is already crying, and Eduardo looks at him in stunned silence. "I didn't know," he whispers. He drops his gaze to Mateo's hand and takes it quickly. "It's nice to finally meet you too, Mateo."

Mateo smiles at Emma and looks back at me. I nod, and Mateo releases Eduardo's hand and quickly pulls Emma into a tight embrace. They hold each other for what seems like minutes but is actually only probably seconds as Emma continues to hold on to him. Finally, she lets go, but not until she rubs her face against his shirt to wipe away her tears.

Mateo raises an eyebrow at her and then looks at his shirt. "Sis, did you just wipe your snot on my shirt?" His lips quirk up in amusement, and Eduardo scoffs.

"Get used to it. It's part of her charm." I can't help but snort, and we all burst out laughing. The noise is a welcome juxtaposition to what occurred only moments ago.

Jameson presses his chest against my back, wrapping his arms around me from behind. His warm breath lands on my neck, and I shudder at his proximity.

"You have a lot of explaining to do, Eve." I chuckle at his name for me. I once told him I was Eve, man's downfall from the Garden of Eden. It was one of our first conversations that night at the club when he asked my name before we parted ways, wanting to know if he could see me again. I gave him the only truth I could at that time. It wasn't far off from my real name then, and that's all I could do.

I didn't think that one night would turn out to be so much more.

"I agree. I do." That's all I can say to Jameson now, as I know that conversation is one I need to have alone with him. Now is not the time.

I glance at my sister and see her acutely aware of what transpires between Jameson and me. I finally point out the obvious. "As much as I'd really like to sing campfire songs and do some face painting right now, I think that we should probably get out of here and get rid of these bodies." I point to the two bodies that are laid out on the cement floor, not getting any fresher.

Eduardo speaks up first. "I can make some calls." He reaches for his phone in his pocket, but I stop him.

"I have a plan. Can you get this place cleaned up, though, Eduardo? Mateo and I will dispose of the bodies. In fact, I have 'the perfect plan,' creating the catalyst to bring out the demons who have been hiding in the dark, into the light."

CHAPTER TWO

EVIE

"PSYCHO KILLER" BY TALKING HEADS

They all go to Eduardo's and Emma's house while Mateo and I load up the bodies and head to Brownsville. We will have to wait for nightfall to see the plan through, but how splendid it will be. What fireworks to see. I become giddy with anticipation at the thought of their reaction.

But before I get ahead of myself, we first need to get some sleep before we can set this black wave in motion, return to Houston, and explain where we've been all this time. Emma deserves to know what happened the night of the fire when our parents died, but somehow I survived. I also need to come clean to Jameson. All the twisted tides pulling us into an oceanic graveyard of the condemned and damned.

Eduardo phones a team to have the area at the warehouse scrubbed, and Jameson is working on security along with Eduardo's personal security team to ensure that the surveillance won't show us being at that location.

Fortunately for us, the warehouse did not have any cameras, and I suspect that's why Julian chose that specific location to hold Emma. Now, the fucker and Cherry are corpses in the back of our van.

I smile as I file my nails into little sharp points. Mateo glances over at me, and I feel his stare. My head whips up as I hold the file in one hand. His eyebrow quirks up.

"Are you feeling a little stabby, my twisted sister?"

I laugh and continue filing my nails. Feeling like I have gotten the perfect angled points, I throw it into my bag of mass destruction.

"Always, Mateo." I look out the window at the petroleum refineries twinkling their pretty lights out in the distance. Who would think that such environmental destruction, with toxic fumes spewing into the midnight sky, could create such a perversely beautiful scene?

The lights go by, and I watch them in the passenger side mirror until they vanish from sight.

The van's cabin is quiet—too quiet—so I decided to put on some tunes. I always hated the silence. The void needs to be filled, even with someone I love and I can be entirely myself. It's my mind that never shuts off that I need to block out. The intrusive thoughts that must be kept at bay make me wonder if I will ever feel peace.

I sigh. "What do you feel like listening to, Mateo? Perhaps some Taylor Swift to lighten the mood?" I say this in jest because Mateo is not a 'Swiffy' fan, although he thinks she is hot.

He laughs. "Let's try something else, huh, Evie?"

I pretend to think it over but get my phone out and scroll, searching for the perfect song that popped into my head.

"What did you pick?" he asks impatiently, sparing me a glance. He then looks at my phone as if he can tell in that second before he darts his sight back to the straight Texas highway road.

"So impatient, bro."

I hit play. Suddenly, the driving basslines of this classic tune float through the air, with the drums flowing shortly after.

Mateo laughs aloud, a full-belly laugh as he hits the steering wheel in beat with the bass riffs. "'Psycho Killer?' Perfect. This song is a banger, Evie."

"Right? Everyone secretly always roots for the bad guys." I spare a glance at the back of the van where two cold bodies are carefully concealed. "But what about us? Some killers aren't all bad."

We repeatedly sing the famous French phrases in the song, belting out the lyrics as we drive into the night.

We pull into a dilapidated motel that is sketchy as fuck. These rooms are definitely rented by the hour, judging by the sign that reads 'Rooms for a night or a lifetime.' It's missing a few letters.

Clothes hang strung over the second-floor balcony, and bicycles on the patio are thrown haphazardly, as if they aren't worth stealing. Paint peels from every surface.

This place is where dreams go to die.

I shudder thinking about the diseases that line every surface of the rooms and what's been done in them. I, for one, will be sleeping in all my clothes on top of the bed, thank you very much. I just hope it's cleaner than the supposedly washed sheets.

I inwardly cringe at the thought of bed bugs because I suspect I will have to burn my clothes after this. Mateo and I check into our room for a couple of hours of much-needed sleep. We just can't sleep at the same time. We don't want anyone to try to steal our van and discover some dead bodies.

I let Mateo sleep first, and he verbalizes no complaint. I take my e-book reader and finish my favorite dark romance hitchhiker novel.

I look up to find Mateo staring at me as I read the epilogue's last part. "Fucking cliffhangers. Ugh. The worst." I shut my e-reader, but not before downloading the next book in the series. I stretch and get up from the chair to take his place.

He places his hoodie over his head, pulling his arms through the sleeves and tugging it down. "I'm going to grab some coffee in the lobby. I'll be right back."

He leaves, but not before I tell him to hurry back. Of course, he knows this, but I can't help it. As soon as my head hits my arm on the bed, I fall into a deep sleep.

Finally, we arrive at the location Jameson told us to be at. They drove Cherry's conspicuous bright-red car over earlier and are already returning to Houston.

We transfer the bodies and strap them into the back seats with firmly locked seat belts in place. Their heads are duct-taped to hold them up.

I take a step back and look at my work. I bring my finger up to my chin in a pensive stare.

"What do you think, Mateo? Do they look okay?" I look over at him and find him looking at me with annoyance. "What?" What died up his ass?

"Evie, what does it fucking matter? We are going to set this motherfucking car on fire in a few minutes." He raises his hand, grabs his hair, tugging it upward, and walks around in a circle.

"Calm down, Mattie. Don't get your chonies in a bunch."

He stops me from speaking further with a raise of his hand. "Please do not refer to my underwear as 'chonies.' I'm not twelve."

I laugh at the Mexican slang word we use for men's underwear.

"I just want it to look good when they burn, okay? Is that too much to ask? Have you no pride in your work?" I place a hand on my hip for emphasis.

"Fine, just stop talking about my underwear. It's weird." He huffs.

"Fine. You got it. No chonies," I retort.

I close the door and drive off, exasperated with Mateo. In the rearview mirror, I see him trailing a short distance away in the van. "He's lucky I love him and that he is my brother," I say aloud to myself, shaking my head in annoyance.

I pull up outside of the Martinez family estate—the home that Julian forced my sister to stay in with his mother and father. Pretentious fucks don't bother to live in a gated community. They think they are untouchable with their reputation, but when people think you're dead, they aren't suspecting you'll bring their dead son to their doorstep, so to speak.

I step out of the piece-of-shit sedan Cherry owned and shuffle over to the passenger seat where the window is rolled down halfway. I shut the door quietly so as not to make a racket, light a piece of Julian's shirt that I cut out and saturated in petrol and flick it through the window.

I run in between the carefully maintained privet hedges. My combat boots slap the pavement as I sprint around the block and down the street where Mateo is waiting in the parked van. I shut the door just as I hear the explosion. We drive off, headed back to Houston having completed what we set out to do.

We drive silently, saying little until Mateo verbalizes precisely what I am contemplating. "How long do you think we have until Mr. Martinez discovers it was us?"

I look over at him and shrug. "Your guess is as good as mine, but now there is no going back. We've killed his son."

Mateo's fingers on the steering wheel tighten, and his jaw ticks. He is really pissed about something. Right when I am about to ask him what's wrong, he cuts me off.

"He's going to go after Emma and Eduardo for sure. It's just a matter of time before he finds out about us, too."

It will be all out there. There is no going back.

"I'm not hiding in the shadows anymore, bro. I am all out and ready to end this."

"Me, too. I've been hiding longer than you, and I want a normal life." He tugs at his hair, and I swear the guy will regret that action when he starts to go bald.

I snort. "Normal? You think that is possible for us?"

He looks over at me, giving me a sad attempt at a half-smile. "I sure hope so, Evie. I sure hope so."

The rest of the drive is spent taking turns driving back in one go with minimal stops. Around lunchtime, we finally arrive at Emma and Eduardo's place after having offloaded the van at a location provided by Eduardo's family. A sick-looking BMW M8 in a green metallic color is waiting for us.

Mateo walks around the car and whistles. "Wow, that is one badass ride, Evie."

I snort. "Sure, that doesn't draw any attention to us, Mateo." I touch the car with my leather gloves. "If I do say so myself, it matches my eyes." I look up and find him bent over in laughter. Pointing at me, he coughs, having choked on his words.

"What?" I feign annoyance. "Spit it out already, Mattie."

"Nothing, that was just too much, Evie. Love you, sis, but come on, I'm driving first."

"Fine. Whatever." I hop in the passenger seat and grab the handle atop the window as Mateo throws it into drive, taking the corner hard. "Bro, you know I have motion sickness. Can you tone it down a notch?" I fake the vomiting motions, and he slows the car to an average speed. "Plus, we don't want to get pulled over, right?"

He looks at me and nods. "You know, you are beginning to be such a fun sucker, Evie."

"Sorry for wanting to avoid the cops after we just killed someone. And I smell..." I hesitate, sniffing my shirt. "Faintly of dead bodies and gasoline."

"Okay, fine. I get it."

Upon our arrival, he pulls into the private parking space Eduardo instructed us to occupy, and we step out of the car. I stretch out, elongating my muscles as they ache from lugging around literal dead weight tonight. I intertwine my hand with my brother's as we head into the elevator on our way up to our sister's and soon-to-be brother-in-law's place.

We attempt to knock on the door, and it opens simultaneously. Emma pulls us in, and I push her away before she can hug us again. "Emma, we need to burn these clothes. You don't want to know what's on these garments."

"Girlie pop. I am not afraid of a little blood, babes. I am an emergency room nurse. I see the worst of the worst–"

"Really? How do you feel about bed bugs?" I cut her off before she drolls on and on. "Because I swear, I felt one crawling—" I don't finish my sentence this time because she jumps backward, face contorted in disgust, shrieking her head off and calling for Eduardo.

Mateo and I start laughing uncontrollably. "Eduardo! Eduardo, come in here quick!" she screams, her arms flailing above her head as she jumps back and forth.

Eduardo quickly enters the room in gray sweatpants with no shirt. His body is sweaty, and I stop laughing, trying not to ogle my future brother-in-law. But dang-gray sweatpants and his chest glistening... my sister is one lucky woman.

"What! What is it?" He looks around, searching for the threat, and Mateo lifts his hand to calm him down.

"It's nothing, man. It's just Emma talking about how she can handle anything because she is an ER nurse. When she tries to hug us, Evie tells her it could be bed bugs from the motel room we stayed in that rents rooms hourly. We stayed there before we disposed of the bodies and haven't changed clothing since."

This time, it's Eduardo's turn to jump back, holding on to Emma.

"Okay, just hand us a bag to dump these clothes, and we'll shower." I go to move, and Eduardo halts me.

"Do not come into this house any farther." He makes us strip down in the hallway, throws our clothes into a sealed garbage bag, and leads us to the showers. Emma proceeds to spray us with Lysol as we walk by.

"Oh, God, babe. My car?" I see her twitch and rub at something on her arm.

Mateo and I chuckle as we walk over to the shower.

"We'll get you a new one," he shouts back at her as he leads us away.

Once we are out of earshot, he speaks up. "That was cruel, Evie." He shakes his head, but I know it could be possible, but more than unlikely.

"I'd rather be safe than sorry. If that were actually true though..." He finishes my thoughts.

"We'd have to burn our house." I eye him wickedly, letting the irony fall into full effect. He chortles.

"Right?" My eyes sparkle with deviance.

"Let's kill some bed bugs." He fist pumps the air. "Death by soap."

CHAPTER THREE

JAMESON

"STORY OF MY LIFE" BY SOCIAL DISTORTION

I arrive at my place exhausted. I toe off my shoes and throw my keys in a dish, then strip down out of my clothes as I move into the bedroom and throw them in the hamper. I look at the rumpled sheets of the unmade bed, wondering what she is doing now, remembering how she felt on top of me, commanding my every move and the thrill that ran through me as her sharp, pointy nails scratched down my chest.

I grab my cock and tug. A moan leaves my lips, and I hang my head down. That moment months ago got me through my ups and downs of not being with her, but now she is here, and there is no more hiding.

I enter the bathroom, let the steamy water billow across it, and step into the hot spray of the showerheads, shooting water at me from different angles. I lean against the shower tiles and lift my head up to let the spray of water hit my face as I gather it in my mouth and spit it out in front of me.

I think of Evie as she dripped whiskey into my mouth and claimed me in a soul-searing kiss. The darkness surrounded us, and the only thing visible from her mask was her jade-green eyes, similar to her sister's. How did I not see it before? Her eyes weren't as vibrant as her sister's though. Where Emma's eyes are an emerald green, Evie's have a slight circle of yellow around her pupil, giving off a feline appearance. I researched it. It's called central heterochromia. I want to know every little detail about her, down to her complex eye color.

The attraction I felt for Emma was nothing compared to my need for her sister. A need that I had to fill with my cock over and over. The feel of her wet heat saturating my dick and the feel of her mouth wrapping and sucking me so hard I had to hold on to the headboard.

I rub shampoo through my hair, facing away from the jets to wash it out, and then soap up my body. When I get to my cock, I stroke it and think of her hands. The way she would withhold my orgasm over and over, edging me to the point I thought I would stop breathing. The need for release was all I could think about. The need to come so strong that I would do anything she said just to find the release I crave. That I *need.*

I start to stroke my cock faster and twist it at the head, rubbing my thumb over the slit where the tip is already leaking. I pick up the momentum. My hand, slick with soap and water, provides lubrication, enabling quicker movements.

My breathing picks up, and I envision her eyes and lips curling up on one side, knowing what she is doing to me, how she drives me out of control, and how she is the only one I could ever want. She is the only one I could ever need.

My head falls back in a roar as my orgasm hits, and I shoot ropes of cum as I pump my cock, until I lower my head and my breathing slows.

I shake my head, flicking drops of water away from rolling into my eyes, and rinse the remaining soap and cum from my body and shower wall. The next time I do this in here, it will be me filling Evie with my cum. No more masks, no more secrets.

I shut the water off and towel off. I hang the towel on the hook on the back of the bathroom door then step out and pull some boxers and a T-shirt from the dresser to sleep in. I pull back the disheveled comforter and climb into my bed, inhaling the smell of our last time together still stuck in the sheets and fall into a deep sleep.

I hear a ding from my phone and blink the sleep from my eyes. I move around in bed and stretch over to my bedside table for my phone, seeing that I do, in fact, have a message. I click it and see that it's Eve. I sit up straighter in bed, not fully awake, and open it.

Evie: Hey. We are all meeting at Eduardo and Emma's place to talk. I hope you can be there.

I see another message sent just a few minutes after as if second-guessing herself.

Evie: If not, it's cool...

I smile when she lays it out and leaves the ball in my court.

I jump out of bed and quickly dress, checking the time on my phone—six o'clock. It's the perfect time to hit evening traffic. Luckily, I don't have far to go.

I throw some product in my hair to tame the way it shoots in all directions and brush my teeth before heading out to see my girl.

At their place, I park in the guest area and lock my car door as I run up the steps. The concierge greets me as I pass through the door.

"Hi, Miguel," I greet the middle-aged man as I walk in, having been here many times over the years.

Eduardo and I have been friends since college. He was one of my frat brothers, and I even thought about hooking up with his fiancée before she was his, but there was really never going to be an us. They have their second chance, and I have... well, I have the girl I was always meant to be with—Emma's twin sister, Evie.

I wonder if the feelings and protectiveness I had for her sister had anything to do with the fact that I felt an immediate connection to Eve—or Evie, as I found out recently. That night we met was the best sex of my life, and the connection we had was so strong. I knew then that I would do anything to make that girl mine.

I take the back elevator that leads to their floor and punch in the code. Seconds later, the doors open, and I step out into the hallway that houses only a few apartments in this high-rise. I rap my knuckles on the door and hear someone coming to answer. Emma answers the door, and I look down at her.

"Jameson?" she asks.

"Hey, Emma." She opens the door, and I step through.

"What are you—"

"I invited him over, Emma," Evie cuts her off. "I thought he should be here when we explain the story from the beginning. Everyone we need to tell should be present so we can do it all at once. It is a lot to take in."

She scrunches her nose up in confusion, looking between us. Evie walks over to me, places her arm around my head, and brings it down to hers for a kiss. She plunges her tongue into my mouth forcefully, taking me by surprise at her blatant display of PDA, and quickly releases me before I try to deepen the kiss, but not before biting on my lip and retreating.

I lick my lips, tasting the coppery metallic blood that is beading on my lower lip. I wipe it away as she grabs my hand and leads me over to the sound of other voices coming from the kitchen.

"Okay then," I hear Emma say as the sound of the front door closes behind me. A low giggle is cut short when Evie looks back at her with a wicked gleam in her eye.

We walk into the kitchen, and she is still holding my hand when I see her brother, Eduardo, along with Philip and Eli, gathered around the kitchen island. Eduardo's eyebrows rise at the sight of Evie holding my hand as I stand beside her. I hold his stare and shrug my shoulders. A smile forms on his face as he looks behind me to where Emma is returning to the kitchen.

"Do you guys want anything to drink?" she asks as she waltzes in, and I notice her shorts riding up one side of her butt cheek.

I turn away quickly and focus my attention on Evie.

She has already noticed and is looking at me intently, her grip tightening on my hand. Maybe she could sense I was about to let go, but she misread my intention because I just wanted to pull her in front of me. Instead, I give her a side smile and move her over to sit on one of the barstools.

I look over at Eduardo and nudge my chin over to where Emma is now stretching upward to grab some glasses from the cupboard. Eli is looking over at her, pretending not to look, but it's obvious he is. Eduardo looks at Eli and then turns around to see Emma's shorts rise even farther as she arches on tiptoes, twisting a bit to grab the glass.

"What the fuck, babe?" Eduardo gets up from his seat quickly and places himself over her back. As he whispers something in her ear, he grabs the glasses for her, places them on the counter, and pushes Emma toward their bedroom. "Excuse us. We'll be right back." He all but pushes her down the hall, and we see them disappear around the corner, but not before we hear him growl and Emma giggle as the door shuts abruptly with a bang.

Mateo scoffs, and I can't help but laugh aloud, especially when we hear a banging sound coming from down the hall a few minutes later. The rhythmic sound tells us what is happening behind their closed bedroom door.

"Okay, then." Evie shoots out of the chair to play some music. Mateo wipes his hand across his face as if the thought of his sister getting railed in the next room is something he'd like to scrub from his memory.

"Anyone want a drink?"

I look up at Evie speaking and nod.

"Anyone else? I think this calls for some tequila shots."

"I'll get the limes and salimón," I announce and head toward the refrigerator.

I cut some limes into miniature wedges, and Evie grabs the bottle of Don Julio 1942, setting it and several glasses around the kitchen island. We each have our glasses ready to go, and Evie clears her throat. I pour some chilé on my hand between my thumb and index finger, prepared to taste and toss back this liquor.

"To getting our revenge," Mateo announces.

We all chant after him in unison, clink our glasses, and take the shots. I grab my lime and suck on it when I catch Evie staring intently at me. I wonder if she is thinking of me sucking on her clit until she drenches me in her juices.

She licks the salt hanging on her bottom lip, and I feel my cock jerk in my pants. I attempt to discreetly rearrange my cock, and it pushes tight against my pants, but it doesn't escape Evie. She moves to sit back on the barstool in front of me, and I stand at her back with my hard-on pressing into her.

A minute later, Emma comes into the room, face flushed, wearing leggings and a hoodie. She doesn't make eye contact with anyone, and Eduardo walks in, sweat trickling from his brow—no one comments.

Evie speaks up first. "Hey, Em, want a shot? We took some tequila shots while Eduardo was taking his shot."

I snort, and the guys try to suppress the laughter at Emma's expense.

Emma's face reddens.

"Fuck off, Evie," Eduardo playfully remarks.

"We'll both take a shot with everyone, and then we need you to tell us the whole story." This effectively ends the drama that would have surely ensued between the sisters.

I pull my girl back to hold her, letting her know I am here for her and not going anywhere.

We line the shots up again, and Evie makes another toast. "To all the twisted lies coming to light."

We down the shots and throw our discarded limes on the plate before us. I intertwine my hand with hers and wait for her to tell me the truth.

PART I

THE PAST

CHAPTER FOUR

EVIE

"SACRIFICE" BY LONDON AFTER MIDNIGHT

"Mom. Dad. I'm home." I slam the door and hear my parents calling me from the kitchen. I see a young teacher who works with my parents in the kitchen with them.

"Hey, Eves. This is Rebekah. She is one of the new teachers who recently started working at the school." The young woman, who can't be over twenty-two, waves at me.

"Hey, Evie. It's nice to meet you." She looks like she could be friends with Emma and me from high school instead of teaching in one.

"Hi. So nice to meet you, too." I look at Mom, wondering what the girl is doing here. Tomorrow is the big day when we leave for Mexico, and we really don't have time to entertain guests. We should be packing and planning our exit out of here.

Mom senses my thoughts and looks over at my dad.

"Evie, Rebekah here will be house-sitting for us indefinitely. She is new to the area and needs a place to stay. She doesn't have any family to help her, and I thought since we would be taking a sabbatical, we could use someone to care for things while we are gone."

I shake my head, contemplating this, and agree with a nod that this is not a bad idea. I wonder if she told anyone. Not sparing another thought about this anymore and trusting that Mom has everything taken care of, I look around. "Guys, where's Emma?" I attempt to walk out and call for her, but my mom stops me.

"Evie, she left a few minutes ago. You missed her."

My face falls as I hope it wasn't with who I think it is.

"Who did she leave with, and where did she go?" I say, trying to control my rage.

My parents look at me, and before they answer, I know she's with Julian. They don't even have to tell me to confirm what I know to be the worst possible circumstance.

"She'll be fine, Evie. They just went out to dinner. She'll be home before you know it, and you guys can get packed together."

I gulp down the feeling of impending doom I have and chalk it up to my usual anxiety, nothing more. But this feels so different. It feels like something ominous is looming over the house, shrouding us in darkness. I shiver at the coldness that runs through me and my skin breaks out in goose bumps.

"O-kay," I say, but the words get lodged in my throat, making it hard to get out.

Just then, the doorbell rings, and I look worriedly at my parents. My mother sighs.

"It's just pizza, Evie. I ordered your favorite. Why don't you go get your bag packed, and then you can grab a couple of slices and show Rebekah around before Emma gets back."

Rebekah looks from my mother and then back to me, trying to get a read of the room. If she guessed secrets, so many secrets... then ding, ding, ding, we have a winner.

I nod, wanting to escape the mixed stares I am getting from my parents and Rebekah. I trot up the stairs, quickly close the door, and grab my emergency backpack from the closet. Since my assault a few years ago, I have always been prepared in the event of an emergency, and this threat with Julian on my sister has caused me to take extra precautions.

I'm throwing some of my favorite toiletries I can't live without into my bag when I hear a thud, as if something has fallen. I stop packing, standing motionless, waiting to hear anything else—voices, footsteps, but nothing but silence.

"What the fuck was that?" I say aloud as I come to my senses and run out of the room, but not before grabbing my backpack and heading down the stairs.

I drop my bag when I get to the kitchen and gasp as I bring my hands up to my mouth in horror at the sight before me. My mom has her face in her slice of pizza. My dad is on the floor, and Rebekah is leaning backward in the chair. I don't have to look any further because I know with certainty that they are dead.

I stand there in shock, looking at them, unable to move. That is until I see movement in the slider patio door. It opens swiftly, and a black figure enters and shuts the door behind him.

I pick up my bag and run back toward the front door. I've seen too many horror movies to know that I will get trapped and suffer a similar fate as my parents if I head upstairs and lock myself in my bedroom, somehow ensuring my demise.

"Evie," I hear my name called, and that stops me in my tracks. "Wait, it's me."

The voice is so familiar that it sends chills up my spine, making the baby-fine blond hairs on my neck stand at attention.

I turn around against my better judgment and look into the eyes of the stranger who saved me years back. That night of my assault almost destroyed me, and it would have without all the therapy I underwent.

"What do you want?" I ask, even though I should be running far away from here.

My throat feels dry. "Evie, we don't have much time. I need you to trust me if you want to live and get your sister back."

I nod because, at this point, what choice do I have?

He holds his hand out. "Here, give me your ring."

I go to take it off and hesitate. But instead of asking questions, I remove it and hand the ring to him.

"What finger did you wear it on?"

I raise my hand where it once resided, and he moves quickly and places it on the same ring finger on Rebekah as she lies lifeless, mouth hanging open and frothy saliva trickling down her chin.

"Grab your bag, Evie, we need to leave. I didn't think I would make it in time, and I almost didn't. At least I can save you." He holds his hand out to me, and I hesitate briefly, looking at my family fallen dead at the dinner table with pizza that was barely eaten still on their plate.

"Poison," the stranger confirms.

I take his hand, and we leave through the back. I stop, remembering the most important thing.

"What about Emma?" I ask, not wanting to leave, despite knowing that staying any longer here is ensuring my death.

"We'll have to get her later. She won't be coming back here."

"I want to see first if she returns," I beg, and he takes pity on me.

"Okay, but we have to hide quickly. It isn't safe here."

We run out into the shadows and hide amongst the trees and foliage in the newly sold house on the corner lot. The new owners haven't moved in yet, so I know we are safe here. We barely get to the side of the house when a loud explosion shakes the ground, and its heat makes my skin buzz.

"What the..." I turn around to see my house engulfed in flames. I stand there, rocked to the core that if this stranger hadn't saved me yet again, I would be dead in the house along with my parents, but I guess that was the point of the explosion.

People come running out of their houses, and soon, the street is buzzing with activity. Shortly after, sirens sound, and a fire truck is coming, attempting to get control of the flames.

This subdivision has acre lots, unlike in the bigger cities where the homes are on top of each other. If that was the case, there might have been other casualties, but more trucks come, and they seem to be getting this more under control; although the house is still ablaze, it's just not spreading at this point.

The stranger speaks, and I can barely make out the words over the ringing in my ears. He turns me to face him, and he touches my face tenderly.

I think I am in shock. I feel funny, like I drank too much caffeine, and my body is light with energy that I can't contain, but my skin feels cold. I shiver, and the stranger notices.

"Here". He takes his hoodie off and places it over me.

I notice his broad chest and muscles that fill out his T-shirt and the black utility belt that holds up his cargo pants down to his black combat boots. He looks like an assassin.

"Evie."

My eyes shoot up to meet his, and his lip pulls into a smile, showing his straight white teeth. There is something oddly familiar about him, something that makes me want to lean my head on his shoulder.

"Don't worry, Evie. Uncle Andrés will send someone to meet us."

My eyes widen. "What do you mean, Uncle Andrés?" I ask, completely confused. "Who are you?" I squint my eyes to narrow my vision, hoping that if I stare hard enough, the answers will present themselves, making who this stranger is more apparent.

He takes a deep breath and stares me in the eyes. "I'm your brother Mateo. Yes, I just saw our mom get murdered. Believe me when I say that I am not okay right now."

I gasp in shock. "No. It can't be. How do I have a brother? Where have you been? Why don't we know about you?" I don't realize I am crying as tears roll down my face. He goes to answer me, but I place my hand over his cheek. "Have you been okay? Were you happy and loved, Mateo?"

His eyes snap up to mine, and he gulps. Clearly, this is not the question he was expecting me to ask. "It could have been better, Evie."

I throw my arms around him, and he hesitates briefly before returning my embrace, and there, in the middle of the night, I hold my long-lost brother, who, along with me, witnessed our parents die just moments ago.

"How did Mom and Dad let you go, Mateo?"

He hesitates but decides to tell me as we watch the chaos erupt across the street. "My dad doesn't know about me, and Mom gave me up when she had me when she was eighteen. Then she went to college, continued with her life, and met your dad there. The rest is your life, not mine."

I shake my head in disbelief. "But why not tell us about you? I don't understand," I beg to comprehend.

"It's more complicated than that, and I know we have to talk about it, but let's do that later, okay? Maybe when we are away from here."

I nod in silent agreement.

He leans over and tries to get a better look at the black SUV that makes its way over and stops down the street. I see my sister run over to the house with Julian trailing behind her. She falls to the ground, and I stand abruptly when my arm is tugged and my body is forced back down.

"No, Evie. You can't go over there. It isn't safe, and that defeats the purpose of making it look like you died in that fire along with your parents."

I turn my head toward Mateo slowly, absorbing the gravity of his words. Then it dawns on me. "That's why you had me hand over my ring?"

He nods. "Yes, the Martinez family is more than likely responsible for this, and they won't bother checking very closely to see if it's you. Julian will recognize the ring on your finger and assume the girl is you."

I hear Emma screaming, and I notice something glinting in the light. Emma slumps over, and I see Julian picking her unconscious body up and taking her to the SUV. Her head lolls to the side, her body limp in his arms, and she is once again at his mercy.

"He fucking drugged her." I point at them and look over at Mateo, disbelieving.

"Does that surprise you, Evie?" He shakes his head in disgust.

"I hate that fucker."

Mateo nods, agreeing with me. "Yeah, he's an asshole for sure."

I look over at him. Trying to get a better read on him. "That's an understatement, Mateo," I counter, but his phone vibrates, effectively cutting off our conversation.

"It's time to go."

He helps me stand with him as we head to the back of the house. Across the street, the park is shrouded in darkness, but a black pickup truck with tinted windows is idling. We look both ways and see no oncoming traffic.

"Come on," Mateo calls out and extends his hand out from behind, and I place my hand in his, effectively blindly trusting my brother that I've just learned about.

He opens the back door, helps me enter, and hops in after me. I take the backpack off my shoulders and place it between my feet.

"Buckle up, Evie," I hear a voice from the driver's seat, and my head snaps up to see Adrian, my cousin.

"Oh, my God," I gasp. "Adrian! What are you doing here?"

He smiles at me. "Well, my dear Eve's, it appears that I am saving your ass, and your sister is next."

CHAPTER FIVE

JAMESON

"LAZY EYE" BY SILVERSUN PICKUPS

I sit alone in the bar, waiting for Dax to arrive. He said that he would meet me here straight after work. I glance at my watch, knowing he should be coming through those doors any minute.

I called him up because I wanted to talk to him about Emma. I thought we had a connection, and when I left her place that night after partying at Eduardo's club, I had suspicions that he was into her. I saw him at her apartment after she sent me home insisting that she was okay and didn't need anyone, but what she meant was anyone other than Eduardo.

I saw their bodies close together as I peered up, looking into her living room window from the parking lot like a stalker. I could've blamed it on the alcohol or my mind playing tricks on me, but I hadn't had much to drink. Any lingering effects of alcohol had vanished while ensuring Emma was okay at the club. If I hadn't forgotten my wallet and tried to return to her apartment after she insisted that I go home, I would have never known she was into him.

After college, we stayed close. I worked and continued to work with Eduardo on projects at his club. He helped me once to start up my business. I know the ins and outs of his club. Some are legit, and others are not so legit, but he pays me well for my security work there, so I can't complain. I know him enough to realize that his money comes from the Mexican cartel, or at least some of it. Not that I would come out and ask him, but it is pretty obvious.

Deep in thought, I am about to sip my drink when a hand clasps me around the shoulder. "Why does it look like your fuckin' dog died, brother?" Dax drops into the seat next to me.

Before I can answer him, the waitress, Simone, saunters toward us, her breasts up close and personal. She clearly has a thing for Dax.

"Hey, handsome. What can I get you to whet your lips?"

I groan in aggravation.

She cocks an eyebrow upward to be sexy, but it has the opposite effect. Honestly, Dax and I have commented that 'less is more' regarding women and their makeup application. Still, with her painted-on eyebrows, heavy eyeshadow, and red lipstick, she looks like the Joker from *Batman.*

"I'll take a Stella beer." He tips his head in my direction. "Jameson, are you ready for another one?"

I swig back the rest and nod, placing the empty bottle on the table for her to take. "Yeah, I'll take another. Why not?"

She picks it up and nods in acknowledgment.

I think about how to bring this up when Dax interrupts my thoughts.

"You okay, bro?"

Before I can answer, Simone is back with our drinks. I wipe my hand down my face and just want her to hurry the fuck up and leave so that I can chat with Dax. She pours my drink in a frosted glass this time, and I wait patiently, trying not to rip the bottle from her hand.

This time, for fear of being interrupted again, I blurt it out. "I think Emma is fucking around with that guy Eduardo," I release all in one breath.

Dax's eyebrows pinch together in confusion. "Your frat brother?" I nod. "He told us they met in the emergency department, something similar to you and Liv, but she is on his radar now. I don't know if I want to even attempt to compete with him."

Dax shrugs. "You don't know for sure, right?"

I shake my head. "No, he is fucking her." I explain what happened and how his Porsche was parked outside after I left.

He seems to think this over and reluctantly agrees there was something there between them that night. "There was chemistry there," he comments, and then, before he elaborates, he seems to second-guess himself but decides to continue, "a familiarity perhaps." He strokes his lip as if thinking about something or someone else.

"Liv had mentioned it to me and something about flowers he sent her recently. I just thought I should let you know."

I smile half-heartedly at his reluctance to betray Liv's trust. "Thanks, man. I appreciate you having my back. It's just weird, though. I thought we had this connection. I can't explain what I feel for her. I want to protect and keep her close, but this one moment we had at the beach during spring break was… awkward? I can't find the word to describe it." Frustrated, I run my hand through my hair and can't explain it, so I stop trying.

"You know what you need, Jameson?" Dax looks at me smugly. "You need to go out and get laid. Why don't you go to The Viceroy and use the full perks of the VIP card Eduardo gave you?"

This does perk me up a little bit. "Yeah, that sounds great. Do you care for a little excitement tonight? You can be my wingman." I rub my hands together in anticipation of how this will go down as I drink the rest of my beer, ready to leave, and head to the club.

Dax hesitates, avoiding eye contact. His hand rubs the back of his neck, and he looks at me sheepishly. "Well, I can't go because Liv and I are together now."

I look at him, stunned. "She's your girlfriend?"

Dax nods in confirmation and he fucking beams. The guy seems so happy, and I can't blame him.

"I'm happy for you." I clap him on his back and throw some bills on the table.

"Where are you going, Jameson?" I hear Dax ask as I start to walk away.

I smirk, eyes alight with mischief. "To find my happy ending."

After going home to change into attire more fitting for The Heavenly Pearl, the exclusive membership-only sex club within Eduardo's dance club, The Viceroy, I enter through the discreet, private entrance that can only be accessed by using a card pressed into a scanner.

Upon entering, a hostess stands at a desk, much like at a hotel. For safety reasons, she checks my card in the system to show the times I've been there, and my fingerprint must be placed on the small scanner to accept my entry.

Members must comply with all the rules as exceptions are rarely granted. Then, when the hostess lets them pass through the second set of doors, the bouncer takes their phone, checks them for anything that isn't allowed in the club, and bags it for them. They get their items when they check out.

It all seems pretty straightforward, focusing solely on client safety. If you have to wonder if an item is allowed, then more than likely it isn't, so I don't bring anything that isn't essential.

I watch with rapt attention to see if anything is amiss during the intake process, but it runs flawlessly, and I smile. I was given a membership after I helped establish a security protocol for this place and ensured the members' privacy and, above all, the patron's safety. I can't say I always use this privilege, but I am grateful for times like these where I can let loose. The membership fee is expensive, but Eduardo wouldn't let me pay, so I likely wouldn't be here otherwise. I'm not ultra-rich like they are, even though my business does well for someone my age.

The idea of working for someone in a cubicle would have driven me mad, so when I approached Eduardo with my business venture before graduation, he was only too happy to invest in my start-up. Unfortunately, having him as a business associate means I know of his dealings—some legal and some not so legal—although I only participate in the legal ones he maintains on his own.

I'm no fool. I know where the money comes from; I just choose not to involve myself in that side of things, and I'm not sure Eduardo would let me even if I was given the opportunity.

Pulled away from my thoughts, I see a woman with a long trench coat, and I can only imagine what is underneath that. I take her in from head to toe as her long black hair swings back and forth like a thick mane in a ponytail worn high on her head. I gaze downward as she walks in front of me. Her black leather boots disappear underneath it, and I can imagine the point of her heel pressing into my chest as she stands above me. We walk in one after another and I watch her walk straight to the bar.

My mask is firmly in place, as is everyone else's, since it is a requirement for entry into the club. I follow her swaying hips as she perches on a seat and begins to talk to another woman beside her.

It would be more tempting if her hair were blonde, but it's dark here anyway. I've never really been attracted to women with dark hair. I have nothing against brunettes, but I have a thing for blonde hair. I go to the bar and order a drink.

I look around at all the scantily clad women. Ironically, women don't have to wear much and are not required to have memberships here. If they are vetted online, they can come, providing proper documentation showing proof of identity, a formal orientation to the club along with non-disclosure agreements that must be signed, and, most importantly, providing test results of no STIs. All of that is done online before their first visit.

The mutual requirement is that everyone must wear a mask. Some people like their identity to remain anonymous. I don't have a problem with that. Sometimes, it's better not to form attachments. I frown, pondering my words filtering through my head.

I turn sideways to get through a few people talking in clusters and hail the bartender over, ordering an old-fashioned. One thing I love about this place is that they make a mean old-fashioned.

I move my hand, and it lands accidentally on a woman's shoulder. I feel a jolt, as if I have been burned as her face whips around to see who dared touch her. That's when her jade-green eyes land on mine, and I'm suddenly bewitched.

I attempt to look away, but her hypnotizing almond-shaped eyes are captivating, and I want to yield to her every whim. As she narrows them on me, I zone in on the yellowish coloring around the pupil, causing the remainder of her green eyes to appear brighter. The tempestuous emerald green is so striking that I could drown in it for days.

I look at her, speechless, trying to form a coherent thought, and I see her lip twitch in amusement.

Way to play it cool, Jameson, I think to myself.

"Hi." That is all I can come up with.

She coolly picks up her amber-colored liquid on the rocks and sips it, eyeing me up and down. I wonder if she likes what she sees. I wait for her to say anything in return, perhaps tell me a 'hi' back, but she doesn't. She just stares, and I suddenly feel like my mouth is as dry as a desert, and I know without a doubt that I am thoroughly fucked.

"Do you come here often?" I inwardly groan at the thought of what I just asked.

Her eyebrows lift in shock as a smile plays on her lips.

Okay, that's strike two. "What's your name?" I groan aloud this time and run my hand through my hair, wishing I could recover from my mortification.

She puts her drink down and turns toward me this time to address me fully.

She seems to size me up and crosses one muscular leg over the other.

I bite my lip inwardly, begging my expressions not to betray my immense attraction to her. Her black leather corset and mini skirt squeak as she moves.

"I thought the purpose of this club was anonymity. Is it not? You know, the masks and all." Her hand makes a movement, mimicking a circle around her face.

She doesn't seem irritated by my line of potentially offensive questions, but I can sense she is as leary of me as she should be. She doesn't know who I am, and I think I might have blown my chances at getting to know her, even if it is for just tonight. I ponder on how to answer the question, and I know that she will be able to sense bullshit a mile away, so I decide to go for the truth.

"Yes." I nod in agreement. "I want to know what I should call you."

She leans a little farther into my personal space. Her scent permeates the air; I smell a mixture of spicy vanilla and bourbon. I close my eyes, trying to remain unaffected while waiting for her response.

She seems to think about it and looks me in the eye, leaning over as if she is going to tell me a secret. "You can call me Eve."

I repeat the name softly, and the one syllable rolls off my tongue easily.

"Eve." I chuckle at her response, shaking my head. "I take it that's not your real name?"

Her eyebrows scrunch together, confusion marring her delicate features. "Why are you so insistent on knowing me?" she asks.

"I just…" I sigh, knowing I must try telling her the truth, even if everything in my mind tells me to be cautious. "Do."

"I like Eve." She searches my face for an expression that will give her a reason to walk away, but she won't find one there.

CHAPTER SIX

EVIE

"CONCRETE JUNGLE" BY BAD OMENS

I straighten in my chair, giving him my partial truth, as I shimmy myself farther up my barstool. "It reminds me of man's downfall from the Garden of Eden." My tone is seductive, and I love how his eyes blaze with a commanding authority that makes my skin prickle with awareness. I feel so dopey, drunk on his essence that I want to drown in it, but I control my emotions, appearing unaffected.

He takes another drink of his old-fashioned, and I lick my lips. I imagine tasting the orange and smokey oak flavors while sucking the cherry remnants from his tongue.

I lap up a bead of alcohol on my lip before it threatens to roll off my own. My throat feels hot, and the amber liquid in my glass is only helping to stoke the fire instead of extinguish it. I'm burning, alight with lust and want that I haven't felt before.

He groans at my remark, showing just how affected he is by my words.

"Somehow, I don't doubt that at all, Eve."

I hold my head up, supported by my hand. My pensive stare holds his own, until I cannot bear to look at him any longer for fear of leaning in and kissing this stranger at the bar.

"And what about you? What should I call you, pretty boy?" But I don't have to wait long for his response.

He lifts his head and, without hesitation, replies, "Jameson."

"Jameson," I repeat, and he silently nods. I take another swallow of my drink, and I feel it go down hard, burning all the way down into the pit of my stomach.

He gulps, watching me devour the remaining amber liquid in one go. Maybe I affect him like he affects me.

"Why do I get the feeling that that is your *real name*—Jameson?" I want to see how he answers this question. I will be able to tell if he is lying.

He leans in closer. I sit motionless, feeling the heat of his breath caress my cheek.

"Because it is."

I turn slightly to look him in the eye and fight the urge to look away. Our stare is so intense that I feel as though I can read his innermost desires. I pause for a minute, contemplating my following words. "Why did you tell me your real name?" I'm confused by his brutal honesty. He is a puzzle that I want to solve.

So he tells me without reservation, "I just want to hear my name on your lips."

And there it is—the truth. My lips part, but I don't speak while his unspoken words swirl in the air, coating me with a silent embrace.

I just want to hear your name on my lips. I hear it echo over and over again in my head. I go to twist the ring on my finger out of instinct, but it isn't there, reminding me of all we lost. I clench my fists.

It was the moment that changed my life.

Sometimes, I rage so hard that I need to gain some semblance of control. The guardian angel that saved me that day was a protective force in my life and my constant the days after—my brother Mateo.

The therapy helped me cope after my assault with my frequently occurring anxiety attacks, and the self-defense classes helped to curb my ever-present anger. This anger never diminished in intensity, so I am here tonight—at The Heavenly Pearl sex club—about to lose myself in a man I just met but want to get lost in forever. His blatant honesty was refreshing. I can't wait to feel him inside me.

I clench my thighs together at the thought, except it no longer is a thought. It's a very real possibility.

I lean into Jameson and swear he thinks I'm about to kiss him. Instead, I stand and walk away from the bar. The coldness settles in as his body's warmth diminishes with each step I take away from him. I turn back to see his head hanging, and he turns to look at me with almost what can be described as sadness.

He also looks like he is stopping himself from running after me.

My lips curl up into a smile, and I lift my hand out to him in an invitation to join me. He doesn't hesitate and immediately takes long strides to reach me.

He takes my hand in his, and his eyes sparkle with excitement. I look at our hands entwined, and I feel a buzz cascading over my skin, causing my body to break out in a shiver. A warmth spreads over me, and I feel like I need to shed my clothing for entirely different reasons than just to cool off.

I lead Jameson past the bar and the small dance floor, but nobody bothers to look our way. We reach a hall, and I walk past the room numbers until I get to the one I reserved for tonight. Did I expect to use it? I was still deciding on that possibility, but after my conversation with Jameson at the bar, things have escalated pretty quickly, and I want nothing more than to use it now, with him.

I press my finger on the door keypad, and it clicks open. Due to safety concerns, cards get lost, keys are never used as they could be lost, and pockets aren't a thing here. No money is used in transactions; everything is automatically deducted from your card in real time. Your fingerprint is taken at entry to confirm and activate any rooms you may have requested in advance or at least the fingerprint associated with your name. It makes sense, and I love how much thought whoever designed the system had put into it. It's obvious safety was this person's priority, and I love that.

I push the door open, and dim lighting illuminates the room's features. Walking in, I release Jameson's hand. It falls silently, and I already miss the connection. He stands there looking at me. I undo my corset and let the string hang around the sides. I shimmy out of my short skirt and kick it off my body, tossing it onto a chair. I remove the corset and let my breasts hang as I place it near my skirt. I leave my spiked boots with red soles on because they look hot as fuck.

I can see Jameson gulp, and he stands there unmoving. His eyes roam over my body, and the desire he feels toward me is evident by his growing erection tenting his pants. He moves his hand over his hard length, attempting to be subtle, but I notice everything.

Before he can move toward me, I speak my first order. "Take off your clothes and sit on the bed, Jameson."

He tilts his head to the side, trying to understand the situation, and I raise an eyebrow at him in challenge. He quirks his lip up and nods in understanding and does as he is told. He doesn't look away but slowly undoes the buttons of his shirt, pulls his arms free, and grabs behind him to pull his undershirt off, placing it on the chair beside my clothes. He toes his shoes off and unfastens his belt and pants. I hear the zipper make a loud noise followed by his pants as they hit the floor. He picks them up and removes his socks, placing the remainder of his clothes on the chair with the rest. He remains in his red silk boxers as he goes to sit on the edge of the bed right in front of me.

Walking over to the bed, crawling onto the mattress, and moving my body to kneel behind him, I lean over and whisper in his ear, "Good boy, Jameson." I kiss over his ear and lick down his neck, sucking his flesh into my mouth. His head tilts back, lips parted.

I run my pointed fingernails up and down his back, and this time, when I come up, I move my hand into his hair and massage his scalp. My hand roams down his shoulders and his arms, kneading and touching my way around his body. Goose bumps spread across his flesh as my nails scratch around the front of his chest, drawing a circle around each nipple.

A moan escapes his mouth, and I smile, knowing how aroused he must be. The tip of his cock is leaking precum from the slit as it gifts me an appearance of this man's well-endowed cock from this angle. I am in the moment of a pure nurture mode. I want to hold and comfort him. Instead, I put my body flush with his, and my breasts touch his back.

He lifts his hand, and I wrap my arms around him, placing his hand back on his legs. I lick around his shoulder, trailing a path upward to his neck and back to his shoulder. I apply pressure with my teeth and bite him. He moans and I lift my head to look and see where my teeth broke through the skin. I love that I marked him.

When we part ways tomorrow, I will have left him with a reminder of tonight. When he sees this in the mirror, he'll remember when he was mine, even if it was only for a night.

I repeat this over several areas of his neck and back. He tilts his head back, as I kiss around, moving up to his cheek. He tilts his head forward as his lips meet mine. His hand reaches up, grabbing my hair, pushing my mouth into his. He takes over the kiss, and his tongue forces its way toward mine. Dueling for dominance, I feel consumed and struggle to regain control of my feelings.

I bite his lip hard, interrupting the moment.

Jameson sucks in a deep breath and breaks the kiss. He looks at me, and I notice blood beads on his lower lip where I nicked it, and he rubs at it. I stand and move away from the bed. He touches and licks at his lip where I bet he is wondering why I did that. I could feel myself falling and couldn't allow myself to feel more than that for someone I really don't know.

I stand before him, and he stares at me, watching and waiting for my next move. "Can you do as you're told, Jameson?"

He tilts his head, realizing what game I'm playing. He nods.

"I need your words, babe."

"I can." His eyes never leave mine.

This is the only way I can do this, but I can't tell him. I lower my thong, flicking it toward the rest of my clothing. Jameson watches closely as I discard the scrap of material. He raises his line of sight to rest on my shaved pussy. He continues to stare when I part my folds with my fingers, circling my clit. I dip a finger into my pussy and trail its wetness back up and use it to circle my clit once more. Jameson licks his lips.

"Do you want a taste, babe?"

His eyes meet mine, and the lust behind them is intoxicating. He nods. "Yes, please."

I smile at his good manners. "Well, since you asked so nicely..." I walk closer to him and stop. He wants to reach out to me, but I shake my head at him, giving him my next set of instructions. "Take your boxers off, climb onto the bed, and lie down on your back."

He immediately complies as he stands to take off his boxers, placing them next to my wet panties and crawling up the bed. I see his sack hanging heavy as his thick cock juts outward. He lays back on the bed as instructed, and I walk over to him, crawling from the base of the bed up his body.

I feel his body tighten, struggling to control his urge to flip me over and ravish mine. If I was any ordinary girl, I'd probably love that, but I'm not. I'm fucked up, and I can't let him have control. I'll unravel, and he doesn't know me or my history. I need to protect myself from him and everyone else.

"Give me your hands."

He looks at me, and I point to the cuffs hanging by the bed. They are soft and meant to restrain but not harm.

"You don't want me to touch you?" His question holds a note of hurt, but

I swallow down the words I should say. Ones meant to be cold and direct. Instead, I allow him a little truth.

"I'd like you to one day, but not today."

He searches my eyes for the truth, and they soften briefly, allowing him a small glimpse of my vulnerability. He nods, accepting this very well, knowing there may not be more than today.

He holds out his hands for me to secure to the sides of the bed. I smile at his complacency. "Good boy."

I take one hand, restrain it in the cuff, and do the same to the other. He gives them each a tug to demonstrate that he is indeed secured, and I am glad he understands my need for this tonight.

He sits back, awaiting my next move. As I move to sit on his chest, my wetness coats him, and his gaze drops down between my legs. I lean back and spread my legs, allowing him an up-close view. He inhales deeply and moans. Then he blows on my exposed lips. I feel a shiver rack my body as I look at the desire he feels for me. "Do you want to lick me, Jameson?"

He nods, making eye contact with me. "You know I do, sweetheart."

I smile at his term of endearment. I shimmy upward and see his head lift off the pillows, but it isn't necessary. I hover above him, giving him all the access he needs to lick me up and down. "Fuck, Jameson, just like that." I throw my head back, as he repeats the action. I spread my lips for him, and he takes my clit into his mouth and sucks. My orgasm that was building explodes as I almost lose consciousness. I feel weak as the last of my climax ebbs while I'm still shamelessly riding his face. My hips ease their bucking and I feel satiated. I took what I needed, and I am unapologetic for it.

As I still my movements, I feel him smile underneath me. "What are you smiling about, Jameson?" I chuckle at him, knowing how self-assured he is in the fact that he got me off—and what an orgasm it was. I shake my head as I lift off him.

With a smirk he says, "And no hands, huh?"

My cheeks are flushed, and the smile on his face is enough to knock the wind out of me.

God, he's so beautiful.

I move down where his long length is there for the taking. "Let's see if you're still smiling after I suck your soul through your cock."

CHAPTER SEVEN

JAMESON

"SOMEBODY THAT I USED TO KNOW" BY GOTYE

I went home feeling worse than when I left for the club. My spirits were lifted at the prospect of a good night to get my mind off things with Emma and Eduardo. I guess I achieved that because I had a good time and my mind is no longer fixated on my previous dilemma.

Except now it's onto something—or rather someone—else.

I realize the girl I want to see again is gone, and I may never see her again. She's fucked-up, and I'm just as fucked because I didn't want to let her go, but she makes that choice for me. She wouldn't even let me really touch her, and I wonder if there's a specific reason why she doesn't allow comfort or touch from her partner. Except that I am not her partner. I am nothing to her.

That's precisely what I felt after we left the room. I asked Eve if she wanted to go to the bar. She looked at me and said she needed to go to the bathroom. I knew from the look in her eye that she wasn't coming back, but still, I nodded and went to the bar to order myself a drink and a bourbon for her, hoping I was wrong.

Fifteen minutes passed, and I sat, staring in the direction she'd left in. Just as she rounded the corner, I stood there watching her. She paused, looking back, and smiled at me. It was a smile that said good to have known you. Maybe even held some regret.

Still, I waited. I finished her drink and left an hour later without knowing who that girl was or if I would ever see her again. It's unbelievable how, just a few hours ago, I was upset that Emma was with Eduardo. Although I didn't feel the connection I had with Eve, that raw chemistry I thought only existed in movies, I still felt this longing to protect Emma. I cared for her in a way that I can't explain. I was drawn to her, but I felt nothing that night at the beach on Padre Island during spring break when we kissed.

The kiss I had with Eve was brutal in every aspect it could be. The punishing ease with which she kissed me and took what she wanted from me was unapologetically damning to my psyche. She owned me. The brutal way she sucked my cock was the best head I have ever received, and the way she licked me all over and pulled my balls while doing it, placing each one in her mouth and kissing the area in between made me see stars.

I rub my aching cock as I remember how good it felt. How good she felt. The worst was the way she brutally dismissed me after. I thought she might change her mind when she turned around, hoping and praying to a god that wouldn't deliver. I was wrong.

I finally fall into a restless sleep, dreaming of being pulled beneath the water and carried under by punishing emerald-colored twisting tides.

Waking up to my alarm going off the following day, I hit the snooze button several times before finally rolling out of bed. I flip the light on in the bathroom almost on auto-pilot with my mundane morning routine. I turn the water on to shower, I brush my teeth at the sink as the steam lingers in the small space. I rub the condensation off the mirror and drop my toothbrush into the sink.

"What the fuck," I mumble through a mouth full of toothpaste. I move my head from side to side and see the bite marks on my neck and shoulders as I turn left and right to get a better visual of the damage that little vixen inflicted.

I hang my head back, staring at the ceiling as celestial visions of the night pass in a flurry of moving pictures. Snapshots flick through of her riding my face while I remained restrained, the way she went down on me, and the way she left me there as if it was just another night at the sex club.

I guess that's all it was to her, and I need to put it out of my mind, move on, and start dating—no more random hookups.

I see how happy my buddy Dax is with his woman Liv, and I want the same. He wouldn't have dared turn down a boy's night out, but now that he is in a committed relationship, he won't even chance it. He almost lost Liv but was given a second chance. If I ever get a second chance with Eve, I won't hesitate to hold on and fight for it tooth and nail.

Arriving at work, I try to concentrate on my tasks with a renewed purpose. The day passes surprisingly fast, and by the time I know it, it's lunchtime—my favorite part of the day because it means my work day is half over. Now, what the fuck do I eat for lunch?

My finger rests on my forehead as I scroll through my phone in search of some nourishment. Just as I decide to grab a sandwich for lunch, Eric pops his head in my office.

"Hey. I was in the area and thought maybe you'd like to grab some lunch with me?"

I laugh. "Sure. I was just scrolling through for some delivery, but I'll go with you. What were you thinking?" I try to sway his choice to what I wanted to eat before he got here. "Maybe a smoked meats sandwich or something like that?"

He snaps his fingers. "Oh, yeah. How about Schwartz's deli?"

I pretend to think about it, but hell yeah that's exactly where I wanted to go. "I could go for that." I downplay my excitement before grabbing my wallet and following Eric out of the office.

We grab lunch from my favorite deli that boasts the best Montréal smoked meats sandwiches, but instead of sitting at my desk, I am sitting with my friend. I was scrolling through social media and pulling up my newly downloaded dating app.

Eric takes a huge bite of his sandwich. "What are you doing?" he asks through a mouthful of food.

"Here goes nothing." I upload a picture that Eric took of me at the beach on spring break last year.

I take a bite of my sandwich and watch as the picture uploads to my profile. I toss my phone toward him and he takes a look.

He whistles. "Nice, man. It's about time."

I nod in agreement. "It is." I retrieve my phone, hitting the silence button, pocketing it before we head back to the office.

The day has finally come to an end, time to clock out for the day. As I shut my computer down for the night. I am looking around for my phone, remembering that I had silenced it and threw it in the drawer so I wouldn't get distracted. Reaching into the drawer to grab it so I can head out for the night, I see I have a message from the guys in our group text, so I click on it as I head for the elevators.

Eric and Theo: Hey! Meet us at the usual spot. Happy hour.

"Perfect," I say aloud. I quickly type out a response.

Jameson: Sure. I'll be there soon.

I pack up my shit and head out with a purpose. I'm not going to fixate on something I can't have. I will have some drinks with my friends and get out of this funk I've been in. I repeat this mantra all the way to our favorite sports bar, which is already packed.

I look around for where Theo and Eric usually sit and immediately spot them. Theo is waving his hand for me to come over, and I sidestep several people to get there. I immediately spot Simone, the waitress infatuated with Dax, and duck out of her line of sight.

The guys stand from their seats and give me a clasp-side hug as we sit, and I flag down the waitress for a beer, pointing at what they are having. She nods and goes back to the bar.

"Where's Dax?" I ask the guys, looking around as if he will magically appear. They laugh, and Theo rolls his eyes.

"Pfft. We texted him, too, but he's not coming out."

I look at him, confused. "Late night at work in the OR?" I glance around, seeing the waitress taking another order.

"Nope," Theo replies coolly. "He has plans with Liv."

Eric laughs into his beer. "I can't say I blame him. If I had a woman that hot, I'd stay home, too."

I nod in agreement. "And then there were three, huh."

"Yep," Eric says. "Just wait. I'm going to find myself one of those book girls." He says this as if he knows something we don't.

"Huh?" Theo looks at him quizzically. "Book girls?"

"You know, one of those women who reads smutty books," Eric attempts to clarify. "I've always been drawn to the sexy librarian vibe."

Before I can comment, the waitress approaches our table with my beer, ending any further questioning about book girls. As I take a long swig, something catches my eye, and I cough on my beer.

"Hey, woah," Eric states. "Are you alright there, Jameson?"

I shake my head and hit my chest, trying to say I am okay, but I aspirated a bunch of hazy IPA, so it's a garbled mess. Finally, I sputter, "Yep, just went down the wrong pipe, that's all."

Theo smacks me on the back.

I look around to find her, but she isn't there. Great, now I am seeing Eve when she is, in fact, not here. I only saw her with a mask on, but those eyes were so vibrant, I'd know her anywhere if I looked into them. *Wouldn't I?* I have got to get it together. I rub a hand down my face and stand.

The guys look up at me.

"Bro, are you leaving?" Theo asks.

"Naw, I'm just heading to the bathroom." I tap the chair and walk off, avoiding the gaze of a group of hospital employees letting loose after work hours a few tables over.

I am almost to the bathroom door when I feel someone staring at me. I look around just as someone grabs my hand. I stop in my tracks and turn to see big brown eyes searching mine.

"Amanda?" I ask. She fucking beams at me, and I just want to crawl away.

"Hey, you remembered." She twirls her hair around her finger, and I smile back.

"Yeah, of course. How are you?" I'm being polite, but I don't give a fuck about her. We had sex a while back. Although it wasn't very memorable, but the mess she left all over my sheets was. She also threw up in my bathroom afterward, claiming lactose intolerance. No one told her to drink sours. That's her punishment. We weren't drunk, but we both had a few drinks that night, and I took care of her and drove her home the following day after stopping for a breakfast burrito. This time without cheese. She was so apologetic, and I felt terrible for her then. Now, I just want to get back to my friends and our table, have a few beers before walking out the door, and going home.

"Who are you with?" she asks, looking around.

"Oh, just Theo and Eric. We were leaving soon." I try to get away, but she steps closer, hugging me and pressing her big tits into my chest.

She lifts herself onto her tiptoes and kisses me on the cheek very close to my mouth. "Maybe we can go out sometime if you want? I was just about to leave myself." She looks at me hopefully, and I hate to be rude to her.

I decide for a bit of honesty. "Um. Sorry, but I kind of met someone." I scratch my head and look over to the bathrooms.

"Oh, yeah, sure." She withdraws from me as if my fake girlfriend will suddenly appear.

"No problem. It was nice seeing you again."

She looks embarrassed. I want to tell her not to worry about it, but I also don't want to lead her on any further, so I just step backward, ready to leave. I smile at her. "Same. Take care."

This time, I make a beeline for the bathroom, and afterward, promptly head back to the table to hang out with my friends.

We try to play some trivia, but soon, they decide to head out, and I am pretty tired after the night before. We ask for the check, and the waitress returns, saying it's all set.

"What do you mean?" I look at the guys, and they seem as surprised as I am. "Well, who do we have to thank?" I look around and don't see anyone that is looking our way.

The waitress chuckles. "She didn't say. She just said to cover the drinks, dropped some cash, and left about a minute ago."

The guys are already heading to the door, but I can't shake the feeling I had of being watched all night, and I have to know.

I stop the waitress as she begins to walk away with our glasses and tug her arm momentarily. "Sorry to bother you, but can I ask what she looked like?"

She shrugs and says, "Short, but wearing high-heeled boots, blonde hair, nothing uncommon except for her eyes. They were bright green." She walks off, and I'm stuck there open-mouthed.

I hear my name called and look around, but I know the waitress said she left. What are the chances she was here? Does she live around here, too?

Theo calls out, "Hey, we're out of here. Catch you later, bro."

I nod and walk toward the entrance as he walks out the door. Eric is probably already home. When that guy says he's out, he doesn't hesitate. As I walk to my car, the feeling of being watched intensifies. I can't shake the feeling that I'm not alone. I'm being ridiculous, but God, I just wish I could see her again.

I open the door, throw my keys on the counter, and head to the bathroom, forcing myself to shower even though all I want to do is crash.

I'm physically and emotionally drained after meeting this woman. A total mindfuck.

I pull back the crisp sheets of my bed and dive in. I set my alarm and notice there is a message on my dating app. I click on the message and immediately sit up. The picture is of a girl with short blonde hair slicked back. She's facing away from the camera. She looks like an emo girl with all-black clothes and black combat boots. Even though she is facing away from the camera, I recognize her body. A body I had the privilege of getting acquainted with most intimately. Without a doubt, I know that if she turned around in that picture, her eyes would be mesmerizingly green.

"Fuck." I take a deep breath and open the message.

CHAPTER EIGHT

EVIE

"CHERRY WAVES" BY DEFTONES

I knew I should have left him alone. There were so many things that I should have done, yet I don't regret a single thing. I don't regret taking him up on his drink offer at the club. I don't regret having mind-blowing orgasms with him. I don't regret making sure he got home okay after I pretended to be unaffected by his touch while I left him there wondering if I was coming back.

However, I do regret not being able to keep him.

Leaving him there was one of the hardest things I've had to do, and considering all I lost, that is saying a lot.

I can't believe he waited for me all that time, knowing I would probably not return. I stared at him, holding myself back from returning, but I knew it would be a mistake, so I forced myself to put one foot in front of the other and numb myself to the repressed emotions that threatened to resurface after spending only one evening together.

I've never had that kind of connection to anyone before. Following Jameson to work, and then to the bar afterward, was wrong, but no one said I was normal. I've accepted that I wasn't an ordinary girl long ago. I was made this way out of deception, lies, and abuse. I was forced to develop my own form of coping skills.

So here I am, at the bar Emma frequents, watching Jameson meet his friends sitting at a high-top with him in my line of vision.

Emma left as we arrived, sitting with her usual coworkers, but he didn't notice. I took a seat, sipping my seltzer water and watching from my spot in the corner with a view of the whole bar. Mateo was put off by my new obsession, but for someone who looks out for the same things I do, he's one to talk.

As fucked-up as I am, I didn't feel that way last night with Jameson. I felt seen. After hiding and pretending I was dead along with my parents in that fire, I must remain invisible to everyone. I rarely talk to anyone besides Mateo, and have never had a relationship.

After Mateo saved me from being attacked long ago in that alley, I was traumatized, but with the help of a therapist, I was able to pull myself from drowning in flashbacks of that night. Even though I was just bruised, my injuries were invisible—and my spirit was broken. I had to learn how to take back the control that was taken from me that night. I did that by speaking about my anxiety, and self-defense classes to combat my fears. I swore I would never let anyone have that kind of power over me again. I will be the only one in control of every aspect of my life.

I have held true to that, even when it comes to being intimate with someone.

Let's be honest. There is no intimacy with the one-night stands that I have. Sex for me is an act used to release tension that has built up to the point of rage. I have had sex with men in the past, but never anything more than that—except for last night. I felt seen and treasured when he looked into my eyes like I was someone who mattered to him. I wasn't just Evie, the sister who died and stayed unseen to protect Emma.

I was an actual person who sought the things all women want. I want to be the center of someone's world. I want to be held and cherished as if I am the most essential thing to their existence. I felt that possibility for a small amount of time, and even if I never have that again and all our plans go to shit, I can say that without a doubt, for that moment, I mattered to someone. I felt cared for and treasured, which is absolutely absurd, since we were both at a sex club. I'm sure we won't be telling this story to any grandkids.

Finding him on that app was pure luck, but once I saw his profile, I knew that I had to reconnect with him again. Maybe just one more time to indulge myself in something I can't have. So I threw caution to the wind and decided to send him a private message.

I want to explain to him that I didn't want to leave but that it was for the best. It's a mistake to talk to him and get him involved any further than he already is, but I can't stop wanting him. He's like a drug, and I need my fix. I pick up my phone and hit send.

Eve: I want to see you again.

One small phrase that should get my point across.

I've never been a jealous type, but when I saw that girl push up against him at the bar, I wanted to scream in her face that he is mine and rip her hands off him. They had a familiarity of having been intimate. I've never felt so many emotions at once: anger for touching what's mine, jealousy that someone else knew him in a similar way I had, and a longing that makes me want to be held the way I imagined he would have night—the night when I walked away from the one thing I wanted to be selfish with.
I drive home where I reside with my brother Mateo. The traffic here is insane, and I wish for a simpler life. I'd like to pick a place I want to live versus someone dictating where I have to live. Living in Houston isn't the best, and I loved the simplicity of living on Padre Island, but Julian found Emma, and Adrian convinced her to move here with Liv, so here we are. The timing was perfect, and the reason held true—to be a friend to Liv and help her with her transition to a new city after the accident at the beach. I can still hear the screaming.

I remember that day and the first time I saw Jameson at the beach.

I blended in with the crowded beach area, pretending to be any girl indulging in the moment. I hid behind my sunglasses and hat while Mateo hung out with girls wrapped around him. He said it helped provide cover, but it sure looked like something else from where I sat.

I watched my sister with her friends and felt a twinge of sadness that I couldn't tell her that I was there. Instead, I watched from afar and bided my time—all to keep her safe.

Day turned into night, and the party continued. The crowds had lessened, and Mateo and I were farther away from where we originally sat, closer to the shore. We had the van parked farther back now as the tide came in, but we were still close enough that I could keep an eye on Emma.

A thump startled me from my thoughts, followed by a high-pitched wail, and finally muffled sounds all coming from the van. Thank God he shoved his hand over that bitch's mouth.

Just when I thought I could get a moment of reprieve, it started rocking, and I snorted, "Fuck this." I put on my Van sneakers and walked in the shadows when someone called out my sister's name.

"Emma?" I heard a voice call out. She looked zoned out until she realized someone was calling her. "Do you have to pee or something? You can't keep still?"

I looked to see where she was and turned to talk to a guy with brownish-colored hair, average height, and a toned body.

Her laugh carried on the humid coastal breeze. "What gave it away?" she asked playfully, and my lips turned up in a smile.

"Oh, I don't know. It looked like you had ants in your pants," he retorted, displaying a beautiful smile across his chiseled jaw. He was handsome and anything but average in my eyes.

Emma threw her hand around. "Ha! I hope not. What do you think about escorting me to the bathrooms? I need to pee, but I don't like that it's so secluded over there and..." I saw her throat bob as she formulated her following words. "Dark."

My heart broke hearing that she was still acutely aware of the dangers that lurk in the dark. I wanted to go to her. To shout, 'I'm here, Emma.' Instead, I stood silent and continued to watch over her.

He smiled at her and reached for her hand. "I'd be happy to escort you." He swung her arm back and forth playfully. "Come on. Let's go." They walked hand-in-hand, like school-aged children, to the portable bathroom stall closer to the sand dunes.

I walked behind the dunes, watching and waiting to see if I needed to intervene.

"Do you want me to wait here?" he asked respectfully. "I'll give you some privacy."

Emma chuckled. "Nope, no privacy needed," she retorted. "Can you wait right here, right here?" She said it twice for emphasis as she pointed to the spot in front of the stall before stepping in to relieve herself.

"Of course," he replied, standing there waiting for her. I heard the stall door close. Then I saw them coming my way, but before they got to the sand dune to cut back to their friends, I saw him stop and face her, bringing her into him. He placed both hands on her cheeks, staring down at her. I couldn't see his eyes, but I could feel the desire he felt for her radiating off in waves.

I swallowed in anticipation of what she'd do. I couldn't help but feel a longing. I saw myself there with him. I envisioned him gazing down at me. I felt his hands on my cheeks, and he watched me with the same longing desire, but this time for me, burning me up inside. My clit pulsed, and I saw him pick her up. Her legs wrapped around him. I sucked in a breath, begging for them to silently stop. I wanted to throw up.

One arm went to grab her ass, holding her up, and my face turned red. The other arm reached across her back, and he looked intently at her as if he saw no one else.

Has anyone ever looked at me that way?

I felt it when their lips touched, and I touched my lips as they tingled from the sensation that mocked me. He deepened the kiss, kissing her passionately. I watched them through blurred vision. Wetness coated my eyelashes, and I've never wanted anything so bad. The ache in my heart widened as the need for this man took hold of my heart and squeezed it painfully—a reminder that I couldn't have him. Their kiss ended as fast as it started, and he stared at her in confusion.

He dropped her legs from his embrace, and Emma righted herself. She looked around, then back at him awkwardly. "Um," I heard her say. "We should get back. They will wonder where we went soon."

He nodded and held her stare as she looked anywhere but at him. "Sure," he said, rubbing his hand at the back of his neck. I'm sure he wondered what the fuck just happened.

"Me, too," I said aloud to no one in particular. Just then, I felt a hand on my shoulder. I stiffened. "Pfft, took you long enough, asshole." I didn't have to look around to know that Mateo had seen me staring at this guy. I watched them walk away, and before I could give Mateo hell for fucking someone in the van, we heard a scream.

"Help! Someone help!" Mateo and I followed Emma, who ran alongside Jameson, to where a large crowd had gathered.

The sound of my phone interrupts my intrusive thoughts. I lie there staring at the ceiling. I got tired of waiting for a response, but then I thought maybe he hadn't seen the message yet.

I hesitate to pick up my phone. A series of questions float through my mind. What if he doesn't want to see me? What if he is already dating someone from the app? What if I didn't really matter to him, and he is this way with everyone? What if I'm not that special?

I pick up my phone and hover over the little pinkish square of the dating app. I see a message from Jameson and let out a breath before opening it.

Jameson: Sure. Coffee?

I look at the cuteness of the place he wants to meet. Unfortunately, I can't meet him for coffee. Maybe not ever.

Eve: I have a better idea. I'll come to you.

His reply is instant, and his confusion is apparent. I smile, thinking about how that night will go.

Jameson: What? When?

I hover over the text and type out a reply before I can second-guess myself.

Eve: I'll come to you—your place. I'll be in touch soon.

I'm about to click out of the app before another message with his address comes through. I can't help the laugh that escapes me now.

"Cute, he thinks I don't know where he lives." I shake my head at his innocence and feel like I have something to look forward to for the first time in forever.

I get under the covers. This time sleep comes the easiest it has in a very long time, and I dream of Jameson smiling up at me as I come undone, riding his thick cock.

CHAPTER NINE

JAMESON

"EMERGENCY CONTACT" BY PIERCE THE VEIL

I hate to say that I've been checking my phone frequently on the off chance that Eve has sent me a time when we will meet up. It was unexpected to hear from her after I had already told myself that I probably would never see her again after that one amazing evening together. I reluctantly watched her leave and immediately regretted letting her turn that corner and walk away. Still, it's been weeks, and I haven't heard from her after that last text message via the dating app, so maybe she had a change of heart.

My phone rings, and I look down at the name flashing across the screen. *Eduardo.* I quickly think of all the reasons he may want to talk to me, and all the reasons involve Emma. With her on my mind, I hit the answer button without a second thought.

The traffic was brutal, so finally an hour later, I am pulling into the rear parking lot outside of Eduardo's nightclub, The Viceroy, as I was instructed to do. He'd said he needed to talk to me about Emma's safety, so I'd left before we even hung up to see what he needed from me.

I'm escorted through Eduardo's office door and notice two security guards present. I know one is Philip, who is responsible for following Emma and driving her places. The other is staring at him with disconcertment.

"Jameson, good to see you, brother. I am glad you were able to get here so soon. Like I said earlier, it's important." He sits forward in his chair. "Eli, I'll call you when we are done with Philip."

The door to his office closes, and I hear footsteps retreating from the entryway. I eye him skeptically, wondering where he is going with this. "You mentioned safety and Emma's name in the same sentence, which is why I am here so fast," I clarify. It makes him furious as fuck, and I wonder why I even said that. It's not as if I am in love with his girlfriend, but I feel a strong connection to her—one that I can't explain.

"Right," he says with as much indifference as the guy can muster, but I notice the tic of his jaw and the clenching of his teeth holding him back from saying what he wants to.

He gets up from his desk and moves to the front, bracing his hands against the front of the desk and kicking his legs out in front of him, crossing them at the ankles, appearing aloof and unaffected. I know that move is one of power and intimidation, but he is my frat brother—I've also cleaned his puke out of the backseat of my car.

I cock one eyebrow upward, urging him to get on with it. He nods in understanding.

"Jameson, I called you here because you care about Emma, and we need your help. What I am about to disclose to you is to stay between us in this room and no one else. It is about her safety, and I can't jeopardize that."

I sit up immediately, interest piqued as I look between the security guards and Eduardo. He waits to hear me verbalize my understanding.

"I understand," I inform him as I sit in my chair, waiting for more details. "What can I do to help? Is she in trouble?"

He hesitates, biting his bottom lip before he responds. "I don't know the history between you two..." He pauses, and I wait for him to elaborate, but he doesn't. He wants me to tell him without drawing inaccurate conclusions. That fucker.

"Yeah," he continues, "I have known Emma for most of my life."

I must look confused because he tells me that their families were business associates and they recently reconnected. He tells me about her abusive relationship with a man named Julian and then about her parents' death and twin sister.

My head shoots up. "Twin sister?"

He nods. "She had a twin sister named Evie, her best friend. She misses her terribly and blames herself for their deaths."

I take this in and slump a little in my chair, letting my hand rub up and down on my pant legs. The rage inside is palpable.

I stand up. "He is still after her? He was here tonight?"

He nods in confirmation. That's all I need to know. I already know that I will help him however he needs me to.

"I need your help looking at the security feed to see if I missed anything, and I also need you to wipe it a little bit or just a certain section of it."

My confusion is evident as he continues to explain the reasoning. "Well, since you installed it, you know more about the system than anyone else would, right?"

I nod, confirming that he isn't wrong. "Um… why do you need it wiped?"

His smile is one of a criminal thug at his finest. He looks over to Philip then to me, and he says, "Philip here has to die, and I don't want there to be any evidence."

Okay, that is not what I imagined he was going to say, and I can't be an accomplice to murder. Can I? I am just contemplating Philip's murder, and he must notice because he snorts, breaking my concentration.

"You're fucking joking, right?" Because now I think they are fucking with me.

"Mostly," Eduardo counters. Seeing my ethos winning the internal war that wages on my morals, he rolls his eyes, putting me out of my misery. "I need it to *look* like I killed Philip, but he will stay hidden and keep an eye on Emma—from the shadows," he clarifies, rolling his eyes.

"With everyone thinking that he is dead, that will give him the upper hand so he can go unnoticed. People won't suspect he is secretly watching out for the person giving Julian information if he is considered dead. We need to find out who that is before they lead him to her and he gets to Emma."

I glance over at Phil and then back at Eduardo before quickly responding, "Okay, I'm in."

After Philip is presumed dead and I wipe the surveillance feed, Eduardo invites me back to his office for another chat. He is more direct this time. "I want to know what happened between you and Emma. I know that you have feelings for her."

I sense the struggle between wanting to know and knowing he may not want to know about his girlfriend. He is staring at me as he blows a long breath and visibly tenses.

I look up at him, running my hand through my hair. "Nothing." He waits patiently as I find the words to describe it. "We met on Padre Island during spring break. That's when Dax met Liv. He was a patient in the ER and we all met up at the beach the next day. We shared a moment, but then she came here. And she saw you. I don't know."

His breathing has increased, and I can sense that he thinks I fucked his girlfriend. I decide to put him out of his misery. His fist clenches and unclenches on the desk, and I know he will lose it very soon if I don't clarify. There were times when his volatile temper got the better of him in college.

"A moment?" He tilts his head and glares at me. "Did you fuck my girlfriend?" And there it is. His voice is laced with barely controlled anger. He finally asked me what he really wants to know.

"No," I reply without hesitation, meeting his glare so that he understands that it is the truth. "We had an awkward kiss, and that is it. I think Dax and Liv thought there was more between us, and I wanted there to be, but now she is with you."

He steps away from the desk, rubbing his face. "Awkward kiss?" he questions, wanting to know every fucking detail. Why does he want to torture himself with all of this?

I rub the back of my neck, trying to explain the kiss we shared in the least embarrassing way. "Yes, bro. Awkward as fuck. It felt like I was kissing my sister, despite being super attracted to her." He snorts. "I can't explain it, but I feel super protective of her, too, but not in a romantic way."

He smiles. "Okay, sister fucker."

We laugh.

"Nice, bro. Thanks." And that breaks the ice a little. "You have nothing to worry about. I care about Emma, but if she is happy with you, I just want her to be happy." I shrug noncommittally.

He stands and clasps my shoulder. "I'm glad to hear that. Now, I need your help with a tracker for Emma."

"Unbelievable," I mutter as I walk through my door a little after midnight. The things that motherfucker roped me into doing tonight. "Only slightly illegal," I loudly mock Eduardo's tone.

In need of some alcohol, I turn on the lights and head to the fridge to grab a beer when my phone buzzes in my pocket. I take a long swig and look at the message. I swear, if he needs one more thing, I will lose it.

I hit the button and see that it's definitely not from Eduardo. I smile, seeing that it's from Eve. I almost drop my phone, thinking about seeing her and the excitement that elicits.

Eve: Can I come over?

Those four words make my heart race in excitement. I stare at the phone in wonderment. It's as if she knew the exact moment I got home.

I take my beer, walk over to my balcony, open the slider, and walk out. I stand there looking over the street, wondering where she is. I take another swig of my beer, wondering what to tell her. I'll be damned if I am going to turn down her request to come over tonight. She reached out, so who am I to deny her?

I shrug the doubt away and decide to respond sooner rather than later, having been so anxious to hear back from her in the past weeks. I don't want her to disappear again, but I don't want her to think she can just come and go. Reluctantly, I need to know, so I text her back.

Jameson: I didn't think you were going to reach out. It's been a while.

I immediately hit send, then regret doing it. What am I doing? A sexy woman wants to come over to my house, and I'm guilt-tripping her for leaving me hanging for weeks. I groan and hope that I didn't just ruin everything. Minutes go by, and I swear that I fucked up royally. Why couldn't I have just said, '*Hell yes.*'

Eve: I was away but reached out as soon as I was free. Is that a no?

I don't want there to be any more confusion. I want her. I wanted her yesterday, and surprisingly, I want her for my future. So, I respond as directly as possible to prevent any other confusion.

Jameson: That's a fuck yes. Come.

I laugh at the double entendre in that sentence. God, what I wouldn't give to have her come over and over on my tongue and around my cock as I thrust into her. I rub my aching dick as it pushes against the tight confines of my denim jeans, trying to alleviate the throbbing, and needing a release.

> Eve: I'll be there as soon as I can. Leave the door open and the lights off. Be a good boy and wait for me naked in your room.

> Evie: Don't touch yourself. That's my job ;)

My body thrums with excitement as I read her message and then re-read it to make sure I didn't miss anything. Eve that night was a woman who knew what she wanted, and I was turned on as fuck as she rode my face. Her take-charge attitude was a complete turn-on, and I loved every second.

I groan, thinking about that night and wondering what tonight holds for us, and with that, I take a quick shower. Stepping out of the fastest shower I have ever taken, I throw a towel around my waist, unlock the door just as she instructed, pick up my beer from the table, and finish the rest. I shut off the lights and head into my bedroom, stripping off my towel just as I step into the room.

Whenever a woman tells you to wait for her naked and in bed, it's best if you just oblige.

CHAPTER TEN

EVIE

"LOVE THE WAY YOU LIE" BY EMINEM

I've been busy these past few weeks and haven't been able to reach out to Jameson since I sent that last text message on the dating app. Pretending you are dead and trying not to be seen is more complicated than one would think. My Uncle Andrés summoned us to meet with him in Mexico about the incident with Emma in her apartment.

Emma and Liv were catching up and visiting, since Liv spends most of her time at Dax's place. Julian must have been in Emma's apartment and wrote a message on her mirror. This prompted Eduardo to race to her apartment and drag her out with a bag. I had been watching the apartment as they drove away.

After that incident, it is clear he is in Houston and has found her. We just don't know how, but we have to be smart about when to anticipate his next move.

She's been at Eduardo's ever since that night. He has provided around-the-clock security detail for her. Someone takes her to work, or he personally takes her places. She is even working the night shift at the hospital now. We hope it is safer that way.

Emma was back at the apartment today, and we were on high alert. Their friends from Padre Island are here and unpacked their stuff hours ago. Watching them tonight proved to be an act of patience. I was at The Viceroy Club with Mateo, watching Emma and her friends from afar. Eduardo allowed her out of his sight as long as she brought the girls to his club, where he could have his security and bouncers watch over them closely.

I had been waiting at the club. Her friends from Padre Island and her best friend, Liv, walk in. The girls are excited about tonight, but Emma is frowning, looking at her best friend. Concern etches her face as she tries to have fun but will not leave Liv's side. I immediately notice Liv looking a little peaked. Despite her best performance, the girl seems one step away from puking in a trashcan.

Always watching and never participating, I feel like I'm living my life through Emma and her friends, except I'm not; I'm nobody. I sigh.

Suddenly, I see a man approaching Emma and her friends dancing. On high alert, I sit up straight on my barstool and send a message to Mateo, but he's already on the dance floor watching Emma as this random girl grinds on him. I'm also watching Emma, and she seems to notice something is off.

Security is around the dance floor talking into their headsets. I walk toward the dance floor's perimeter, wondering if this is when my cover is blown, but Mateo and I make eye contact. The girl he is dancing with has her head buried in his chest and is holding onto him. He shakes his head at me, and I immediately go back.

A big, muscular guy wearing a tight-fitted Henley shirt with tattoos in places similar to Eduardo's approaches Emma with a predatory gleam in his eye. He starts to dance closely against her, and a small commotion occurs on the dance floor. A very pissed-off Eduardo tells the guy something in his ear while looking at my sister. He nods in recognition when he realizes his error. Emma is led off the dance floor hand-in-hand with Eduardo, and I visibly relax. Then she turns back and rips her hand away, running to Liv.

Liv is holding onto a barstool, swaying as if she is one breath away from passing out of the floor. She motions for Eduardo, and he quickly calls for security. Liv is picked up and taken upstairs to what I assume is Eduardo's office. Emma and the girls follow her upstairs past the VIP areas and into the back hallway. Mateo abandons his partner on the dance floor and walks to me with purpose.

I toss back a shot of tequila and pass one over to Mateo. He takes it from me and throws it back in a similar fashion. He wipes his mouth with the back of his hand. I lean over to talk with him. The music is unforgiving, but I can't wait and need to know now.

"What happened? Did you see what went on?" I lean in closer to hear him better, but then pull back. "Ugh, you smell like a brothel." The cheap perfume is so sickly sweet that it's nausea-inducing. "Is this what Liv smelled?"

He shakes his head.

"You're so dramatic, Evie." He moves closer, despite my wrinkling my nose and the stench emanating from his shirt.

"It really does smell bad. I'm allergic to cheap perfume."

He ignores me.

"Yeah, that guy with Emma was a distraction. I saw another guy walking around that was staring at Emma. It's probably a good thing Liv had to be carried away. It brought extra security around them, honestly."

I see a bouncer escorting a man through the crowd and walking toward the VIP rooms. I nod.

"Wanna bet that's Liv's boyfriend?" Mateo snorts at his own question.

"Wanna bet that girl's pregnant?" I counter and look over at my brother with one raised eyebrow.

"You think so?" He looks at me like that is impossible. He shudders. "Kids."

"Who knows?" I've already lost interest in Emma's 'best friend.' "I guess it could be a stomach bug." I roll my eyes for emphasis, just in case he didn't pick up on my sarcasm.

"Maybe," he answers in more of a question than a statement, still not grasping my condescending tone.

I look up to the balcony, and see Emma hanging over, looking down at the crowd dancing below. Her friends are around, and she is watching someone walk in. I look at her line of sight and freeze when I see Jameson approaching Eduardo's office. Mateo catches my eye.

"What are you doing, Evie?" I want to get up and run after him, but I can't. My fist is clenched, and the other holds on to the barstool, preventing me from running after him. I look back up and see that Emma has returned to her friends.

"Let's wait and go back to see what we can learn from there." I go to stand, and Mateo grabs my hand. He must see the anxiety rising to the surface, coming over in waves. I take a deep breath to calm myself.

"Come on, sis. I got you."

We leave the club, and I hold onto my brother like a lifeline—the only man who has been there for me.

We waited but never saw Jameson and Philip exit the club. I did see another man they called Eli drive off with Emma and the girls, undoubtedly to take them home. Mateo followed them, and I took off to our apartment alone.

Instead of going there, I detour, taking the on-ramp heading to Jameson's place. I'm parked outside, stalking him, and I'm excited to see him. I didn't think it would be this long before I saw him again, but here I am debating on whether or not to end the torture I've felt, not being able to reach out to him because I was out of the country.

Seeing him walk into the club, and how good he looked made me stabby—even seeing my sister taking him in sent jealousy coursing through me. She has her own man, but the reminder of her legs wrapped around him at the beach sends a bolt of anger rushing through me as my face begins to feel too hot. I turn up the air conditioning and adjust the vent to hit my face, trying to calm the surge of anger.

He pulls into the parking lot, and I watch him jump out of the car and lock it with the key fob. He's sending a message, and I immediately wonder who he is messaging. I look down at my phone. Nothing. It's not me, but why would it be. I've left him hanging.

I rub at my temples, with the impending headache that threatens to erupt. I open the app where my text message was sent to Jameson some time ago.

'Come.' One word has me shivering from head to toe. Goosebumps break out along my arms. I know he sent the message like that because he knew how it would affect me. I have been recounting the events of our first evening together—reliving the experience with Jameson.

My connection with him was one that I have never felt before or with anyone else. I have never allowed myself to become attached to anyone, but with him, I want to try. He makes me feel so much, too much, and that in itself is a scary thought.

Eve: I'll be there as soon as I can. Leave the door open and the lights off. Be a good boy and wait for me naked in your room ;)

I grab the mask I wore the last time I was with him at the Heavenly Pearl Club. I shouldn't even be seeing him. I should stay away, but I can't.

I get out of my car. I parked down the street from his house, and the lights have been off for over an hour. I take in a deep breath, as I open the door, fighting all of the reasons why I should get back in my car and just drive away. Instead, I push open the door and walk into his place.

The lights are off, and I touch my mask to ensure it is in place. I lock the door behind me and take in my surroundings. I walk over to the balcony where I saw him standing weeks ago and take in the view. I want to see it from his point of view. I imagine myself watching him from my car and him looking out, unaware of me.

I touch his sofa. My hand brushes along the soft leather. Its coolness nips against my skin as I walk down the hall toward his bedroom.

And there he is. Lying on his bed. Just as I asked, he is naked and lying flat on his stomach. His even breaths let me know that he is asleep. Did he go to sleep thinking that I had stood him up, that I wouldn't come?

I go to his chair and sit across from him, staring at his perfect form in front of me. His muscular ass is barely visible in the dim moonlight coming in through the window blinds.

When I look back up to his face, I see his eyes open and looking right back into mine. A small smile plays on his lips, and I can't help but reciprocate. I reach down and take off my combat boots. I shimmy out of my knee-highs and leather skirt. My tank top is pulled over my head, and I stand there in nothing else except my lacy black bra and a matching thong.

Jameson turns over without breaking eye contact, and his fully erect cock is there for the taking. His tip glistens with precum; I salivate at the thought of tasting him. I reach around and undo my bra, letting it fall to the floor.

I pull down my thong, and wetness pools around my center. The sight of him turns me on.

He groans. "Eve, you're killing me here."

I walk over to him and crouch over his body. I lick at the tip of his thick erection as a milky drop leaks from the slit, and I lap it up, tasting his saltiness. He lifts his hips, and I take him in my mouth. Before he can grab my hair, I release him with a pop.

I move slowly up his body, leaving kisses along the way, and when I reach his neck he grabs my face between his hands and he kisses me with everything he has. Our kiss turns sloppy and hungry as if he can't get enough of me. I understand the feeling. I run my center up and down his dick, soaking it with my wetness. I line him up and drop down onto his thickness, feeling so full.

"God, Jameson, I've needed this," I admit shamelessly, showing him a vulnerability that I refuse to give anyone else. I want him to know that he is different, that what I feel for him means something to me, and that in turn, he means something to me.

I moan and start riding him. His hands go to my hips, pushing me down hard with a punishing force. I place my hand over his, not turning away his touch, but for the first time embracing it.

God, how long has it been since I've allowed anyone to touch me like this? It turns me on so much, and I hold his hands there, pinning them to me. I'm lost to the sensations as I bounce up and down on his cock. I hear his breathing become labored.

"Eve, I need you to slow down." His hand goes up over his head, and his head moves back and forth as if he can fight off the impending orgasm from crashing over him.

"I can't slow down, it feels too good. I need this Jameson. Please let me have this." Because I'm almost right there with him. My hands are on his shoulders, and I rock into him as he pushes up into me, meeting me thrust for thrust, both of us lost to the sensations.

"Oh, God." I pant. "Jameson."

He brings my face down to him and kisses me, thrusting his tongue in and out along with the pace of his cock. His chest is covered in a sheen of sweat, and my juices run down his cock, soaking his balls. The sloppy sounds of our fucking fill the room. He grabs my ass and brings me down more forcefully, and I swear he is so deep, hitting that sweet spot no one could ever find.

"That's it, Jameson. Keep doing that." I throw my head back, and he meets me thrust for thrust. My walls start to convulse as I come so hard that I almost black out.

He fucks me through the orgasm, and he comes after a few more deep thrusts. He brings me down to him, threading our hands together as he kisses me. I collapse onto his chest, and he strokes my back gently. And I allow it. Wetness fills my vision, and everything is blurry.

"Where have you been all this time, Eve?" he whispers, but I don't think he expects an answer, and I certainly don't offer him one.

Not once does he ask about my mask.

CHAPTER ELEVEN

EVIE

"DECODE" BY PARAMORE

I watch Jameson sleep, and I can't help but stare at him. He looks so peaceful, and I bet he does it without a care in the world. He probably doesn't even dream. I envy him for that. To be able to sleep without waking up from a nightmare that you relive whenever you begin to think you feel safe, but I haven't felt safe in a very long time.

Retrieving my clothes, I quickly dress and stare at his sleeping form before leaving. I'm trying to take a mental picture of him this way. Instead, I take out my phone. *Click.*

Without looking back, because if I do I may do something crazy like crawling back into bed and staying. For once, I felt seen, and I don't want to go back to being invisible.

No more masks.

Grabbing the mask, looking down at it one last time before letting it fall onto the table. I vow that the next time I see him, he will see all of me—no more hiding, at least not from him. Reality, on the other hand, has different plans for me. I have to put my happiness on the back burner if I want to help my family. The only family I have left are my siblings.

I take one more look around his apartment and walk out the door with a silent prayer falling from my lips that maybe one day I can have him. I can choose to be selfish and have my happy ending, too, but for now, I can't let this continue. I have to keep Emma safe. This thing we are doing is a luxury that I can't have. If I just keep repeating it over and over to myself, I just might start to believe it. Our need to get revenge is more important. I can't have any more distractions, and Jameson is a huge distraction for me.

When I get back to my car, I slide into the driver seat and just sit there with the engine idling. I don't want to leave, but I force myself to pull away and drive back to my place, leaving a piece of my tattered heart behind as I drive away.

As I pull into my parking spot just before dawn, I see someone jogging out of the complex, and another is leaving for work. I always feel like a loser when I arrive home in the early hours of the morning after a night out at the club. My sister calls it the 'walk of shame,' and it's tough to head to bed while everyone else is just starting their day.

I drag myself up the stairs and open the door when a big yawn escapes me, scratch my head, and throw my bag on the kitchen island. I fill a glass of water, turning around to lean against the counter, when I come face to face with Mateo staring at me.

"Dear God!" I jump back, sloshing half of the water out of my glass. "Bro, what is wrong with you? You almost gave me a heart attack. Don't sneak up on me like that." I flick the water off my tank top, now sporting a huge wet spot in the center. I frown looking down at it, then grab a towel to pat myself dry. I chug the remaining water and place the glass in the sink. Mateo is still staring at me. "What?" I look at him, trying to decipher what his deal is.

"Oh, looks like someone had a rendezvous. Did you see that guy again?"

I look quizzically at him. "Who?"

He snorts. "Don't play dumb, sister. It doesn't suit you."

I smile, displaying my straight, white teeth. "You'll have to be more specific, Mattie. I'm not twelve." We laugh and then realize the implications of that comment as our laughter dies out.

We didn't get that chance to have that relationship because he was sent away. I didn't even know I had a brother until recently. Now, he and my sister have become the most important people in my life. Another part of me thinks that maybe Jameson can be my person, too.

A hand lands on my shoulder. I jump at the unexpected touch.

"Relax. I didn't mean to startle you." He brings me into him and kisses the top of my head.

I force myself to relax into his embrace.

As if hearing my thoughts, Mateo speaks. "I love you, Evie."

I raise my hand to my heart and rub the ache that threatens to take up residence there. The physical aching from someone telling me I am loved is a welcome feeling.

"I love you too, Mateo."

He takes a sniff. "Now, who smells like a brothel? You smell like sex." He pushes me away.

"Yeah, alright. I am going to shower. Great moment." I walk away, and he calls me back.

"Oh, Uncle Andrés called right before you got here. I guess Eduardo called him up asking for Emma's hand in marriage."

"No shit. Um, wow. She's getting married?" I don't know how to feel about that.

"He told Tió that he would keep her safe."

I think about how much time has passed since they were younger. I guess when you know, you know. "Maybe I'll get to go to the wedding," I reply snarkily.

Mateo nods. "Yeah, and maybe I'll finally meet my sister," he speaks hesitantly.

God, I am such a bitch. When I think about all I've lost, I realize that Mateo has had it so much harder than I have.

"One could only hope, Mattie." I smile sadly at him as I walk off toward my bedroom and close the door behind me.

Flopping on my comfy but empty bed, I slip on my favorite sleep shorts and tank before throwing my outfit from last night in the hamper, mimicking a two-point shot. *Swish.* Snuggling down under the covers, I wrap myself in my blankets, refusing to shower so Jameson's scent can envelop me in a feeling of peace where my mind can finally be at rest.

I wake up to the bright sun shining through the blinds. I lazily walk to the bathroom, turning on the shower to let it heat up so I can shower quickly and get some things done. Walking out of my room and into the living room, I see Mateo sitting on the couch watching television. He stands quickly, turning the TV off.

"Come on. Let's get some tacos. I'm starving."

I walk over to grab my bag. "You don't have to tell me twice, bro. I love tacos."

When we get to our fave Mexican spot, we ask to sit outside on the covered patio. The ceiling fans are going, giving us a nice breeze. When our waitress comes over, we order a plate of tacos. Mateo gets a beer, and I get an iced tea.

"No beer?" Mateo questions.

"Nah, I am thirsty, and nothing quenches my thirst like an iced tea."

He tries to hide his laughter but just shakes his head at me. As the waitress returns with our drinks shortly after taking our order, I eagerly grab my iced tea and take a big sip, feeling the coolness of the drink refresh me. However, as I put the glass back down, I notice some moisture pooling on the surface, making me shudder a bit. I quickly reach for a tuxedo wrap and wipe off the excess moisture. Mateo shifts in his chair.

"You really hate condensation, don't you?" He takes another drink, shaking his head at me in jest.

"Ha, you have no idea. Emma and I both do." A smile plays on my lips, thinking of my sister with good memories instead of the bad ones.

I gaze at my brother's profile, searching for any resemblance between us. Despite looking light-skinned while he is an olive tone, and having green eyes while his are as dark as night, I can't help but wonder where his features come from. As he catches my stare, his expression softens, and he smiles, revealing Emma's smile. This gentle reminder tugs at my heart, reminding me that everything could change at any moment. However, I hold onto the belief that we will be reunited soon.

"So, tell me about Jameson?"

My eyes shoot up to his as I ponder his question. What do I tell him about Jameson? Hell, I don't even know much about him, or how I feel about him, except that I found a deep connection to him that I just can't explain. I was able to let some of the control go as he held me. He actually fucking held me. It was almost sweet, as if he understood that I had some issues, yet he still wanted to consume me. It didn't feel like just a fuck. It felt like something more.

"I pick at the napkin around my glass, avoiding his gaze. "I like him." I stop and meet his eyes. They soften.

"I can tell, and I'm happy for you, Evie. You deserve to be happy."

I frown. "I just need this to be over so that I can tell him everything, but when will that be, Mateo? You know, I saw him that night at the beach when Brodie had that accident. I liked him from that moment without even knowing him, but he was interested in my sister then." I look over at Mateo, and his head tilts to the side.

"What do you want to ask me, Evie?" He stares at me instead. I push through and ask my question, verbalizing my biggest fear.

"What if he likes me because somehow I remind him of Emma? I mean, she is my twin." I bite my lip. I hate the vulnerability in my voice. I look across the street at people walking by, taking in the ease with which they walk without a care in the world. I see a woman walking up to a man. He wraps her in a hug, kissing her, and grabs her hand possessively as they walk off. God, what I wouldn't give to have that—to be the center of someone's whole world.

"Evie, do you really believe that?" he asks with concern etched on his features.

"I don't know, Mateo. I mean, no, not really, but he did have a thing for Emma, but she is with Eduardo now. What if I am just second best?" I immediately hate the words when they escape my mouth, but now that they are out there, my worst fears are voiced.

"No, Evie. You are nothing like Emma. You may share looks, but other than that, you are so very different from her. I see a strong woman in front of me. One that loves fiercely and protects what she loves at all costs."

I smile. "Thanks, Mattie. That means a lot to me. I wouldn't know what to do without you."

He shifts awkwardly in his chair but smiles at the compliment.

"Enough about me. Tell me about you. Any special lady in your life?"

He shakes his head. "Now? Nope, no one special."

I shrug, deciding to pry further and invade his privacy. "So what do you do when you leave the house and come out here?"

He chuckles. "You promise not to laugh?" He shakes his head.

"Oh, boy. Now, I have to know. What do you do?" I repeat, almost bouncing in my seat with excitement, and I know that I am so going to enjoy this.

He begins but then stops mid-sentence, pondering his following words. "Fuck it." He rubs his hand over his face. "I went for a walk to think, and I found this cafe by the water. I started having my coffee there and watching the ocean waves. It brings me a bit of peace, you know?"

I nod my head in acknowledgment because I totally understand how peaceful the waves can make you feel.

"I met this older man, he was playing chess alone. I would just sit and watch him play, then one day, he asked me if I wanted to join him."

Wow, that wasn't what I thought he would say at all. I look at my brother, shocked. "You've been playing chess with an old man in your spare time?"

He rubs his hand across the back of his neck. "I mean, I guess, yeah." He snorts, almost embarrassed. "We talk about nothing and everything. His wife died, and he doesn't talk to his son. I think he is just lonely."

I nod in understanding.

"I mean, he is nice, and it quiets my mind."

Silence falls between us. Looking over at my brother, my heart aches as I realize the depth of his loneliness. It's heart-wrenching to imagine how he must be feeling, especially after being abandoned by those who were supposed to be there for him. He didn't have a real family, despite my uncle and aunt raising him as best they could. I can't imagine how tough it must have been for him not to have parents wishing him a happy birthday. Looking back, I now realize how fortunate Emma and I were. I also know how he feels when he says that it quiets his mind. Isn't that what I seek out, too?

"Is it fun?" I ask, wanting to know.

He laughs. "I mean, yeah. I enjoy it. I actually look forward to our time together. Is it weird to have a friend who could be your grandfather?"

I finish my drink. "Nope. Not at all. Hey, do you think maybe I could join you sometime?"

Surprise registers on his face. "Um. Yeah, sure. If you'd like to hang out with us, we meet once a week," he responds shyly. He smiles and shifts his attention to the waitress coming over with a tray of tacos.

The smell hits me, and my mouth begins to water. I swear I can taste the crispy mahi-mahi from here. The conversation halts as the waitress lays out our food in front of us, and I moan at the first bite of my crispy meal. Mateo and I sit there in silence, devouring our weight in tacos.

CHAPTER TWELVE

JAMESON

"CREEP" BY RADIOHEAD

I wake up the next day hoping that Eve will still be there, but as I go to touch the other side of my bed, I already know what I will find. My fingertips brush the cool sheets, and it's obvious Eve has been gone for a while. I stretch out and swear I can still smell her on me. The spicy vanilla scent is the one I wish I could spray on my sheets so that every time I lay my head down, I can envision her being here with me.

I turn my head into the pillow her head rested on last night and inhale deeply, committing it to memory in case it's the last time. I look up at the ceiling, not wanting to think about that but knowing very well that it's a possibility.

As I get out of bed, I whip the covers off my body. I try to remove the crumpled bedsheet from my bed, but I find myself hesitating as I find myself transfixed on the empty space where I had Eve lying just a few hours earlier. I drop my head and realize how fucked I really am if I can't strip my bed and rid myself of her scent just yet.

"Just one more day, and then I'll change the sheets," I mutter like a lovesick fool. I can't help the smile that pulls at my lips as I straighten the sheets and duvet as best I can before jumping into the shower. As I get dressed, I reflect on yesterday's events.

Last night at the club was so messed up. I didn't appreciate the danger that Emma is in with that psychopath ex of hers. Has she been dealing with this all this time? Was that why she appeared so skittish and afraid of the dark when I first met her during spring break on Padre Island?

My phone vibrates with an incoming text message, and I stop thinking about Emma. Instead, I only have thoughts of Eve and hope that it is her texting me. When I turn it around and click on the message, my shoulders slump forward when I see it is from Dax.

Dax: Hey. Can you meet me for lunch? It's kind of important.

I wonder what could be so important, but then I remember that Liv was taken to the emergency department last night. Geez. I run a hand through my hair. I hope she is okay. Dax is so in love with her.

I frown when I remember Eduardo's request, reminding me I must go to work today to sort out the details of Emma's tracker. I also know I have to be there for Dax, so I decide I need to meet him today as well.

Jameson: Sure. I have to go to work for a bit, and then I'll be there.

I finish lacing up my sneakers as I open the refrigerator door, wondering if there is anything I can take with me to eat that isn't spoiled. Another text comes in, and I pick up my phone and see the details from Dax.

Dax: Usual spot. Noon.

I type out my reply and shove my phone into my pocket.

Jameson: Gotcha. I'll be there.

"Not much to eat here." I close the refrigerator door and open the pantry, searching aimlessly until I see an almost empty box off to the side. I grab a protein bar and rip it open after deciding I'll meet him for lunch today so I will get a proper meal in a few hours, so I probably don't need much to eat before then.

"That should do it," I voice aloud my happiness at my progress in developing a tracker for Emma. I turn it around in my hands, admiring my work.

The GPS tracker should be easy to place in a pendant or locket. It can be worn with a necklace or a bracelet. It even has an SOS button on it.

I look down at my watch and notice it's 11:30. I start picking up my items and placing them into a little velvet purse-stringed bag to take to Eduardo's place. I know he wanted to give Emma a present.

I chuckle at the murderous look Eduardo gave me when I had to tell him about the awkward kiss Emma and I shared, but it was only a kiss. They are obviously madly in love with each other, so it really shouldn't even matter. But there's only one woman who consumes my thoughts on a daily basis, her presence lingering in my mind with every passing moment.

I arrive at the sports bar we usually frequent after work for happy hour. Dax hasn't been here in months, since he has been spending all his time with his girlfriend, Liv. I knew that from the moment he met her in the emergency department that day during spring break, he was a lost cause. He was a wreck after he left her that night, but they seemed to have their second chance, and I couldn't be happier for him.

I see him sitting at our usual table and plop myself down, clasping my hand to his shoulder.

"Hey, bro. How are you?" He looks tired but smiles like the cat that caught the canary. I steeple my hands, placing them in front of my face. "So, it looks like you have some good news. I was worried about Liv when she was taken to the hospital. I assume everything is okay?"

He nods enthusiastically. "Liv's pregnant. We are going to have a baby."

I am just about to speak when Dax looks past me, and I turn my head slightly, seeing Simone, the waitress that has a thing for Dax, stare at him with her mouth agape, opening and closing it like damn fish. She goes to speak and then stops. We both stare at her until she says, "I'll give you some more time to order," and scurries off, obviously shaken at the news of Dax becoming a daddy.

"So," I chuckle, "I guess you are officially off the market, huh?" I drink my ice water, relishing the cold drink from recently after getting out of the hot Texas heat.

Dax laughs. "Yeah, I am. That girl owns me, and the thought of her belly swollen with my baby very soon is making me all kinds of possessive of her." He runs a hand down his face. "Fuck, honestly, I can't wait to do it again."

I look at him in shock because this is not the same person I knew a while back. The guy who would not fuck anyone without a condom.

"Congrats. I am happy for you, man." I clap him on the back and he gives me one in return.

"Thanks man. I just wanted to tell you in person. We are both still in shock, but we are so excited. I'm also going to ask her to marry me. I just went out this morning and bought her the perfect ring."

He looks proud of himself, and I can't help but sputter in disbelief. "You're getting married?"

He nods, confirming my question with a wide smile.

I run my hand through my hair. "Wow, this is a lot to take in." I laugh, and he just shrugs.

"This baby's going to come sooner than later, and I want Liv to know I am all in. I don't want there to be any doubt in her mind." He removes something from his pocket and shows me a velvet box. As he carefully opens the box, my eyes are immediately drawn to the shimmering engagement ring. She is going to absolutely love it.

I whistle. "That's a huge rock."

Simone comes back to take our order and sees Dax with the ring. We both look at her as she walks off without taking our order.

"Bro, thanks a lot. Now we are never going to eat."

He laughs. "Do you think we should go somewhere else?" He looks around the sports bar.

"Naw, it's all good."

Simone never returned to our table, which was okay with us. After finally placing our order with a different server, we ate quickly as most of the time was taken up by waiting to place our order. We made plans to get together before he left on holiday break.

I'm just walking to my car when Eduardo calls me. He usually sends a text, so I wonder what the urgency is. I quickly answer the phone as now we are working together with a singular purpose.

"Hey, man, what's up?" I hit the button on my key fob, start the car, and wait until the phone picks up on Bluetooth.

"Hello," I hear Eduardo say into the speakers.

"Yeah, I'm here. I just got in the car and am headed to your place. Are you at work? The club?" I stop at the light and something catches my eye one block from the restaurant—a woman with short blonde hair wearing combat boots, leggings, and a crop top. Oversized sunglasses cover her eyes. The light turns green, and I speed up as she enters a bookstore. "Fuck," I curse, hitting the steering wheel.

"Jameson, you all right?"

Silence.

"Huh? Oh, yeah, sorry. I thought I saw someone I know, but I lost them."

Eduardo chuckles. "Alright then. Are you coming over to drop off the trackers? You finished already?" Hope radiates in his voice.

"Yes, I worked all morning on them, and I have what you need. I'll drop them off and explain what we need to do and how they work."

This seems to make him happy, and I can sense the worry leaving his voice.

"Great, I appreciate this, man. More than you know."

I end the call and pull up to his club, parking in the back.

Eli meets me at the door, patting me down. I am annoyed that I have to go through these measures, but in the world Eduardo lives in, I guess no one, even people you've known for years, can be trusted.

I pass through the hall that leads up to the Heavenly Pearl and wonder if Eve has been by the club recently. Has she been with anyone else? The thought makes me murderous, and I clench and unclench my hands as we walk up to the hall that leads to Eduardo's office.

Eli knocks on the door, and I hear the lock click meaning Eduardo hit the button on his desk to open the door for us. Eli walks in, and I follow, plopping myself into one of the chairs.

I run a hand over my face, and Eduardo stares at me.

"I'll ask you again. You okay, Jameson? Is there something you need to tell me about Emma?"

I see the worry on his face, and I shake my head. "No, I was just thinking about someone I met a while back."

He smiles and runs his hand over his face, rubbing at the scruff. His eyes are alight with amusement. "You met someone?"

I hear the door close and realize Eli left us alone together. I nod, confirming as much but not willing to give anymore details right now. I pat my pockets, pulling out the velvet purse-stringed bag.

"Here. I have what you asked for," handing it to him.

He takes a seat across from me and empties the contents on his desk. He looks up at me. I quickly explain what it is.

"This is the GPS tracker for Emma?"

I nod. "You just need the jewelry. You need to buy something like a pendant to put on a bracelet or necklace." I motion with my hand at the small tracker.

Eduardo's smile is wide as he opens his desk drawer and removes a large blue velvet box. "You mean like this?" He opens the box to reveal a stunning emerald pendant. There is a necklace and bracelet in the box.

"May I?" I ask before I pick it up.

"Of course." Eduardo hands the box over to me, and I pick up the pendant.

"This is perfect, Eduardo."

He smiles. "Yeah, it reminded me of Emma's eyes, and I had to have them."

I hold onto it, and a strange familiarity works its way into my memory of similar eyes that shone through a mask at me, once at the club and once at my home. I touch the green of the pendant and run my hand across the flawless gemstone. I straighten my shoulders. "Let's get this thing installed, and I'll show you what to do."

CHAPTER THIRTEEN

EVIE

"THROUGH GLASS" BY STONE SOUR

I've spent most of my days stalking Cherry after I found out she was harassing my sister and her friend while they were shopping. I saw her in the shop talking to my sister with a snarled expression, like the bunny boiler that she is. That girl is certifiable, and I swear if I didn't need her alive to lead me to Julian, I'd dispose of her properly.

I'm torn between following her to see what she is up to, but then I would have to leave my sister. I immediately call Mateo, but he isn't in the area, and I've lost that god-awful box red-dyed hair of a disaster walking out through the crowded city streets.

"Ugh." I stomp my foot, causing a woman to startle, jumping back and cursing at me under her breath. I see Liv laughing, arm in arm with her best friend as they enter a restaurant to have lunch. I've become an intruder in their life. I am no longer my sister's best friend; I am just a lonely woman looking through the glass and watching what should have been my life, too.

My nights are not spent any better. My mind is consumed with pining over Jameson or watching him from afar. The holidays are approaching, and I've never felt more alone.

At least I have my brother.

Mattie and I have plans of our own. He was invited to spend the holiday with the older gentleman who he plays chess with. I am supposed to meet him today, and I am glad that my brother has found a friend, albeit a seventy-year-old elderly one. Apparently, he is alone for the holidays as well, so it seems like the logical choice, throw in being by the shoreline and we will take it. I am hopeful that this will be our last year in hiding.

Walking along the boardwalk, I see Mateo on the pier overlooking the water. I stop where I am to take in the sight of him. He's tall, over six feet, with a solid build. The guy is not someone I would describe as lean, more so the type that is built for cage fighting. He is ruggedly handsome with his olive complexion and soft, wavy hair that falls into his eyes. His dark brown eyes stare at you with the innocence of a child, but I have also heard Mateo with some of his conquests and innocent is something he definitely is not. I also know he wasn't afforded that luxury, having grown up in our family and being a soldier for our uncle.

At times, something about this appearance is familiar, but it is probably because I have spent more time with him in our hunt for Julian and to keep our sister safe.

Some college-age girls pass by him and attempt to gain his attention, giggling as they pass. I smile at them, wondering if my brother would have had a girlfriend like that. If he had gone to college instead of working for our uncle, he would never be free to choose his path.

He senses me approaching and turns, his eyes soften when he sees me, and I can't help but skip a little as it turns into running towards him. He laughs, shaking his head at my antics.

"You're late." The lines around the corner of his eyes show his increasing age and sun-kissed skin, and he places his hand over his eyes to shield them from the bright Texan rays.

"I was busy," I counter, a pout forming.

He rolls his eyes along with his head and then shoots me a look that screams bullshit. "Does it by any chance have to do with a certain guy named Jameson?"

I stab my pointed fingernail into his solid chest. "None of your business, Mattie."

He leans away from the pier, standing tall as I fight the sunshine reflecting off the water to stare up at him.

"Right, then. Let's go. I want to introduce you to my friend."

I loop my arm in his as we approach their frequent meeting place.

The bell chimes above the door as we enter the cafe, and I am immediately hit by the aroma of rich coffee mixed with the scent of cinnamon. From the entrance, I can see an elderly gentleman placing a cup of coffee on the table by the widow. He beckons us with his hand as he sees us approaching his table. My mouth immediately starts to water. I grab Mattie's arm, and he halts midstep. He looks back at me quizzically.

"Nothing," I state. "I just want to know if you'd like a coffee. I am going to grab one for myself, and I see your friend already has one." I gesture with my hand over to his friend, who is now smiling at us and watching our interactions with amusement, his smile reaching his kind eyes.

"Yeah, thanks. I'll take an iced coffee, nothing in it."

I nod. "Right," I counter, "a black iced coffee to match your soul." I smile cynically, my full lips pulled wide, displaying my straight white teeth.

"Ha. That's a real knee-slapper, sis. Har-har." He smacks his outer thigh for emphasis.

Turning I head to the counter, whipping the ends of my shorter hair across my cheek, not acknowledging his stupid joke. I scan the menu that is displayed across the counter, squinting at the almost illegible scrawled cursive-colored chalk, *until* I see the Mexican latte that makes my mouth water.

I order a kolache to go along with my latte and Mateo's black iced coffee, then move down to hang out by the end of the counter while I wait for my order to be ready. I click on the dating app and notice a message from Jameson. My heart races with anticipation.

Jameson: When can I see you again?

I stare at it, knowing I can't see him again, but I want to. I left my mask there the last time with the full intention of never returning, but I am going to make a liar out of myself, and that man will be my sole reason.

Eve: I'm still trying to figure it out.

I bite my lower lip, thinking about it. I begin to type and then backtrack and stop. Do I lead him on? What if I can't see him ever again, and it makes me a liar? Without second-guessing whether I should see him again, I reply.

Eve: Soon, hopefully. Very soon.

I click out of the app and place the phone in my pocket, my emotions somber. I hate this and the way it makes me feel.

My order is ready, and I see the handsome guy in front of me. He is smiling at me. He seems... I pause, trying to find the right word for him.

Sweet.

I smile and grab my items from him with a thank you, pocketing my kolache for later, and tipping my cup at him. I approach the table where Mateo and his elderly friend sit, setting up their chess game. I hand Mateo his coffee.

"Thanks. Evie, I want you to meet Ramón Martin. Ramón, this is Evie, my sister." He looks between us and smiles.

"Evie, it's very nice to meet you," he says with accented English.

"Likewise, Mr. Martin. My brother seems to enjoy your company. I hope he isn't too much of a chore to entertain. He's quite serious, you know." I place my head on Mateo's shoulder, letting him know that I'm joking.

He pats my hand, resting on the table lovingly. Mateo laughs, pointing at my drink. I look at him as though he's lost his mind.

"Please," Mr. Martin replies, "call me Ramón."

"Okay, Ramón. It's very nice to meet you." I look over to Mateo who is fixated on my cup before returning to my conversation.

The elderly gentleman graces me with a smile.

"What's the matter with you?" Mateo startles me away from my pleasantries. He turns my drink around and I look at the guy's number written in black marker on the side with his name.

I look over to the guy at the counter and he is staring at me, face flushed with embarrassment. I turn back to look at the name.

"Dylan," I say aloud. I shrug and take a drink of my coffee. It's delicious, and the burst of spicy cinnamon chocolate hits my taste buds with a flourish.

I am struck with a sense of nostalgia, reminding me of a time when I was young during the Christmas holidays in Mexico. My abuela would make the best hot chocolate over the stove by melting a thick, dark Mexican bar of chocolate. She'd allow me to stir the tantalizing concoction until it was fully melted, mixing in some milk and a little sugar and a dash of spicy red pepper at the end that always made my mouth water in anticipation.

I remove the lid on my coffee on autopilot, still submerged in my visions, blowing on the top to cool the caramel-colored liquid as I take another drink from my cup.

"Mmm," I hum in appreciation.

Ramón breaks me from my trip down memory lane, and I look at him, realizing he said something. "What was that?" I ask.

He places his chess pieces on the board and lifts his chin toward the guy who gave me his phone number.

"I'd throw away that number away if I were you," he says nonchalantly.

I cross my arms over my chest defensively, look at Mateo, and then back at him. Sitting back, I kick one foot out in a relaxed pose.

"And why is that, Ramón?"

He sits forward as if he has some secret to tell me, and I find myself leaning forward, mimicking his position as if he is one of my friends from high school.

"I saw his wife with their baby in here the other day..." He lets that sink in, and I immediately sit up straight, my nostrils flaring.

"So he's a cheater?"

He places his hands up defensively.

"Hey, I don't know if it is his wife, but it sure seemed like it, especially when she left with the kid waving its little cute chubby hand in the air, saying, 'Say bye to Daddy.'"

Mateo almost chokes on his iced coffee, and I glance at him, daring him to breathe another word.

"Geez, calm down. I wasn't going to call him, but now I'm annoyed that his name and number are on my cup." I point at the offending cup with my hand. I look at the scribbled marker, and a thought comes into my mind of taking his number and giving it to an escort service who...

Mateo has his hand on my arm, stopping me from plotting and scheming the downfall of Dylan, the barista.

"Evie, whatever you are thinking, let it go." His penetrating gaze reminds me so much of my sister's. She would give me a similar look when I wanted to take revenge on someone or get even. I nod once and smile up at him.

"No problem, Mattie. It's already forgotten." I glance over at Ramón.

His look tells me he isn't so sure, but he nods at the chessboard and speaks to Mateo. "Are you ready to lose, buddy?"

After Mattie and Ramón played a few games resulting in Ramón sweeping Mattie best two out of three, we say our goodbyes, and make plans to get together again soon. We are in the car driving to our apartment, which resides between the beach and the city. It was a compromise for both of us because we knew where we wanted to be and where we had to be. Conflicted, we opted for the halfway mark, much like we do with everything in our lives. Breaking the silence engulfing the car, I look toward Mateo, his expression one of contemplation.

"Mattie?"

His eyes crinkle in confusion as I pull him away from wherever his mind is. "Yeah, Eves?"

I fidget with my hands. "I like your friend. He, um, seemed… nice."

His eyes soften. "Well, he seems as lonely as we are, so I thought maybe we could all get together and maybe not be so lonely together."

I nod in understanding.

He takes his eyes away from traffic again, sparing me a quick glance. "You look like you want to ask me something." He poses this as a statement when it's more of a question.

I swallow, done with the motions and vulnerability, deciding to take a chance. "I'd really like to see Jameson."

He shakes his head. "I don't know, Evie. He's friends with Eduardo. The whole point is to keep you hidden, to keep Emma safe."

I attempt to bite my nails in frustration but just end up stabbing my lip. I look down at them and frown—maybe a little too pointed. I flick my hand out, admiring my filing job. "Okay," I almost whisper.

He pulls my hand away from my mouth. "Maybe wait a little while longer, yeah? See if he can be trusted. Maybe feel him out by talking to him first. The holidays are coming, so get to know him and size up his character."

I smile, now having something to look forward to for the first time in a very long time. "I could do that."

He smiles back at me. "Just keep me posted, okay?"

I happily agree because this gives me hope—hope that I could be something more than what I am now, hope that I could be something to someone. So, I grab my phone out of my bag and I send a message—one of many that will get me through the time and the holidays until I can see him again.

CHAPTER FOURTEEN

EVIE

"DEEP WATER" BY STRAWBERRY SWITCHBLADE

Ramón has become a permanent fixture in Mateo's life, and he seems equally smitten with the old man. They have a weird connection that makes me jealous.

We spent the holidays at his house, and I'm delighted that we did. It was clear that he was indeed lonely, and I think we brought him a sense of family interactions that he was missing. For some reason, he no longer sees his son, and I don't really know much about it. It's not really any of my business to pry. What I do know is that he doesn't have any other family besides him. His wife passed away, leaving him to spend his days in the company of a young man and his sister.

In a way, I think we all helped each other have a feeling of the things we miss around the holidays. This won't last forever. When we end this, I am confident that we will have the biggest family get-togethers. But until then, I'll be longing for the times when we can have a moment of peace all to ourselves. If I keep believing this, perhaps I can manifest it. Maybe we will even bring Ramón with us into our family—our found family.

There hasn't been any other interest in Emma these past couple of months. Ever since Eduardo proposed and gave her a massive engagement ring, she has had a couple of people who dated Eduardo make some unsavory comments toward her about his past.

I am concerned with the woman who used to work at Eduardo's club. Cherry threatened Emma when she saw her out at a store when she and Liv were shopping. When I found out, I was livid. Adrian told us that Eduardo admitted he used to screw her at the club, and I swear if he weren't as devoted to Emma as he is now, I would have made sure he suffered for that. It all happened before he reconnected with Emma, but the fact that she is coming at my sister because he is with Emma now is disturbing.

During Emma's and Eduardo's stay in Mexico over the holidays, we were surprised to discover that Philip is still alive and undercover, watching Emma's every move. It would appear that Emma has a few people walking amongst the shadows, watching her and looking for unsuspecting threats.

Tonight will be difficult to navigate without being noticed. They are going to a gala to benefit the hospital where Liv's husband is employed. His parents support the organization, and his mother is the chairperson for the gala. All the proceeds are utilized to provide a selected unit within the organization with state-of-the-art equipment that helps their hospital stand out in the community, making a difference in patient care.

I awoke late in the morning after spending a long night on the phone with Jameson. We have fallen asleep together, and I imagine myself sleeping next to him. I heard his light snores coming from the phone earlier, and I touched my lips and then the phone, wishing it was his mouth I was kissing before getting up from bed.

I haven't seen him since that night when we were physically together, but we have had phone sex. We seem to be having a lot of that, and I long for the days I can have him again. I get to explore things with him that I doubt I could do in person.

I found that I know the sounds he makes before and when he comes. He tells me what he wants, and I feel empowered to give it to him. I let him tell me the things he wants to do to me, and I imagine my hands are his, moving over and inside me. The control that I desperately need is in my hands.

I don't know if he realizes this is like therapy for me. I can only hope that when I am with him again, I can relinquish the control that I require and allow him to take it. To be able to take me and make me his in the physical sense, because I already know that I am his in my mind. We are getting to know one another, and I hate that I give him half-truths, but someday, I can tell him everything. I just hope he sticks around to learn it all, because I know we can have it all if he does.

I'm just stepping out of the shower, towel drying my hair, when I hear Mateo on the phone with someone.

"Yes, Tió. I will." He spares a glance at me with an evil smirk while he is apparently speaking with my uncle. "She is very excited to go to the gala tonight. You know Evie. She loves a good party."

If he hadn't turned his face away from me, I am sure I would have punched him from spreading such vicious lies about me. He knows I hate parties. Also, there is no way that I would find attending a fundraiser to be a good time. "Tió Andrés is very concerned about the gala tonight," Mateo says as he disconnects the call with our tió. The mocking tone is evident in his commentary.

I pick up the coffee pot and pour a mugful, noting the lack of steam rising. I touch the pot and find it's cold.

"Ugh. No coffee?" I hold out the offending pot to Mateo.

He shrugs. "There was some earlier, but someone slept in."

I don't have to guess who that someone is, but it is apparent he is set on talking in riddles this 'late' morning. I walk with the mug to pour it down the drain but stop, thinking better of it. Instead, I just pop a cup into the microwave.

"Are you listening?" Mateo side-eyes me, but I can't be bothered because I haven't had my motherfuckin' coffee yet. I will shank this bitch. Don't even test me.

I raise my hand to halt his words because I literally can't right now. "I need coffee first, Mateo."

My head is hung, and my arms are slumped over, resting on the counter. The microwave chimes, and I grab my coffee from it. I lift the steamy brew up to my mouth to sip the strong cup of black coffee. I pull out one of the two barstools from the kitchen island and plop myself there. I push my shoulders back, waiting for what he has to say.

I crack my neck from side to side and look in his direction. "Okay, what?" When he doesn't speak, I lift my arm to him, rolling my hand around so he can get on with it.

He shakes his head back and forth as if clearing a lousy memory. "I have a bad feeling about tonight."

I continue to sip my coffee, staring at him. "What do you mean?" My eyebrows pull in, unsure of what to make of this statement.

He begins to pace around, biting his fingernails. It's a nervous tic he has that makes me cringe at the irritating sound grating on my every nerve. His comment makes me feel uneasy. His eyes soften when they meet mine.

"We haven't heard from Cherry, and things have been quiet. I don't want to lose my sister before I have had the chance to meet and get to know her." He drops his head and braces himself on the island where he stands next to me. I soothingly run my hand on his back.

"Mattie..." Emotion clogs my throat and I clear it away. "I genuinely believe that we will all be together again."

He raises his head, meeting my eyes once again. When he looks at me, the sadness there is heartbreaking. "I just want my family, Evie."

My heart breaks for the boy who didn't have one. I at least knew what it was like to have a family and be brought up with loving parents, but he didn't.

"You'll have us always, Mattie, and once Emma and I are reunited, we will always be *your* family."

He turns around and pulls me into a hug. I gulp down the emotions threatening to leak from my eyes, and I hold my brother, determined more than ever to reunite us and get our revenge against the monster that took it from us.

The event is held in Galveston along the seawall, and the historic-looking hotel is breathtaking. The decorations are nothing short of elaborate. I wish we could arrive and valet park, but that would draw too much attention to us, so we park a short distance away and walk in through the outside area where a small group of people are congregated.

It gives us access to anyone who is pulling up as well.

I am sipping on my tonic and lime when I see Eduardo stepping out of his SUV, holding his hand out for Emma to be assisted out of the back seat. He holds her arm lovingly, she looks at him as if he has hung the moon and stars just for her. I almost audibly sigh because it's just so fucking cute, and then I realize where I am.

"Okay," Mateo explains the plan. "So we know they are here, so let's just stay out of their line of sight. If they see me, it doesn't really matter, but *you* need to remain hidden, and when I tell you, make sure to keep your head down."

I pick at my hair and feel the weird texture assaulting my fingers. "Do you really think they will notice me with my short hair in this wig?"

He stops to take a look at me. "No, it looks good on you though. I was more concerned about your eyes, but with the contacts in, it's not too much of a problem now."

We walk past another couple, and they smile at us, clearly thinking we are together.

"I look like shit."

He takes my arm, guiding me around another couple of people stopped in conversation regarding the hospital.

"You do not. You look beautiful as always." As he says this, a tall woman in a red dress with long blonde hair makes eye contact with him, licking her lips. He winks at her, and I snort.

"Great, now that's not awkward as fuck."

He huffs. "Why do you say that?"

I throw my hand out as we reach the other side of the bar, hidden away from the larger crowds gathered inside. "It looks like my date is cheating on me."

He laughs. "You're my sister."

"That's not the point!"

He shakes his head. "I don't get it."

"Of course, you don't. The point is that she has no respect for me. She doesn't know that I am your sister."

He turns to face me. "I swear you always try to pick a fight with me."

"I do not," I counter, pouting at him for calling me out. "Forget it, let's focus here, Mattie."

He stares a minute longer at me and then looks over my head at something that caught his eye. I know the moment he spots Emma and Eduardo because he stiffens.

"Let's move to our seats. I think the speaker is walking up to the stage, and I see people returning to their tables." He leads me to the table we are assigned to in the back corner.

Thank goodness. I notice Liv, who is noticeably pregnant now, and Dax walking over to my sister. Dax walks beside Liv with a hand around her lower waist, guiding her possessively to their table. Emma shoots up from her seat, embracing Liv.

The speaker announces herself as Isabella, and everyone turns their attention to her. I keep an eye on Emma and her friend. Something is going on over there, and I see Liv put the phone up to her ear. She draws the attention of a few others as she does the same thing a few minutes later, except this time, she leaves the table, heading toward the bathroom.

Mateo and I excuse ourselves, keeping my head down as Mateo instructed as I walk out in the same direction Liv went.

Emma excuses herself and makes her way into the bathroom, as we wait nearby to see where she goes next. Moments later she walks out of the bathroom, when a man dressed in a suit bumps into her. His hands raise to apologize, then they drop into a defensive stance. Her face whitens, and then she runs off, chasing Liv out the door.

The man looks as if he is going to follow her but decides not to at the last minute. I want to see who he is. I want to see who it is that has scared her this way.

We approach him. As he turns around, I am so caught off guard that I almost stumble back as Mateo holds onto me.

"Mateo..." I stop, realizing my error as his razor-sharp eyes look at me in recognition and then at my brother.

CHAPTER FIFTEEN

EVIE

"WRITTEN IN BLOOD" BY SHE WANTS REVENGE

I swear all the air is sucked out of my lungs. I gasp, and I must look like a flopping fish out of the water, an angler who holds me bound by an invisible line suspended mid-air as he stares at me with an unadulterated hunger.

He steps closer, and I instinctively take a step back, self-preservation mode kicking in. He smirks, clearly enjoying the recoil his mere presence brings, much like his sons'.

This must be what it feels like when a predator holds his prey, and you are locked in their sights with nowhere to flee.

Mateo grabs my arm and stops my retreat. He raises his chin to the man with similar eyes. I never knew it before, but that is what I always found familiar when I'd stare at my brother. The sudden realization makes me want to vomit.

I see the evil glint in his eye, almost giddy at seeing my brother. He knows this is something big, and I wish we never found out this way, but there is no denying it. If I didn't know him better, I'd assume he was almost... proud.

"Mateo," he drawls, and I hate how he says it.

Mattie squares his shoulders, attempting a stand-off with this man, and I visibly stiffen.

"Yes, and who are you?" my brother asks.

But I don't want him to know the truth. I already know it, and I don't like it. Does Mateo not see it? I want to say to him that we should run. We should run far away from here, take my sister, and move back to Mexico, but then this would all be for nothing.

The man smiles sinisterly at him and puffs his chest out. "Well, that really is the question, but you should always be weary of the questions you ask, Mateo."

Mateo snorts, his arms crossed over his chest in a defensive stance. "Oh, really? And why is that?"

I grab his arm, pulling it down, and that makes the man's face light up with amusement. He spares me a glance before returning his focus to who he is really interested in now.

"You might not like the answer," he states with a touch of humor that seems to annoy Mateo.

"Oh, is that right?" my brother growls.

I watch this volleying of responses. A long moment lingers between us, and when I don't think he will answer, I contemplate walking away and leaving, but I can't. I find myself stuck in this spot, unable to move. I wonder if I will have to be physically dragged from here. I always considered myself to be strong, but his revelation has ungrounded me. It has made me question everything that my family ever told me. It has made me aware of the fact that maybe I didn't really know my parents at all, especially my mom. She has a story that I will never get to hear from her. So many twisted lies and secrets that just keep coming to light, and it's blinding.

Finally, after the tense moment, he speaks, confirming all my thoughts that Mateo is now going to be living a nightmare. "Let me introduce myself. My name is Mr. Martinez, Julian's father."

I see Mateo clench his fists and unclench them. His jaw is set so hard that I think I can hear his teeth grinding. But what he says next is the most unsettling.

"*Your* father."

I gasp, and Mr. Martinez looks at me quickly before his gaze returns back to Mateo. "I'm glad to meet you finally, son."

I see the shock register on Mateo's face, and then disgust oozes from every pore. He stands back, full of contempt. "I'll never be your son."

He grabs my hand, but we hear a commotion from outside before Mr. Martinez can make a rebuttal. I see Eduardo running out of the door, Eli and Dax crouched down, and Liv slumped to the floor, crying hysterically. Dax picks her up bridal style and carries her out. Her head is pulled into his chest, and Eli has his arm around Emma. As they walk out the side, I see Eduardo pulling up with the SUV, and they all climb into it and take off.

Mateo and I are close-behind as we get into our cars and pull away from the venue.

We pull into the emergency department entrance to see everyone in the SUV running in through their front door. The words 'trauma bay' are illuminated above that entrance where there are several ambulances parked outside. I don't know what caused everyone to come here so quickly, but I can guess it has something to do with Liv's friends, since she was the one crouched down, sobbing inconsolably against the wall.

We sit there after they enter the emergency department and wait to see what happens next. The silence continues until I can't take it anymore. "Are we going to talk about the big news we were just blasted with, Mateo?"

I look away and stare out the window. I can hear Mattie's breathing pick up. I know that he is still processing the clusterfuck that is the news of hearing that Julian's father is his father and, worse, that the person who had been hurting his sister was, in fact, his half-brother, Julian. If I am frank, I also have a hard time with this.

"I can't," he finally says. He shakes his head, and I understand. It is all too much, but what I can do is offer my brother the support he needs.

We sit there in silence for a couple more hours until I see my sister wrapped up in Eduardo's arms and Emma's pregnant friend, Liv, being held up by Dax. She is crying hysterically, and I can only assume it is not good news. They pull out of the parking lot and follow suit, returning to our place.

A week passes, and we find ourselves at my least favorite place. There is peace you should have knowing that your loved ones are no longer suffering and their souls are laid to rest, but that isn't always the case. Some of the souls were taken before their time, driven from their bodies by someone or something that took their life. They took them from their families, children, and left them to figure out things independently. To live a life without them. The last time I was here was when my parents died.

The last time I was here was to attend my own funeral. I got to experience what a person would feel like if they could hear everything that was said, and experience all the sadness of the life they left behind.

I listened to my sister crying, and I wasn't able to console her. Julian had her wrapped around him forcefully. He fully supported her financially, but without her consent in anything, and he appeared to everyone as the ever-doting boyfriend.

Not everything is as it appears.

Loud thunder cracks across the sky, pulling me from my morbid thoughts. It is fitting that a storm should be approaching. It feels like an omen of what's to come. It's as if the angels are weeping with us. I see my sister and all she has had to go through. She is so supportive of her friend, but she truly had no one there to support her when we were laid to rest? Julian may have been there, but that was all for show. That was before Eduardo came into the picture, and before she became best friends with Liv. But our cousin got her out and away from Julian, and she found her way back to Eduardo who has been keeping her safe ever since.

Jameson is there, too. He is sitting silently near Eduardo and Dax. He is alone and stares out across the cemetery. I can't take my eyes off him; he looks so beautiful—and mine.

I want to go to him and let him know that I am here. I want to have him support me as Eduardo holds onto Emma, like she is something so precious to him. I close my eyes and imagine that Jameson is holding me. His strong arms envelop me in a solid embrace. I tilt my head back a bit. I can almost smell his musky scent of steamy nights mixed in with my earthy scent of questionable intentions, making the perfect scent for just us.

I decide to send him a text to let him know that I miss him, but his reply is always the same.

Jameson: When can I see you again?

I want to go to him, but I can't. I decide that after I return, I won't let myself be away from him any longer.

Evie: I have to go away for a while, but when I get back, I would like to see you.

It feels good to tell him this, but I just hope he can wait.

Jameson: How long will you be gone?

I bite my lip, not looking at the phone, trying to determine how long we will be away.

Evie: I'm still trying to figure it out. It will take a couple of months at the most. I have some family business I need to tend to.

I am waiting for his reply, but I don't get one. I look over at him, see him reading the text, and then placing the phone in his pocket. I slump my shoulders in defeat. Does this mean he isn't going to wait for me? Are we over before we have begun? I panic, not even thinking before I send off the message.

Evie: Please wait for me...

That's all I can say, and I hope I'm not too late. I curse myself, and this makes Mateo look at me with concern. I shake my head, not wanting to talk about it. It will just make me sadder than I already feel. Besides, Mateo has enough going on in his mind to worry about something that should be a priority at this point. Literally, everything else is more important than this, except it isn't to me. It's just my happiness, but that is something I haven't been allowed to indulge in.

The priest talks about the Kingdom of God in a long-winded speech about His son returning to be united with Him. I look around at all the people who made the trip for this young man whose life was taken too soon.

As the ceremony ends, everyone is walking to their cars. I have already been sitting in ours as Emma is in the SUV watching from the window at her friend suffering alone by the gravesite, refusing to leave.

She stands there holding her single red rose and staring down into the grave. It's as if she doesn't want to throw her flower in the grave because that will be it—the final goodbye. She releases it, and I can't help the gasp that leaves my lips. I almost didn't expect her to do it. I almost wish she would have walked away with it, but what's the point? Acceptance is all there really is to move forward now. She looks up at the sky as if she is cursing at her God.

Tears fall down my cheeks, witnessing such a private moment. I swallow the sobs that threaten to escape. I wipe my tears from my cheeks and look at my brother. I grab his hand for support.

"Come on, Mattie. Let's go home."

We have a lot to discuss when we get home—the only home that we have to go to now. Just when I think I can't feel any worse, I feel my phone vibrate.

Jameson: I'll try for you.

I take a deep breath, and I feel like I am losing him. I feel him pull away; if I didn't know that, I could see it. I watch him answering his texts just as we are pulling away to head to the airport. He hesitates, looks away, and then pockets his phone. He rubs his temples as if I make his head hurt. He is tired of waiting on me, and why should he? He is an attractive man. I know that, but I can't help but want to selfishly keep him, and make him mine. I wish to possess his mind, body, and soul. I have never felt this connection with anyone. I also wish I could relay all my thoughts and the intensity of my feelings for him without scaring him away.

Taking our seats on the airplane, the flight attendant comes around to make sure our items are stowed away correctly. I rest my head against the seat and think about everything that happened earlier today and hope that I am not away for too long. I take out my phone and send one last text to him.

Evie: Please.

I set my phone down, the flight attendant giving me a dirty look as I was told repeatedly to turn off our electronic devices. I tuck my bag under the seat, but keep my phone out. I'm getting ready to turn it off when I see a message pop up.

Jameson: I'll wait for you.

That's all it says, and that's enough to put a smile on my face and ease some of my tension for now.

CHAPTER SIXTEEN

EVIE

"RUNNING UP THAT HILL" BY KATE BUSH

The plane touches down in Mexico, and I feel the anxiety creeping in. Mateo and I didn't speak much during the flight. The night that we found out about Mr. Martinez being Mateo's father, I knew that a long-overdue visit to Mexico was needed to finally find out what the actual fuck was going on. We have so many questions that need answering, and I want to be able to see our uncle's face when he tells us the truth.

"How many more lies are they keeping from us?" I mumble under my breath. It's not a question because I know that there is definitely more to come to light.

Mateo glances over at me, but doesn't respond. He runs his finger over his lip, probably wondering the same thing. I look out the window as the plane is taxing into the gate.

This is *our* family, and there should not be any secrets between us if we are to succeed in bringing the Martinez family down. I know every family harbors some secrets, but this is beyond normal. This is the mother of all secrets, so to speak, and I can't believe my own mother kept this from us and that, worse, no one told us anything about it after her passing. Wasn't it significant enough to warrant a discussion? I want to find out why my brother was sent away from us and we never knew anything about him.

We grab our luggage from the carousel and walk side by side out of the baggage claim area. As soon as we get outside, I am assaulted with the heat that only comes from a desert-like climate. Spring is hot in Texas and is similar to south of the border, but what a heat wave it is. The heat creates a visible mirage glaring off the pavement in wavy lines. I place my hand over my brow to reduce some of the glare when I see Adrian pull up.

"Eek!" I drop my luggage handle and run over to hug him. I know that Mateo and I are close, and it stings something fierce to know that they are cousins, too. The unfair balance of family dynamics is unsettling and puts a damper on my reunion.

He runs around to the side of the truck, and I can't help but jump into his embrace, messenger bag and all.

"Hey, cousin. How are you?" I drop down from my koala-like hug and fling my messenger bag over his shoulder before he can reply. I jump into the front seat of his truck before Mateo can get in there.

"Shotgun!" I ring out as loudly as I can. I hear Adrian greet Mateo while simultaneously throwing our luggage and my messenger bag in the back.

"I see she is just as pleasant as ever," he remarks, and Mateo snorts.

"Oh, you have no idea. Remember, I live with her."

Adrian laughs. "Right, my condolences."

They both get into the truck, glancing my way.

"Hey, I can hear you guys. You know that right?"

"Um, Evie, we were not saying anything you didn't already know, and we weren't exactly trying to keep that from you." Adrian chuckles, placing the truck into drive.

No, but what else are you keeping from me, cousin?

I roll down the window as we take off toward our uncle's house, the only consistent home I've ever had and filled with many good memories. I stare out the window, wondering at the possibilities.

We are barely settled in at the house and are about to have lunch when our conversation is interrupted by a phone call from Eduardo. My uncle heads to his office, and Mateo, Adrian, and I all run toward him, following like children to eavesdrop when he takes the call.

My uncle ushers us in, as he shuts the door when I slip in last, taking my seat. The emotions on my face quickly decline as my mind turns into a downward spiral of what-ifs. Mateo tucks me into his embrace, standing by my side as always while we wait to hear what Eduardo has to say. He places the call on the speaker and places his finger to his mouth, a gesture letting us know to be quiet.

"Eduardo. To what do I owe the pleasure of this phone call?"

The urgency in Eduardo's voice makes me want to run back to Houston to see if my sister is okay for myself. Mateo squeezes my arm, trying to comfort me.

"I just spoke to Emma, and she informed me that Mr. Martinez, Julian's father, was at the gala last week, and he cornered her outside of the bathroom. She just told me after a week. A whole fucking week, Andrés!"

He sounds upset. My shoulders relax as Mateo and I saw this account firsthand. I know he didn't have time to tell her anything, but he does know where she is now. Unfortunately, that's the least of our concerns at the moment. After our brief, but informative visit with Mr. Martinez, we now see much more is going on, which is more unsettling than today's news. After all, that is why we are here visiting our uncle.

Uncle Andrés knows this too, and judging by his expression, there's more. They discuss strategy, and he lets Eduardo know that he is coming up with a plan but has an emergency he needs to take care of at the moment. They disconnect the call and Tió points to the chairs that he would like for us to take a seat at. I'm already sitting, but before Adrian joins us, he decides we might need a different approach.

Adrian walks over to his dad's cabinet and pulls out a bottle of scotch. He grabs four glasses, pours some Buchanan's into each glass, giving one to each of us. I, for one, don't waste a minute before I throw back the entire contents in one go, smacking my lips in the process. Adrian wrinkles his nose as he looks at me like I am a disgrace to the family.

"Pfft, please." He wouldn't be incorrect, but there's a lot of 'disgrace' going on in this family. I place my glass on the table before smacking my lips at the flavors assaulting my taste buds. My uncle looks at me with a slight quirk on his lip. "Something you wanted to say, Uncle?"

He steeples his hands, observing us, and Mateo's knees bounce in anticipation of what he will say. I look him up and down. Maybe he should have drank the scotch in one go also. Bro looks like he can use about one or twelve.

I frown, looking his way, but he doesn't notice. He doesn't notice anything except the person sitting at that desk about to make his worst nightmare come true. He is focused on anything that may leave our uncle's mouth. I turn back to him, and then he confirms what we feared.

"Mr. Martinez is your father."

Mateo blinks a few times before he drops his head down, and I move my chair over to offer my brother some emotional support. To be told that that monster is your father is the worst news that anyone can get.

Tió continues, "Julian is your half-brother."

And I think I lied to myself because it definitely did get worse. Mattie shakes his head in disbelief, but he knows it's true. He just doesn't want to admit it, and I second that.

"How?" he says. "When?" He shakes his head in disbelief, but he knows it's true. He just doesn't want to admit it.

"Your mother dated Julian's father during her first year of college. She was on her own, like father and son, he had a similar infatuation with your mom as Julian did with Emma. She found out she was pregnant with you and came home one weekend to speak with us about it. She explained that she had been sexually active with Mr. Martinez in a consensual way, but when she told him she was leaving college to return home, he wanted her to take time off and have her stay there with him. He was very insistent, and she was wary of his intentions. She swears he must have tampered with the condom, but before she could end the relationship, she found out she was pregnant with you. She was in her first trimester, and we discussed various options."

Mateo visibly tenses with this, and I know immediately what he is referring to by this. I hold onto Mattie's hand out of instinct, and he leans into me, unsure if he wants to hear anything further. Tió holds his hand up to let him continue with what he is saying.

"I want to be clear. She always wanted to keep you, and anything else than not having you wasn't an option for her, but she also knew that if she told him about you that he wouldn't let her leave and his controlling behavior would just get worse. He would hold you over her forever, so she left the beach of South Padre, which she loved so much, and lived here with us."

"I did believe her when she told us that Mr. Martinez had tampered with the contraception. This wasn't what she had planned. Our parents were pissed, but they supported her decisions, when she came back home to have

Mateo. She also discovered that her best friend and dorm mate was now sleeping with Mateo's biological father, so she felt he would soon forget about her."

"But he didn't forget about her, did he?" Mateo mutters under his breath.

"Our father thought it was best for her to go to another college farther away, and they decided to raise Mateo along with my wife and me."

"So, why didn't she give me up for adoption?" I look over at my brother and selfishly thank my mother for keeping him close. He saved me, too, so there's that. If it wasn't for him, who knows what would have happened to me, but I do know. He would have broken me, and then I'd be dead, too—like my parents.

"She couldn't possibly let him get to you, and I think she wanted to keep you close because she couldn't let go. Anyway, later, she received a letter forwarded from the PO Box we had on file at the school containing a wedding invitation from her ex-boyfriend and ex-best friend. We thought that was the end of it, and for a long time, it was.

"When your mom went to this new college, she met a man there and fell in love with him—your father, Evie. She wanted to come back and be closer to you, but we all decided that you could never know about her, Mateo, and that she was your mother. She begged and pleaded with us, but we were insistent and wouldn't hear of it. You were safer that way. We all were."

He takes a big gulp of his drink before placing it down. "She eventually moved back to the town she loved so much after she had you girls, which was still close to us. She wanted her kids to be born in the US, and her husband was a US citizen. They had you girls and came to visit frequently, but then Eduardo and Emma became close."

He left that to simmer for a bit. "He seemed almost obsessed with her, and he came from another mafia family. Your mom didn't want that life for Emma."

I notice Mateo visibly stiffening in his chair. Anger radiates off him, and I can understand that. "But she didn't care about that life for me?" He slams his fist on our uncle's desk.

"Let me be clear. We discovered Mr. Martinez wanted to trap your mother because of her family ties. He realized she was the daughter of a major mafia player in the Gulf Coast area, and he wanted to tie himself to the family through an heir. That was why he could never know about you."

I turn to look at Mateo and my uncle. I understand his reaction. He has a lot of anger, and things are undoubtedly unfair. He never had the chance to meet his mom and have the family he deserved. In fact, when we were there in Mexico with our mother, Mateo wasn't. He was sent off to boarding school, and now we know why.

"So why was I sent off?" he spews, but I already know. "Was it because they didn't want me around when her new family was here?" The anger is palpable, and I recoil at the viciousness his words yield.

My uncle is quick to reply. "No, it's more than that, Sobrino." His eyes soften, and this is the first time he has referred to Mateo as his nephew.

I almost choke out a sob and try to rein it in, looking away from my brother. His expression would gut me. I see from my peripheral vision as Mateo's head drops, and I know that he realizes as much as I do that there is something broken in my uncle's voice that is more like regret and sadness.

"I don't remember her being here," Mateo admits. His voice cracks, and I almost want to cry for the little boy that wasn't with his real family. "I remember you and Adrian, but I don't know them." He looks over at me, and sadness stretches between us. I glance up to meet his eyes—a bridge of tears that brings us closer to understanding the truth of what happened all those years ago.

"We left and went on trips. You always loved the beach." He smiles, remembering all of it as his memories wash over him in nostalgic waves. He pauses. "As the girls got bigger and my wife passed, I couldn't handle it anymore. Grandpops passed away, and my mother had suffered from dementia for years and was in an assisted living facility with round-the-clock care. Her memories were stolen from her, and she didn't even know who we were."

Adrian stands up and pours us all another glass of scotch. Tió empties his glass's remaining contents and holds it out to his son for a refill.

"I decided to send you off to school so that you could have a better education. Then, when your mother cut off ties with us, we brought you back and made you part of the organization—a soldier—in case we needed you to take a stand.

"Mr. Martinez might have suspected you could be alive, but he never saw any indication that the rumors were true, until he recently had everything confirmed with his own eyes."

I look at my brother in panic, and he stares back at me, the same emotions flaring to life.

"Emma was falling down the same path with Eduardo, and I think your mom overreacted and never returned to Mexico. Eduardo's family is heavily involved in the mafia, and she wanted a different life for her kids."

"Well, that worked out well, clearly." I point around us. "You know what they say about the 'best-laid plan' and all."

"It might have been. Except Eduardo was always in love with Emma. That time the kid returned the following year, and he left heartbroken. A shell of himself. I had to tell him to respect your mother's wishes. But who knew that history would repeat itself and Julian would get his claws into Emma." He pauses, looking around at us.

"This is so fucked up." I stand up and walk around the office. Mateo is still sitting there, until he finally speaks.

"Does Julian really need Emma now that I am alive and have a real connection to him and this family? The bond that ties us all?"

Uncle Andrés finishes the rest of his drink and stands. "Now that, my nephew, is the real question, and more importantly, what happens now?"

CHAPTER SEVENTEEN

JAMESON

"JUST PRETEND" BY BAD OMENS

As promised, Evie has kept in touch, and when she returns back from her family business she had to attend to, we will finally make plans to meet up.

There isn't a day that has passed that we haven't chatted since she asked me to wait for her and I said I would. Sometimes, I send a quick text about what I think about getting for lunch. Sometimes, she texts me with a food recommendation about what I *should* get for lunch. I like learning about all of her interests. I long for the day that we will get to meet for lunch, and we can order together.

Theo and Eric think I am nuts waiting for a girl for months without physically touching her. I think back to the times that I did and our connection with each other. You can't fake that type of chemistry; the physical attraction is off the charts. If I had to wait an eternity for this girl, I would. Nothing has felt more right.

Today, she sent something that surprised me. She snapped a picture of two people holding hands. I don't know who they were because the image was not meant to show their faces but what they represent. It displays their backs, as if she discreetly took a private moment from them from behind and sent it over to me. The text under the caption read: *'I can't wait until this is us.'*

I stop and look at it, wondering what she is implying. Is it the couple? Us being a couple out in the open for everyone to witness. Is it me holding her hand casually? Or is it something deeper? Whatever her reasons, I will make sure that it becomes a reality. I want to be the person who helps her achieve all her dreams and be the partner she trusts completely. I think we both need that more than anything.

I know the girl has her secrets, and that they had to be the reason why she sought control over everything, especially in the bedroom, which I didn't mind too much. Despite that, I am bewildered as to why this can't be us now.

For a brief moment, I wonder if maybe she is secretly married to someone else or in a relationship, stringing me along, but there is nothing that makes me question this chemistry between us.

When I looked into her eyes that she hid behind that mask, as she rode me from above, my hands held back with a tie; I almost felt like I had seen her before. It was powerful, and it was raw. The emotions she carefully hid behind her mask showed me a person who wanted to be held. To be cared for. And most of all, to be free of fear so that we could live out the rest of our lives without this invisible weight she carries.

How we would get to that point, since she wouldn't let me even touch her, was beyond me, but that night at my house, something changed.

She left her mask, and I thought that that was the last time I would see her again, but she clarified her meaning by saying that she would never hide from me again. That next time it would be without any mask, inside and out.

I find it ironic that she has been gone all this time, and I just have to believe her when she said that it was for work and family business. Besides, tonight I won't have to wonder anymore because I feel that after we see each other with no sneaking around or wearing masks at clubs, we can finally move on to having a real relationship.

She's told me different things about herself without fully divulging too much. It's only a sliver of what I want, and I'm greedy enough to devour it all. Whatever she is, I want to know it.

She wants me to know her real self, no more pretenses or masks to hide behind.

Speaking of masks and covering up faces with costumes, there is a Ghost concert that Eduardo is taking Emma to tonight, and in case he needs me for anything, which I doubt, I plan to be somewhere nearby to get to them.

Emma is obsessed with this band, their lore, and the comradery of their fan base. Thankfully Emma wore and loved the jewelry with the GPS tracker, and SOS button I had made for Eduardo. She wears it religiously, making him and herself feel more secure, knowing he can get to her location should anything happen. Philip and Eli will also be there tonight, so I am confident they have everything planned to optimize Emma's safety.

Eve and I plan to meet for dinner and drinks. As I arrive at the restaurant and take a seat at one of the high-top tables by the bar. I have a clear view of the entrance and can see anyone approaching from the giant glass windows that span the entirety of the front of the restaurant.

The server takes my drink order, and places a glass of water in Eve's empty seat. After fifteen minutes, I notice a woman with blonde hair and wearing boots approaching through the doors. I sit up a little straighter in my chair, excited to finally get to see Eve up close after months of torture and only phone sex to occupy my nights. She follows behind a hostess, and when I see her face, I immediately deflate, looking at her brown eyes and round face. Eve has more of a heart-shaped face, and her green eyes are unmistakable.

After another fifteen minutes pass by, I realize she isn't coming. I flag down the server for the check because I know when I've been stood up and I don't want to embarrass myself anymore by waiting another minute. I pay the bill and feel my phone ding with a text notification, but before I can look at it, my phone begins to ring.

I look at the name and answer the phone call from Eli. "Hey, what's up?" He sounds anxious on the other end, and I hear footsteps like he is running, and a door slam.

"Jameson, they've taken Emma. Eduardo is following her on the GPS tracker."

I start running to my car.

"Where is she? I'll meet Eduardo. Wait, I'm calling him now." I disconnect the call and ring Eduardo. "What's going on?" I ask directly into the line, needing to know what is happening.

"Jameson," Eduardo answers out of breath, "where are you? Someone has Emma, I just know it."

I had pulled up the app Eduardo insisted I have on my phone in case something like this happened—a double safety feature should this actually happen and Emma was taken. I look at the address. "I am at the restaurant down the street. I'm leaving now. I'm on my way." I thought he was being overprotective and utterly ridiculous when he insisted I have it just in case, and now I realize that he was so right about all of this.

He responds quickly. "I see her in this warehouse not far from here. Do you see her, too?"

The star-shaped icon on screen continues to move. Just when I think it couldn't get worse, we all get the SOS alert from the location where Emma has now stopped moving on the map.

Eduardo verbalizes my concerns. "Oh, shit. Emma is in trouble."

I just hope we are not too late. I speed to the location where the SOS came from.

Arriving at the warehouse where the tracking icon had stopped and hasn't moved since, we scan the area. Nothing looks out of the ordinary and the warehouse is dark. As I run across the street to regroup with Eduardo and Eli, Eduardo has a few of his men around the perimeter that are ready to intervene if necessary.

As Eli, Eduardo, and I go to enter the building, trying to be as discreet as possible. Eduardo pulls his gun, as does Eli, they give me one should the situation arise and I need it. It's better to be safe than sorry.

The door is open as we step into the almost pitch black room. However, I catch sight of golden hair and see the moment Eduardo recognizes his whole world is tied to a supporting column in the middle of the room.

A light shines, and I see Cherry; her face is messed up. Eduardo is standing here, assessing Emma for injuries, but there don't appear to be any. However, Cherry's eyes are bruised over, and it seems her nose may be broken. From the looks that Cherry is giving Emma, I believe that Emma acted in self-defense, and I have never been more glad to see her okay than at this moment.

Emma's eyes look over to us and then lock on Eduardo's.

Julian steps in from the corner with his gun pointed at us. "Drop your weapons and kick them forward."

We all lower our guns and drop them, doing as he says. Just as Cherry puts a knife to Emma's neck, and I place my arm out to stop Eduardo from charging over there to rip that bitch a new one, but now between that and

Julian having our firearms, there is not much we can do.

Julian steps in front of Emma, blocking his view. "Don't even look at her. She's mine and for my eyes only. You remember that."

Eduardo clenches his jaw, and I swear I hear his molars crack. The murderous look in his eyes would have lesser men recoiling.

I notice Cherry's head snapping up and staring at Julian in disbelief. "What do you mean she's yours?" she spits spitefully. The feral, unhinged look in her eyes is scary even for us to witness, and I see Emma cringe inwardly. Cherry snaps her sights on Emma. She is defenseless as Cherry lunges for her.

She screams out, "I'll fucking kill that bitch! She can't have you, either! I did everything for you, Julian!" She goes to attack Emma, and I see Emma brace for it, but Julian intercepts her and pushes Cherry onto the floor.

"No one else hurts Emma. She is only mine to hurt." The spit flies from his mouth, and he is indeed the monster Emma thought he was.

Cherry lies on the floor and attempts to get up. We watch, frozen in our spot. Julian walks over to her, and instead of helping her up, he points his gun at her.

"I can see you are going to be a problem. I was hoping we could have some fun together, but I don't think it will work out anymore, Cherry." With that, he lifts his gun and shoots her twice in the chest.

She lands backward as red appears on the ground, pouring from her chest wounds, making the red of her shirt even darker. She places a hand on her chest as blood comes out of her mouth in a cough that sprays blood all over the floor. Julian lifts his gun once more and shoots her in the head. Three bullets, and Cherry is gone.

Emma stares at her dead body. Cherry's eyes are fixed, locked on something she no longer sees. I know that she is gone. Emma shoots her gaze to Julian, who has already lost interest in Cherry—if she ever held any interest to that man.

He walks over to Emma, and Eduardo is trying so hard to restrain himself from lunging forward. Julian stands by her side. "I think this has gone on long enough, Emma, don't you? Why don't you tell Eduardo who you really love?" He looks over at Emma expectantly. Eduardo attempts to lunge forward, and Julian watches as I hold him back.

He lifts his gun at Emma. "I wouldn't do that if I were you, Eduardo." He tsks. "If you claim to love her as much as you say, it would be in your best interest not to move any closer." He moves closer to us and kicks our weapons out of the way.

I look over at Eduardo and Eli. We all have the same pained expression of anger and sadness in our eyes.

"Say it, Emma!" he screams at her, and she looks him in the eyes, not backing down.

"I'll never say that to you, Julian," she says low enough, but we all hear it. It has its desired cruising effects on Julian.

His eyes narrow, and then he lifts his gun to her. Emma locks her eyes with Eduardo and mouths, *'I love you always.'*

PART II

THE PRESENT

CHAPTER EIGHTEEN

EVIE

"TEAR YOU APART" BY SHE WANTS REVENGE

We stand there in shared silence trying to process the events that have happened from our point of view and lives that led up to this moment. Jameson pulls me back to hold me, letting me know he is here for me and not going anywhere. We line the shots up again, and I make another toast.

"To all the twisted lies coming to light." I lock eyes with Emma and she nods.

"I'll drink to that." She lifts her drink up and taps the table like I've seen her do so many times with her friends.

I frown, recalling this as Emma commits such a common action with no thought to it, as she tosses her shot back. We down the shots and throw our discarded limes on the plate before us. Jameson intertwines my fingers with his, sensing my downward spiraling mood. He silently encourages me with this action, but patiently waits for me to tell them the truth.

I look at our entwined hands and it gives me strength to get it out there. To place my past before us. To verbalize the words that I want to suppress more than anything because of all the feelings that arise from the torment of reliving it through my vivid memories of past events.

And I do—the long, sordid tale of those past events and leading up to all that transpired just yesterday. I speak of what happened while we were disposing of the bodies. The empty vessels. The people who caused us so much pain, but we know that it doesn't end there. We know what's to come, just not when. That is an unspoken truth that lingers in the air like the calm before the storm.

Hours later, he is still holding my hand. I stop and look around at everyone, and I suddenly feel so sleepy. It's as if all my energy has been zapped from my body. I know that I am, in fact, more emotionally drained than physically. The thought of just telling everyone the entirety of our sordid tale has taken so much out of me, and to be honest, it has the same effect on Evie and Mateo as I stare at their resolute expressions.

Eduardo is the first to break the silence. He claps his hands together. "Okay, I think that we should all get a good night's sleep and then reconvene in the morning. It has been a long couple of days." He brings Emma in and kisses the top of her head.

We look around at each other to process the conversation and decide to table it for another day. I look at Mateo, and he shakes his head, reading my thoughts of silently imploring him to take us back to the apartment. "Not a chance in hell, Evie. I am staying here tonight."

Eduardo grabs Emma's hand. "You are all welcome to stay. In fact, I insist. There is room for everyone." Emma kisses Eduardo's hand before releasing it.

"Babe, will you help me get everyone settled into a room?" He looks at her lovingly.

"Of course, baby. Do you need me to grab you any extra sheets from the linen cabinet?"

She nods. "Yes, and a fitted sheet for the sofa, too."

Mateo starts to walk toward it, already choosing his place to retire for the night. "I'll take the sofa, Emma." He drops his bag near it, and Eduardo comes back from down the hall, carrying linen for the bedding. Mateo takes the items and makes himself comfortable on the sofa.

"Eli and Philip can take the game room and the couches there," she indicates with a nod of her head, turning toward the hall, then she turns to speak to Gus.

He lifts his hands. "I'm going home. I have somewhere to be."

Eduardo laughs. "You mean someone to do?"

Gus shrugs the comment off. "Same thing. Laters." He walks out the door, I grab Jameson by the hand, dragging him toward the hallway.

Emma calls out before we make it to one of the rooms, stopping us. She runs over, grabbing me in a solid embrace. "I'm so glad you are here." She kisses my cheek as I hold onto Jameson's hand, my eyes glistening.

"Me too, Emma."

I spare a glance at Eduardo, who is looking on with adoration just as Jameson is looking at me. I know they think that we are unbelievably brave, and I know that we are going to need to continue to be strong and support each other if we are going to get through this.

I enter the spacious room with a sleigh-style bed in the middle of the room against the wall. The room is tastefully decorated in beige, gray, and neutral tones. The earthy color scheme boasts a beautifully understated and classically elegant style, except for the crystal chandelier that hangs in the middle of the ceiling. Two tufted chairs are placed in front of the window, and a table is in the middle where one can look at the cityscape below and gaze at the wonder of a multitude of flickering lights, while looking out onto the city.

"Wow, what a view."

The billowing curtain sways with the air vents that are currently pumping out some central climate control in the room.

I perch on the seating provided at the foot of the bed to remove my shoes. I place my feet on the rug and tuck my boots into the corner of the seat. I run my feet back and forth on the luxurious fabric before I stand and walk to where Eduardo has left my bag. I step around and look up to find Jameson staring at me.

He smiles. "I'm going to take a quick shower, okay?"

I nod, blinking away my lust-filled thoughts, and continue to organize my stuff. I hear the shower turn on, and the steam billows around the bathroom, creeping out into the bedroom space.

I stand there, conflicted. My clothes are in my hand, and I don't want to intrude on his shower, but I really want to join him. I figure if he did want company, then he would have asked. So, I continue to stand there waiting.

I hear the shower shut off and a repeated squeaking sound coming from the bathroom. I look up and see his reflection in the mirror as he wipes the condensation and the surge of stormy fog away from the mirror. Our eyes meet in the reflection, and I can't look away.

Water drops from his wet hair, landing on his chest. His blondish-brown hair appears darker when saturated with water. I can't help but ogle his body and how incredibly handsome he is—the first two times we were intimate had been under a disguise. I was hiding my face and, more than that, my emotions under a literal mask.

After all the time we had apart, we had explored each other without touching. His voice echoing through the speakerphone, telling me to touch myself—to pretend it was him. The way my hands obliged and pretended they were, in fact, his as I made myself come over and over the past months I was away from him.

Seeing him here right now, naked and wet in front of me, is surreal. Although nothing was confirmed about our relationship status, I know in my heart that I am his and he is mine. I hope that the intimacy we shared remotely can be reciprocated tonight. I want to release the control I've come to need and give it over to him.

Let him take me. Claim me. Make me his.

I walk into the bathroom, facing the shower. I undress without looking back at him. I step into the shower as he stands there, watching me enter. The transparent glass leaves nothing to the imagination. I wash the day's grime away from my body and the twisted lies that spewed forth from my mouth earlier as they swirl in a bubbly tide of water down the drain.

He doesn't move from his spot; he just continues to watch me. The fact that I hold him captive is alluring and empowering to me. I run the conditioner through my shorter hair, and it doesn't take long to rinse it out.

I shut off the water and hear a cabinet open and close. When I step out of the shower, Jameson is holding a towel open for me, and I turn around as he wraps it and his arms around me. I am immediately enveloped in the fluffy cotton and his warm embrace.

I hold it hitched around me as he takes another smaller one and towels off my hair. He wrings the water from it and fluffs it around, much like he did on his own hair. I can't help but smile at the simple yet kind domestic act. I rock up on my tiptoes and back down again like a kid waiting for their birthday surprise. He pulls me in for a hug and holds me there, as if he's afraid I will pull another disappearing act. I ease his concerns.

"I'm not going anywhere, Jameson." I let him know so he understands I am staying here this time. That this time is different. He kisses the top of my head, as I release the towel from my grasp. He feels it fall from my body, his body tensing in response, and then he looks down at it pooling around my feet. I step back and look up at him. I smile seductively.

I drop my head down, unable to meet his eyes. "I want you to touch me." He lifts my chin upward to meet his. The fire in his eyes makes me shudder. I gulp before speaking, licking my lips. "Will you show me how much you've missed me while I've been away?"

His eyes alight with desire, accepting the challenge. "Baby, I would like nothing more. I can't wait to make you come on my tongue, fingers, and cock."

He bends forward and takes my hand in his. His other hand caresses my cheek as his lips touch mine. He presses soft kisses to my lips, down my cheek and neck. He slowly licks his way up my neck to my ear, pressing light kisses that make me giggle as his facial hair tickles my sensitive skin. When he sucks my earlobe into his mouth, tugging lightly before he returns his path to my mouth, I meet him without hesitation. I open for him as his tongue swirls with mine in a tangle for dominance.

He moves his hand in between my legs, brushing a finger across and then through my folds. He pushes further inward, parting me, moving the moisture that has pooled around my core and bringing the wetness upward to make little circles around my clit.

My head falls back slightly as he bends lower to kiss my neck, sucking in the exposed skin. I am sure it will make little marks where his mouth has been.

He pushes a finger inside me, and I can't help the moan that leaves me. He takes his other hand, and places it on my breast. He moves his fingertips over my erect nipples while tugging and flicking over the sensitive peaks. He adds another finger, scissoring them inside me, making me even wetter. When he adds a third finger, I gasp as he fucks me, making me feel so deliciously full. I start to pant with longing, seeking the much-needed release only he can provide.

"What do you need, Evie? Tell me, baby," he almost pleads, desperate to hear my answer.

I don't make him wait, the truth falling from my lips. "I only need what you can give me, Jameson." I can sense this pleases him. The upturn of his smile tells me so against my bare skin. "I need your fingers," I continue as his fingers thrust in faster, and I feel my climax approaching. "I need your mouth." I whimper as he sucks hard on my neck, undoubtedly leaving evidence of his claiming my body. "I need you to make me come."

He curls his finger upward as he hits the exact spot I need to make me see stars as I come undone from his ministrations.

"Oh, God." I take a few breaths to regulate my racing heart. He removes his fingers, and I see evidence of my climax on his wet fingers as he takes a fingertip and traces my lips with it.

I lick my lips, tasting myself on them, and his eyes flare with pure, unadulterated lust, as he watches the motion. "I need..." I hesitate, wondering if it is wise to reveal so much vulnerability because that would give up any bargaining chips.

He would know my true feelings, bearing it all to him.

Instead, I throw caution to the wind and, for once in my life, decide to relinquish the control I so desperately crave and need. I choose to rip myself open at the seams for the possibility of what we could be.

"I need your heart."

His eyes meet mine, and the surprise that registers is quickly replaced by a fierce determination.

He smiles widely and then kisses me so deeply that I feel it all the way down to my toes, and I know that, somehow, we are going to be alright.

He takes my hand and leads me out of the bathroom and onto the bed. For once in my life, I put my body and soul into someone else's control. As we lay there wrapped in each other's arms, I can feel the weight lift from my shoulders. The regret that I live with, the same that Emma lives with, feels lighter as I release the burden I have always carried. The lies between everyone is a cross that no one should bear. And for once in my life, I feel free.

Jameson grabs my hand in his as we lie in bed. Our legs draped over one another as our bodies mold together. I close my eyes, drifting off to the sound of his steady breathing, and I realize that this is our new beginning.

CHAPTER NINETEEN

JAMESON

"CULT OF PERSONALITY" BY LIVING COLOUR

Mateo and I decide to bring back some breakfast for our family. Eli and Philip left this morning with nothing but a cup of coffee to join Gus—Eduardo's primary personal security detail and long-time trusted friend. I mean the entire group that had gathered around the island, our found family, have returned to ensure everything is running smoothly at the clubs while we strategically plan our next move. We are still waiting for Mr. Martinez's response to our blatant attempt at retaliation and expect him to bring hell to our doorstep, but his fury has yet to make an appearance and come our way.

Mateo pushes the seat back in my vehicle to accommodate his large frame as I start the car. I connect my Carplay, and one of my favorite songs starts playing. I hit the air conditioning button several times to full arctic blast mode to combat this Texan heat in a city that just seems to bake on the concrete slab it resides upon. I saw Theo cook an egg on the hood of his car once in high school, proving it could be done. Unfortunately, it also took away some of the paint.

I smile. Lesson earned.

Mateo glances over at me, seeing me lost in my thoughts about my idiot friends, as he turns up the dial and starts bobbing his head to the music.

Well, look at that, bro has good taste in music.

I look over at him and witness my girlfriend's brother. He shakes his head, singing and playing air drums. "The only thing we have to fear is fear itself." Taken from the "Day of Infamy" speech is one of my favorites, and apparently Mateo is fond of it too, especially in this particular rock song.

I slow down as I approach the local taqueria and ease up on the gas as I pull into their drive-thru entrance. There is a long line, but things progress quickly, and I lean back so Mateo can lean over toward my window and order when it is our turn. He has the list, and he knows what he wants, too.

I pull up when our turn comes and scrunch up my nose at his order. "What the hell is nopalitos?" There's another car in front of us receiving their order, and he looks at me and laughs.

"Cactus," he replies cooly.

I pretend to gag, now knowing what it is. "Why the fuck would you eat that? Great fiber?" I'm now trying any excuse to guess at why he chose that out of everything they have on the menu.

"Well, I like it for one, and it is better than what your girlfriend ordered," he counters.

I gulp dramatically. Curiosity winning, I take the bait. "Okay, enlighten me. What did she order?"

He looks me up and down, trying to decide if he wants to tell me. He smirks evilly at me and then replies, "Tacos de lengua."

I shrug. "I have no idea what that is. It sounds good, though." I counter.

Mateo nods, agreeing with me. "Yes, delicious, if you like beef tongue."

I look at him in horror.

"That's what it is?"

He nods, confirming. "I've had that before. It tastes…" I look for the right word. "Salty."

He nods again, agreeing.

"Yep, I agree. Definitely salty."

Suddenly, all the saliva floods my mouth, and not in a good way. I need to change the conversation. I don't have to wait as the server at the window repeats our orders. Mateo looks over at her, winking, and I see the blush forming on her cheeks.

"Here you go, boys, and I threw in something extra."

I grab the bags, hand them to Mateo, and thank her for the food.

"Do you want to know what tripas are?"

I hold my hand up, halting this conversation. "Definitely not."

He laughs loudly, slapping his leg. Tears spring from the edges of his eyes as he fights back the fit of laughter.

"Save it. I'm so done. If it tastes good, that's all I need to know."

He tightens his hold on my shoulder as he slaps my back while I am driving. "Bro, welcome to the family."

I smile. Indeed.

We walk through the door with the bags. Evie and Emma come over to take them from us. They unpackage everything, and I see Evie frown. I look over at what she is holding, and she lifts a paper.

"Sylvia?" she reads. "What the fuck is this?" She looks at me, and I feel like taking her against the counter in response to her outright act of jealousy.

I find it to be such a turn-on, knowing that the thought of another woman flirting with me consumes her with fury. I already know my little vixen has a temper, and I'd love to test it out, but maybe without an audience this time.

Unless, of course, it is back at Eduardo's club in a voyeur room.

I inwardly moan at the thought of angry sex with Evie, if it is anything to go by that night we shared back at his club. I shake my head, blocking that thought because if anyone else saw her naked, I'd have to gouge their eyes out.

I realize I have zoned out and laugh.

Evie is still staring at me, assessing and, no doubt, plotting my demise. "It's not mine," I reply, lifting my hands in surrender. "Ask your brother."

She looks at Mateo, who seems unfazed by her dramatics. He rolls his eyes. I guess that's what happens when you live together for a while. He reaches her, snatching the paper out of her hands, and quickly shoves the paper napkin into his pocket.

"For a rainy day," he remarks absently. "Now, let's eat."

We sit around the island like last night, but it's time for breakfast and coffee instead of tequila and limes. I look over at Eduardo, who is striding into the kitchen, freshly showered and ready to start his day of mafia dealings. Now that everyone is on the same page, there is no use in sugarcoating anything.

Eduardo is eating his tacos, and he moans around the food. "I love when my tripas are extra crispy."

Mateo snorts. "I know, but don't tell Jamesy here what it is. He doesn't want to know." His hands are raised in a halting motion, and he is not attempting to hide his mocking tone.

I look at my plain bacon, egg, and cheese taco, shrugging off the comment. "Some things are better left unsaid."

"Agree." Eduardo laughs, knowing my sensitive palate full well. "It's bad enough that I discovered Evie ordered cow tongue tacos." I place my food down, taking a big swig of orange juice.

"You said you liked my tacos." She looks at me, puzzled, and dare I say offended.

"I do, but they are salty."

She leans forward and murmurs in my ear, "I love salty things, baby." She licks my ear, and Emma coughs, speaking up.

"Okay, can we please get through breakfast?"

Evie shoots her an ugly look, and Emma beams at her.

"What the fuck kind of family have I gotten into?" I say, barely audible, but apparently not low enough because Eduardo chuckles. Great, now I am sitting here with my taco and a hard-on after Evie's comment. I adjust myself as discreetly as possible.

My phone chimes, distracting my thoughts just as Emma's does simultaneously, and we both share a look.

Eduardo straightens upright and looks between us with an expression of displeasure and wondering what the message could be that involves Emma and me, but not him.

Evie's jaw tightens, and I touch her face and turn her toward me to kiss her quickly before showing her my phone. "Here, read it for me. My hands are greasy."

She smiles, knowing full well that I am doing this to show her that I have nothing to hide from her.

I know we have many things to work on, and the first one is trust. I need to continue building trust between us, and this time, there will be no more secrets. It is a group text from Liv and Dax. I see the recognition on her face as she reads it, and then a smile spreads when she sees the picture of a baby boy taking up the screen, and his weight and length are displayed under his name.

"Kaden Brodie Johnson," she reads aloud. "He's beautiful, Emma."

I look up to see Emma touching her phone. Tears run down her face, and Eduardo kisses her cheek and licks away her tears. I look at his devotion to her and finally understand his feelings toward Emma. I only wished back then that I could have those feelings of love, protectiveness, and utter devotion to someone. They were childhood friends and then became so much more.

Evie senses me looking at something and looks over at her sister as well. I see the same realization on her face. It's not one of jealousy. Her features soften, and I squeeze her hand. She looks up at me, and when our eyes connect, I express with as much emotion as I can the feeling I have and the hope for us to have a similar connection. She squeezes my hand before releasing it and walks over to Emma.

Eduardo shrugs. "You guys go. I have some things to take care of here, and if you are there with them, Jameson, I would feel much better." He clasps me on the shoulder and starts to walk off.

"Wait," I hear Emma call out to him.

He stops quickly and turns toward her, immediately concerned for the panic rising in her voice.

"Yes, babe. What is it?"

She walks over to him. She bites her lip, and I can see the wheels in her head spinning about how to phrase her following words.

"Um." She twists her engagement ring around. "I was hoping that maybe I could tell Liv the truth. I have been feeling guilty for lying to her for a while now, and I really want her to know how much I value her friendship and maybe allow her to get to know the real me."

Her shoulders slump forward, and I realize how much she looks like Evie in this instant. The thought that they have gone through so much is terrifying to me. All Evie has been through was also without anyone there to hold her and love her. I know she had her brother with her, but it is not the same. Eduardo is so devoted to Emma, and she has relied on his strength to get them through some of the most challenging times, but who did Evie have?

"Hey, sis. Do you want some company to go and see your friend?" I see Evie's look of uncertainty flash across her face before she shuts it down and looks to Emma for an answer. She thinks Emma will blow her off. The vulnerability she tries to hide behind a strong façade is heartbreaking. She braces for her response as if the words Emma speaks could physically crush her.

Emma doesn't hesitate before she replies. "You mean, do I finally get to introduce my sister to my other bestie?"

Evie lifts her head in surprise and happiness. Emma quirks an eyebrow upward, and Evie cannot contain the laugh that bursts forth.

Looking at them both, I can tell they will get there sooner rather than later. Their pieces are now whole; now that Mateo is in the picture, they have come full circle and have their family back together.

I walk over to my girlfriend and take her hand, bringing it to my lips. I kiss it gently and then drop it. "We should all go," I say, looking at Emma. "Me, Evie, and you?" I ask so they don't think I would leave Mateo out. "Do you want to go, Mateo?"

He is quick to reply with a, "Fuck no. I need to sleep, and I mean for a whole day. I'm tired as fuck."

I place my hand behind Evie's neck. "We should probably go and get some rest, too." I look over to Emma. "When do you think we should go?"

Emma scrunches her nose up in thought. "Well, she just got home from the hospital, and we need some time to plan for any retaliation from Mr. Martinez that should be coming our way soon." She looks over to Eduardo, and he confirms.

"Yes, babe. Maybe give her some time to rest, and then you can all go over to visit, or if Jameson can't go, then I can take you girls to catch up." He thinks about it for a second. "How about this weekend? I have some work at the club, and you can spend some time with your friend and let her know to plan for them to visit her and to..." He pauses and swirls his hand in the air. "Whatever it is you want to tell her."

The girls nod in unison and agree to make a date to visit this weekend to see Dax and Liv's newborn.

"I can take them then," I confirm with Eduardo, and he agrees that it is still a better choice. "I'd like to catch up with Dax if he's home." Which I suspect the fucker took advantage of some paternity leave if he could.

Eduardo claps his hands. "Okay, it is settled then. Jameson will take you girls, but now I need to see what I can find out about Mr. Martinez."

Mateo stands. "I'll meet up with you in a bit. I have somewhere I need to be, and then I'll meet you at the club?" he asks, and Eduardo nods. "Jameson?"

I shake my head no.

I grab Evie by the hand and drag her out. "We have some catching up to do."

Evie barely has time to grab her bag as I'm ushering her out by the arm. I hear Eduardo laugh, and I get it. If I spend the rest of my life telling her how much I love and cherish her, it still won't be enough for the rest of the time I wasn't there with her. The only thing I can do from this point on is devote myself to her.

CHAPTER TWENTY

EVIE

"ALL AROUND ME" BY FLYLEAF

"Hurry up, Evie. I don't want to be late to meet Ramón!" Mateo shouts from the kitchen.

Where did I put my bag? I lift the pile of clothing from my bed and see the offending object. "Okay, just a sec."

I hear him pacing around out there. Bro needs to calm down before he goes bald from tugging at his hair. Sure enough, as I proceed to sling my cross-body bag across my shoulders, letting it rest over my right front hip, I see his hair standing erect on one side. I walk over to him, lick my hand, and smooth the hair down on that side.

He steps back, I'd say disgusted if going off his facial expression. "What-the-ever-loving-fuck?"

I shrug. "Your hair was sticking straight out on the side."

He lifts his hand up in protest. "So, you thought you should just..." He motions with his hands flying back and forth between my hand and face.

"Lick your hand and rub at my hair?"

I chuckle. "Um. Yep, that's exactly what I did, bro." I grab my water cup and swallow the ice-cold brew that resides there instead of the H2O that *should* occupy the space, but I'm not one to do things I *should* do.

He shakes his head in defeat. "Whatever. I just can't with you today." He walks out, and I follow him, locking the door behind me. I hurry to catch up with his long strides.

"Mattie, are you okay? You seem all…" I move my hand upright, making a circle around his person. "Tense," I finish.

He continues walking, sparing me a side glance so I can see just enough of his exaggerated eye roll as he continues ignoring my question.

"Are you suffering from FSB or something?"

At this, he stops mid-trek to the car. He pivots and turns around to me. "I'm afraid to ask…" He rubs a hand down his face. "But I will against my better judgment anyway. What the fuck is FSB?"

I smile slyly. "Why, fatal sperm build-up, of course."

He rolls his eyes upward as if they will pop right out of his head at any moment. He pivots and turns around without further comment. I can see the remark hit its desired mark because, if I am not mistaken, I see his shoulders rising as he tries to stifle a laugh.

Walking up to his usual coffee spot where he meets Ramón for chess, as I follow behind like a scolded child. I guess he is still sore about the saliva thing.

I walk in and see Dylan at the front counter. He sees me and smiles brightly. I don't return the enthusiasm, but I am not a total bitch, even though every bone in my body wants to scream '*cheater.*'

I notice Mateo is already seated with Ramón, and I once again feel like an outsider hanging out with them, as if I am intruding, except now that we had spent some time with him over the holidays. I see how much he enjoys his time with Mateo and how lonely he is. Two men finding a sense of purpose with one another—filling a missing familial void.

I get a text message and glance quickly to notice that it is from Jameson. My smile widens, but the text message has me a little confused.

Jameson: Where are you?

I look at my phone, wondering why he is asking this when I already told him we were coming to see my brother's friend.

Evie: I am with Mateo.

I snort as I type this. What is he getting at? Does he think I am lying?

Jameson: Where are you both?

Okay, I didn't tell him where, but we are still near Houston.

Evie: We are in Galveston?

I type it out because I don't want him to worry. This line of questioning is kind of worrisome. He has never been like this, and it is starting to make me nervous. I can see that he is typing, as the three little dots show under his message.

Jameson: Who are you with, and where?
I need all the information Evie.

I am now starting to panic. I look around the coffee shop and don't see anything conflicting or unusual that would make me suspicious. I am pretty good at sensing danger at this point. Nothing is screaming 'dangerous situation' at me.

I feel Mateo looking at me. I meet his gaze, and his expression remains neutral, but his eyes are questioning. I ignore it and look back at my phone, typing out a response.

Evie: I am at the usual coffee shop with
Mateo and his friend Ramón.

His response comes quickly.

Jameson: Perfect.

I make a jerky body movement, and annoyance starts to creep in. I type a nonthreatening questioning response.

Evie: WTF?

I see his following message and throw my phone down on the table.

Jameson: I'll explain later...

I don't bother responding this time. I'm just annoyed, but I am sure there has to be a good reason for that line of intense and very specific questioning. I cross my arms over my chest and kick my feet out in front of me in a pissed-off stance.

I look over to my brother and see him and Ramón staring at me and wondering why I have been reacting to my messages in that manner.

"Jameson is being vague. And super annoying," I say to them with an eye roll.

Mateo laughs, and Ramón smiles. "Ah, young love," he comments with a faraway look in his eyes, as if he is remembering a moment that is now just a distant memory—a blip in time. Maybe he is thinking about his wife. Whatever it is, he doesn't elaborate or comment further.

They return to their game, and I sit there wondering what is going on right now.

Bored with my situation, I stand up and leave them to their game—Ramon is clearly winning this round—and walk over to the water station and fill up a cup of iced water, adding a lemon to it.

I stand looking over at the sun reflecting off the water outside. I feel someone looking at me, and I turn to see Dylan. I lift a challenging brow. He looks as if he is going to walk my way, and I almost want him to do so, so I can let him know what I think of him. I am saved by the bell when a young woman comes through with a stroller, her eyes bright and cheerful. Dylan turns to her in surprise and then spares a quick glance my way, schooling his features.

I sip my drink, watching the interaction from a few feet away. She removes the clasp on the carrier and lifts a little girl from the stroller. She is wearing a little pink dress with a pink hairband holding back her little blonde curls surrounding her cherub-like face. She is beautiful, moving her chubby little hands back and forth and sticking her tongue out.

"We just came to see Daddy before lunch with Grandma and Grandpa." She coos at the little girl, adoration and love spilling forth for her little bundle of joy.

Dylan is rigid, knowing that he is officially busted. I take a long swig, watching the exchange and wishing I could help his unsuspecting wife in a way that lets her know she deserves better.

I turn to look at Mateo, and he is watching me. His eyes are pleading, asking me not to cause a scene. I nod once, and he visibly relaxes and returns his attention to his lost cause of a chess game.

Dylan takes his baby girl and kisses her on the top of her head. I see that he loves her because of the way he carries on about her. I mean, who wouldn't? She is so perfect.

It's at this moment my resolve softens, and as much as I think Dylan is the scum of the earth for attempting to give me his number, I don't know his situation. Looking at them, I don't see wedding rings on either of their fingers. *Interesting.*

I walk over to them, drawn to the sight of the baby and all its cuteness. I decide to just pass by and walk to our table when the baby drops the little doll that she had just had in her mouth. A long line of saliva falls, chasing after the little toy.

I pick it up for the young mother and hand it to her. She smiles at me, and Dylan just watches me to see what I am going to say. The little girl looks at me and shows a complete, gummy smile that radiates sunshine and happiness.

"She's beautiful," I whisper, not intending for that to slip out. I straighten my posture rigidly. I speak up. "You are both so lucky." I smile at them, and the mom beams at the compliment.

Dylan speaks. "Thank you. She is the best thing that happened to us."

I walk away and hear the woman ask Dylan if he has any plans tonight or if he is free to watch their daughter. It is then that I realize maybe they aren't together and I might have misjudged the situation. I frown as I walk back to the table.

When I hear the woman leave, I look at Dylan. My eyes soften, understanding the complexity of his situation. Dylan's cheeks blush as he looks down and walks off. I watch him retreat, wishing him positive vibes so that he can find happiness and find a person who will love him and that sweet girl unconditionally.

It's then that my jaded heart cracks just a little more with sympathy and compassion for another person instead of jumping to conclusions and seeing only the worst in everyone.

I sit there and reflect on the events in the coffee shop, waiting for my brother and Ramón to finish their game of chess. Mateo, in fact, loses the game. Shocker. They pack up their chess game, carefully putting away the pieces into the velvety cloth drawstring pouch. He helps Ramón put it into his messenger bag as we stand to walk out.

Dylan is at the counter, trying not to make eye contact with me. I walk over to him, and he looks up in surprise.

"Hi," he says shyly.

"Hey," I counter. "I just wanted to let you know that I have a boyfriend, but if I didn't, it would be such a turn-on to see such a man taking responsibility and caring for his daughter. I'm Evie, by the way." I extend my hand out to him, and he takes it, smiling.

"Thank you, Evie. I appreciate that."

I turn around, and before I leave, I wave. "See you around, Dylan."

The door chimes as I step out into the blazing heat. My hair is frizzing by the second. I pluck the sunglasses from my head and place them over my eyes to combat the blinding sun rays. I see Mateo and Ramón standing by the pier waiting for me.

Mateo shakes his head at me. "You just couldn't help yourself, could you?" He looks almost disappointed in me.

"I didn't say anything wrong. He isn't married, and he seems like a doting father. I just wanted to let him know I have a boyfriend, and his little girl was cute." I shrug.

Mateo looks at me. "Hm." That is all he says, and I see him look at Ramón, who smiles without comment. "Okay then. Let's go. We will drop off Ramón at his house after his doctor appointment, then head home, okay?"

I place my hand in my pocket. "Sure, no problem."

With that, we walk over to where we parked and get into our very hot car. Mateo opens the windows to allow some of the heat to escape. As we drive, I look over at the boats on the bay, the calmness, and the sound of seagulls flying carefree. It brings me a sense of peace when everything around me is spiraling out of control. I like things I can control.

Jameson: Are you dropping off Ramón now?

I look up at the door, frowning at the question. I turn around and look out at the empty street, but I don't understand this line of questioning. *Can he see me?*

Evie: Yes, we are headed there now. It took a while after his appointment. He had to see a doctor today.

I need to know what is happening, but I sense that we will not like the answers. He starts typing then stops. I stare at my phone and frown, but don't comment. No further messages come through.

Mateo pulls into Ramón's driveway, and he assists the older gentleman, helping to get him to his door. Mateo disappears inside the condo, and I wait for him. My phone dings moments later, and I notice another text message from Jameson.

Jameson: You and Mateo meet me at The Viceroy after. Eduardo and I will be waiting for you.

I'm reading the last message as the door opens, and Mateo slides into the driver's seat. He looks over at me, then backs out of the driveway, pulling onto the feeder road to get on the highway. He looks over at me, sensing something is wrong.

"What? What's going on, Evie?"

I shake my head, confused as to what they need to discuss with us and why all the evasive questions.

"Not sure, but Jameson said we should go over to Eduardo's club. They want to talk to us there." I look over at my brother to see what he thinks about this.

"Did they hear back from Mr. Martinez yet?"

I bite my nail, shrugging my shoulders. "He didn't say, but I have a bad feeling about this, Mattie."

"We can speculate all we want, but it's best just to go now and see what they have to say."

I nod in agreement. We ride the entire way into the city, absorbed in our thoughts, wondering when the other shoe will drop.

CHAPTER TWENTY-ONE

JAMESON

"TOO SWEET" BY HOZIER

I get a call from Eduardo to meet him at his club. He doesn't explain the reason for the meet-up, but I know it is important if he called me at work to meet him.

I promptly gather up my belongings and rush out of the office, rushing to his club. I park right next to the door in the back alley and hit the button on my key fob to lock my car door as I am met by Gus. He leads me down the hallway and up the familiar set of stairs to Eduardo's office. Gus doesn't knock. He opens the door, and I see Eli and Philip already there. I enter, looking back at Gus, and take the only remaining seat across from Eduardo's desk.

"You aren't at the gym today?" I know he isn't, so it's more of a rhetorical question, if anything.

Still, he shakes his head in a nonverbal answer to my stupid question that really didn't need an explanation in the first place. His hands steeple over his mouth in a contemplative gesture as he carefully chooses his following words.

"I received a phone call today from Evie and Emma's uncle in Mexico."

I straighten in my chair, immediately on edge as to what this could now mean for us. "Did you speak with Emma? Does Evie know?" I look back at Gus, who walks closer to us and leans on the wall, crossing one foot over the other—his half-effort at getting comfortable.

Eduardo shakes his head. "No, he just called and told me about something exciting, and because of this new development, I need you to get me a camera." He looks over to Eli and Philip.

"What is this about? How can I help?" I look back and forth at anyone who could put me at ease because I don't like how my stomach drops at the uncertainty of the situation.

He hangs his head and then directs his focus at me. "I just found out that Mr. Martin is actually Mr. Martinez."

I look over at Eduardo, who is waiting for me to react. I just don't know what he's talking about. Perhaps if I had more information, I would respond differently.

"I'm confused. Mr. Martinez?"

Seeing my confusion, Eduardo quickly brings me up to speed for the urgency of this meeting. "The same as Julian and his father. As in the same grandfather to Julian. That Mr. Martinez."

I sit there frozen. "Ramón?"

My brain takes a moment to compute the gravity of the situation. This past year, Mateo has found a friend in this older man. I thought it was odd that this gentleman wanted to hang out with him so much.

"That's his grandfather?" My hand falls over my mouth. "Evie has been over there multiple times, and they were with him over the holidays because the man didn't have any family," I say, my pitch getting higher, as my anxiety rises through the roof.

Good God, how could we not have known? All this time that Mateo was spending time with this man along with my girlfriend was because he didn't have any family, when in fact, Mateo *is* his family. This is so fucked.

"Is he the enemy? Are they in danger?" I jump up quickly, my chair toppling to the floor as I move haphazardly, unsure of which direction to go. I imagine myself having a meltdown.

My body moves one way, and my mind moves another. My movements are jerky and erratic, causing me to almost misstep and tumble over the toppled chair. A loud thud echoes in the lofty office space.

I lean forward on his desk. My breathing picks up as my head hangs down. I try to calm the panic that Evie could be in danger. She has been going to this man's house and hanging out with him and Mateo frequently. If I recall correctly, they were even meeting him today.

I lift my gaze to Eduardo and see the same concern for his fiancée's safety. He holds his hand up as I am starting to ask another question.

"From what I can tell, he has been without contact from Julian before he died or from Mr. Martinez. I just don't know how he met Mateo and Evie. I think it seems just a tad bit coincidental that he meets them both and hangs out with his grandson without him actually knowing that Mateo is his biological grandson."

I look over at Eduardo's security detail and trusted friends. "Is that why you want the camera? To see if something is going on?" I take the object from my bag and place it on the desk. "What do we do now?" I throw that question into the air and see who grabs at an answer. The room remains silent. *Does no one know what we should do?*

I look to Eduardo for guidance. He has been doing this longer, and while Emma was my friend and I helped to keep her safe, this hits a bit differently. Now it's Evie, my woman, who is in trouble.

Eduardo sighs and rubs at his temples, like he is waging a war against an impending migraine. Everything is headache-inducing. The situation is complex and tiresome. Will we ever be able to just relax and hang out without worry? College was long ago; even days spent on Padre Island seem eons ago.

"Do you have everything I asked you to bring?"

I'm pulled from my thoughts and look at him, nodding that I do and pointing to his desk where I placed a bag with the contents of a camera inside.

He smiles. "I have an idea, but where are Mateo and Evie now?"

I take out my phone and send a text to Evie. I thought she was with Mateo in Galveston today, but I want to be sure. A moment later, she replies. My annoyance must show, so I quickly thumb through the reply, followed by two more. I put my phone down.

"She's with Mateo and the old man in Galveston."

Eduardo shoots a quick look at his best friend, Gus.

Gus steps off the wall and puts his hand out. He must sense my question to his outstretched hand. "I need the camera."

I look to Eduardo, who smiles and then begins to explain. He hands the camera over to Gus, who hooks the bag over his shoulder.

"We are going to plant it in Mr. Martin's house and see what he's up to. It just seems all too coincidental, don't you think?"

I nod in agreement. "I do. Coincidental as fuck." I point at the camera I brought and explain how it works, but there isn't much to it.

With that, Gus leaves for what I assume is Mr. Martin's place. Since he is out of the condo now, it should be an okay time to get this done.

I send one more text to Evie and ask her to let me know when they are on their way from dropping off Mr. Martin. We need to come up with something and make a plan to handle this new and unexpected development.

The phone rings in Eduardo's office. I look over in puzzlement at the source of the intrusion. Eduardo picks it up and smiles slyly. "Excellent, Gus." He looks over at me. "I'm sure Jameson can get it up and running here, and we will see you soon." He hangs up the phone, and I'm still staring at him, waiting to see what this conversation was about.

He feels me watching but ignores me to grab himself a drink as he hovers over the bar area in the corner. He grabs a glass and pours some amber drink into a glass. He looks over at me and tosses it back.

"What?" He stares at me in confusion.

I start to laugh. "I didn't think you still had a landline."

He looks at the phone and then back at me. "So." He shrugs. "It's for the club, and if anyone needs to call me."

I nod, accepting this excuse. I look around.

"What are you looking for?" He seems to be helping search for the unknown item.

"Nothing, I was just curious where your fax machine was." I start laughing, and he pours himself another drink.

"You know, I was going to offer you a drink, but now, I'm not feeling so charitable." He chuckles. "Dick."

"I'm just kidding, bro, but what did you need me to do? I heard you mention something to Gus."

Eduardo's smile spreads into an evil grin. "Yes, we have the camera up in Mr. Martin's house. It's time to find out what that old bird has been hiding."

I get the app up, and we look through the phone to see Mr. Martin standing in his kitchen. Eduardo called him an old bird, which isn't far from the truth. Ramón is under six feet, but that's not what makes Eduardo's comment accurate. He has a hook nose that mimics a beak. His eyes are beady and elongated in an obsidian black color, much like the color of

Mateo's eyes and Mr. Martinez's black ones that match his heartless soul. This combination gives him a bird-like quality that makes his comment laughable and highly on point.

I motion with my hand over to Eduardo. He peers over my shoulder. "Put it on speaker."

I do as he asks and place the phone on his desk. Eli and Philip move over to see him on the screen moving about in his kitchen. The clanking of dishes in the sink sounds through the phone as he sets the clean dishes down on the rack to air dry. Suddenly, a sound pierces the room, and Philip looks over at Eli.

"What's that noise?" Philip comments.

I laugh at his question. "I know, right? You should ask Eduardo," is all I say as Eduardo scowls at me.

Mr. Martin dries his hands on a towel as he walks over to answer the phone on the wall. They start laughing, but it dies down as soon as Mr. Martin answers the phone.

"Hello." He folds the dish towel over the sink and braces himself on the island. "Yes, I went to the doctor today, and Mateo took me." He adds the last part hesitantly. He appears to be in physical pain as he shifts his weight from one leg to the other. Whether the pain is related to his doctor's appointment or this phone conversation, we don't know.

We hear in a hushed tone, "Please don't ask that of me." His head is bent down as his hand rubs at his hair, much like Mateo does.

I look over at Eduardo, and he listens intently to every word of this one-sided conversation. It funnels in through the speaker in a whirl of acrid sounds as if he is afraid to miss any detail. "Okay, son. Yes, I will."

With that last sentence, I let out a breath I didn't realize I was holding. He hangs up the phone on the receiver. I sit up straight and watch as Ramón hangs his head and cups his face. He stands abruptly and walks off out of view into the bedroom.

A moment of silence passes before Eduardo speaks, confirming what we all know to be another truth. Ramón definitely speaks to or is in cahoots with Mr. Martinez, Mateo's father.

"Well, I guess we have our answer." Eduardo looks over at us as we consider the gravity of the situation.

"So, who is going to tell them?" I ask.

As soon as Eduardo's office door opens, Mateo and Evie walk in.

"Who's going to tell them what?" Evie says just as Eduardo groans.

"Fuck. You always did have perfect timing, Evie."

CHAPTER TWENTY-TWO

EVIE

"FOR WHOM THE BELL TOLLS" BY METALLICA

I walk into who knows what conversation as Mateo trails a few steps behind me.

"Perfect timing to tell me what the fuck is going on," he grumbles.

"With pleasure, Mateo. That's why we asked you over here. It certainly isn't for your smashing personality." Eduardo retorts.

He walks over to us, ushering Mateo and me into the already cramped office space. Mateo looks around at the solemn faces and whirls around to Eduardo.

"Why do I sense that we are going to get another piece of fucking information that I know we aren't going to like?" Mateo pulls at his hair again.

I grab his hand. "Stop that. You're going to go bald. I know you will hate that look."

He stops to roll his eyes at me, but I can tell I at least distracted him from escalating further.

Eduardo goes to his desk, grabs another drink, and pours a large amount of an amber liquid into a glass, as he puts the bottle back. Before I think what he will do with it, he hands the glass over to Mateo. He stares at it questioningly. One eyebrow arches up, but Mateo accepts the glass from Eduardo, although hesitantly.

"O-kay." That's all Mateo says as he waits to hear what happened.

Eduardo walks around to his desk and sits behind it before delivering the news that I'm sure will wreck us.

Mateo takes a sip and waits patiently, without rushing the words Eduardo really needs to spit it out already because he is drawing out the waiting period agonizingly slow, if you ask me.

His fingers drum on the edge of his desk. He shares a look with Jameson and he frowns at me. I swallow all the saliva that has now pooled in my mouth, suppressing the feeling of an imminent vomiting episode. I gulp, and Mateo takes the rest of his drink and downs it in one go.

"Tell me already," he says as he places the empty glass on Eduardo's desk with a resounding *thunk*.

Eduardo moves away from his desk. He stands with his feet placed apart and his hands crossed over his chest in a confrontational manner. "There is no easy way to say this, and I want you to hear me out before you jump to questions."

Mateo nods once, and that must give Eduardo the encouragement he needs to continue. "We had suspicions that Mr. Martinez was getting his information from someone, and it was confirmed when your uncle called to inform us that Ramón is the one who has been feeding him the information about you and Evie."

He pauses and the room is silent. It takes a minute for Mateo to process what Eduardo says, his breathing increases in intensity, as if he is trying to take a deep breath to contain his brewing anger.

I can't take it anymore. I speak up before this gets ugly. "Why do they think that…" I pause as the words I want to say escape me. "I mean, are you sure?" I look at Mateo, who is not moving, but his fists are clenched and knuckles are white as he holds onto the chair with a death grip.

Eduardo looks over to Jameson and Mateo, and I turn my attention over to him. "What's going on, Jameson?"

He walks over to me and grabs my hands. "When I asked you about your whereabouts today, it was so we could plant a camera in Mr. Martin's home."

Mateo stands, knocking the chair back. Jameson startles at the sound and looks his way.

"You went into his home and invaded his privacy? For what, a hunch?"

He is furious and wants to take his anger out on someone; however, his anger is misplaced. He is still protective of Ramón, and I can understand why. He was the closest thing to a father figure, and once again, he feels betrayed.

I can't help, but I feel the same way. I understand what it feels like to be lied to, and everything that you knew or thought you knew was all just a lie concocted for the benefit of someone else. Good intentions are a waste, if you ask me. To believe that we were conned by an elderly gentleman and then were in his home for the holidays… how could he have faked that kind of emotion?

Jameson doesn't miss a beat. "It was more than a hunch, and we confirmed it when he was talking with your father on the video feed. Albeit reluctantly, he was, and it sounded like he was asked to do something he didn't want to do."

Mateo rushes at Jameson and grabs him by the shirt. "Don't you ever call that fucking monster my father!" Spit flies from his mouth as he attempts to control the rage that courses through him in waves. I immediately step in between them.

"Mateo. Get your hands off of Jameson. We need to hear the rest."

Mateo slowly releases Jameson's shirt from his fists and steps back. The anger is still there, while he is attempting to control his emotions. The fury is just barely contained under his skin, waiting to erupt at any given moment.

Mateo turns to Eduardo, and I take the opportunity to throw my arms around my boyfriend, relieved that no punches were thrown.

Eduardo lifts his hands. "Mateo, there is more, but I need you to keep your cool as I tell you the rest because it is a lot to take in."

My brother returns to sitting in the chair and leans forward, hands steepled together like a kid praying at the altar. I hope he is praying to a god right now to have mercy because I can't imagine anything else being as wrong as what we heard. The betrayal that he must feel right now, his trust once again broken. My heart aches for the life my brother has had to endure, and I want nothing more than to take the pain and ease the burden from him.

Eduardo stares at him, waiting for him to regain his composure, and whatever Eduardo is looking for he must see because he continues and delivers the final blow. "Ramón is your grandfather."

And there it is, the final death punch.

Mateo hangs his head in defeat. I suck in a breath, causing Jameson to look at me in concern. I must sound like I am having an asthma attack, but no air comes out. I look around and the faces that stare at Mateo are solemn. They know how close my brother has become to Ramón, and now this news? It is just too much.

I leave Jameson's side and run over to my brother. I throw my arms around him in a protective embrace, leaning into him, and rubbing circles around his back. His hands go up to his face, and from the rise and fall of his back, he is crying. One by one, the guys clear out of the room and leave us as Mattie, my strong and protective brother, falls apart in my arms.

Jameson gives me a kiss on the forehead. He whispers near my ear, "I'll be right outside if you need me." With that, I hear footsteps retreat and the soft closing of a door as Mateo and I are left alone in Eudardo's office.

I stroke his hair. "I love you, brother. So much. It's okay. You have us, and we love you so much."

His sobs increase and a heart-wrenching cry comes out of his mouth, causing tears to flood my eyes as my vision becomes blurry. I have never felt something so heartbreaking. The loss of my parents, finding out the truth of their deception, what they did to my brother, and even Emma being kidnapped is nothing compared to the feeling I have for the man who is breaking down in my arms.

I want to protect him like he protected me, and I vow that I will hunt this man down and make him pay for all the pain he has caused my family. I wish I could go back in time and knock some sense into my mother and tell her not to go out with Mr. Martinez, but then I wouldn't have Mateo, so what is done is done. We can only move forward from here and end it once and for all.

I don't know how long we stay like that, but the door opens again, and I expect it to be Jameson or Eduardo coming in to see how we are doing. What I don't expect to see is my sister walk in and rush over to us, throwing herself into Mateo's lap. She hugs him so fiercely, and he shakes all over again. Emma tells him how much she loves him just like I did, and we all hug each other in a tight embrace.

Emma stands and reaches for me, and I grab her hand, pulling her into my side. We extend our hands to Mateo, and he looks at us with red-rimmed, swollen eyes. We smile at him in adoration of the boy who protected us, despite being denied the family he should have had all along. We each hold out a hand to him as he rises and takes them. We form a complete circle. Our family.

Emma speaks, looking straight up at Mateo. "We are here for you always, Mattie. You are our brother, and we love and support you no matter what. We will finish this."

I nod and squeeze both of their hands. Mateo goes to hug Emma and rests his head on her shoulder. He runs his nose along her collared shirt, and my hand rises to my mouth as I stifle a laugh. Emma visibly tenses, slowly releasing Mateo's embrace, and her head shoots to the side where Mateo has left a slimed trail of mucus along her blouse. Her eyes narrow and shoot over to him accusingly. He wipes his face with his hands, and a smile is left on his face as they lower to his side.

"You did that on purpose, Mattie." She pretends to be angry.

He smiles. "Must run in the family, sis."

She laughs with her head thrown back. "Touché, bro."

I let out a laugh, as does Mateo. We hear the door open, and Eduardo peeks his head in. His eyes go to each of us, and sensing the mood in the room, he motions outside to his entourage to come back into his office.

"Everything okay in here?" Eduardo looks to Emma, and she saunters over to him. His expression is guarded. It pains him to see Emma angry, and he would do anything to prevent her from feeling anything other than happiness.

He pulls her into him and kisses the top of her head. Her arms are wrapped around his lower back as she snuggles into his embrace and sighs in contentment.

I look over to Jameson, who is watching me keenly. I shrug, and he comes over to sit in one of the chairs, pulling me on top of his lap.

Mateo clears his throat, breaking the silence. "So what do we do with this information, Eduardo? What's the plan?"

Eduardo looks at my brother and studies him for a moment. "What do you want to do, Mateo? Do you want to confront him?"

He seems to think about it and eventually nods. "Yeah, I think I do. We are meeting next week at the café. I plan on asking him there."

Jameson looks over my shoulder at Eduardo. "I think that is a good idea, and maybe this week we will find out something else from the camera feed."

I glance quickly over at Mateo and his jaw clenches. I can tell he isn't too keen on the idea, but it must be done. I think he recognizes this and nods.

"Yeah, okay. Sounds good." With that he stands. "I think I have had enough excitement tonight. I'm going to head home. You need a ride, Evie?"

I stand and pull him into an embrace. "No, but I will meet you back at home tonight."

Emma comes over to hug him goodbye, and he waves as he leaves the office. No one says anything for a while, but Eduardo looks over to Emma, who is biting her lip with worry.

"Don't worry, babe." He grabs her hand. "It will all work out."

I stand and pull Jameson's arm to bring him to an upright position. "Let's go. I'm so tired, and I need to think."

He nods, telling Eduardo to call him if he needs anything else as we leave not much after Mateo does. Climbing into Jameson's truck, we pull out into the bustling traffic.

"Your place or mine?" he asks me because I know, after all that went down at Eduardo's office, he doesn't want to leave me alone tonight. That was a lot to take in, and his need to make sure I'm okay is palpable.

"Mine. I want to make sure Mattie is okay." I turn my head to look out the window, and after the bomb that was dropped, my mind is a whirlwind of rising emotions.

CHAPTER TWENTY-THREE

EVIE

"I JUST WANNA RUN" BY THE DOWNTOWN FICTION

We get to the apartment to find Mateo isn't home. I check his room and find it just as he left it earlier, which means that he never came home after leaving the club.

I hate to admit that I am worried. I have never seen Mateo cry. Not even after our mother died, when he learned about Emma and I being his siblings, and even when he learned about our mother giving him up to be raised by her grandparents. None of that had the reaction that I saw from him today in Eduardo's office, when he cried over the news about Ramón that was difficult to watch.

Is he really that close to Ramón? Maybe it was just that last scoop added onto the heaping pile of shit that is our life. Maybe it was just too much for him to handle—the straw that broke the proverbial camel's back and all. The last Jenga piece placed haphazardly that caused the whole tower of emotions to come tumbling down in one fell swoop.

I return to the kitchen where Jameson is standing with his hands in his pockets watching me with a myriad of emotions displayed on his face. I walk over and stand in front of him with my arms crossed over my chest. He looks into my eyes, and I keep his stare, but it is hard to return it. I want to break like Mateo did, but I can't. I won't let myself be weak any longer. I made a promise to myself years ago that no one would ever break me again. I guess we all go through shit, and some things just tip us over at some point.

Today was one of those days.

I feel like Jameson can see into my soul and all the rot that takes up residence there rent free. He sighs and removes his hand from his pockets and places them on each side of my arms, running them up and down as if he is trying to warm me up from a chill.

He smiles coyly at me. "How are you holding up?"

I shrug, and he keeps running his hands up and down my arms. Now I do feel chilled. It elicits goose bumps on my arms from where his touch leaves and then returns. I involuntarily step closer as if I am being pulled by an invisible thread that tethers his heart to mine.

"It was a lot to take in."

He searches my eyes for the truth. "Was he okay when we left the room?"

My voice cracks at first, and then I clear my throat. "Not really. He has been through a lot. It was heartbreaking." I press my cheek up against his chest. The sound of his heart thumps louder. The rhythm is strong and soothing to my rising anxiety.

He places his chin on the top of my head, and my arms feel cold when his hand leaves them to rub circles on my back. I feel like I'm shivering yet burning up as he stokes a flame that needs just a bit more fuel to fully combust.

"I wish I could save him the way that he saved me."

I hear him start to say something and then stop.

I lift my head from his chest and look up at him. Jameson gulps and then looks away. "Did you want to say something?"

He turns back and nods. "I want to know everything about you, Evie. I want to know the good and the bad. I want to be there for you and be someone you can trust and rely on."

Now it's my turn to gulp back the lump that forms in my throat as the intrusive memories try to resurface. All the memories I have been attempting to suppress rise along with my stomach bile. I fight the nausea, and it makes me flinch as if it just happened yesterday.

I pull away from him and he tenses, thinking he did something wrong, that maybe he pushed me too far, but he doesn't realize how much he has already helped me.

I tug at his hand and pull him toward the couch. "Come on. Let's talk about this while I'm sitting on the couch. I need to be a bit more comfortable for what you want to know about me."

We walk over to the couch and sit side by side. Jameson turns his knees angled in toward me, and I do the same to give him my full attention.

"You know, I loved art. I wanted to be an artist. That is until everything happened and I could only see the ugly in the world. I refused to make anything that was as dark as all the emotions that shredded my heart and the depravity of what I thought in my head. I wouldn't give it a name or face, so I stopped painting and drawing."

He takes my hand in his. "Take your time, babe."

I clear my throat and continue. "When I was fifteen, I had to stay after school to finish up a project I was doing for art class. We didn't live that far from school, so I thought I would just walk home. I took a shortcut through the center of town and through an alley. I was almost through it when two men came out of nowhere."

I can sense Jameson getting angry, but I ignore it and continue. "One grabbed me from behind, and the other stepped so close he sandwiched me between them. I bit one of the guy's hands when he clasped it over my mouth and nose. I felt like I couldn't breathe. I thought I was going to pass out, and I was in self-preservation mode. Maybe not thinking clearly, but at that point what was the right choice here? Getting raped? He called me a bitch for it. I screamed before the other one slapped me so hard across the face, my vision blurred." I wince, remembering the sting of that slap and the tingle that spread across my body at the violation my body felt afterward.

"He... ugh." I pause, looking away from Jameson as I get through the next part. He runs his thumb across the top of my hand to soothe the emotions running through me. I'm finally calm enough to finish.

"He said, 'I'll give you something to scream about' as he cupped his hand hard in between my legs as he mimicked thrusting his erection on my leg."

I feel Jameson tense and I spare a glance at him. He nudges me with his hand on my leg to continue. I tense, remembering the feeling, and he removes his hand from my leg and holds both my hands in his. It is as if he can sense my discomfort and tries to lessen my burden.

This feels so intimate and stifling, but I know that he is only trying to provide me with comfort, and I know that I can get through this. I can do this for him. "I didn't hear anything, but more like I felt his presence. Then something landed on my shirt. Something warm and wet, and when I looked down, there was blood on the front of my shirt.

"I was pushed forward and almost tripped over the dead guy who just had his hands on my most intimate parts a moment ago. He was lying on the ground in a pool of blood. His life gone. I saw a young man walking toward me, and the assaulter who held me against him along with his dead accomplice started running to get away. He tripped, and I turned to look up at my guardian angel of death before he put a bullet in his head and killed the second assaulter."

"I heard sirens, and the young man that just saved me from an unknown fate comes up to me and tells me I am going to be alright. The sirens get closer; I look over to the police running my way. I turn back to thank him, but he is gone."

Jameson pulls me into a hug. "That was Mateo?"

I nod. "I just didn't know it then."

Jameson looks at me quizzically, but encourages me to go on with my recounting of events that night.

"Later on, when Emma met Julian, I was hit and left unconscious in another alley. You think I would have learned my lesson about alleys, but I was with Emma, and she wanted to get some food from our favorite street truck after her shift at the coffee shop... I mean, it was still daylight out," I stammer, still trying to comprehend how I let this happen to me again, as if the excuses I make have anything to do with the ordeal being my fault. I didn't ask for any of that.

I shake my head thinking about it. "Julian and his dickhead driver pulled up, and he tried to make Emma go with him. Long story short, the driver punched me and Julian took Emma. I came to, awakening with Mateo holding me in the alley until I was able to go home. He walked me home and then took off."

Jameson curses, and I look to see how angry he is. "Did you know that he was your brother?"

I shake my head. "No, I mean, I didn't even think that. I thought he was just someone my uncle had watching over us after I told my mom about it." I laugh, but it sounds evil when I get it all out.

"After we told my mom about Julian and Emma, she mentioned it being Uncle Andrés's security detail. Not my fucking brother or her son. Can you believe that?"

"No," he replies. "That's just so fucked-up, Eve's."

I nod in agreement. "It is, and I didn't see him again until he saved me from the house explosion and finally told me that he was my brother. My own parents didn't even tell me. They never told us the truth."

All the twisted lies. I run my hand down my face, and Jameson grabs my hands in his.

"You are so incredibly brave, baby, and I love you so much for all of it."

I freeze. I don't think he realizes that he just told me he loves me, but I can feel it.

"You love me?"

He looks me in the eyes and brings my face to his. He kisses me. "Yes, Eve. So, so much." He pulls away and studies my expression.

I bite my lip and smile up at him. "I love you, too."

He swallows. "Is this why you didn't like for me to touch you when we first met? The times we were intimate?"

I stand and pace away before I turn to him. "I went to Krav Maga classes after the incident. I didn't ever want to feel that out of control of my life again. To have those feelings like I had years ago. Defenseless. Helpless. I felt so down on life, and I hated being a victim. I thought that I could take back my life if I could control everything about me. Maybe a little too much." I shrug, and he stands up.

"I have an idea. Do you trust me, baby?" He looks at me with so much devotion in his eyes that I can't say anything but the truth.

"Yes, completely."

He smiles, showing a full set of pearly whites, and my heart dances around in my chest, excited to see what he has in store for us.

"I'll be back in half an hour. Go run yourself a bath, and I'll be back before you know it." He winks at me and then leaves the apartment on a mission, for whatever he has planned, I know that he would never hurt me.

CHAPTER TWENTY-FOUR

JAMESON

"COME UNDONE" BY BAD OMENS

I drive back over to Eduardo's club and park out back. I open the back door and run up the stairs that lead to his office. I see Gus walking out and he eyes me suspiciously.

"Everything okay?"

I smile. "Yes. Is Eduardo in there? I have to ask him something, but it's of a personal nature."

He nods. "Sure thing. Just knock per usual. You know he doesn't usually lock his door. No one would be stupid enough to go in there."

Not that they'd live to tell about it. I think of that psychopath, Cherry, and shudder.

"Got it." I thank him and run off.

I knock on the door and Eduardo's voice gives me a resounding, "Enter." He looks up from his computer as I walk in. His expression turns to worry and I put my hand up.

"It's nothing, I just want a personal favor for Evie."

One eyebrow lifts up, and I wonder if he realizes that he does that so well. It's almost comical.

He sits back in his chair and steeples his fingers together. "Go on. What is it?"

Taking a breath before I ask, "Now, I hate to ask this, but I think it could really benefit Evie, and if I am being totally honest, it would help me a whole lot, too."

He just stares at me, waiting it out to see where I am going with this.

"I was hoping to borrow some supplies from the club next door," I get out all in one breath.

He tilts his head to the side. "My sex club?" I nod. A smile spreads across his face. "And why is that, James?"

"Just call it therapy," I counter.

He laughs. "Sure. I'll let them know that you are going in and will 'borrow' some items." He emphasizes the word *borrow* in air quotes. "Just make sure that you return them and disinfect them before we also disinfect them. Okay?"

I'm already heading to the door. As I open it, I give him a thumbs-up, and I can hear him laugh as I close the door behind me.

I enter the club with a mask on, disguising my face much like I did when I first met Eve here. Wow. To think so much has changed since then.

I approach the hostess station, scan my card, and let them know that I am here to borrow a few things. She seems skeptical, but after a quick call to her boss, I am escorted to one of the rooms where I pick a few items out that she helps to place in a garment-like bag. Once it is zipped up and discreetly hidden away from prying eyes, I leave the club through the back entrance and tuck the items in the back seat of the pickup and leave in a hurry to start my first session with my willing girlfriend.

I don't really have an idea if this will work, but I have to give it a chance. I want Evie to trust me while simultaneously helping her overcome her fears. We have made such good progress, but I want to be able to do more. Although she may not ever fully recover from her trauma and hold onto tidbits of that memory and fear, I can help her overcome the part that affects us and our relationship.

As I contemplate all the therapy sessions we will have tonight, I barely register pulling into the parking lot. I grab the bag out of the back seat and run up the stairs, taking them two at a time. I unlock the door with the key that Evie gave me before I left and place it back on the foyer table, calling out to her as I make my way into her bedroom. "Evie? I'm back."

"In here," she says.

She is towel drying her hair and rubs some products into it that smell like lavender and other botanicals. She tosses the towel to hang over the hook behind the door as I place the garment bag on her bed. As I fully unzip the bag for her, she looks at each item I have, receiving an eyeful of the toys I intend to pleasure her with.

Before she can ask, I let her know my plan. I walk over to her and take her hands in mine. "Remember when we met at the club that night for the first time?"

She smiles mischievously at the recollection of the events that unfolded that night, and I know exactly what part she is remembering.

"Of course."

I smile in return. "Well, I stopped by the club earlier and thought maybe we could create some more memories in the safety of your bedroom."

Her smile increases. "I like that plan. What do I get to use on you? Do you have a certain thing in mind?"

"I do," I reply. "I want for you to have an open mind."

She eyes me suspiciously and I can't help but encourage her. "Do you trust me?"

"You know I do."

But I can tell her hackles are raised and she is hesitant to learn of what I have planned because she is right. It is something to be concerned about, and I just hope that I am not making a colossal mistake and taking her too far out of her comfort zone.

I remove the first item from the bag—a pole with a leather padded attachment called a flogger. I place it on the bed, and I see her stare at it. I bring the next item out of the bag—a silk scarf. That is obvious, but the last one causes her to shuffle backward.

I remove the leather restraints from the bag and place the four items together on the duvet. Lastly, a pole is placed with the cuffs. "It's a spreader. It keeps your legs apart."

She looks at the items and then at me. "I don't understand."

"I think you do," I counter.

I approach her, and her body stiffens. I bring her closer to me. My hand is on her waist, and I look down into her eyes. They seem guarded, and they should be because we are going to test some limits, and I want her to get past this fear. If I can help her, maybe she can heal and learn to trust me as her partner and lover.

I run my hand down her cheek, and she leans into my touch. She stares up at me. I bring my lips to her and kiss her softly. "You know that I won't hurt you, right, Eve?" She nods, but doesn't speak. "We can stop at any time if you are uncomfortable. You know that too, right?"

She nods again. "Do I need a safe word, Jameson?"

I kiss her lips and trail kisses down her chin and neck. I pepper light kisses along her chest as she tosses her head to the side, granting me more access to the place she wants me to move. I oblige and then answer her.

"No. No safe word, baby. You just tell me to stop and I will. That's all it will take."

She smiles. "Okay. I want to try it for you."

I grab her hands and place them above her head. She keeps them up as I pull her tank top off her body and throw it over her head. I kneel at her feet and look up at her, bringing her sleep shorts and panties down her legs as she steps out of them. I toss them behind me and place a wet kiss on her pussy, swiping my tongue through her folds. She stares down at me with a hooded gaze. I stand up and point at the bed.

"Lay on your back in the middle of the bed, baby."

She quickly turns around and jumps on the bed, eager to follow directions. I strip all my clothes off agonizingly slowly, even though I want to peel them as soon as I can from my body so I can bury myself in her tight cunt.

I groan at the thought and palm my dick to stifle the ache that is building at the idea of her wet heat engulfing my cock. A bead of precum drips off the tip, and I need to progress this if I want to make it through all the things I want to do to her.

I pick up the scarf and twirl it in my hand. "I am going to cover your eyes, so you are going to need to trust me, okay."

"Okay. I can do that." She looks at the other things on the bed as I kneel on it and move on all fours toward her.

"You have already seen what I took out of the bag, so you know what is coming, okay. This is about you turning control over to me and learning to trust. I would never hurt you, Evie."

I place the scarf over her eyes, and she lifts her head so I can tie it around her head loosely, but effectively. "Can you see, baby?"

She shakes her head now, and I smile.

"Okay. I am going to put the cuffs on your hands and feet now." I pick up the cuffs, and the chains make a noise that causes her to flinch. I trail my finger over her legs and bend over to kiss her feet before placing the cuff on one leg and then repeat the same action on the other one. Once I have the cuffs on her legs, I attach them to the spreader that will keep them apart as I lock it in place.

I move over her body, my hand rests on her flat stomach, and I touch her lightly, running my hands under her breasts and everywhere except where she wants them. I see her lift her chest up in offering, hoping that I will put one nipple into my mouth, but that will come later.

I lift off and entwine my hands with hers as I raise them above her body and attach the cuff to them. My erect dick leaves a trail of wetness on her chest and hovers just over her neck as I move forward to attach the restraint to her metal headboard. As I tighten the last one, I feel her tongue dart out to lick my cock as she runs her tongue along the side.

"Fuck, Evie. You want to be a good girl and suck me off, baby?" This was not the plan, but if she is offering… I want to make her happy.

"I do." She licks her lips at the drop that falls from my tip.

"Open wide for me and stick out your tongue, so I can feed you my fat cock."

She obliges, and I grip it at the base as I scoot up and place the tip on her tongue. She licks the tip, and I inch more into her mouth as she hollows out her cheeks and takes me in deeper, until I hit the back of her throat. She doesn't gag like I thought she would, and I retreat out a bit before I push it back in.

Her tongue swirls around at the tip and licks the underside as I pump in and out of her mouth, but this wasn't the plan, so I pull out of her mouth with a pop as saliva trails down her chin.

She pouts.

"This isn't about me, baby. It's about you. Your mouth is sinful, Eve."

She smiles when I call her that.

"You are definitely my downfall, and I'll ride that train straight to hell if you're driving, sweetheart." I kiss her, and she lifts her head to deepen the kiss when I pull away and step off the bed. I pick up the flogger.

"What are you doing, Jameson?" she asks nervously.

"Nothing you won't like, baby."

I see the rise and fall of her chest quicken as she becomes anxious of what's to come. I don't keep her waiting long as I grip the flogger and place the cool leather trailing a path up her arm and down her chest. I circle her nipple with it and then repeat the same action on the other side. I trail it around and then bring it down quickly on the underside of her breast in a quick snap to her flesh. She gasps, but realizes what happened.

"Jameson," she moans.

I trail the flogger down her leg and up the other until I reach her pussy. I give it a quick snap with the flogger and wetness pools down her leg. She tries to bring her legs together to relieve some of the ache that is forming between them, but the spreader bar is there preventing her from moving the way she would like to. I place my head between her thighs and blow on her glistening pussy.

"You are so wet for me, baby."

"Please, Jameson. The anticipation is killing me."

I don't give her a chance to say anything else before I devour her. I hold her lips open as I fuck her with my tongue then come back out, finding her clit as I pull and suck it into my mouth. She comes with a scream. I tuck one arm under her hips to help bring her closer to me as she bucks and thrashes around while I continue to suck on her clit.

Wetness pools underneath her as I wipe the mess from my chin. Her breathing starts to slow, and I undo the spreader bar. I toss it off the bed and climb forward as I run my dick through her wetness. I line up with her opening and surge forward, causing Evie to cry out. I stall.

"You okay?" She shakes her head. "Use your words, baby."

"Please fuck me, Jameson."

And I do. I won't last long. But I want her to come again, so I suck on her nipple and toy with the other as I fuck her hard, hitting that spot that makes her see stars. I know I've reached it when she gasps.

She screams, "Right there. Keep going." She squeezes my cock as she comes, and I follow, climaxing along with her.

I collapse on top of her and swirl my tongue around her over sensitive nipple. With my dick still inside her, I undo the restraints on the headboard and hover over her as I remove the blindfold from her eyes. I look into her eyes and she smiles.

I kiss her and feel my cock harden again. I start to move and she wraps her legs around my waist. This time I fuck her softly, letting the gravity of what we just did register. She trusted me, and hopefully that's enough. She loves me, and I know that's everything.

CHAPTER TWENTY-FIVE

EVIE

"ONLY HAPPY WHEN IT RAINS" BY GARBAGE

I don't know when we fell asleep, but I was fucked into unconsciousness. I'm awake at three AM, the witching hour. It is the time of night that nothing good happens, when evil is meant to be at its strongest and the supernatural run rampant, spreading lies and deceit through the remaining hours of nightfall.

I hear a crash and sit up quickly. Jameson is already out the bedroom door to investigate the disturbance. I throw on his shirt when I see him helping my drunk-as-shit brother up off the floor. The guy is piss drunk and reeks of cheap thrills taken in a dive bar bathroom stall.

I hope that I am exaggerating, but he does smell heavily of booze and sickly sweet perfume. His zipper is down and his dick is sticking out slightly and I wince, looking away just as quickly. I hope that he was trying to take a piss somewhere and it's not from anything else.

"Yikes. Commando. Agh. My eyes." I rub at them, but some things cannot be unseen.

"Evie." Jameson startles me from my verbal diarrhea. "Help me get him to his bed, please."

I jump into action as I round the other side of Mateo and fling his arm around my shoulder. Jameson and I struggle but manage to bring his dead weight over to his room and attempt to lay him on his bed, but he bounces as we drop him there. He groans as if in pain.

Just wait until tomorrow. I shake the thought away with a violent shudder, remembering how that time felt and vowing never to feel that hungover again. That out of control.

"Yeah, that wasn't fun for me either, bro."

I tug his shoes off, and Jameson helps to remove his pants. I don't want to see any more of my brother than I already had to this early morning, so I run over to the other side, lifting the covers as Jameson lifts his legs up and I swoop the covers from under and pull them upward and over his body.

I go the kitchen to grab a Gatorade and water bottle along with some pain medication. I know he will need it to help with what I am sure will be a raging headache when he finally wakes to welcome a more sobering day.

He will definitely regret this later.

After we place him on his side with a trash can in case he decides to puke, we close the door. I follow Jameson back to my room, and I swear I can still smell his scent of questionable morals lingering in a claustrophobic blanket of despair over my body.

Jameson is behind me now, waking me from my thoughts. He quickly kisses my neck, nuzzling and breathing in deeply. "Wow, he stunk," Jameson says as he steps away from me, frowning as he sniffs his arm. "Can you still smell it?" he asks me, and I giggle, nodding.

"Right?" He grimaces. "Damn. I thought so."

"Should we shower?" I think about it, but I am beat and want to go back to bed.

"We are getting up soon, so why bother? We can shower in a couple of hours when we have to get up anyway."

He nods in silent agreement.

He rummages through the bathroom cabinet. "I found it." He looks victorious as he waves my favorite lemon verbena spray and starts spraying our room and sheets with it. "There." He puts the bottle down, sniffing the air.

"Good lord, it does smell a little better now." He sniffs his arm again, but the overpowering fresh scent of lemon is all I can smell.

"Can we finally go back to bed now?"

It doesn't take much to convince Jameson as he pulls the covers over his shoulder, tucks himself into me, and is asleep before his head touches the pillow.

Hearing him breathe so relaxed and deep makes me tumble into an equally deep slumber where dreams evade me and my mind is clear from the dark waves of emotions that constantly wash over me.

Emma called and asked if I wanted to join her to visit Liv. I had my reservations, but she convinced me to go. Jameson is going to drive us, since he is friends with Dax, Liv's husband. They are going to catch up while he is home on a brief paternity leave with Liv.

I am sitting, having my morning coffee and cursing Mateo, when she pulls up to my house at around ten. Jameson says something about disinfecting some equipment before returning it to Eduardo's club.

He walks out of the bedroom and places the garment-looking bag on the side of the couch. My face reddens looking at it and thinking about how we used most of the equipment in varying positions. I got used to feeling restrained around him, and the way Jameson fucked me like a champ all night left me pleasantly sore between my legs. I slept so soundly afterwards, until I didn't.

The doorbell rings, and I get up to answer it. Emma is at the door and waves to someone as she enters.

"Was that Eduardo?" I close the door behind her, and she waves to Jameson, who is scrolling through his phone with his cup of coffee.

She places her mug on the table. "Yes, of course, it was. You know how he is." She looks around and walks to the refrigerator. She opens it and she fist pumps the air. "My favorite cold brew. How did you know?"

She opens it and pours a generous serving along with my oatmilk, which is hidden off to the side and covered by Mattie's gallon of whole milk. So infuriating. Why did I somehow miss the lactose enzyme? She places her top back on her cup and takes a long sip.

She sighs dramatically. "Absolute heaven." She looks around. "Hey, where is Mateo?"

I shoot a glance over to Jameson, and he looks at me, then proceeds to avoid eye contact with Emma.

She stands. "What was that look for, Jameson?"

He won't look at her. "I have no idea what you mean, Em." He continues to scroll through his socials, and I scoff.

"Geez, at least I know you are a bad liar." Emma focuses her attention on me. "What is it, Evie? Is our brother okay?"

"No, he isn't okay. He was given some pretty devastating news yesterday, remember?"

Emma starts to walk over to his room, but I pull her by the hand away from the door.

"He came home so drunk last night, or rather this morning, around three AM. We had to help him to bed, and it was a sad sight. He smelled horrific, and I swear I need to burn his sheets."

She rolls her eyes. "Don't be so dramatic, sis."

Jameson finally looks up and holds his hand up. "Hey, I have to agree with Eve on that. He was so saturated in booze and cheap perfume that I think it is better just to do that. In fact, I think he should bathe in more alcohol to burn the germs off. I just hope he was careful and didn't fuck anyone without protection."

Emma winces at the visual that Jameson painted for her.

"I told you. He was in a bad way, Em. I was going to check on him, but I honestly thought it would be better for him to sleep. He'll need to sleep off that hellacious hangover."

"I agree," Jameson says.

Emma looks toward Mateo's door and frowns in displeasure. She relents. "Okay, I guess you're right. Let's let the guy sleep, but later, he is free game."

I feel bad for Mateo if he has to hear her bitch at him this afternoon.

I stand, placing my now empty mug of coffee in the sink, and Jameson follows suit. He comes over to me and gives me a quick peck on the lips, pulling himself close to me and wrapping his arm around my waist before he lets go. He claps his hands together, rubbing them together.

"Are you girls ready to leave here and see a baby?"

Jameson agrees to drive us over there, and I climb into the front of his truck. Emma hops in the back, and Jameson gets in on his side, starting up the truck. I roll down my window to let some of the heat out. Jameson blasts the air conditioning, but it doesn't feel cool until he pulls onto the interstate. The cooling seats are magnificent, as the leather doesn't seem quite as hot as before.

My thoughts go back to last night and all the delicious things Jameson did to me. I wanted to admit I wasn't okay, but I didn't want to upset him. I felt better when I practiced my breathing techniques and remembered that I was in a controlled environment.

Even though I gave control to him, I never felt like I wasn't in control. He told me if I wanted to stop, we could. There were too many reassurances for me to feel anything other than safe in his arms.

I understand it is because I trust him, and the comfort level is there. I had so much therapy before, and my partners were never someone as close as Jameson is to me. We are in a relationship built on love, respect, and now trust. He knows all my secrets, fears, and, more importantly, my dreams. He wants to be a part of that, and it's more than I could have ever hoped for in a relationship.

I smile, thinking of him coming with a roar in my ear as he nuzzles into my neck, causing a tickle there that made me squirm and laugh. If he had tickled me while I was tied up, I would have been pissed.

"What are you smiling at, Evie?"

His question pulls me from my thoughts, and I look over at him. I'm biting my nail, and I'm sure my cheeks are pink from the memory of him fucking me hard as the headboard knocked against the wall.

Oh my goodness. My poor neighbors.

"Never mind," he says as he looks over my shoulder to merge into the other lane.

Emma chimes in. "I don't think I want to know."

We pull into Dax and Liv's place, and Emma starts toward the door, while Jameson comes over to my side of the truck, where I step down onto the pavement. I look up at him as he pushes me against the truck. His erection grinds into my stomach as he bends over to kiss me. I push him away and swat at his arm.

"Stop."

He laughs and closes the door, locking it with the key fob and adjusting his erection as Emma watches us, shaking her head with her hands lifted above her head. She knocks on the door, and Dax opens it. I'm already ahead of Jameson, and he jogs to catch up. "Hey, ladies. Liv is through that way in the room off the kitchen."

Jameson mouths 'Have fun,' as I follow Emma to see Liv's new baby, Kaden Brodie Johnson.

Liv is snuggled into a chair with baby Kaden in her arms. She stands when she sees us. She shuffles over to Emma, and Emma wraps her arms around her best friend and looks over at the little boy in her arms. She looks up to stare at me and looks over at Emma.

"Holy shit. You have a twin sister?"

Emma winces. "Yes, Liv, this is my other best friend and sister, Evie."

Liv looks at me, and then Emma and I can sense the hurt radiating from Liv and how she never knew about me. It's not as if Emma could have told her, but I am beginning to understand why I am here and the support Emma needs to tell her best friends the truth. It's time for all the lies to stop.

"Liv, I am here today not only to see you and the baby but also to tell you the truth." She bites her lip and looks over at me. I stand near Emma to give her support.

Liv nods and then points to the chair for us to sit. She settles the baby into her lap, and I put my hands out to offer to hold the baby for her.

Liv looks over at me hesitantly before handing her baby boy over to me. She crosses her feet under her and places her hand in her lap, waiting for Emma to speak.

"Liv, there is so much I want to tell you, and I have kept so much from you, but you are my best friend. It is time to tell you the truth. I can finally tell you the truth about my family and why I was so secretive. There were so many times that you asked me something, and I wanted to tell you, but I couldn't because it wasn't safe for me to do so."

Liv leans closer, as if the secrets will appear if she squints hard enough. Emma twists her hands in her lap, and I move side to side, trying to comfort a sleeping baby, but perhaps I'm the one who needs the soothing.

"I knew Eduardo from when we were kids, and my mother kept us apart. The reason is that his family is in the mafia."

Liv blinks and then looks away. "Emma, I kind of already knew that. I mean, Jameson said that he went to college with Eduardo and didn't come out and say it, but that's what I suspected."

Emma smiles. "Yes, you are right, but what you don't know is that my family is, too." This news shocks her, and her hand goes up to her mouth, stifling a gasp.

"I was on the run, Liv. I had a stalker ex-boyfriend that abused me, and he and his father killed my family. I was taken by him, held captive, and escaped when my family in Mexico came for me. I recently learned that my sister wasn't dead and that I have a brother."

Liv jumps off the couch and throws herself at Emma. "Oh my God, Emma. Why didn't you tell me you were in danger?" She pulls back, and Emma is trying to hold back tears that threaten to fall from her eyes at any given moment.

"I didn't want to put *you* in any danger, Liv. I thought I was doing what was the safest for you, especially since Julian was still trying to find me."

Liv shakes her head. "Is he still after you? Are you safe now?"

Emma looks over to me. I speak maybe out of turn, but I want to give Emma a moment to recover.

"Julian is no longer a threat." Liv audibly gulps, and I continue. "But his father is. We are handling it, but Emma brought it up at our family meeting, and here we are. She wanted to purge the secrets she's kept from you, so I hope you will keep this to yourself?"

Liv is quick to reply. "Of course. Of course."

I smile, satisfied that she will keep our secret. "It's also really nice to meet you, Liv. I feel like I know you, too. I used to watch over Emma and always wanted to hang out with you guys and your other friends at the beach and club, but you know… being dead and all," I trail off, and I swear I see her hide a smile.

"Yes, I see how that could be a problem, Evie." She looks over at Emma, who is analyzing our interaction.

"Now you see why she hid from me and I had to keep her a secret? Troublemaker, this one." Emma laughs, pointing a thumb in my direction. The tension in the room seems to lighten after our banter.

"So…" Liv starts. "You and Jameson, huh?" She waggles her eyebrows up and down.

Baby Kaden starts to fuss after being placed back in Liv's arms. I snort. "Yeah, I know."

Liv and Emma start laughing as baby Kaden begins to cry. Jameson walks in with Dax and looks over at me. "Ya know what, Evie?" he repeats my words, asking a question, although with a hint of mischief in his eyes.

CHAPTER TWENTY-SIX

JAMESON

"BAD COMPANY" BY FIVE FINGER DEATH PUNCH

"So, you and Evie, huh?" After spending some time catching up with our mutual friends and hearing about Dax's new position as a full-fledged partner in his father's practice, I'm surprised it took him this long to discuss the elephant in the room.

I take the soda he offered me, electing for a more alcohol-free drink this morning full of sugar and caffeine. I swear I still smell that jackass's stench on me. Dax must see the downturn of my mouth and interprets this as something wrong with Evie and me.

"Am I wrong?" he asks, concerned.

"Huh? No, sorry, but we had a little problem last night, and I was just trying to think of the best solution to fix it." Dax rubs his hand over his chin, trying to ascertain if I need help or not. I hold my hand up to him.

"It's better if you don't know." He looks at me and then nods in understanding.

"Of course, but if you..." he trails off, letting me know that he is here for me should I need him, and those unspoken words mean the world to me.

I place my hand on his shoulder. "Thanks, bro. I appreciate that."

He smiles, and I hear a wail coming from the other room. Dax stands immediately to tend to his son, and I follow.

"Man, that kid has some lungs." The crying, along with Evie's dipshit brother coming in at the asscrack of dawn, has my head pounding.

Dax chuckles. "You have no idea, Jameson. Just wait. It will happen to you, too."

We enter the room just in time to hear the end of their conversation. I wonder what was said before I entered the room. Whatever it was will have to wait, and baby Kaden is having a complete meltdown, and Liv needs to feed him. We take this as our cue to leave.

We make rushed goodbyes with a promise to meet up very soon. We walk down the stairs, and I look back, extending my hand to Evie's as we walk to my truck.

I shake her hand, nudging her to look at me. "You okay?

She shakes her head. "Yeah, but dang, there was a lot of screaming in there."

I bring her hand up to my lips. "You mean you aren't ready to have little Evie or Jameson running around yet?"

She stops mid-stride, and realizing she is no longer walking with me, I turn back to look at her. The sheer terror on her face makes me go back to her.

I approach her carefully, like a skittish cat that will run off if you advance too soon. "Baby, I was just kidding. I'm not ready to have kids right now. It was a joke, and by the looks of it, maybe a very bad one."

She relaxes into my embrace. "I'd make a terrible mother," she almost whispers.

I take her face in both hands and bring her close. "You are brave, protective, and love so fiercely, Evie. I think those are the best traits for a mother, and I think you would be the best mom someday."

She searches my eyes for the truth. And I know when she finds it there as she melts into my embrace. Sometimes, I forget that even though she puts on a brave act, she is still vulnerable and needs reassurance, just like we all do.

She tilts her head in my hands, and I bring her lips to mine in a soft kiss. She leans into me, and I hug her, kissing the top of her head. When we turn around, Emma is standing there with tears in her eyes. She looks away and walks ahead of us to the truck without looking back.

The ride back to Evie's and Mateo's place is quiet. Entirely too quiet as we are all lost in our thoughts. I look in the rearview mirror and see Emma looking out the window. She must sense me staring because she looks my way. Her eyes meet mine and she beams at Evie and smiles. Then she looks back at me before returning her attention to the passing cars on the interstate.

We pull into the complex and see Mateo is still there. Emma is out of the car as soon as it stops, jumping from the back seat like she is propelling herself at a forty-five-degree angle, posing as a stunt double in an action-packed movie.

I cock my head sideways as her little legs take her up to their apartment. Where she is curvy, my Evie is toned and just perfect. I stifle a laugh, and Evie swats my arm.

"Stop already with the short jokes. It hurts her feelings."

I raise my hands defensively.

"You know we are twins, right?"

"Okay. Okay, but I didn't say anything. And for the record, you do not look identical."

We've almost caught up to Emma as she has to wait for us at the door since we have the keys. I wave them at her, and her nostrils flare with annoyance. She takes both of her hands and twists them in a scooping fashion toward the door, urging us to hurry up. Evie scoffs, taking them from me and tosses them to her. She opens the door seconds before we arrive and, immediately, the cold air-conditioning hits my face.

"Geez, what is it, like sixty degrees in here?" Evie goes over to the thermostat, turns it up, and the air conditioning cycles off.

Mateo walks into the living room with gray sweatpants and no shirt while he towel dries his hair. We all stare at him as he rolls his eyes at us and saunters off.

"Oh, no, you don't, Mattie." Emma starts marching over there.

"I'll be right out, and you can yell at me in a second. I just need to put this towel away." He disappears into his room but reappears with a bottle of water.

He slumps into the recliner, placing the cold water bottle on his forehead. Evie and Emma sit on the couch as I stand up, leaning against the wall staring at us. Mateo downs half the water bottle's contents and leans forward to place it on the coffee table in front of him. He slumps forward and runs his hand through his hair, tugging at the ends. He moves them to steeple under his chin and waits patiently for the chastising to begin.

No one says anything.

I look over at Evie, and she seems genuinely sad for him, while Emma looks pissed.

Emma shoots up off the couch, startling Mateo, causing him to lean back and away from his firecracker of a sister with an equally volatile temper. She raises her hands in the air. "What the fuck Mateo! You cannot get shit-faced like that and just disappear."

Mateo hangs his head like a child being scolded.

"You scared Evie half to death coming in last night drunk off your ass and smelling like it, too, from what I hear. You cannot bury yourself in booze and pussy because you were feeling sorry for yourself."

He looks up at Emma with a scathing look. "And why not, Emma? Huh? Maybe I just need to forget what my life is like sometimes. Maybe I just wanted to feel something, or maybe I just wanted to feel nothing at all."

Emma sits back down on the couch, crossing her arms over her chest.

Evie leans forward, this time to say her peace. "Mattie, I was so scared when you came home like that. I worry about you. Just like you worry about me. You are my brother. My family. And I've lost so much already. I couldn't bear to lose you, too. I don't think I could recover if I lost *my guardian angel.* My protector. My brother." Evie hits her chest with each spoken word, like a vow she makes to him in return.

Mateo gulps as a multitude of emotions flash over him. He withers into the chair like he is empty and defeated. Beat down.

Evie walks over to him and squats at his level. She takes his hand in hers, and I want to hold her. I want to tell her how amazing she is, but I just sit there, taking in the scene as she comforts her brother.

"Mattie. It's okay to feel alone, to feel shattered, and to take others' feelings for granted. You have been through a lot. We all have. Just remember that you have us. You're family, and we love you. You are not alone anymore. Collect your broken pieces and fix you, Mattie, because if you don't, one day your life will be nothing but regrets."

His eyes shimmer with unshed tears, and then Evie leans in and hugs her brother.

Emma walks over to Mateo and throws her arms around him. "Please don't forget that again, Mattie. We love you." Emma speaks softly into his shoulder as she leans on the recliner side, hugging Mateo.

He pulls her in closer and kisses her on the cheek. "I love you too, Emma."

She smiles in return and then smacks him on the arm. "But if you ever do that again, Mattie..." She doesn't finish that sentence before Mateo tickles her side, and she falls off the chair laughing.

I walk over to the couch that is now free as the girls are huddled over with their brother on the recliner. "Mateo," I speak up, and the room is silent as Evie glances over at me, forehead scrunching. "I have a concern."

They all look over to me, and Mateo nods, encouraging me to speak my piece. Emma bites her lip, forcing herself not to speak up to defend her brother and wait until I get out what I have to say.

"What will we do about Ramón now that we know he is working with Mr. Martinez?"

The girls both look to Mateo for answers as I wait patiently to hear his response.

He clears his throat. "Well, I think I need to confront him, but I don't think his house is the best place. Maybe at the cafe where we usually play chess?" He looks to me for what I can only assume is my opinion on the matter.

I nod. "I just worry about Evie because she always goes with you. Maybe I can tag along, or Emma, Eduardo, and I can show up there for your next meet-up?"

He seems to ponder the idea over and nods in agreement. "Yeah, I think maybe that would be best."

Evie squeezes his hand, walks over to me, and sits on my lap. "When do we see him again, Mateo?" She shifts her hips over my thigh, making my cock jump into action. She feels it as she wiggles her ass over the rigid outline as it is trying to push upward as if it has a mind of its own.

I hold her from shifting further and stifle a groan. She giggles, and Emma squints her eyes as if she has x-ray vision that allows her to see through clothing.

Mateo speaks, interrupting my thoughts of slipping my rock-hard cock into Evie's slick heat. "We are set to meet on Friday around midday."

I look at Emma, and she nods. "I can be there. I'll bring Eduardo. Just give us the details, and we'll see you there." She stands, and Mateo rises with her.

"You leaving, Em?"

"Yes. I have to work tonight. It's such a zoo there, and nights are the worst, but Eduardo thinks it is safer. I don't work much now, but it's part-time. At least for now, until I do other things."

Evie and I look over at her, and Emma walks toward the door. Evie turns to me and mouths 'other things.' I shrug, not knowing what that means as we walk to say goodbye to Emma.

She kisses her hand and then waves. "Love you, but I gotta run, or Eduardo will throw a fit before he takes me to work." With that, she closes the door, and we stand in the window watching her sashay to her BMW Eduardo had dropped off to her earlier, as she drives away.

Evie scoffs. "Let's not pretend that Eduardo doesn't always know where she is."

As if right on cue, another vehicle with someone who strangely resembles Philip follows Emma out of the parking lot and onto the street.

"Told you," Evie barks out, pointing to the car driving off after Emma.

"Baby, that's not the half of it. And I can't say I blame him."

Evie looks over at me, searching my eyes for something she won't find. Because if there is one thing that I have learned from Eduardo, it is that there is nothing we wouldn't do to protect the women we love.

I pull her to me as I hear Mateo move away.

"I think I'm going to order some greasy food and go back to bed," he says.

I tug Evie toward me. "I think we will skip the first part of that and go straight on to the second." I lead Evie back to her room and close the door.

CHAPTER TWENTY-SEVEN

EVIE

"LOVERS ROCK" BY TV GIRL

Midweek, I decide to call Emma and see if she wants to have a girl's day. I know she doesn't work tonight, so she agrees. We are meeting up with everyone this evening for dinner to brainstorm ideas for when Mateo will confront his grandfather, Ramón, on Friday. The anxiety of that meeting has me on edge, and I need a distraction. What better way to do that than to go for afternoon margaritas at our favorite Tex-Mex restaurant? It might be fun to see if Liv wants to come along.

I remember all the times when I witnessed Emma and her friends out and about having a good time eating lunch or clubbing at night. I felt that pang of jealousy as I watched from the shadows, never to be invited or even known about. The sister who died more than anyone else would ever realize. I died a thousand deaths in the shadows, feeling dead inside.

Now, all these feelings rise to the surface, overpowering me as a turbulent storm of emotions which constantly swirls around me, trying to break through my carefully crafted façade. Since Emma told Liv about us and our family, it seems like a weight has been lifted.

I feel lighter. I feel free. I feel seen.

I thought the day would never come when I was able to sit at their table, talking and laughing with my sister and her friends. To partake in conversation and camaraderie is something I have longed for and will never take for granted.

"I'll take the Texas Skinny margarita, please," Liv tells the waiter and gently places the menu on the table.

I frown at her choice because she just had a baby and that shouldn't mean that she needs to go on a diet. I don't know her well enough to tell her that I think she looks fantastic after giving birth, so I offer her a small smile instead.

Emma takes forever to pick something, and it makes me roll my eyes. I want to cut in but mind my manners as the waiter ogles her, and she remains oblivious. I look over at Liv, and she suppresses a laugh with her hand, hiding her smile as she looks away. Emma bites her lip in concentration, and he licks his lips. I can only imagine what he is thinking at the moment, and I cock my head to the side, assessing to see if I need to intervene.

"I'll take the Some Like it Hot margarita." She places her menu down and doesn't even look at the guy. She nods at me as if letting me know it's my turn to order. She must feel his stare on her; this is her way of kindly turning him down.

So done with this, I roll my eyes and snap my menu down, startling the waiter and Liv, who snaps straight and makes a startled noise similar to a baby bird. The waiter faces me, seeing the smirk that forms on my lips, letting him know I saw him. Emma's eyes twinkle with hidden laughter. I look at his name tag as if I am getting a hard look at it, squinting my eyes for the full effect.

"I'll take the Smoky Mezcal, please, and if we could get a vat of guacamole with chips and salsa, please, Cole."

He nods and leaves us without another word.

Emma scoffs. "I hope he comes back soon with our order. I think you might have scared him off."

Liv watches the exchange between us and doesn't comment.

I roll my eyes at her naivety. "Sorry, but I really didn't want it to get back to Eduardo, and then I have to listen to it because we are all meeting tonight for dinner, and we have much more pressing issues to discuss."

She nods her understanding. "Agreed."

The waiter returns with our drinks and apps, and we give him the rest of our food order. I take a big scoop of guac and practically orgasm as the taste of spices and cilantro hits my mouth.

I sip my margarita and look up at Liv and Emma, who are curiously eyeing me. I dab the salt off the sides of my mouth and sip my margarita once more. I put it down and look at Liv, who is staring at me like I'm Uncle Eddie in my favorite Chevy Chase Christmas movie.

"Sorry, but that is the best guacamole ever."

Liv gives me a genuine smile and loads up her tortilla chip before she bites into it, sending crumbs splattering over the table. She makes a similar noise of pleasure.

"Agreed." She says this with a mouth full of food, mimicking Emma's comment earlier.

Emma laughs, throwing her hands in the air. "Okay, now it's my turn." She holds her chip mid-flight as I scoop up more with my tortilla chip. "Don't you dare try to stab me with your chip." She snorts.

"I would never stab my own sister, Emma." I wink at Liv as she snaps her attention over to me and then to Emma, as if she sees Emma in her truest form for the first time.

I grin widely. "She's just kidding, Liv. I am usually the stabby one."

Liv almost chokes on her drink as Emma moans loudly, licking the excess avocado from her lip. We all look up to see our waiter, Cole, standing there with a food tray in his hand and his mouth open as he stares at Emma.

"Oh, hey, Cole, just in time," she comments as he distributes our food quickly and leaves without further comment.

Liv's hand goes to her mouth as she laughs. This causes Emma to snort, and I watch them in amusement, thinking that I have not had a better day in what feels like forever.

As we finish up our food and drinks, Cole approaches us, asking if we need anything else.

"Then thank you, ladies. The bill and tip have been paid in full, and I thank you for your generosity. I hope to see you again soon." He leaves us, and Emma throws her napkin on the table.

"I don't know about you, but I need to be assisted out of here. I ate so much. I don't think I can breathe, much less stand."

We all get up to leave as Philip brings the car around the front of the restaurant to take us home. Liv gets into the back seat with Emma, and I sit in the front. As I buckle up my seatbelt, Liv touches my arm, startling me, and I fight the urge to pull back. Her touch is gentle and non-threatening. "Evie," she says softly.

I turn back toward her. "Yes."

She looks over to Emma and then to me. "I just want you to know that I had so much fun with you and Emma today, and I am thrilled to have another friend."

I look over to Emma, who is smiling at me and Liv. I am not used to feeling this way, and the thought of having another friend catches me off guard. I haven't had many close connections, and this feels like a huge step into living.

I touch her hand in return. "Thank you, Liv. That means more to me than you know. I really appreciate your friendship."

Emma turns her attention to Liv. "Hey, I wanted to let you know now that I can talk freely in the car that we may be gone for a while. Something has happened that may be a bit dangerous, and we need to leave."

Liv looks between us. "Where are you going?"

Philip looks at Emma in the rearview mirror, and Emma nods. Ignoring Philip's pleas to stay silent she, of course, does the exact opposite.

"I told Liv no more secrets, Philip." She brushes back her hair that has fallen out of her loose bun and inhales deeply, closing her eyes.

Liv waits patiently, as if she's almost afraid to blink.

"The man that killed my family lives in Brownsville, and we are going to hide out, assessing the situation to ensure the next part of our plan to take revenge for our family is implemented.

Liv snorts. "Damn, Em. You say that like it's a nursing care plan you used to write for school."

Emma laughs, and I look at them, not understanding the joke, but I am sure I won't get many of their private jokes.

"Well, I do have a fully furnished condo near Brownsville, and it sits empty now, if you need a place to hide out, just so you know."

Philip looks at me, and I place my hands together.

"Oh, a secret hideaway lair. How perfect." I rub my hands together like an evil overlord plotting Earth's demise.

Emma slaps Liv's leg, startling her. "Liv, that might just be what we are looking for. Do you need to ask Dax, though?"

She shakes her head. "Nah, we can't use it now anyway, and I'm sure he's offered it to Jameson also. Not a problem. Just let me know, and it's yours if you need it."

"It's right on the beach, too, huh?" I ask anxiously.

Liv nods. "Yep, you'll love it."

She sits back, and we laugh and talk about normal things women our age would. They catch me up on their friends back in Padre Island, since we are on the topic of it.

Soon, the trip is over, and we make plans to do it again soon. They drop me off next, and I tell Emma that I'll see her later. As I am walking to the door, I hear the car door open. Emma comes running over to me and tightly hugs me.

"I am so glad that we have the chance to do this, Evie."

I hug her back. "Me too, Em."

With that, she gets back into the car and drives off as soon as I enter my apartment. With everything that will happen in the near future and all the unforeseen complications with Mr. Martinez and now Mateo's grandfather, it was nice to have a sense of normalcy, even if it is just for a brief moment.

Jameson, Mateo, and I drive over to Eduardo's and Emma's place since we planned on meeting there to discuss our next step with Ramón. We found out that Ramón is Mateo's biological grandfather and Mr. Martinez's father, so we have to decide what this could mean for all of us. Eli, Gus, and Philip are there. We are all gathered around the island. Eduardo comes out of his office with his laptop.

"I have a few people who are going to be on a video conference with us."

"Who is it, babe?" Emma plops herself onto Eduardo's lap, and he pulls her in tight, moving her off to the side as he tries to shift himself discreetly. Emma tries to move over, and he halts her, whispering something into her ear. Her face blushes, and she nods once.

Mateo's eyes narrow, and I cough to hide the laugh that threatens to leave me.

Eduardo clears his throat. "My dad, for one, my brother Ramiro and his fiancée, Anna—" Emma cuts in.

"Oh, that call. Our Uncle Andrés and cousin Adrian, too then?" Emma announces.

I can't help the question that leaves my mouth. "Why is your brother's fiancée listening in?"

Eduardo leans over the island, pushing Emma along with him. "We don't keep secrets from each other anymore, Evie. We are family, and all of us here, whether related by blood or not, are family. Our own family is built on love, trust, and respect for one another. No more secrets."

Emma leans over to him, nuzzling her face into his neck. "I couldn't have said it better, my love."

Eduardo claps his hands. "Okay, ready to get this started?" He logs into the video conference call, and faces pop up on the computer, letting us know that they are all there and ready. After a few rounds of 'can you hear me?' and 'how do I turn on my camera?' we are finally ready to formulate a plan together.

"Absolutely not!" Eduardo booms loudly through the kitchen as he stands up abruptly, almost knocking Emma to the ground before he catches her around the waist as if she weighs nothing. He kisses the top of her head, placing her gently on her feet. "I won't put Emma in harm's way."

I look at Jameson, and by his expression and the tic of his jaw, I don't think he likes the idea either as he shoots daggers at my brother. If looks could kill, Mateo would be dust already.

"Look, Liv offered her condo down in the valley to us, and it's literally right there by Brownsville. No one would know that we were there."

"I think it is the best idea where we are all close together. Until I meet with Ramón and find out what he and Mr. Martinez want from me, I'd like to have my sisters close-by and hidden." Eduardo rubs his hand over his face.

"I have an idea," Ram's voice comes through the speaker.

"I sure hope it is better than Mateo's." He shoots my brother a look that would make another man wither, but my brother is no other man. He was a soldier for my uncle and brought up the same way Eduardo was.

"I'll come up and take over the business for you while you go down to Brownsville with the girls. With you and Jameson there and their family just a stone's throw over the border, I would feel okay with the plan."

"Oh, you would have no problem if this was Anna? If it was your fiancée there instead of Emma?"

Ram hangs his head down and looks over to his wife. He grabs her hand and kisses it. "Maybe, but I think that this is the best solution."

CHAPTER TWENTY-EIGHT

JAMESON

"ROMEO AND JULIET" BY DIRE STRAITS

Last night, I dreamt that I lost Evie to that monster. I can't imagine how Emma felt thinking her sister was dead all this time, especially after losing her parents as well. I know that she was the closest to Evie, and as she lies beside me, I can't help but hold her, bringing her closer.

I kiss her neck as my hand splays across her abdomen. She pushes her ass into my hard cock, causing it to weep. I trail my fingers lower to her panties, feeling her sweet heat. Then I throw one leg over her, bringing her closer to me still, and feel her waken as I palm her pussy. She moans, and I slide my hand under the hem of her panties, pushing through her folds as I move my finger through her slick seam. She turns her head slightly, and I move over her more, kissing her. She brings one arm around my neck, pulling me to her, and I think back to when she couldn't do something as simple as this.

It took a while of being away from each other, getting used to her touching herself, pretending it was me, and then slowly taking my hand over hers until we got to this—the point where she trusts me completely not to hurt her, and I would rather end my life than hurt this woman. Who knew she would be so perfectly damaged and fit my own missing piece of a puzzle?

I circle her clit with my thumb and plunge one finger into her hot, wet pussy as it sucks me in greedily. I add another finger, and she opens her legs wider for me, allowing me more access. I add a third finger, and she throws her head back. Wetness drips down my fingers as I finger fuck her, and she rides my hand as I suck on her neck, marking her.

I pull my fingers out of her, and she whimpers at the loss. I flip us and place her on top of me. I bring my fingers to my mouth and suck off her sticky wetness one by one. She watches me with hooded eyes, yet I am the one drunk on her. She rocks back and forth, seeking friction from my hard cock as her panties dampen further.

"Gotta take these off, baby."

I grab both sides of the sparse material and pull it apart, leaving a little mark on her hip. It pulls there, and I tap her bottom. "Come up here, Eve, and ride my face. I want you to come all over my mouth. I'm dying for you, sweetheart."

I lift her ass up and move her along as she almost falls forward. Her breasts land right in my face, and I lick and suck. She grabs my hair and pulls me to her. I tweak her nipple with my other hand, pulling and tugging as her pussy drips onto my abdomen. "Can't let that sweet juice go to waste, can we?"

I pull her all the way up, and she hovers right above me. I can smell her, and it is heaven. I push her legs apart with my forearms and hook them around her thighs as I bring her core right to my face. I swipe my tongue through her folds. "Part those sweet pussy lips for me, baby. I want to eat you."

Evie uses one hand to place on the headboard, and the other hand goes to separate herself for me so I can easily get to her pretty, glistening cunt. I admire it for a split second before shoving my face into her as she soaks me in her juices. She throws her head back.

"Ride my face, baby." I bring her down more and nip and lick her. I eat her like she's my last meal. I am starving for her and only her.

"Oh God." She is lost to the sensation.

I shove my tongue in, swirling it around, and sweep upward, biting at her clit. I feel her quiver, and I suck hard while she convulses under me. I feel a squirt and stick my tongue in her pussy, licking up as much of her wetness as I can before she goes still, and then I lap at her clit before she starts to shake again.

I sweep her off me, and she falls onto the bed like a dead weight. I drop down on the bed and hook her legs over my shoulders, bringing her back to me. I thrust three fingers in at once while I suck her clit into my mouth. Her body bows off the bed as she cries out with another orgasm.

I sit up, wiping my mouth as I stand up off the bed, pulling her down toward the end where I stand in between her legs, placing them over my shoulder. I lean down and lap at her beautiful tits before kissing her, letting her taste herself on my lips.

I stand back, lining my painfully hard erection up with her slickness as I drag myself through her cum. She rocks her hips, trying to get close to me, and I don't make her wait any longer as I impale her on my cock, taking her to the hilt in one go. She's so wet after two orgasms that I slide in without much effort.

I play with her tits as I plunge into her, mercilessly fucking her hard. The headboard hits the wall over and over again. I'm sure Mateo, as well as the neighbors, can hear it, but I don't give a fuck as I chase my release. I swirl my hips around and then lower her legs and myself to her as I rut into her over and over. I tongue fuck her mouth as I feel her walls spasm, gripping my cock, and I come, cursing as I fill her. I pull out of her as I start to soften up.

There is sweat glistening over her body, and I see my cum dripping from her opening. I run my finger over it and drop down to my knees, bringing her close to me. I lick her softly, as I push my cum back into her.

"Jameson, what are you doing to me?" she whispers.

I swirl my tongue around her swollen clit, and she shudders. I suck gently on her bud as she throws her head back, riding out another orgasm. I drop to my ass, sitting on the bedroom floor as she has one arm flung across her face.

I hear the front door slam and Evie snorts a laugh. "I think you pissed off Mattie."

"Whew, I think I will skip the gym this morning." Sitting back, I'm unable to move.

"I think I am going to go back to bed. I think you broke me," she says as I rise to stand over her bending to kiss her. She pulls me in, and I kiss her again as my dick springs back to life. I pull her up with me, and she falls into me with a laugh.

"Come on, you little hellion. You're going to shower with me. You got me hard, and now you're going to drop to your knees and suck me, swallowing my cum." I swat her ass, and she laughs as she walks over to the shower, winking at me as she sways that sweet ass into the bathroom.

Jameson: I need to drop by this morning. Are you around the office?

I sit at my desk, wishing I had my coffee, which is probably sitting just where I left it this morning. I was in such a hurry to leave after giving Evie a few orgasms, then she sucked my cock so thoroughly that I forgot about everything else, including my favorite beverage.

Dax: Yeah. Come by, and I'll have them send you back.

The receptionist walks through the door, dropping off a package left at the front.

She stands there waiting, but I continue with my message. If I don't get Dax now, then I could miss my window of opportunity, and then he will be off seeing patients.

Jameson: What time?

He replies immediately, and I mentally give myself a fist pump. I'd like to get the keys to that condo, just in case we need them sooner rather than later. You never know when the need to leave will arise.

Dax: 10:30. I have a free moment before I have to go to the hospital for a scheduled surgery.

I look at my watch, noticing that I'll have to leave soon if I want to make it to his office with lunch-hour traffic by that time frame.

Jameson: Great. See you then.

I place my phone down. "Hey, Marie. What's up?"

She fiddles nervously with her blouse and approaches me. "I've worked here for a while…" Marie saunters over to me. "And I thought maybe you'd ask me out, but you didn't." She puts her head down and looks upward at me through her curled lashes, a pout on her lips. "I thought you were interested at one point, but then you haven't looked at me since, so I thought I'd make the first move."

She picks her head up and walks over to me, her intentions clear. I put my hand up to stop her advances when I see someone standing in the doorway. I immediately stand to stop her advance, but she doesn't see Evie there. When she comes closer to me and raises her hand to my chest, I grab it just as Evie walks in with my coffee. I immediately drop Marie's hand, dismissing her, and walk over to Evie who is watching me with a mixture of trepidation and annoyance.

"Oh my God." I take a sniff of the magnificent smell that is rising from the cup. "Baby, did you bring me my coffee? I left it at home. You distracted me so much."

She laughs. "Yes. I felt bad seeing it on the counter this morning."

I see movement in my peripheral vision, realizing I totally forgot that Marie was there propositioning me. I'm not going to lie, I did think she was hot, but that was before I met Evie, and well, now that isn't an option for me anymore.

"Marie, this is my girlfriend Evie. Evie, this is Marie, our receptionist."

Evie looks her over and waves her little pointed fingernails painted red with black tips.

"Nice to meet you, Evie. I'll just be going." She mouths, 'Sorry' as she is leaving, and I shake my head and drop it to my chest.

Evie lifts it for me to look at her. "If I hadn't come in when I did..." she trails off, not finishing her sentence or needing to, for that matter, because I can sense the question and apprehension, but what kills me is the vulnerability in her eyes. She gave herself over to me entirely, and now she wonders if that is too much.

I bring her to me. "Evie, you have nothing to worry about. I am totally in love with you, baby."

She brings her forehead to my chest and then looks up at me.

"I am yours, and you are mine," I assure her.

"I love you, too. It scares me so much," she confesses in a whisper.

I kiss her forehead and bend to kiss her lips as she reaches up to meet mine. "I know," I whisper back. "Hey," I say a little more loudly, electing to lighten the mood. "Want to give me a ride to Dax's office? There is something I need to pick up there on the way."

CHAPTER TWENTY-NINE

EVIE

"A BEAUTIFUL LIE" BY THIRTY SECONDS TO MARS

As I walk down the pier with Mateo, I can't help but feel like someone is watching us. Throughout the years, it has happened, and I've become acutely aware when something just isn't right. There are some telltale signs. The way that my skin tingles. The prickly sensation that causes the hair on my arms to stand on end, much like static electricity. Except, this is more of a feeling, an instinct of self-preservation. I doubt anyone is, but I also wasn't aware of Mr. Martin. Not once did he give me bad vibes. Mr. Martinez, Julian, and Marcus, Julian's driver, always gave me the instinct to flee and to do so fast.

I should feel creeped out that this older man whom Mattie has come to love so much could betray us so badly. I'm trying to give him the benefit of the doubt because I know that Jameson mentioned that he looked defeated, dropping his head down when he repeated that he didn't want to do that while he was on the phone with his son, Mr. Martinez.

The camera they secretly installed in his place captured that one-sided conversation. It made it seem like he wasn't complacent in this, but instead, he was doing it out of necessity.

We won't know the whole story until we walk in there and learn the truth from Ramón.

Mateo opens the door, spotting the little traitor in the corner with his coffee and chess set. His bright eyes, usually alight with humor, are dulled. There is a worried expression replaced by a furrowed brow, his thoughts miles away from this café.

He's taking the board out as Mateo walks over to him, and I turn around to grab our usual coffee orders. That's when I notice Dylan, the barista who wrote his name on my cup months ago, standing there.

I misjudged him, thinking he was cheating on his wife when she was, yes, the mother of his child that they were co-parenting and not in an actual relationship with. He looks skittish, displaying a recent black-and-blue eye. He won't look at me, and it sets me on high-alert for some reason.

"Dylan."

He looks up at me before looking around, but no one else is in here right now except for us this Friday afternoon.

"Are you okay?"

He ignores the question, acting like he doesn't know me. "What can I get you?" He avoids making eye contact with me as I repeat the same thing I order every time I come in here. He turns around to get us the coffee and rings me up. Taking my payment, I slide him a note telling him to meet me around the back by the bathrooms. He nods once, and I take the coffees over to Mateo and place mine there as well.

"Hi, Ramón," I say to the man who shares the same blood as my brother. I give a little wave, and he smiles, not knowing that he is about to meet with a few intimidating people in a few minutes. "I'm gonna run to the bathroom quickly before I watch Mattie lose."

Mateo makes a 'hmph' noise as I walk off in search of Dylan.

As I turn the corner, an arm pulls me into the back, and I almost lose my footing, ready to give the guy another black eye.

"Evie, I wanted to warn you, but I'm afraid."

My hackles rise. "What do you mean, Dylan?"

He looks around, as if potential danger lurks in the broom closet. "I was approached by a man the other day asking about you and your sister. He said his name was Mr. Martinez."

I look at his black eye. "Did he give you this?" I reach out to touch it and he winces.

"Yeah, well, not him, but another guy that was with him. He also had a couple more men at the door watching. He snuck in at the last minute when I was closing up. I don't really know why he was asking these questions, but he threatened me and my family. He wanted to know when you came in again."

I nod.

"Evie, if I don't tell him, he is going to hurt me or, worse, my baby."

I shush him as I think about it some more. "I appreciate you telling me. I have my family coming here in a few minutes. After we leave, you call him and let him know that Mateo and I are here."

He shakes his head. "No, Evie, I can't let you get hurt because of me."

I smile at him and how sweet he is. To think how badly I really misjudged him. "It's okay, Dylan. You tell him, and then you will have done what he asked of you. He won't hurt you or your family, okay? Can you do that for me?"

He bites his lip, thinking it over. "Okay, but be safe."

I assure him I will as I head back to the table, knowing that this will take a different turn very soon. It's obvious that Dylan's black eye happened recently, meaning he is still in town, so he knows where we are.

I return to my seat, and Mattie looks at me. He can sense the change in my posture, despite my attempts to keep my mood light. I don't get the chance to direct the attention elsewhere because Eli and Philip flank Eduardo, Emma, and Jameson as they walk in through the coffee shop like they own the place.

Dylan scoots back from the register and busies himself, pretending to refill coffee beans. I shake my head and smile, trying to reassure him that no harm will come to him, but he can sense the danger these men bring to the table.

They take a seat surrounding two tables, moving them closer to us as chairs screech across the floor. Jameson puts his arm around me, bringing me into him. A blanket of warmth and safety envelops me, making me remember when Mateo was the only one who helped save me. Now he needs our help, and I'll do anything for him, including laying my life down to protect him like he did for me those times before.

Ramón looks over to Mateo in question. He just shrugs. "I think we have some things to discuss, pops."

The look of shock and what I can only describe as fear, envelopes Ramón as he crumples his shoulders in defeat. His head hangs low, but when he raises it, there are tears in his eyes.

"You have no idea how much I wanted to hear you call me that. I have come to know you over the past months, but for you to say that to me now means that you know something, but not everything. I can assure you things are not always as they seem. But today, I will ensure you learn all of it."

His determined expression shows that he was strong in his day, a force to be reckoned with. He did raise Mr. Martinez and with a grandson like Julian... I can't even finish that thought.

Goosebumps rise on my arms, and Jameson interprets this as me being cold. He moves his arms back and forth on me in an attempt to warm me up. Emma sits there silently, and Eduardo looks murderous.

"I think you should get talking, *Mr. Martin.*" Eduardo stresses his name, letting us all know that his real name is Martinez, much like the animal he sired.

He nods. "I knew your mother."

Okay, woah. That is not where I thought this was going.

"She came to me when she learned she was pregnant with my son's baby and asked for my help. I was a lawyer, much like my son who is following in my footsteps, but that is where it ended. He had big aspirations, and one of those was to marry your mother and have an heir that would give him the connection to the Ortiz mafia family, which he needed so much to further his political endeavors.

"I learned that he was physically abusive, and she wouldn't let her unborn son be used over her as leverage to return to him, so she came to me asking for help to get away. I kept her secret, and we formed a plan to move my son's focus onto the gold digger, who was her best friend at the time and roommate—Julian's mother.

"Your mom already knew that he was sleeping with her, and it wasn't too much later that she ended up pregnant. They even sent your mom a wedding invitation to show her how much of an afterthought she was."

Mateo looks over at me, and I shrug.

"So she planned that?" Matteo asks in confirmation.

"Yes," he states. "And her plan worked. She had you and kept you hidden. She went off to college and met Evie and Emma's father, who wanted no part of that life. I think that it was a relief for her to discover that. She didn't want that for her other children either."

Emma squeezes Eduardo's hand. "Yeah, she almost cost us our happiness in the process."

"I think she cost us a lot of unhappiness." Mateo hits his hand to the table.

Mr. Martin nods. "I think it was hard for her, and unfortunately we may never know what she truly would say to it all. What her answer would be to those questions because of my son's actions."

Jameson scoots his chair closer. His fingers tighten around my hip. "Your son terrorized my girlfriend, and she almost died in that fire alongside her parents, if it wasn't for Mateo. He saved her on more than one occasion."

He holds his hand up to halt the conversation. "I haven't talked to my son in years. I disowned him and my grandson when I saw their depravity. They were evil, and I wanted no part of them. I didn't know what he was doing until recently when he told me his son died and that you left his body placed in a car belonging to some woman and set it in a fiery blaze outside his home to find."

Evie feigns indifference. "It was the least we could do to that sick fuck after what he did to my sister, and it's only fitting that he died similar to my parents. An eye for an eye, right?"

Mateo glances over at Eduardo. "So what now?"

Eduardo stands with Emma, and they both look at Ramón. I can sense that Eduardo would have no remorse if he killed him if it meant that Emma would be safe.

"That depends on what you have to say for yourself, Mr. Martin. Are you working with your son to take us down?"

Mr. Martin looks at Mateo but answers Eduardo's question. "Absolutely not. He is forcing me to help him, or he threatened to hurt my grandson. I was hoping to get him to work with me, but I just couldn't bring it up. I had a phone call the other day, and he is in the area now. This needs to end, and that means my son needs to die."

Eduardo nods at his two men, and they get up and walk to the front and back entrances of the coffee shop to look out. "We heard your conversation with your son at your home."

Ramón looks up in disbelief. "You bugged my house? When?"

Eduardo waves his hand away, and Jameson beams, proud of the part he played in keeping us safe by stealing a page out of Eduardo's playbook. "That's not important. What is important is what he said to you."

Eduardo and Mateo exchange a look, which I don't understand.

Ramón nods in understanding. Recollection of that conversation is fresh in his mind, and he spares not a single minute to share the details of it. "He wants you to take over for him. To be the heir he wanted all along to solidify himself a place in the mafia world. His true heir. With those types of connections, he feels his political standing will soar, as will his wealth in the illegal drug trade across the border. He wants you, Mateo, and I am entrusted to deliver you to him." He stands up.

"No, Mattie. You can't go. I won't let you." Emma stands, too, pleading. "He is a monster, and I've seen it with my own eyes. I've been on the receiving end of it with his son, too. You can't leave us."

Mr. Martin looks at Mateo. "I don't think any of you understand here. He doesn't just want his son, his only heir, to take over his business. He wants his sisters, too."

The room is so quiet you can hear a pin drop. The anger that radiates off Eduardo is palpable. The air grows thick. He stands abruptly, toppling the chair over.

"Over my fucking dead body will he take Emma from me." His words are deadly and vicious. His chest heaves as he restrains himself from having a fit of explosive rage.

Emma places her hand on his, and he breathes in deeply. He closes his eyes, trying to collect his hot temper, which only a few have had the displeasure of witnessing.

He looks over to Emma, and he seems to calm a little at her soothing touch. She calms his inner monster and makes him a better person. We all know this.

I look over to Jameson, and he is entirely rigid—his lips parted. I swear he has stopped breathing. I place my hand over his cheek, and he sucks in a deep breath, like he is revived by my touch alone.

"Fuck, no," he says angrily. "He can't have you." I look over at him but talk to everyone around us.

"He has already been here. He knows where we are, and he wants us. You see that guy behind the counter with the black eye?"

They all turn to look at Dylan, and he visibly pales at the attention of the angry group in my blended family.

"He knows that we come here. Dylan told me when I got here. He threatened *his* family, and I told him to call Mr. Martinez and let him know when we leave."

Everyone looks at me, saying my name in unison. Jameson turns my face to look at him, ignoring the angry cries contesting my decision, but it's already been made.

"Why, baby? Why would you tell him to do that?"

I look down before meeting his eyes. "So many people have been hurt to help us, and he has a baby. A baby, Jameson. A defenseless baby that Mr. Martinez threatened to hurt."

Emma gasps, and a small sob comes out of her as Eduardo soothes her, running his hand through her hair, murmuring loving words to her.

"It's time, Mattie. You have to go with Ramón. You have to end this. If that means we must go with you, then so be it. He stole our past. It's time we reclaim our future."

CHAPTER THIRTY

JAMESON

"NITRO (YOUTH ENERGY)" BY THE OFFSPRING

"When did you get this?" I hand the keys over to Eduardo.

"Evie stopped by the office the other day, and she gave me a ride over to pick it up. Dax didn't ask any questions, but Liv told him we needed the condo in Padre Island to hide if things went bad. I think this is truly the definition of 'if things went bad. Don't you?"

He nods in agreement, biting his lip in concentration. "Yeah, I think it is."

I planned this thinking that it would just be a precautionary measure, that we wouldn't need it. I mean, I hoped we didn't need the keys, but I am glad I had the foresight to get them. Otherwise, it would be hard to know if we are being watched and then needed the keys before Emma and Evie are forced to leave with Mateo. Because they are going to have to leave with him. I am still unsure about Evie and Emma having to go, but we will get a better idea when we hear it directly from the source. When we have an idea of what he really wants with our family.

Dylan, true to his word, called Mr. Martinez as soon as we left, and now Mateo and Ramón are headed to his place to meet the monster we call Mr. Martinez. Hearing that Mr. Martinez threatened Dylan and his baby solidified the notion for me that he would stop at nothing to get what he wants. I don't think it is really about family but about him getting what he wants from the wealth and power his alliance and connections with a mafia family would provide.

Mateo has a burner phone hidden. He thought it would be a good idea to have a separate phone that isn't tracked, just in case his phone is looked at by his father or any of the security details that his father has back at his house. Being a politician allows him to have security for his home, but more people realize that it is more to his connection in an illegal trade that requires this level of protection and secrecy.

I recently placed cameras, which allow us to at least listen in on the conversation. We will have a heads-up to see what is coming our way. Will they make them leave right away? Ramón mentioned that he wanted Evie and Emma to go with Mateo, but I can't imagine why. Will he keep them as collateral to keep Mateo in line, or will it be for some other advantage?

We've had preemptive talks with Mateo and Ramón, so they know to keep the conversation flowing around the island or near the kitchen so that we can hear what they say more clearly. Now it's time to see how well Mateo has perfected his acting career.

We speed to Eduardo's office and huddle around his desk, watching the screen. We text Mateo when we get here so that we don't miss a thing. He and Ramón plan to finish up their chess game, allowing us time to make it back to Houston. The drive back is quiet. Each of us is in our heads and not speaking about the what-ifs.

Eduardo calls his brother on the way, putting it on speaker, and I watch my friend closely. "Hello? Ram?" There is a moment of silence on the line as the international call connects.

"Hey, little brother. To what do I—"

"Ram, I need you," Eduardo cuts him off, " and I need you to call Father and let him know that things have turned for the worse over here in Houston."

Without hesitation, Ramiro asks, "What do you need? I can be there soon to take over the business if you need to go."

Eduardo looks over to Emma and tells his brother everything without another thought.

"I'll be there and have Dad call you. Do not worry about anything over here. Just go to keep Emma safe and do what you have to do. They are messing with the wrong people. Dad will call Emma's uncle and join forces to do whatever needs to be done. She is your fiancée, and no harm will come to her if we have a say in it."

Eduardo grabs Emma's hand and kisses it. "Okay, Ram. Thank you, and hurry, brother. See you soon."

"See you soon," is echoed on the other line before it dies.

Now we wait to see what they say at Ramón's.

They leisurely head to Ramón's place to put the plan into action as if there are no pressing issues, such as a psychopath waiting to take them away at any given moment.

We hear the door open, and Ramón walks through, followed by Mateo on his heels. They are around the kitchen island talking about predictions for when they will have to leave for Brownsville.

"I should grab my bag from my room just in case we have to leave soon." A look of confusion passes on Mateo's face as he disappears down the hall, but then his head jerks toward the door opening a moment later.

And then we all actually see him—Mr. Martinez.

He approaches Mateo slowly, like a predator circling his prey, except Mateo is no one's prey. His eyes narrow, calculating and assessing his biological father as he steps closer and is now standing before Mateo.

It is hard to dismiss his similarities to this horrible man. They are of similar size and stature: brown skin, brown eyes, and a full head of hair. Mateo's hair is dark brown, and Mr. Martinez's is streaked with gray, but it doesn't take away from his striking features. He could easily pass for his son, but whereas Julian had more of his mother's facial features, Mateo has strong lines and a square jaw.

Mr. Martinez studies Mateo, sizing him up. Mateo assesses him in return. When their staredown is interpreted by Ramón coming back from the room with his bag, he sets it by the sofa, and Mr. Martinez raises one eyebrow in question.

"Going somewhere, Father?"

Ramón simply shrugs. "I'm not sure, son. Are we going somewhere?"

Mr. Martinez raises his hand. "Not until I have had the opportunity to talk to Mateo. Have you told my son anything yet?"

We see through the camera's eye Mateo stiffen at the use of the word 'son,' but Mr. Martinez doesn't seem to notice. Ramón shakes his head, saying no.

"I told him you wanted to talk with him and that he would learn of everything soon."

This seems to please him, and he turns his focus to Mateo. "Well, this has been a long time coming. Your mother kept you from me, and now that my son, Julian, is gone..." he trails off, looking at Mateo. If he is looking for any admission, he won't find it on our brother's stoic face. "You are my only remaining son, my only heir." He reaches to place his arm on Mateo's shoulder. "My firstborn."

"You mean I am the only heir, and my mother's family is also part of the Ortiz mafia that suits your financial endeavors, am I right?"

His smile widens. "Yes, well, that, too," he admits, running his finger over his bottom lip. "I believe we can do great things together, son."

"Did you kill my mother?"

His hand falls off Mateo's shoulder. Mr. Martinez's eyes narrow, and he visibly shakes.

"That lying cunt stole you from me. She left and married that pathetic and weak excuse of a man who couldn't offer her anything. We could have had it all, but she chose poorly and suffered the consequences. She left you and me."

Mateo nods, trying to appease the crazy in this man who claims to be his father.

We move closer to the screen, and I watch Mateo's features. Emma has her hand over her mouth, waiting to hear what he will say next.

"Yeah, she did leave us both." His head is bowed down when he says this, and I know that the emotions shown on his face are real. This is his family and he doesn't hide his feeling from them and only them. He looks like he feels every bit of her leaving him, and he may never get over that fact. For whatever reason, she thought it was in his best interest to do so.

But when he raises his head to meet Mr. Martinez, his following words are spoken as an act, but still gut his family as they fall from his lips. "What do you need me to do, Father?"

Emma chokes on a sob, and Eduardo brings her closer to him as we stare at Mateo on the screen.

Mr. Martinez laughs sinisterly. "I knew you'd come around, son. We are going to leave here and go to our new home. Everything I have will be yours now, and we will grow our business, and then... you will take over. We will force the Ortiz family to play nice and accept our terms. I need the connections to bring my drugs over the border, and they have the connection that I need. I have them here." He lifts his palm up to Mateo to signify that he has them in the palm of his hand. "You see, it's a mutually beneficial agreement."

Mateo rubs his chin, pondering the things Mr. Martinez has said. "I don't know if you are aware of this, but they sent me to boarding school, and I don't think they will be willing to accept that deal from me. They barely acknowledge me as their own."

For some reason, I see the shared look on Evie and Emma's face, it's obvious that they, too, feel the raw emotion that comes through in his spoken words. Despite the performance he is portraying for Mr. Martinez for our benefit, there is some truth radiating from the harshness of his tone.

Ramón steps closer, and so does Mr. Martinez. He leans forward on the kitchen island.

"Well..." He cocks his head to the side. "They might not be with you, but when we take your sisters with us, then they might have to reconsider."

Eduardo stiffens, rage building in him. Gus, Eli, and Philip exchange glances with each other, and the room is so quiet you can hear a pin drop.

I hold Evie closer, and she leans into my embrace. We listen and wait for the rest of the story.

"You'll make them come with us, and then we will marry them off to the highest bidder."

There is the slightest tic to Mateo's jaw, indicating that he is much displeased with this direction of conversation, but he doesn't say as much. We look at the screen, dumbfounded.

Eduardo stands up, and Emma almost falls off his lap. However, his usual firm grip around her waist allows her feet to land on the floor instead. He is shaking with uncontrolled rage.

"Motherfucker! I will fucking kill you! You're dead!" Eduardo is yelling at the screen with spittle flying like a rabid dog. He's fuming and shaking with so much unrelenting anger, and Emma hits his arm, trying her best to calm him enough so we can hear the rest of the conversation.

"Highest bidder, huh? I don't know about that. Father, I don't want my sisters being offered up like cattle."

Mr. Martinez shrugs. "Makes no difference to me." He pretends to pick an imaginary strand of lint from his suit jacket.

Mateo is deep in thought and then snaps his fingers when he is struck with an idea, although I don't think he had thought about it long.

"I got it," he says, and Mr. Martinez looks over at him. "What if we have a party announcing their 'availability' and then have suitors come and discuss a mutually beneficial agreement."

He seems to think about this, and then his smile broadens. "You know, son, I think that would be a great idea."

Mateo nods. "We need strong allies if we are going to make this business venture beneficial with powerful players in place, but also, we want to be able to control the narrative. We should pick the best suitors who would make a more profitable alliance, right?"

Mr. Martinez soaks this up, and at the moment, I am afraid that Mateo may have switched sides. He is so determined to bring us down that I believe him.

He turns toward the camera and winks. Emma reaches over to Evie, and she nods that she saw that, too. Evie sinks into my lap in relief because Mateo's story was too believable for our liking.

Mr. Martinez must buy the act too because he claps his hands together in an excited fashion. "Okay. When do we leave?"

Mateo makes his way toward the door. "No time like the present."

Ramón has been watching this entire exchange without interruption, but as Mateo moves to leave and passes him by, he stops him.

"Where are you going?" Ramón looks over to his son sheepishly and then at his bag. "Do you need me to go with you, Mateo?" The look in Ramón's eyes says that he is afraid to be alone with his son while Mateo is away.

For some reason, I believe that his grandfather cares for him. A person can't have that level of concern for another without it meaning something. I just hope, for Mateo's sake, that they have some salvageable relationship after this is over.

Mateo looks over at the camera as if he is speaking to it. "I am going to bring my sister's back over here so that we can begin a new life."

With that, he exits Ramón's place and gets in his car to drive back to Houston, where our whole world is about to get a lot more complicated.

"I'll be waiting, son."

Everyone hears as the door shuts as Mateo walks out.

CHAPTER THIRTY-ONE

EVIE

"LET'S HAVE A WAR" BY FEAR

We sit there stunned into silence. My breathing picks up, and Jameson's grasp on me tightens. I practice my breathing like I was taught so long ago in therapy. When my thoughts go dark, I think about the therapist who helped me so much back then, but it feels like all the same emotions are just beneath the surface, threatening to break me. Amid a violent storm that threatens your life amongst the chaotic seas that rocks you to your core, you must get through it because at the end of the storm, there is calmness and peace.

The sun breaks through the stormy clouds, and the water reflects the light off the peaceful waters. This storm has been brewing for years, and now we must face it. No matter how strong I tried to make myself, I knew that this time would come when I would face all my fears and our family would have to come together to win a war—a war that was started so long ago over greed and power at the cost of those that weren't born yet.

And we will have to suffer the burden to end it all.

I am pulled from my thoughts as Eduardo roars and throws everything off his desk. It all comes crashing down—his anger, frustrations, and helplessness at the failure to get his reason for existing, as he says to her so often in anyone's company, are all his emotions swirling as he refuses to let her go.

Emma sobs into her hand, and he goes over to her, kneeling at her feet. He takes her hands in his, pulling them from her tear-stained face.

"I thought I was free, but will we ever be free from this, Eduardo?" she asks him so innocently that my heart breaks for her.

She suffered so much brutality from Julian. We ended his life, but his father is still alive and now wants to sell us off as if we are his possessions to do so.

"I am not going to let anything happen to you, baby. I promise."

I rise from Jameson's lap. I extend my hand to my sister much like I did that day we ended Julian's life in that warehouse. I knew that this time was coming. The time when we would have to fight for our family.

She looks up at me, and her face is streaked with tears, but tears no longer flow from her eyes. There is a look on her face that I haven't seen before. She looks pissed.

She places her hand in mine and rises as Eduardo moves aside, allowing her space to stand alongside me. She looks into my eyes, searching for something she must find, and then she looks at Eduardo.

"I am so tired of this fucker, and I want to see him suffer a cruel death deserving of the sins he has committed. I want to see him die, witnessing the moment his life fades from his eyes. I want to know that we did that and that he lost. Everything he wanted. His hopes and dreams are to be extinguished so he can burn in hell with his son."

I've never heard Emma speak this way, and it empowers me to know that she can and will be brave enough to see this through.

Jameson is shaking when he takes my hand, pulling me out of my trance-like state, seeing my sister finally become the woman I knew she could always be. There is no place for weakness now, and knowing that she can be strong enough to do this helps me. I can't be strong for the both of us, and Eduardo, as much as he wants to keep her safe, understands that she needs to be strong, his equal, if she wants this type of life with him. We all do. We are all part of this life together, and together we will fight to keep what is ours.

Someday, Eduardo will take over his father's business and take his place as the head of the family. He was raised for this. Knowing that Emma can be by his side, strong and assured in her role as his wife, is all I ever wanted for my sister. I want all of us to get what we deserve–the happiness and peace we so desperately seek. This is the moment where it starts. It's time to finish this. So, I say, "Let's have a war."

Jameson takes me to my apartment, and Emma will meet me here. Mateo has already texted us and told us he will be here soon, so we can be ready. I step through the door and walk to my bedroom. I stand there looking around the space I have called my own, but not my home.

Jameson comes around me and wraps me in a solid embrace. He is so warm, and I shiver—not from being cold, but from my comfort when he is here with me. I lean into him and tilt my head to the side. His warmth caresses me as he leans in to place soft kisses on my neck.

"When all this is over, Evie, I want you to move in with me. I want us to pick out a place together that is just ours. I want you. If I have learned anything from being with you, it is that life is fleeting. I see the dangerous life we live and the enemies that will stop at nothing to take what doesn't belong to them in the quest for more power and control."

I turn around to look him in the eye. I am amazed to hear his words spoken and the truth that he loves me written on his face. Jameson wears his heart on his sleeve. He may not be the alpha male that Eduardo is, but that doesn't mean that he won't risk his own life or do everything in his power to keep me safe. Eduardo was born into a different life than he was, but being Eduardo's friend means that he needs to be a strong man as well.

"Maybe we can get a place in Eduardo's building? Even Mattie, too. We can all have separate places, but still be there for one another."

He nods. "That sounds amazing, Eves. I like that idea so much, and it will be the only thing I will look forward to when you are in that monster's house. I won't be able to keep an eye on you like I want to, but I will be able to at least track you." He pulls out a box from his pocket. "Here. I had these made and picked them up the other day."

He hands me a little black velvet, heart-shaped box. I stare at it, afraid to open it. "What is it?"

He looks at me, amused. "Well, why don't you open it, and you'll find out?"

I look at him, assessing, until my curiosity wins out. I step away from his embrace, turn to look at him, and open the box.

"Wow, I don't know what to say. They are beautiful." I hold a box open that contains a set of two large emerald hearts. I pick them up, noticing they are a little heavier than I expected. "They are beautiful, Jameson."

"I agree," he says, "and practical, too."

I look at him curiously, wondering where he is going with this. "Well," I say, thinking about it, "I do wear a lot of green, and they do go very well with my eyes, making them very matchy-matchy." He chuckles at my comment. "You don't think so?" I raise an eyebrow at him in question. I take the earrings out of the velvet holder and put them on. "They are also screw backs, so they won't come off." I list all of the valid points as to why they are such a perfect present.

"Sure, I do think about all those things. I also think that they will let us know where you are at all times and let us hear you if we need to." He waves his tracking app on his phone before stuffing it into his pocket.

I laugh aloud. "Of course there is." I shake my head as I tighten the last earring, securing it in place.

He looks delighted with himself as he rocks on his heels and back to the balls of his feet in one fluid motion. His hands are in his pant pockets, and he looks absolutely delicious. I lick my lips and he seems to understand the look of hunger in my eyes as he approaches me slowly, calculating his next move.

"One's a speaker." He touches one of my earrings. "The other is a tracker with an SOS feature, much like Emma's bracelet Eduardo had me make for her."

My hand drops from his gift. "Practical and beautiful," I whisper.

His body is flush with mine, and I breathe in his masculine, earthy scent. It envelops me, and I want to remember it, to bottle it up and take it with me. I want to commit it to memory, so that I can take it with me and cherish it when I am alone and in my bedroom without him, waiting on someone else to determine my future for the last time. I don't voice the thought that I may never see him again because I have to believe in our blended family and know that they will do everything in their power to see him through to the end.

"I agree. So beautiful." His words tickle my ear as he sucks and tugs on my earlobe, sending a tug at my core. I moan and tilt my head, giving him better access. He licks down my neck and places kisses all over my face, until he plants a soft kiss on my lips. He hovers over my mouth, until he brings me in close, parting my open lips farther with his tongue. My body is pulled into his, and I can feel the rigid outline of his cock.

He leads me backward to my bed until my legs hit the edge of the mattress. He pushes me back and takes off each of my shoes, and then my pants and panties in one go. He undoes his belt, letting his pants pool around his ankles as he steps out of them.

"Take off your shirt." His voice is desperate. Pleading. "We don't have much time until everyone gets here."

It's like having cold water thrown on my face to wake me from my lust-filled gaze. He watches me as he pulls his shirt over his head and then grabs my shirt, ripping the thin, lacy material. It smarts against my skin, and I look up at him, ready to say something, but he doesn't let me.

He pushes his cock into my mouth as my teeth scrape lightly along his velvet skin. He is trying to get me out of my own head, and it's working. He always knows to give me what I need, and right now, I need his cock choking me, filling me.

He crouches over me, holding my head up as he fucks my face. I hold onto his ass, and my fingernails in their usual pointed shape dig into his cheeks as he pauses, holding himself to me. He hisses and removes his cock as dribbles of saliva trail down my chin. He drops down to my legs and plunges his tongue into my entrance. My legs spread wide, giving him full access to my pussy.

Jameson licks around my entrance as he lashes out at my clit and sucks hard. My back bows off the bed. I open my eyes, seeing him watch me from below. He places kisses to each side of my leg, wiping his mouth on my inner thigh. He brings himself up and hovers over me, aligning himself with my entrance. He drives in one thrust, and I cry out. He fucks me mercilessly, as if this is the last time.

We are loud and wild. I grab his hair and tug him to me. He kisses me hard and grabs upward, using the wrought iron to pull him into me more forcefully. I've never been fucked harder, and when he hits that spot deep inside of me, twisting his hips, I cry out.

"Fuck me, Jameson, that's it. Right there. Keep—Oh God, keep going. Oh..." My mind stops working, and my body shakes, convulsing with an orgasm so strong, I spasm, turning rigid under him, and he fucks me through it until I open my eyes and see him again.

He kisses me lightly, so different from the man who owned me and possessed every ounce of my body a moment ago. "I love you, Evie. Come back to me."

Something wet hits my cheek, and I see this man crying for me. It is almost my undoing as I shed tears that I haven't in so long, when I vowed never to be weak. To never show my emotions. He drops down onto me, covering me in his full weight.

"I promise," is all I can say because I will do everything I can to come back to this man. To come back to my family and have the life I deserve and the happiness I have now in Jameson's arms.

He doesn't just own my body but my heart and soul, too.

CHAPTER THIRTY-TWO

JAMESON

"ZOMBIE" BY BAD WOLVES

"I better take a shower."

She gets up and walks to her dresser, retrieving a pair of panties and bra set. I take them and toss them onto the bed where her suitcase lies open, waiting to be packed. I tug her back into me. My hand splays over her flat abdomen, and I trail my fingers down to her slick, wet folds. I gather up our cum dripping down her legs, pushing it back up into her. She is sticky, and the thought of her filled with me, with us mixed in our sexual act, has me already hard.

"Leave it. If you must leave me, take a piece of us with you." I breathe out slowly and drop my head onto her shoulder. She tilts her head to look back at me, but I can't meet her eyes. I am in a bad way at having the best thing that has happened to me leave and walk straight into danger. To be sold off to the highest bidder.

What if we can't get there in time to save them? What if I lose her forever?

I shudder underneath as the fearful emotions roll out of me and onto her.

She turns around in my embrace and picks my head up. "Okay." She looks into my eyes, and sadness pools in hers. "I'll take you with me." I nod and kiss her. "Always," she breathes onto my lips.

Our moment is interrupted by the front door closing. We realize our time is up. Our moment finished. We step away from each other.

"I'll just change." She walks into the bathroom, and there is a knock on her door.

"Evie?" Mateo asks from the other side of her bedroom.

I walk to it and step out, closing the door behind me. "She is just finishing up packing."

He nods, and there's another knock on our apartment door. Mateo looks out the window and sees Emma and Eduardo outside. He drops his head for a moment, then opens the door. It's time, and we have run out of it on our end.

Eduardo enters the apartment, bringing in all his tension and rage. The room feels incredibly small with all of us here. The anxiety I am feeling is crippling, especially with the impending doom I feel at Evie and Emma walking through that door with Mateo, knowing that he is going to take them straight over to Mr. Martinez and Ramón. They will all go to Brownsville and be kept at his house until Emma and Evie are to be married off for the benefit of Mr. Martinez's political associations and financial security.

Eduardo is holding Emma's hand in a death grip. Her eyes are wide as she looks over every apartment space to see if Evie will magically appear.

"She's getting ready. Almost packed."

Emma nods. I look over to their clasped hands, and Eduardo's fingers release Emma's hand and then regrip it firmly. He's holding her emerald heart charm in his hand, and I snap my head up, attention piqued.

I've known Eduardo for a long time. Part of being friends for so long is that we can read each other perfectly without any words being said. He's asking me about the bracelet and the earrings I had made for Evie. I nod very subtly and then fix my sights on Mateo. We purposely didn't tell him about this. The fewer people that know, the better it is to keep a close eye and ear on the girls.

They both have SOS options on their trackers. Evie also has a small microphone to pick up conversations in her earring. I am sure their bags will be looked at or maybe even confiscated and disposed of. We don't want to risk the chance that they are taken anyway.

"Emma's suitcase is in the car." Eduardo looks over at Mateo. "I trust you, Mateo, to guard your sisters with your life."

Mateo steps forward, never breaking eye contact with Eduardo. "I have always guarded my sisters with my life and would gladly give up my own for their safety. They are the only reason my life is worth living. Without them, I have nothing else. They are my family."

Emma leaves Eduardo's side and runs to her brother, throwing her arms around him. I look to the door of Evie's bedroom, wondering where she is, but she is there standing, listening to the entire conversation. I don't know how long she has been there, but it must have been long enough because she joins her siblings in a group hug.

Mateo kisses the top of each of their heads. "I promise to do everything in my power to get us through this. He pulls back, looking down at their short statures.

"I just want you two to know that there may be times when I have to act or behave a certain way. I might be cruel or say things that are very out of character from the brother that you know. The brother you know would never say or mean those things, but it is something I might have to do. I have a part to play, and you do, too. Let's do everything we can to stay safe and do what must be done."

Mateo looks over to Eduardo, who is speaking to him. "I have to know that he dies and this is over. There is no other option, Mateo."

"I'll make sure to get word to you when to come."

They nod in agreement. "We will come, Mateo. I promise."

"Okay," he says to Eduardo. "We better go before Mr. Martinez gets suspicious."

We close up the apartment that Evie and Mateo have stayed at the longest together, and I feel like we are closing a chapter in their life. Mateo turns back to look at his place, standing in the middle of the parking lot. He is silent for a while, until he finally speaks as we wait for him to load his vehicle.

"I hope that when we return here, it is to start a different life. A life where we all are free to live, fulfill our passions, and pursue our dreams. I don't know who I am anymore, other than Evie's guardian angel or Emma's savior—their brother. I want to live a life for myself and maybe, just maybe, find the happiness they have with a partner that is so in love with me that we cannot exist without each other. I can only dream of having a life like that one day."

I clasp my hand over Mateo's shoulder. "Let's play our parts and get this done. Then we can all get our own happiness, however that may be."

We load up the cars, and Mateo starts the engine on his. He blasts the air conditioning, trying to cool off the vehicle. It hasn't been that long since we arrived from the coast, but the city has a way of making it hotter than average.

Eduardo and I shake Mateo's hand and watch Evie and Emma get in. Mateo shuts his door and puts it into drive, pulling out of the parking lot. I stare at them as they drive away.

As they turn the corner, I see Emma's hand on the window with tears streaming down her cheek. Evie stares straight ahead. I know that she is trying to be brave. She can't risk falling apart, and if I know her as well as I think I do, she is counting her breaths and holding them in a practiced fashion the way she was taught to do when she is about to have a panic attack. She is so controlled now, more than ever, and someday I wish that she won't have to put on a fake act and be able to show me the most vulnerable side she has. I want to swim in a rocking sea of her salty tears and lick them away from her face as she looks up at me through those tears-stained eyes, knowing that I am the only one that will ever see the real her.

I continue to watch them drive away until there is nothing there except an empty street. I turn my attention to Eduardo. Gus comes out of the car and walks over to us. I lift my chin in an informal hello, and he does the same, but his main focus is on Eduardo.

"Are you ready to go, boss?" he asks. His sights never leave Eduardo's.

"I'll be there every step of the way, too, buddy. We need to stick together. We have a new priority. *'Operation bring them home.*"

Eduardo looks over at me. "I'm glad you said that, Jameson, because I'm going to need you close to bring our women back and get our family back together as soon as possible."

"I want that more than anything." I slap my hand on his back, as he walks over to his car, Gus following. He turns back.

"I expect you to bring your shit and move in until they are back home safely."

I look at him to see if he is joking.

He continues, "I need all the surveillance ready to go and the station with all the manpower to leave at the drop of a hat. Bring your equipment and get everything ready in my place today."

I run my hand through my hair.

"Yeah, I guess that is the best way. Be there in a couple of hours." With that, he drives off.

I am left standing alone, and the gravity of our situation finally hits home. With a newfound sense of purpose, I run to my truck and drive off in a hurry to get to Eduardo's place. But first, a stop at my mine to start *'Operation bring them home.'*

I fight the traffic and lose miserably. I end up three hours later at Eduardo's place, well into the evening. I shoot him a text letting him know that I am here and need help getting my shit into his house. I understand this is a secure area, but I don't want to make several trips back and forth to get everything. The elevator door opens into the garage, and out steps Eli, Philip, and Gus.

Eduardo isn't present, but I expected this. I know that he is home because his car is here. What I don't expect is for him to get out of Emma's metallic-green BMW and walk toward me. I don't have to wonder why he was sitting in there. I know that it was to feel closer to her and breathe in her scent that envelops him in her car.

Avoiding looking at him, I allow him his own private moment and sling my bag over my shoulder and grab my laptop. Each of the guys grabs a box that is filled with monitors and speakers to amplify the sounds from Evie and Emma's trackers. I also have a separate screen showing where they are in the house. I have a blueprint of the mini-mansion that Mr. Martinez calls home. I have also tracked his wife's routines. I like to know where she is at all times. I am sure that with Evie and Emma in her home, things might take a turn for the worse. I want to be able to get to her—mostly to tear her throat out if she so much as lays a finger on our women.

We ride the elevator in silence, and the tension rises with each floor we ascend.

As soon as Eduardo leads me to our workstation, I quickly get everything situated and in working order. I don't know what happened when Evie, Emma, and Mateo left us to meet Mr. Martinez and Ramón back at their place because they never returned there. Shortly after he left their place, Ramón and Mr. Martinez left as well to an undisclosed location. We know that Ramón already had his bag packed, so the element of surprise is gone.

Mr. Martinez doesn't want to risk getting caught at Ramón's place if Mateo breaks his newly formed trust. He wants to ensure that he can witness it for himself. It seems too good to be true that Mateo went along so quickly with everything that his sperm donor said. That's what we have been referring to him as—the sperm donor. Usually, when things are too good to be true, they are, so he has every right to be cautious.

"There," I say, pinning the blueprints of the house on the cork board. I take a look around the workspace that looks like a crime center at first glance.

On the GPS monitor, I see the girls traveling in a car heading on Interstate 37, showing their every movement. Eduardo steps into the room, handing me a can of beer.

"I thought you would be drinking something stronger?" I take the beer can, open it, and take a large pull from it. My throat is dry, and my heart is aching, but I keep it to myself.

Eduardo shakes his head. "No, I have to keep my wits about me in case I need to leave. In case something...." He doesn't finish that sentence, but he doesn't have to. I already know what he was going to say. "Come on. You need to eat. I ordered everyone pizza, then we can get back to work."

CHAPTER THIRTY-THREE

EVIE

"IN THE END" BY LINKIN PARK

Mateo drove us to the place Mr. Martinez told him to on the phone. We heard his phone ring, and when he answered, he looked at us. Without saying a word, we knew the plan had changed.

Now we are in a Walmart parking lot, of all places. It is packed, and I guess that is the point. We were transferred to another vehicle, this time a black SUV similar to the one Julian rode around in when Emma was with him. I say the term "with him" loosely because she did not have a choice toward the end. The end of where we ended his life and then set Cherry on fire in her own car in front of their house.

I notice Emma tense as she walks over to it. Every instinct she has for self-preservation screams for her to run from this SUV. Do not get into the vehicle, which is blaring with loud red sirens.

We ignore that loud warning bell and walk with purpose to the SUV.

We slide into the seats as the doors close in the back, locking us in—as if we would try to run at this point.

Ramón is driving Mateo's vehicle, and Mr. Martinez and Mateo are in the middle section with Marcus, along with another scary-looking man with a bald head and a gold front tooth that eyes me lasciviously from the rearview mirror. He licks his lips, and I look away. Marcus laughs in the front seat, but no one says anything as we drive out of the parking lot.

Our hands have been ziptied since we left Houston, and they ache with the need to rip them apart. To free myself from these physical confines. Having to use the restrooms outside the gas station we stopped at was difficult since we didn't have the luxury of having free hands. Now, I sit here in silence with only another few hours remaining before we get to our new prison.

I don't know how I could have fallen asleep, but I wake up with a jolt as the SUV door slams shut, and Emma looks over at me. Our door opens, and that scary man that was lusting at me in the mirror opens my door, grabbing me over the seat and hoisting me out of the car. His hand lands on my breast, and I flinch, almost falling over as he leans over me, catching my fall while his erection digs into my backside.

As he struggles to stand me up, Mateo is striding over to him, pushing him away from me. He snarls at the man, and he smirks at my brother, knowing very well what he is doing to aggravate and get a rise out of him. Mateo stands straight, demanding respect.

I look over at Emma, who is watching along with Mr. Martinez, who is watching the exchange with amusement.

"My sisters are going to be promised to some very wealthy men. I won't have you tampering with them. We need them, so if I so much as see you look at them in the lustful manner in which you did before, I will cut your eyes out, am I clear?"

The guard looks over at Mr. Martinez.

Mateo slaps his face, getting his attention back to him. "Do not look to my father to save you. I am his son and heir. You will listen and respect me, or I will beat it out of you until you understand. You work for me. You got me?"

He must understand whatever he was looking for in his employer because he changes his tune quickly. "Of course, boss. I understand now."

Mateo nods, and we walk to the house. Still zip-tied, Emma and I walk in front of our brother as Mr. Martinez and Ramón enter the house.

We walk through the opulent and gaudy interior of the home, and I hate to say that it screams *I want to be important.* It is so flashy that my eyes cannot look at one thing. The mismatched designs and bright colors are in opposition with themselves, and I become dizzy trying to make sense of what is going on here. It is the exact opposite of class. The design is... I'm-trying-too-hard with a splash of desperation sprinkled into the home's interior design.

My boots echo on the open foyer as we stop, taking a look at our temporary home. A woman comes through shortly after and greets Mr. Martinez, welcoming him home. She is young and very pretty and I suspect she is there for things other than being the estate's stewardess. I wonder how Mrs. Martinez feels about that.

"Adalia, this is my long-lost son, Mateo. I have finally brought him home."

Mateo nods at Adalia, and she blushes. Of course, she does.

"It's so nice to make your acquaintance, Mateo."

I roll my eyes, and Emma just watches the exchange.

He nods. "Adalia, these are my sisters. I trust that you will keep an eye on them and give them whatever they need to make their short stay here as pleasant as possible."

Adalia spares a glance with a small smile before returning her full attention to my brother. "Of course, sir. I can absolutely do that for you. I can do anything that you need me to."

Ramón coughs. Mr. Martinez looks at her sternly, and I am sure she will be punished for that comment later. I don't wish that on my worst enemy, especially if he is anything like his son.

Emma gulps loudly, and I can only imagine the memories that are brought up now, being in this house once again.

"I'll show them to their rooms, sir," Adalia says.

Emma and I start to walk off, but Ramón calls out for us to stop. He walks over with a pocket knife in his extended hand. Mateo immediately takes the knife from him and comes over to us.

"Here," he says, pointing at the zip-ties.

I wordlessly extend my arms out to him, and he cuts through my ties and then does the same thing to Emma. Immediately, we attempt to ease the tingling in our wrists from being in that fixed position for the last ten hours.

Mateo's eyes hone in on the redness that encircles our wrists, but he doesn't comment. The tic of his jaw is the only sign that he is upset at the pain he was partially responsible for, but we all have our parts to play. His parting words echo in my mind, easing some of the feelings brewing.

We follow Adalia as Mr. Martinez says, "Come on, son. Follow me. I have much to talk to you about."

I hear their footsteps leave us as we hit the home's second level and walk to our gilded cage.

We are in a bedroom that is connected to a bathroom—a Jack-and-Jill style.

"Here you go, ladies," Adalia says as she shows us to our room. "Your suitcases are here, and I believe they have already been checked, so if your things seem to be rummaged through, then you would be correct. Can't be too safe these days."

I want to say safe from who, but I can't find it in me to talk to this poor, brainwashed creature.

"I suggest getting a good night's sleep because breakfast is early." She heads toward the door, but I stop her.

"We are eating breakfast with our brother?"

She turns back to address me, her hands intertwined in front of her. "Oh no, you will be served breakfast and lunch in your rooms."

I nod in understanding. They are truly locking us in here.

But she adds, "You will have dinner tomorrow night with everyone present where they will let you know what is expected of you."

With that, she leaves and closes the door behind her. We hear a lock, and then her footsteps trail off until there is nothing but silence. Suffocating silence.

I study our surroundings and then look at Emma. She sits on the bed, hugging herself. I walk over and sit beside her.

"Will you sleep with me, Evie?"

I nod. I don't want to be alone, either. Even though our rooms are connected through a Jack-and-Jill style bathroom, it feels too far to be away from one another. I'd like for us to stick together in this place.

"Mateo won't let anything happen to us, Emma." I don't know if I say that to reassure her or myself because right now, I am feeling anything but safe in this palatial prison.

I walk to the bathroom with my toiletries and belongings under my arm to shower. As the water runs, I undress. The images of Jameson just a few hours ago seem like a lifetime away, but I can still smell him on me, and that thought brings me comfort.

I reluctantly step into the shower, not wanting to wash his last memory off me, but I need to freshen up from the trip. I let the hot water warm me up. Even though it is a hundred degrees outside, I feel chilled to the bone. The warmth of the water seeps into my skin, absorbing the heat and moisture past its protective dermal barrier.

After I'm done, I step out and towel dry my hair. I touch my earring and remember that Jameson is here with me, and that gives me a sense of comfort. Emma is waiting to shower after me. I brush my hair in front of the mirror. I wonder if he can hear me.

"We made it. Emma is in the shower. We have adjoining rooms on the second floor with a bathroom in between, Jack-and-Jill style. Emma wants me to sleep with her tonight, and honestly, she didn't even have to ask me twice."

I put some product in my hair, slicking it down. "They locked us in here. They said they will feed us breakfast and lunch here, and then we are to join them for dinner to learn what will be expected of us. I am sure they would love to discipline us if given the chance. I'll try my best not to cause any trouble." I pick up the blow-dryer and dry my hair.

I look up to see Emma standing in the doorway of the bathroom, looking at me. I apply some moisturizer to my face, stand, and walk past her returning to the bathroom to brush my teeth. When I step back out, she is braiding her hair where I was just sitting.

"It helps to keep the curls if I do it this way."

I didn't ask her, but I feel it, too. There is a need to say something, anything, to make the feeling of normalcy return to our lives. Except this isn't anything normal. We are locked in a room of the house of an evil man, going to be auctioned off to the highest bidder through a forced marriage all to help Mr. Martinez gain power through our family connections.

Walking over to my bag dropping it to the floor, I start taking things out of my suitcase, standing up pissed. "They took my Kindle, those assholes. I thought maybe I'd get to read, but nope. It's not like I can access the internet. It would just be to read what I had on there. I have a lot of books on there. It would have helped to pass the time." I throw my head back, fighting the tears that threaten to fall.

Emma shrugs. "Well, that is one thing we have..." I pause, looking around and then back to meet my sister's eyes, wondering what she means by that comment.

"Plenty of time," Emma explains. She walks over to the bed, pulling back the covers. She climbs in and pats the side of the bed. "Come on, Evie. We should get a little sleep. Who knows what will happen tomorrow."

I walk over to the bed and climb in. "The bed is comfortable. I'll give them that." I pull the blankets over my chest, and Emma leans into me.

"Good night, Evie."

I place my head on hers. "Good night, Emma. Maybe when we wake up tomorrow, it will all be just a bad dream."

I feel someone pulling me. "No, I don't want to go with you. Please, just stop. You're hurting me."

But he just shakes me over and over.

"Evie," I hear my name being called, and I sit upright in bed in a place I don't recognize. "Evie, it's me, Emma. You were having a nightmare."

I notice a pale light coming through from the window drapery. I lay back down.

"Great, I woke up from one nightmare just to realize I'm living in another one."

I feel the sweat cooling on my skin as I take a deep breath and count my breathing to stop the anxiety and panic from creeping in. I don't want Emma to witness it. I've always tried to keep it from her.

"Do you have dreams like that a lot?" she asks, and I look over at her.

I bit my lip with worry. "Sometimes, I guess." I shrug it off, trying to make light of my nightmares. "I haven't had one in a while."

I've changed, and I think it has a lot to do with Jameson being in my life. He has been there for me, loved me, and made me feel safe. My brother may have saved me from several close encounters, but Jameson saved me from myself. From being in my own head. He gave me the time and patience I needed to learn how to trust someone and relinquish the control that I sought to maintain after I had none with the assault, and later in the situation with Emma's own abuse.

I remember waking up unconscious in an alley from one of Julian's abusive encounters. The memory makes me shiver. I was alone and vulnerable there, unconscious. Anything could have happened, but Mateo saved me.

I just pray he can do it again.

I must have had the same dream because, once again, I feel like I am not in control of my life. I am at the mercy of Mr. Martinez. I just hope that we come out of this. If we do, it will be on the other side, finally waking up from this nightmare.

CHAPTER THIRTY-FOUR

EVIE

"GIRL YOU'LL BE A WOMAN SOON" BY RAFFERTY

We were served in our room like we were told we would be yesterday by Adalia. The food, shockingly, wasn't bad. I would even consider it some of the best I've had in a long time. I expected to be served subpar meals, but then again, nothing has been what I've anticipated since arriving here.

We are getting comfortable the best we can, lounging on the bed, deep in our thoughts, when there is a knock at the door. I flinch, and Emma sucks in a breath. Is this it? Is it time for them to drag us out of here like cattle to the auction barn? We were not expecting anyone after our meals, and we don't know what time it is. The sun is still shining outside.

Emma grabs onto my hand just as the door opens. Adalia enters, breezing in with her skirt flowing behind her and carrying two packages in her hands. She has a beaming smile plastered on her face, and I can't help but wonder if she is possibly drugged. No one can be that delusional, but wait, this whole house is.

Maybe it's something in the water.

I quickly look over at my empty glass as it sits on the counter, condensation pooling around the bottom, and I snicker, thinking how Emma is silently cringing at it. If it didn't bother her, then we indeed have more significant problems.

"Hi, ladies. Your wonderful brother asked me to bring these to you. He is sorry he couldn't visit but he is so busy with his father."

I look over at Emma, whose nose is crinkled up at the tip, trying to hide her disgust but failing miserably. I stand, trying to sound excited. "Oh. I love presents, Adalia. What is it?"

Emma is now staring at me, wondering what I am up to.

Adalia practically jumps up with glee. "Dresses!" she exclaims. "Beautiful dresses." She claps her hands. "Isn't that great?"

"Wonderful."

"Can we open them now, Adalia?" Emma asks, joining us, and I bet it kills her to be this type of fake nice to her.

Adalia picks one package up and hands it to Emma. "Of course, silly goose."

Emma accepts the package and mouths, *'Silly goose.'*

I quickly turn away to hide my chuckle. "Is that mine?" I point to the other remaining package.

Adalia nods and hands it to me. I open the package, and in it is a red fitted dress that should come to land around mid-thigh. It is short. A pair of black patent red-soled stiletto shoes complete the ensemble.

I look over to Emma. She opens her box, which holds a green halter dress with a similar style and length along with chain-style black leather red-soled shoes. She holds up the shoes, and her eyes light up.

"Not bad, Mattie." Emma clicks her tongue.

Adalia squeals in delight. "I knew you'd like them."

I nod in agreement. "It's like Christmas." I look over to Emma, and she snorts.

"Literally, green and red. Our favorite colors."

Adalia looks over at the dress. A slight frown forms on her lips. They purse when she notices the green and red colors clashing like a Walmart Christmas portrait people mock on social media sites.

I reach out to her and grab her by the wrist to get her attention. Her eyes dart over to me, and I drop her wrist.

"They are really lovely dresses, Adalia. Will you please thank our brother for us?" This seems to make her spirits rise a bit. I cringe at my fakeness spewing forth.

"Of course!" she exclaims, clapping her hands together.

Emma and I hold our boxes, wondering what we are supposed to do now. We look at each other and then at Adalia, who is standing there.

"Um," Evie starts off, about to say something.

"Oh, right. The dresses are for the party this weekend. We just want to ensure they fit, so I need to see them on you. I am to report back if anything needs to be switched out."

We look at each other then walk into the large bathroom to change, and as soon as we shut the door, Emma starts to speak.

"What happens—"

I put my hand over her mouth, shaking my head. I place my finger up my mouth and point to the door, indicating that Adalia is listening and will likely report back anything we say.

We get dressed in silence, and I glance in the mirror. The dresses are pretty, but together, they scream 'holiday party.' We walk out, and Adalia frowns.

"Well," I hold my arms out, twirling a little, "What do you think?" Emma doesn't do anything but stand there holding her hands like a little girl seeking approval from her mother.

A sigh comes out of Adalia's mouth. "I don't like the colors together. I am switching them to both be red. What do you girls think?"

I look over to Emma. She shrugs, and I nod. "I think that is a good idea. I do like the colors though."

We step out of the dresses and hand them over to Adalia, and she walks to the door but hesitates before she leaves. She turns around to face us. Her eyes narrow.

"Don't screw this up for Mateo. There will be a lot of important people at that party, so your complete cooperation is expected. Otherwise..." she trails off. Her smile widens. "Mr. Martinez has the final say on who you marry, and he might not be very cautious about whom he picks for you from the potential suitors. We have all ages with varying specifications for their future bride. Or even worse, if he allows Oro to punish you, I can guarantee that you won't be able to walk well for about a week if that happens."

I hear Emma gulp.

"Dinner is in a couple of hours, so be ready. Someone will be up to escort you to the dining room, so I suggest you are both on your best behavior."

I look over to Emma as I hear the door close. I walk over, and she throws her arms around me, hugging me. We change into one of the few outfits we were permitted to bring with us and wait. We sit there in silence, deep in our thoughts, not wanting to talk about what we fear and what may happen this weekend. Without a clock or watch, we have no idea how long we sit there waiting.

Suddenly, the door opens, and our brother walks inside. We both jump off the bed and hug him tightly. I step away to look at my brother as Emma still holds on to him. That's when I notice he isn't hugging us back.

"Emma," I say, and she looks at me in question, still holding onto Mateo, then notices what I noticed moments ago—the resemblance.

She steps back, looking at the man we came to love, and wondering if this is an act or something else. Did he betray us?

"Sisters, follow me." He walks out the door, and his polished shoes click on the tile floor as we follow him down the hall.

The scary-looking guard with the gold tooth, who they referred to as Oro, is leering at Emma. His lip curls in a sinister smile as we walk past. Emma turns her head just as he winks at her, licking his lips and staring at her ass. Mateo doesn't notice, and she doesn't comment if he does notice. We continue to walk behind our brother in what I assume is the direction of the dining room.

Enter the dining room, where a large ornate table lies in the middle of the room under a crystal chandelier, there is a serving station with wine and champagne resting in their respective glacettes. Adalia picks up a bottle of red wine and serves Mrs. Martinez.

Mateo pulls our chairs out, and we take our seats in the spots that he selects for us. He then goes to sit across from his father and grandfather.

Adalia stands there along with the butler, who brings everything out to the table. He has a plate full of raw filet mignon steaks that he brings over to Mr. Martinez for approval. I watch with interest at the exchange. Mr. Martinez nods, and then the butler walks over to the guéridon trolley to begin cooking the steaks.

The steak is placed over heat, and brandy is poured into it to begin the flambé process. The fire roars to life, and the meat sizzles, causing my mouth to water. The smell of perfectly cooked meat fills the air, and I realize how hungry I am.

A multitude of trays line the table under heated flames to keep the food warm while the steaks are cooked to perfection. No one asked me how I like my steak cooked, but as I watch this demonstration, I can rest assured that they will be cooked perfectly to a medium-rare temperature.

Adalia picks up a bottle of wine and some champagne from each glacette and fills our cups. I select the champagne, as does Emma. I feel someone looking at me as I turn toward Mrs. Martinez. She is sizing me up with a look of distaste. Mr. Martinez laughs at something Mateo says, and her gaze moves toward him. If she looks at me with distaste, then the emotion on her face as she stares at Mateo is with a look of pure hatred.

She must sense my continued stare because she turns back to me before I can look away as she finishes the rest of her wine in one gulp. As soon as she puts it on the table, it is promptly refilled. I wonder if I should be worried about her lack of restraint. Nothing good could come of a drunk wife around my brother who has quickly taken her son's place.

I've barely taken my last bite of food as I set my napkin on my lap, when I hear a throat clear. I turn to see Mr. Martinez wiping the corners of his mouth like some kind of aristocrat instead of the corrupt politician that he really is.

"Ladies, I hope you have enjoyed your stay here because it will be short-lived."

Emma and I both look at Mateo, and his expression is emotionless. A robot would have more compassion than my brother.

"As much as I would have liked to have punished you, Mateo assured me you would behave while you were here, and he was right. This weekend, we will have a party for you where you will meet your potential suitors. By the end of the night, we will have chosen the best addition for this family to become your new husband, binding us to the Ortiz mafia connections across the border. This will solidify our ties and ensure a prosperous business venture."

He clasps Mateo on the shoulder and squeezes. "My son is home, and I look forward to the continuation of my legacy. Now to find my son a bride of his choosing."

Adalia perks up at this with her delusional smile plastered to her face.

The smile Mateo gives Mr. Martinez is all white teeth and most award-winning. The happy moment between father and son is short-lived as red wine drips from my brother's face and saturates Mr. Martinez's white shirt. The crimson color streaks the front as it rolls down the fabric and onto the floor. I hear a gasp from Adalia, but Emma and I sit there frozen and unflinching, not wanting any attention to be distracted from the wrath that will be coming.

Mr. Martinez stands up abruptly, and his chair falls back, hitting the floor with a loud thud. Mateo grabs the cloth napkin from his lap and wipes the excess wine away from his face. He is wearing a black dress shirt, so the wine coloring isn't visible, but I can tell most of it was meant for his face.

Mrs. Martinez must be drunk or stupid because even I know to be scared, but any common sense has left the building along with her sanity. She stands up, her finger pointing at him as she leans over the table. I don't know if she is using her grip on the table to hold herself upright or to keep from swaying at this point as she slurs obscenities at her husband.

We watch the exchange with our heads volleying back and forth as if we are watching a tennis match where the winner is an obvious unanimous decision.

"Your son. Your son!" she screeches, and I almost go to put my hands over my ears to ease the high-pitched sound that threatens to rupture my eardrums. "Our son is dead. My son is dead. He was the rightful heir, and this bitch killed him. I want her dead. I want them both dead." She is looking between us and Mateo, but Mr. Martinez just laughs at her.

"Do you think I give a flying fuck about what you want?" He mocks her. *"I want them dead."* He shakes his head. "Was their mother not enough for you? You've always been a jealous bitch and a lousy lay." He looks over to Adalia and winks at her. Now my steak threatens to come up because I know that she is fucking him.

Mrs. Martinez takes her new glass of wine and begins to chug it.

"I think you've had enough to drink for tonight." He takes her drink from her and places it away from her reach.

"Fuck you," she spits at him, and he is so quick that I don't hear the smack until a second after it happens.

She holds her cheek as anger radiates from her body. She stares at him defiantly, and I shift down farther into my seat, not wanting to see what will happen. "Fuck you!" she screams.

He nods. "Maybe that is what you need then."

Her eyes widen almost as if the demon that took over her body has been exorcized, and she is just realizing what she did. Although, now, her eyes widen in fear.

"Oro!" Mr. Martinez yells, and the large tatted-up man enters the room.

"Yes, boss," he says as he stops right in front of Mr. Martinez.

She backs up, realizing her mistake, but it is too late.

"I need you to show my wife what it means to be fucked."

Oro chuckles. "Oh, I can certainly do that, boss."

"No! No!" She begins to back up and looks around. If she is looking for help, she isn't getting any from us. No one is saving her. Her cheek is bright red from the slap Mr. Martinez gave her.

Oro stalks toward her, and she attempts to kick him in the balls, but he anticipates the move. He leans in and punches her in the face, and she goes down like a ton of bricks. He picks her up as if she weighs nothing and flips her over his shoulder. One shoe falls to the floor as they turn the corner and disappear.

Emma and I stay there sitting quietly.

"Let this be a lesson to you to understand what will happen if you don't cooperate this weekend at your party. If you step out of line, I'll let Oro teach you some manners." Mr. Martinez leaves the room.

We hear a door open. The sound of muffled cries echoes down the corridor before it disappears along with my dinner as I throw up the entire contents of my stomach onto the high-polished floor.

CHAPTER THIRTY-FIVE

JAMESON

"HEY MAN, NICE SHOT" BY FILTER

I have hardly slept. Eduardo and I listened to Evie talk to us through her speaker via the microphone earrings I gifted her before she left me. My stomach twists with sickness as the small device picks up her words with almost perfect clarity—both a blessing and a torturous curse simultaneously.

We learn that she and Emma are being kept in a shared room on the second floor, and I see exactly where it is via the GPS tracking device. Emma also has hers, but Eduardo has had no relief in knowing where she is at all times. According to him, he has failed if her heart is not alongside his.

I draw out two hearts in the center of that room, marking it on one of the blueprints hanging in our office, and stare at them, both of us trapped in our own hellish silence.

What really broke me was listening to her scream in the middle of the night and not being there for her. Her nightmares have returned, and for good reason. She's living a nightmare that she can't wake up from.

It killed me, and a part of my soul dies not being with my other half, not being able to comfort her or to find comfort in her embrace.

In this short time, Evie and I have become so close that I swear we are one of those couples I used to envy that could complete the other one's sentence. That's what hurt the most. Emma was there for her and comforted her when I wasn't there to do so, and it damn nearly killed me. I bring my hands up to my face to fight back the tears that blur my vision as the anger rises inside.

"Motherfuckers!" I hear Eduardo shout as his glass hits the wall and shatters into a million pieces along with our sanity.

Emma grounded him. She tamed his inner beast that always hid behind a firm handshake and a narrowed glare. I haven't seen him this volatile since our college days, which were a haze of debauchery and frat parties. That is, until Emma returned to his life. I didn't realize that she was 'the Emma' from his tattooed knuckles that he frequently used to beat the shit out of anyone who gave him the slightest reason.

Evie wasn't lying when she said she hadn't had a nightmare in a while, but I know that it is the feeling of the unknown that caused it. Not being in control of herself and at the mercy of a cruel monster. Being in the same house with Marcus, her assaulter. It brought back all the memories of a time when she was helpless and at the mercy of someone who had dominated her. Anyone would be scared, and if it was a person other than Emma and Evie, they would have fallen apart already, but these sisters are strong and resilient. I know that if anyone can overcome this, it is them. I have to believe it is for me to continue with this plan and not damn near run into the house and drag her out, even at the possibility of not coming out alive to join her.

Eduardo's hand hits my chest, breaking me out of my self-loathing. "Shh. Did you get that?"

Eduardo is already going to the board to write down the name Oro and the date for when they will be sold off to the highest bidder or the suitor with the most assets to give Mr. Martinez the money and resources to optimize his business relationships. I look over to Eduardo and don't understand how he could be so calm now when he was all fury just a moment ago. Now, at the mention of his fiancée being married off like some prized cow, he is almost gleeful. I must look confused when Ram speaks up.

"So what's the plan?" Eduardo's brother asks.

The guys have been here since day one to help out. His brother has taken over at the club so that Eduardo can concentrate on bringing Emma home. That is his sole focus now, as is mine.

I have shut down all contracts because I cannot concentrate on anything work-related when Evie is held prisoner in the Martinez house. To think that I may never see her again…

The memories of our last night together run through my mind on a constant loop, repeating the sound of her moans as she came on my fingers, tongue, and cock. I sent her away with my cum dripping down her leg and wouldn't let her shower. Now, I know it is all down the drain along with our hopes and dreams. I just pray that she will be safe and back in my arms again soon.

"This week, we will bring them home."

I am startled from my thoughts again at the plan Eduardo begins to bring forth.

"How?" is all I say. I want to believe that this time next week, I will have Evie home with me and this will all but be a distant memory while we forge ahead, creating our own memories together.

Forged hearts. Stronger and unbreakable.

"We move out in the morning to Brownsville and move into Dax and Liv's condo."

I nod because we need to be there closer to them. In the morning, we take off.

"I've already contacted Andrés and Adrian, and they are going to meet us there with my father. If we all can't bring them home, then no one can. The girls may have brought on this war, but with all of us combined and as a united front, we will see to it that it ends now."

We all get up early the next morning and make the five-hour trek south. We make no stops and take no breaks. Eduardo insists on driving the entire way. Ram stayed behind to run the business, and by the time we get into town, it is evening.

We pull up to the condo and remark on the beautiful sunset. I'm thinking about how much Evie would love it. I would love to sit out here and watch the waves crashing along with the sun setting in the background. It is breathtaking.

We gather our bags and open the door to our new home for the week. I must remember to thank my best friend, Dax, after this is over. After this weekend, we will be free. There is no option of failure. I can't think of the alternative where Evie isn't with me.

I know Eduardo feels the same about Emma. He hasn't been himself since Emma left, and he doesn't even want to eat, only consuming alcohol. Now, he hasn't touched a drop as he is committed to the plan. The guy is miserable without her, and I now understand how Dax felt with Liv.

When you know, you know.

I set up the equipment in the living room and it appears that the girls are having dinner with the family. It sounds like a pretty good dinner, from what I gather, but then I hear Mrs. Martinez comment about Mateo not being the true heir. The punch that echoes in the room when Oro knocks her out makes me visibly recoil.

We all stop moving around and listen carefully to what transpires next. I hope Mateo is watching out for them. I can't believe they are there. If he lets that happen to his own wife, then what is he capable of if the girls mouth off? For their sake, I really hope they don't make this harder than it has to be.

I know that Mateo won't allow anything to happen to them, and if Mr. Martinez tries something, the plan will be ruined and the guise will be up. I don't hear a peep out of Mateo the entire time, and I would wonder if he is really there if it wasn't for the comments made about him in his presence.

"So, it's happening this weekend?" I ask Eduardo.

He nods as he sips his coffee lost in thought, almost like he isn't really here. He doesn't answer me. He is here only in the physical sense because I know that his mind and soul are with Emma.

Nothing else matters.

We hear a knock at the door, and I get off the couch to answer it.

"There's your answer," Eduardo replies, void of emotion.

I look at the window and then through the peephole to see who is on the other side. When I recognize the faces of Evie and Emma's uncle and cousin, I open the door.

"It's about time," I say, relieved, and welcome them wholeheartedly. I give them each a hug, patting them on the back silently and thanking them for their assistance in getting the girls back home.

"Think nothing of it. This was a long time coming, and I am glad to see this finish so that maybe my sister's soul can finally be laid to rest."

I quirk an eyebrow up, clearly not believing any of this spiritual stuff, but Eduardo does, and he makes the sign of the cross. I almost roll my eyes at the irony of these men who also release people to the spirit world more than I'd like to know about.

"Thank you for coming," Eduardo replies while walking over to them.

Andrés just nods, acknowledging his thanks. They enter the condo and get settled. We discuss the plan and fill them in on what is happening. We relay all our news and show them where the girls are being kept.

"I have some news," Andrés says.

Eduardo nods, urging him to continue. I bite my nails in frustration, not wanting to hear, but then feel compelled to listen to anything that could help bring my girlfriend back home as soon as possible.

"It was brought to my attention that the police chief that is in the pocket of Mr. Martinez is upset."

Eduardo nods, encouraging Andrés to proceed with his discovery. I lean in closer to what he says next, hanging on every word.

"It also came to our attention that his pixie-looking daughter's life was threatened to encourage his complacency with Mr. Martinez, who has been slowly overtaking things here in Brownsville. His insistence on bringing illegal drugs across the border has had the police chief turning his attention to anything other than the drugs that are being smuggled across the border by Mr. Martinez."

"How did he threaten his daughter?" Eduardo asks out of curiosity.

Andrés doesn't hesitate to answer. "Some guy named Oro who is one of his enforcers and security detail. He is considered a brute and does anything Mr. Martinez asks of him. He sexually assaulted the chief's daughter and threatened worse next time if he didn't have his full support in his endeavors."

We nod, remembering the knockout ordeal with Mrs. Martinez for spitting at Mateo and throwing her wine at her husband. It was all so much to take in, but Mr. Martinez didn't have any of it, so he sent her off to be punished by Oro.

I shudder at that mental image of Emma and Evie in that house, along with that monster that threatens them if they step out of line. It makes me want to gut someone, but I control my temper and wait for further instruction. I know that we can all keep them safe. We just have to formulate a plan to ensure it works.

CHAPTER THIRTY-SIX

JAMESON

"INSANELY ILLEGAL CAGE FIGHT" BY DAL AV, JACKSON ROSE

We set a meeting with the chief of police mid-week. He was hesitant when he initially received the request from Eduardo and Andrés, but as soon as they mentioned removing the threat to his daughter, he was full steam ahead in assisting in any way he could.

When the day to meet him finally rolls around, I wake up early and purposefully. I have a few questions of my own for this man, and the thought of him having any information about how to handle this situation or working together toward a common goal would also be considered a win.

The store is empty at this hour. The large chain bookstore has a sizable cafe in the middle that allows us some discretion but isn't too big so that we can't see someone approaching. This is the perfect combination to allow us the opportunity to have this meeting.

We have a clear view of the front doors from where we sit and will notice when he enters. I've never met the man, but by looking at his pictures, we should be able to identify him quickly.

I approach the counter, placing our order for some coffees. I peruse the menu further, considering the 'buy one, get one half-off' cookies, but decide against them.

That's when I notice the barista's book recommendations placed in front of the cashier. A sign that reads, 'Only five dollars with purchase of a beverage' is placed between the cookie display and the coffee cups. It's a romance book.

My upper lip curls in a half smile, making me chuckle aloud. I tilt my head to get a better look and contemplate whether I have seen this particular book at the apartment. I wonder if Evie has read it. She and Emma like to read about kick-ass heroines in polyamorous relationships. I could never be in one of those relationships because the thought of sharing Evie with anyone makes me want to commit all kinds of crimes.

The barista notices me checking out the books on display and raises an eyebrow. I place the book back on its shelf and shrug. "My girlfriend likes to read these types of books." I raise my arm toward the stack for purchase. The cover model is a scantily clad woman. Her harem of men surrounds her while they all touch her, and their stare shows to anyone looking that her presence consumes them.

I have to admit, it looks hot.

"She has them lying around throughout the apartment," I go on, my hand reaching behind me as if our apartment is there and she can see all the books. I pick up the book and fan through it before placing it back on the holder. It appears a little crooked, so I straighten it.

She laughs, causing me to look up at her. "Sure. Whatever you say." She looks behind me, raising her chin upward to the person ready to get the next order.

I feel my face heat and then step away, and when they finally call my order out, I pick up the cups in a holder to return to our table. I hand out the black coffee and wait to see when he approaches.

Right on time, a man in his late forties with a salt-and-pepper military-style buzz cut that matches his mustache enters, head held high, and heads straight for us.

We stand and offer him a seat. It draws the barista's attention, but she pretends not to notice us. Clever girl, I think to myself. Our table screams danger, but we only want to harm those who have taken something that doesn't belong to them, and we intend to right that mistake very soon.

"Please, call me Santi." He holds out his hand to Eduardo, who is leading the meeting. "I was told that we could be mutually beneficial to each other."

Eduardo nods, and we all stay silent and pensive while observing his reactions to Eduardo's following words.

"I understand you have had unpleasant dealings with a certain public figure in Brownsville."

We notice Santi visibly tense, and we spare a quick glance at one another to see if they picked up on it, too. He sits upright, no longer relaxed and wary of his following words.

"I–"

Eduardo holds up his hand. "We are very aware of your problem with Mr. Martinez and him threatening your only daughter. I believe we can help one another because, you see, he has two young women, sisters, that belong to our family. We understand what it is like to have someone take and hurt your family." His eyes shoot up to mine.

"What did he do to your sister?" His hands ball up in anger. His rage is barely contained beneath the surface.

Eduardo shakes his head. "Not my sister, but my fiancée and her twin sister, who is also my friend's girlfriend." He gestures in my direction, and I look at him. I'm sure my eyes are pleading with him to help us.

Andrés speaks up, causing us all to turn our attention to him. "She is my sobrina."

Adrian speaks after his uncle. "My prima."

Santi nods in understanding. "They are your family."

Eduardo looks around at the group gathered at the small table in the cafe. "They are our family, yes, Santi. Mr. Martinez has taken them to sell them off to the highest bidder all because he wants to further his assets and solidify partnerships through their marriage. They are selling them off like cattle, and I want my fiancée and her sister to be back home with us where they belong. With their family."

He nods, determination lining his facial features. "They threatened my daughter, Meli. If I didn't turn my attention away from his drug smuggling, he would retake my daughter, and, this time, she might not come back. Meli—" He stops to compose himself before continuing.

"That monster, Oro, assaulted Meli, and she wonders if she'll be retaken. If that happens, I know she won't survive mentally or physically." He rubs his face as if attempting to erase the bad memory from his mind.

Andrés leans in. "Help us get rid of him, and you have my word. He won't hurt Meli or anyone else again. Any of them."

Santi nods. "What do you need me to do?"

Eduardo looks over to Andrés, and he nods, giving him permission to relay the idea we came up with earlier.

The remaining days pass in a whirlwind of planning and high emotions. We all realize the severity of the consequences if we fail. Eduardo was a wreck the night before, but I convinced him to ride it out without alcohol.

The time frame is too delicate, in case we need to go in there and break them out, but this way is much better than that. We just have to be patient for a few more hours.

Tonight, we strike when they least expect it. They are undoubtedly planning for us to sneak around like thieves in the night to steal Emma and Evie away, but *they* are the thieves, and we are merely there to take back what belongs to us—our family.

"Did you get the tuxedos?" Andrés speaks to Adrian as he waltzes into the condo with a few takeout bags. He places everything on the counter and drops the bag he carries with his teeth onto the table.

"Yes, Father. I just couldn't carry it all." He scoffs. "Can you help out?"

Seeking any excuse to make the time go by, I jump at the offer. "I'll go."

I spring up from the desk chair and practically run out the door to make myself useful. I have been monitoring things at the mansion, but I am so nervous about tonight. I feel the need to release some of this pent-up anxiety. I wish I could go for a run to expel all my nervousness, but I can't bear to be away from the computer screen for too long.

What if I am out running and then miss a crucial element of the conversation and events of tonight?

I know that we pretty much have the situation handled, but I still think knowing everything possible is helpful. There is no room for errors tonight.

I open the door as Adrian unlocks it with his key fob. Seven tuxedos are lying on the back seat. We will all play our part at the party, but we won't be on the guest list. In fact, they won't even know we will be there until it is too late. With blueprints and reinforcements coming in to stay at a safe house located between here and the border, which, mind you, is a few miles away, it should be quite the show.

Adrian and I enter the condo and walk toward the back bedroom where we hand out the tuxedos in the closet. After having a meeting with the police chief, our men, and our family gathered here at the condo, I believe Eduardo when he says that this unified front is enough to bring the girls home and to show these men that they are messing with the wrong family.

Eduardo has reiterated that it isn't about just bringing the girls home but also teaching a lesson to our enemies who may try to repeat events such as these. The family must show them that they are strong and have the power to defeat their enemies and keep the organization strong. It's been a long time since someone has dared to challenge them for power, and, like always, the strongest prevail. Luckily, that is us, our blended family, but it doesn't stop someone from trying to take what is yours.

Eduardo picks up the bag of tacos and takes two. They are passed around until only a bag with a styrofoam-enclosed plate is left. He looks curiously at it. "What's in there?" he asks, going to open it, and I reach out for it.

"It's mine." I take a whiff, and my mouth waters. "It's a taco salad."

Eduardo raises one eyebrow. "A taco salad?"

I open the container, and the spiced chicken and veggies smell permeates the air. Nom. Nom. I smack my lips in anticipation.

"A fucking taco salad?" he asks again.

I take a bite of the salad that rests inside a crispy corn shell. It crunches, and light flakes of corn tortillas fly away from my mouth.

"Hm. Yes, bro. It's the best."

Eduardo just shakes his head, chuckling. "Whatever you say." He finishes his tacos in a few bites and walks out of the room, tossing his bags and trash out on the way.

I call out to him over my mouth full of food. "Where are you going?" I take another heaping forkful of my food, groaning as the flavors assault my taste buds.

He turns back to me. "To get ready. I want to look my best when I rescue my fianceé." He winks at me before he disappears behind the door.

It takes everyone a while to get ready, but there are a couple of bathrooms where we take turns showering and getting changed into our tuxedos. We call up Santi to see how everything is going on his end.

"Santi, is everything a-go for tonight?" Eduardo has him on speaker so that we can all listen to his response.

"Yes, I have all my men in place, and they have been made aware of what will happen tonight."

"What about your wife and daughter? Are they at the safe house now, just out of an abundance of caution? We want to ensure their safety. When we eliminate the threat, they can return home."

There is silence on the other line, but we can hear his breathing pick up. He blows out a breath.

"That would be great. Thank you, Eduardo. We want to help you, too, and it has been a long time coming."

Although we can't see him, I imagine him nodding in agreement.

"It has, and I am glad that it will soon be coming to an end. I'll see you soon, then." He hangs up the call, and Eduardo tucks the phone back into his tuxedo pocket.

"Okay. Let's go over the plan one more time."

I nod, as does the rest of our blended family, and we go over one last time on how we are going to get into the house and bring our family home.

CHAPTER THIRTY-SEVEN

EVIE

"SON OF A PREACHER MAN" BY DUSTY SPRINGFIELD

"Here you go, ladies." Adalia enters the room without knocking. Her sheer, flowing dress billows about as she rushes in with two packages—two boxes I recognize from the other day. She places them on the bed, looks at them, and then back at us. She lifts her hand to the packages. We watch her with curiosity.

"As promised, here are the dresses, both red this time so we don't have the 'holiday theme.'" She makes air quotes and rolls her eyes. "I remember the words you spoke when I brought them in for you to try on."

I open the boxes to see that the dresses now match. "Thank you, Adalia. That was very kind of you." I give my best attempt at sincerity, and she beams at our praise.

With her head held high, Adalia turns to walk out the door with a flourish of iridescent fabric trailing behind. Before she exits, she turns to us.

"You have someone coming in. Make sure you are waxed and made up before you slip into your dresses. I suggest you don't give them a hard time." She waves, and the door shuts behind her.

"Pfft, I was almost going to say she isn't that bad." Emma snorts as we stand in our robes, dumbfounded at the exchange just as another person enters moments later.

This time, a young woman enters wheeling a cart in front of her, and a bag is slung over her shoulder. She doesn't speak; she just goes about her business while we stare at her.

She gently places the bag on the vanity and opens it, and a multitude of makeup and hair products spill forth. Next, I notice the heated wax on the silver cart, which makes me sweat. She grabs a stick and places it into the waxy mixture, then sets it down, testing the readiness of the substance as she claps her hands together in glee, ready to inflict pain on someone's lady parts. As if there was any question about her role in this room, she immediately clarifies it.

"I'm going to help you ladies prepare for your party. Who wants to get waxed first?" She looks excited, and I look like I'd rather bathe in the hot wax as punishment.

The question lingers in the air as neither of us answers. She looks from me to Emma and then back again, wondering when someone will answer her. I glance over at Emma, who is standing there open-mouthed.

"I'll go first," I volunteer for what I suspect will be a Brazilian wax. "How do you want me?"

She points to the bed. "Lay on your back with your knees bent and legs open like a butterfly." She demonstrates the motion with her hands. "Let your knees drop outward."

I do as she says, and Evie looks away, pretending to look over her dress to give us some privacy.

"Yes, that's it."

Moments later, as the hot wax spreads over my most sensitive areas. The hair is removed in one quick sweep. Before I can think of it, I feel the sting, and my eyes fucking water.

"Oh, wow. That was intense." I shift uncomfortably.

She nods in understanding. "We are almost done."

I look up at her. "Really?"

"Nope. Just a few more passes, though."

I almost pass out with the thought of continuing this for a few more rounds. I think my skin has gone numb as a protective mechanism. I didn't know I even had hair there. I must have cleared my mind with my meditation techniques.

Before I know it, Emma is in my place, and the cool, soothing gel really did help to alleviate the minor discomfort of having all my hair ripped out at the follicle.

Emma howls, and I hold her hand, looking away out the window.

"So dramatic, babe." I look down at her as she just glares daggers at me.

Before we know it, we are dressed, hair done, and makeup, too. I take in my appearance in the floor-length mirror and admire her grooming work. I look refined and sophisticated in the outfit. I look every bit the mafia princess worthy of a maximum payout for her hand in marriage.

I just hope Mateo comes through for us. We haven't seen him since that horrific night at the dinner where Oro carted Mrs. Martinez away before our eyes. I shudder at the thought of him punishing her. Although we weren't present to witness what happened to her, the screams that came from the room were enough to imagine the horrors she endured as part of her punishment.

The young woman is putting away her things, and we watch her, wondering what we do now.

"Is someone coming to get us?" I ask, and she raises her head to look up at me before continuing to put away her accessories.

She shrugs. "I don't know. I was just told to get you ready like your life depended on it."

I recoil at her choice of words. She doesn't seem to notice my reaction. She leaves precisely how she came in—without acknowledging us. As she opens the door, we can hear the commotion of an event consisting of chatter and a band playing classy lounge music. I imagine guests walking around with a cocktail or champagne as Emma and I await certain doom.

A knock at the door lets us know that our time has come. Emma winces at the sound, and I hold onto her arm for comfort. She squeezes it in return, thanking me for my support.

In walks Mateo, and boy, is he a sight for sore eyes. Emma is about to run up to him, but the scared look in his eyes lets us know that that is a bad idea.

I hold her back, stopping her from going any farther and for him to have to physically reject the affection. There are bags under his eyes, and it looks like he hasn't slept in ages.

"Are you ready, my sisters?" he asks with a pleading look on his face.

I answer for Emma and me. She is incapable of words at the moment. I don't know what she thought was going to happen. He has a part to play, and so do we. We just have to trust that everything will come out okay.

To put your blind faith in someone is hard. You just have to trust them to come through, and not seeing anyone this week has really made it hard not to feel abandoned. Yet here we are, placing our faith in our brother to end this war that has been a long time coming.

I shake Emma's arm, and she looks at me. Her eyes harden, and I smile.

"Let's do this. Lead the way, brother." I motion with my hand in front of me.

He nods, a slight smile to his mouth as he turns around, and we walk out to the party where shit is about to get real.

We walk down the hall as the music and noise get louder. "Walk behind me, please."

As we arrive at the grand staircase, we are met by Mr. Martinez and his father, Ramón. Mr. Martinez looks us over with his hungry gaze that makes me want to vomit, but I won't show him any weakness. Mateo and Ramón move to flank Mr. Martinez on each side of him, thereby hiding us from view.

"Can I please have your attention?"

The music stops, and the crowd grows silent. I can't see anyone from here, but I know there are many guests present for this. The faces blend into one another as if they are melting.

"I'd like to welcome you to my home and, for some of you, into my family. You know my father, but you may not know my son, Mateo. Much like the prodigal son, he has returned home, and I welcome him with open arms. He is my true heir, and he brought us our very special guests for tonight. They are quite lovely, and I know that two of you here tonight will be fortunate enough to make this collaboration worth every penny. I will pass this over to my son to make further introductions."

He slaps Mateo on the back and hands him the little microphone. He smiles widely with excitement.

"Hello. As my father introduced me a moment ago, I am Mateo, his son. Thank you all for coming, and I look forward to doing business with you in the near future.

"Without further ado, I know that you are here for the lovely women we are offering tonight, so I'd like you to meet them."

Mateo motions for us to come forward, but I cannot move. I am the center of attention, and the hushed whispers make the perspiration drip down my back. Marcus is at the top of the stairs and pushes us forward.

"My sisters, Evie and Emma Ortiz Taylor." Mateo holds out his hand for us to take, one on each side of him.

The music starts up again with a bass riff and a flute, lightly fluttering notes in the background. The singer belts out jazzy vocals as we begin our walk down the long staircase toward an uncertain fate.

CHAPTER THIRTY-EIGHT

EVIE

"SEVENTY THORNS" BY JONATHAN DAVIS AND KIM DRACULA

One thing I notice straight away is that there are a lot of men here. I gulp, holding onto Mateo's hand with a firmer grip. The second thing I notice is Oro, standing by the large picture window, flicking his tongue at me. My nostrils flare. He's provoking me. His laughter rises up above the crowd to mock me. My anger takes over as my primary emotion as I envision his head exploding. Gray matter flies out of his brain with force as a projectile shoots through his skull, causing his head to crack open like a watermelon. I hear the gasps as people duck and run.

I blink, but the image stays.

That's when I realize he *was* shot, and what I was envisioning wasn't my imagination, but it really happened.

The band breaks into another song with harsh lyrics and death metal vocals. I feel like I am in one of my nightmares—a kaleidoscope of images and lights flickering from one scene to the other. Too much is happening that I can't focus on one thing. The images shift and then disappear as bodies fall to the floor as the sound of gunfire echoes in the mansion—dead men who wanted to purchase two young women.

A person jumps through the fractured glass, causing me to gasp in surprise. The glass further shatters the remaining window pane as men in tuxedos and skull face paint begin to surround us.

People run for the door, hit with bullets before exiting and landing facedown, taking their last breath before the light vanishes from their eyes. Blood pools all around, and the screaming and yelling escalate along with the frightening lyrics that continue to play forth from the band, making for a hellish sight. The security guards turn their fire onto the crowd.

I hit the SOS button and see one of the masked men shift his face to me. *Why is he looking at me? Did he hear it? How could he possibly...* Then recognition hits.

It's Jameson. He's here. I look around at the other masked men, now approaching us at an alarming speed. Knowing who they are, I smile, and Jameson's smile mimics mine. He strides toward me with purpose but gets punched by a man with a bald head. He is not one of the paying guests, but as it turns out, he is one of Mr. Martinez's security detail.

I turn around to see Marcus coming at me. He grabs my wrist, and I pull it toward me and push it out of his hold as my other hand hits him with the flat palm of my hand, striking him with a hard upward motion straight to his nose. I feel the crack under my palm. He raises his hands to stop the blood pouring out as I knee him in the balls. He drops forward onto his knees, not knowing what to hold.

Mateo takes his gun out and shoots Marcus, while Emma pushes his collapsing body over the balcony railing, where he falls in a freakish fashion. When he hits the highly polished flooring, his legs and arms are bent unnaturally. His eyes are open, staring into nothing. Blood quickly drains from his lifeless form, pooling underneath and outlining his body.

Mateo has his back turned, so he doesn't see what happens next. Mr. Martinez makes a rush for him. His gun is raised as he points it with his sights locked on Mateo's chest. I hear someone call his name, and he turns to see where the voice came from.

"Mateo. Watch out!"

Mateo turns his head to lock stares with his father, who now has the gun pointed firmly at his chest.

"Son, I thought better of you. I didn't think you, of all people, would betray me. Your own father." He walks closer.

Emma stands still, and I beg her not to move. To cause him to have the trigger pointed at her instead.

"What a disappointment."

We see and hear the gun go off. The bullet is set to hit its target right as Ramón jumps in front of his grandson, pushing him out of the way. The force of the bullet causes Ramón to fall backward and tumble down the stairs. Mateo runs after him, halting his rapid descent.

I watch in disbelief that Ramón saved my brother from his father. I breathe in a deep, meditative breath to calm the anxiety rising up, threatening to throw me into a panic attack. I hear a grunt and open my eyes to see Emma standing over Mr. Martinez.

"You sick fuck. You thought you could sell us. You and your son, Julian, are the worst kind of evil, with no chance for redemption. Now, I can end this, and I hope you meet your son where you both can rot in hell where you belong." Emma holds the gun at Mr. Martinez's head.

He sneers. "You don't have the—"

She fires, as blood splatters over Emma's chest and face. She looks like an avenging goddess covered in her tormentor's blood. She drops the gun and rushes over to me.

"Deep breaths, Evie, I've got you. I've got you like you've always got me." Her hand runs over my forehead as I kneel on the floor, sucking in lungfuls of air without the feeling of my lungs fully expanding. I can't get enough air to breathe, and I'm starting to panic.

"Evie!" I hear a familiar voice as my vision starts to go.

"Emma!"

Jameson and Eduardo are here with us. Eduardo is kissing Emma, despite all the blood covering her chest and face. I am immediately engulfed in a warm embrace, and Jameson's soothing voice helps me calm my breathing.

"Count, Evie. Hold it in for two counts and slowly let it out. Okay, now do it again, baby. I've got you. I'm here. Let's get you both out of here."

I stand on shaky legs. I can take a deep breath once again. I nod. Now, Emma is next to me. She holds onto my hand as we descend the stairs and sees Mateo holding Ramón. Emma runs down the remaining stairs to help him.

"Mateo, how is he?" She drops beside him, feels his skin, and checks for a pulse. Blood coats his arm where a bullet intended for Mateo grazed him, but otherwise, it did not injure him.

Emma rips his shirt and assesses him for other gunshot wounds. "It's just a graze, Mateo, but we should get him to a hospital after that fall. Something could be broken."

Another man in a tuxedo with a skull-painted face approaches.

"Does he need an ambulance?"

Eduardo answers while looking at his fiancée for further direction. "Emma?"

She shakes her head. "I'm not sure of his injuries. If we call an ambulance, it might bring attention to us."

The man talking to Eduardo looks over to me. "The area is secure. No one will say anything, and the property has been searched. We found a dead body in the basement. A middle-aged woman. I believe it was his wife, Mrs. Martinez."

I look over to Emma, and she nods knowingly. I'm glad they are all dead. "Let's get Ramón to a hospital. He saved my brother, and I consider him part of our family now."

Eduardo nods. "Agreed. Let's get him help."

They carry Ramón out of there, and we follow. Jameson holds my hand. I can't help but look at where the band played a while ago and think of how differently this night started.

There is a large SUV waiting for us. Eduardo opens the door, and Emma gets in. Jameson pulls me in and onto his lap. I sit there curled up in his warm embrace as he rubs circles on my back. The vehicle idles. I'm waiting for us to leave when a blaze erupts from my peripheral vision. Jameson's hand tightens around me, and I focus on the beautiful fire that engulfs the house.

"That is how it all started, you know," I say aloud to anyone and no one.

Jameson places a kiss on my neck, trailing up to my ear, and places another soft kiss there. "And this is how it ends," he whispers in my ear.

I bury my head into his chest and cry, and he lets me, just content in holding me tightly to him as I unleash all the emotions I have kept hidden. I cry for my parents, who died in that fire years ago, along with a part of me. Emma thought I was dead, and I might have been if it wasn't for my brother, who saved me that night.

We drive out of the property gates and onto the highway, leaving behind our past forged in fire. The tides turned that day. Julian took everything from us, yet we rose from the ashes and came out stronger after it all.

I once told Emma that when something bad happens and causes everything you once believed in and loved to burn to the ground, you have no choice but to rise with an unbreakable strength amid the flames.

Those intense periods of pain became our black wave—unrelenting. We persevered. We spread our wings and soared away from the past and into our new future, transformed and resilient. Despite it all, we now have a newfound strength to help us heal our family—our forged hearts. The rising, falling, and turning twisted tides broke free, crushing all our enemies in their wake, ensuring that for once, we are finally free.

CHAPTER THIRTY-NINE

JAMESON

"THE SUMMONING" BY SLEEP TOKEN

We meet Mateo at the hospital and sit in the waiting area waiting for an update. I look over to Emma and wonder if she is thinking it's like déjà vu remembering how Liv, her best friend, received some terrible news about her ex-boyfriend. Now, we wait similarly for news about Ramón's progress.

Ramón saved Mateo, there is no denying that. Anyone can see that he loves his grandson. The countless hours he played chess with him, without any agenda other than spending time and getting to know him. For whatever reason, he had to do what he did. I am sure we will hear about the true reason for his actions, when, or if Ramón makes it. I bet there is more to that story than what we know now. I just hope there are no more lies to be revealed. Now is the time for healing and forgiveness. This self-reflection needs to happen if we are going to get through this together.

A few hours later, a surgeon approaches us, as Mateo stands up. We knew that he was in critical condition due to the severity of his fracture, but I also know that Dax highly recommended an amazing surgeon. When I called him to tell him about Mateo's grandfather falling, he didn't ask any questions; he just called up his buddy, and he went to evaluate him in the emergency room and prepped for surgery a few hours later.

"He did extremely well. I don't anticipate any problems with his recovery," the young surgeon states. "He will be waking up from anesthesia shortly, but why don't you go and get a good night's sleep and return in the morning? I will personally let him know that you were all here, but I sent you home to get some rest. I have to talk to him when he wakes up anyway."

Evie lets go of my hand that I have had a firm lock on, as she walks over to her brother. "Come on, Mattie. Let's go home like the doctor said and we will come back after we get some rest. We still have some things to discuss."

Mateo looks down at his sister and brings her to him in an embrace.

He kisses the top of her head as she rubs his back. "It's okay, Mattie. We are all here, bro, and we love you."

He nods and runs his hand over his face. His eyes are red-rimmed and tired. "Yeah, let's go home."

He walks away, and we all get up off our chairs and follow him out of the hospital.

The ride home is a blur. We decide to all head back to the condo to get some much needed sleep. Gus, Eli, and Philip all return to the safe house with Santi, where he and his daughter should be able to go home. Now that Mr. Martinez and his goons are dead, they don't have to worry about her assaulter returning or the threat to comply with his irrational and demanding requests. That will be one hell of a cleanup, but the fire did help escalate it. All evidence was burned and covered up with the help of our families and Santi, who had his daughter to think about.

We each take a room at the condo. Mateo uses the room that was turned into what looked like a crime scene investigation as his sleeping quarters for the night. I pull Evie into one of the rooms and use the bag Eduardo left out for us to dispose of our clothing.

We must have looked like a Halloween horror show gone wrong with our blood-streaked tuxedos and skull-painted faces, but no one said a thing, and I know that we have Santi, the police chief, to thank for that.

I really hope his daughter finds the peace she needs to heal, and knowing that Oro is gone and won't hurt her anymore should be the start to that healing process.

I drag Evie into the shower, and we bathe with purpose to get all the night's activities off our skin. Pink-tinged water circles the drain until it finally runs clear after a couple of washes. The face paint requires more washes though.

I bring Evie to me and kiss her. "Sleep, baby. I will dispose of these clothes and hand them to Eduardo before I come to bed with you." I close the door behind me and see Eduardo coming out of the office and taking a bag from Mateo. I hand my bag to him, and he smiles.

"I'll take care of this, buddy. Go back to your girl."

I run a hand through my wet hair, exhaling loudly. "Yeah. Alright. See you in the morning?"

He nods and walks out of the condo with the trash bags. I have no idea what he's going to do with them, but he is used to this, and I trust him to do the job right.

I return to the room where Evie is fast asleep. I hear her light, easy breathing as I pull back the covers. I climb into bed with her for the first time in a week, and she shifts toward me like an invisible force drawing her closer. I can't help but to reach for her, bringing her body flush with mine. I nuzzle my nose into her hair and breathe in her smell. I sigh in contentment knowing this is the start of our life together. I just hope there are no more truths to be told, but I suspect that there may be one or two more that need to come to light. There always is.

I open my eyes to morning light streaming through the sheer curtains of the condo, along with the sound of beach waves. It reminds me of a time not long ago when Dax and I met Liv and Emma for the first time on Padre Island for spring break. Who would have thought I'd be in bed with her sister? I am totally in love with her twin.

I lean forward and reach for Evie, but I come up empty. My hand touches the rumpled sheets. Her side is cold, as if she hasn't been there in a while. I lift my head up and hear the sound of talking coming from the kitchen. I throw on some sweats and a hoodie, as I walk with purpose toward the voices.

I see my girlfriend, Eduardo, Emma, and Mateo around the kitchen island with steaming mugs of coffee. A box of Mexican sweet bread is placed in the center, and I see Evie eating her favorite hot-pink colored frosted cake. I walk toward her and kiss her quickly before grabbing my cup of much-needed caffeine.

"How's Ramón?" I ask, taking my full, steamy cup and walking back toward Evie. I sit beside her and pull myself closer to her, decreasing the space between us.

"He was awake and in a little pain but seems to be doing well. Provided everything goes okay, he should be able to come home this week. I will stay with him and help him get around, take him to his appointments, and do any other errands he needs."

Emma reaches for her brother. "If you need any help with Grandpa, let us know." Mateo quirks an eyebrow at her, and she laughs. "What? That's what he is to you, right?" she questions him, and Mateo nods.

"Yes, I suppose he is. It's just weird, you know?"

I speak up. "If you need anything, any one of us will be there to help." I grab Evie's hand, and Mateo tracks the motion.

"Nah, I'm good, but thanks for the offer. I think you all need some alone time."

Emma's face flushes red, and Eduardo laughs. Mateo pushes two envelopes toward Emma and Evie. "Ramón gave me these at the hospital today. One is for you, and the other is for me."

Evie drops my hand and reaches for them. "Do you not want to open yours?"

I look at her and think about the way she worded that. It's almost as if she knows he doesn't, but I wonder to myself why.

He shakes his head. "No, it's from your mom."

Emma cringes at his phrasing. Although she wasn't much of one, she is his mother, too.

"Do you want us to open them, Mateo?" She reaches for the envelopes and picks up one manilla envelope, sizing it up its weight in her hand. "This one seems heavy."

She rips the envelope and empties the contents on the kitchen countertop. The metal object bounces with a loud clatter as it hits the granite.

"What the..." Evie trails off as Emma's hands go to touch the slightly damaged ring.

"Oh, wow!" Emma exclaims.

"It's the ring you got me for my birthday." Evie jumps up off the barstool. She picks up the ring and turns it around, studying the object. "This ring saved me."

Mateo reaches for it, and Evie hands it over to him.

"Yeah, it did. Ramón told me that was how they knew it was you in the morgue where they had to identify the bodies. Nothing was recognizable, but they sure did recognize your ring," Evie huffs out.

"What assholes," Emma chimes in.

"You made me leave it there that night, Mattie."

His gaze is far away, as if relieving the night her parents died and she pretended to be dead. "Yes, I did," Mateo confirms. "Ramón took it off of that poor woman they thought was you and kept it for you. I don't know why he did it, but he said to give it to you. It might help you find the closure you need."

Emma and Evie exchange a look and then glance over at the other package.

"You knew what was in it?"

He nods, but Emma continues. "So what's in the other package?" she asks, and Mateo stares out the window, looking at the waves rolling onto the shore.

"More closure," he says softly, as if to himself.

CHAPTER FORTY

EVIE

"MARY ON A CROSS" BY GHOST

I pick up the envelope and open it. Mateo isn't looking at us, but I can feel his anxiety rise to the surface. I empty the envelope's contents, and a single letter falls out of the folder. It is addressed to my brother.

"Mattie, what is this?" I pick it up and try to hand it to him, since it has his name on it. He doesn't make an attempt to take it from me.

He sighs, his face pained. He looks at me, sadness in his eyes and his body slumped.

"It's from Mom."

I recoil at his use of the word 'Mom.' Again, he used it to identify the woman who raised Emma and me but abandoned her firstborn—our brother. He has gone through great lengths to be there for us and keep us safe. A boy who grew up into a man without a family of his own. His whole life, he lived with the feeling that no one wanted him.

My heart hurts for the boy he was and the man he has become because he did it alone. He might have had our uncle and cousin to talk to, but then he was sent away to boarding school. I could see how hurt he was when he found out Ramón was his grandfather. He had someone around who pretended to be his friend. Someone who wanted to spend time with him but got to know him through false pretenses. Who knows what is real anymore with all the lies our mother kept from us?

I frown, turning my attention back to the letter sitting there mockingly.

"Are you going to read it?" I ask, picking up the letter but not wanting to open it. I feel that Mom wanted him to read it first and then maybe share it with the rest of us. He should read it.

"I don't know if I want to open it." He takes the envelope from me, twirling it in his hand.

"We could burn it?" I arch an eyebrow upward, and Emma snorts.

"Yeah. That seems to be a common theme with us these days. Can we stay away from the fire for a bit?" She looks wearily at Eduardo for comfort. He kisses her forehead, and she beams at him approvingly.

"I'm just kidding." I roll my eyes at their seriousness when I was just trying to make light of a depressing situation. "Well, mostly kidding, but you know, bro, if you don't read it, you'll never know what she had to say. You can't ask her. She's dead. These may be the last words you get."

Emma snorts. "Way to be sensitive about it, Eves." She points to the letter, and Mateo picks it up and surprises us by opening it.

He begins to read it aloud—no hesitation—before he can back out.

My Dearest Son,

If you are reading this, things didn't turn out as planned.

If you are reading this, you probably hate me because I never had the chance to change the events in my life.

If you are reading this, at least I know that you are alive and my death was worth it.

When you were born, it was the best day of my life. The nurse handed you to me, and

you grabbed onto my finger as I held onto you. I never wanted to let you go. I never sent you to the nursery while I was there. I didn't want to because I secretly knew. I knew those precious moments with you might be the only ones I was offered in this life.

I had you all to myself for nine months before I had to let you go. The day I brought you home, my brother told me what I must do. I begged for one more day with you.

If he found out about you, he would have held you over me forever and kept me because he knew I could never leave you. You would never be free. He would have molded you into what he wanted, much like how his other son turned out. You wouldn't have been the kind man who takes care of his sisters and follows them around, protecting them from the evils of this world.

The day that I returned to Brownsville, married with twins, he lost it. He always had the suspicion you existed. I confided in Ramón when I learned about the pregnancy, and he promised to find you one day if something happened to me and give this to you. He promised to be the family that you deserve, and I hope you find the love you deserve because, my sweet boy, you are worthy of ALL the love. Maybe one day, if you have children of your own, you will understand the love I gave up so that you could find yours.

Love Always,

Mom

The room is quiet, and there isn't a dry eye in the kitchen amongst us. I walk over to my brother and hug him. "I don't know what Mom was thinking, Mattie, but I know that whatever she did, she thought she was doing what was best. I have to believe that."

Emma strides over and embraces our brother from the other side. "I love you, and am so thankful you are in my life. I may disagree with what Mom did, but if Mr. Martinez was anything like his son, Julian, then I can understand some of the abuse she underwent to have to make the difficult decisions to keep you away from that toxicity. I'd rather die than be married to Julian."

Mateo nods, taking it all in. "I can't imagine what would have happened, but I can't dwell on this anymore. This letter proves that in her own mind, she was validated in abandoning me. I'm so tired of living in the past. I want to put this all behind me and live in the present. I want to forgive and live for my future. I know what we have to do."

Arriving at the cemetery after visiting the liquor store and supermarket, we loaded up on all our favorite food and beverages. We followed each other in two vehicles, along with Phil, Eli, and Gus, who insisted on coming with us. We aren't entirely used to not having to watch our back because there is always a threat in this line of business. You learn to look over your shoulder and anticipate the unexpected, if that makes sense. Clear as mud, my father would say.

Last heard from Santi, he took his daughter to get some much-needed counseling to help her heal. He told us everything had been handled and not to worry.

After this weekend, we will be returning to Houston and to the lives we were living before this final act. What we are looking forward to the most is our future—being united and spending time with our family.

We unload the SUVs and bring out the table, chairs, and food. We get everything set up, and much like in our celebrations in Día de los Muertos, we have a brief reunion with our deceased relatives where they are forever laid to rest.

We all sit around drinking and getting to know one another. Emma and I told stories about growing up—our family traditions. We compared stories of being in Mexico with our uncle. We learned so much about our brother. What it was like growing up for him. It seems that he had a good life, and that after our grandparents weren't around to, our Uncle Andrés and tía gave him the love he needed growing up. They wanted him to learn the way of their world, so they sent him off to boarding school, which was more of a military-type training. He would be prepared to become one of my uncle's soldiers when he returned.

Our uncle told him about us and little did we know that he would have him be our protector as well. If he hadn't been there to save us all those years ago, we might not have fully recovered from that kind of mindfuck trauma that happens with abuse and assault.

As the day turns into evening, the shade of the live oak trees provides a large canopy with its branches overhead. Emma, Mateo, and I stand up from our seats and gather in front of our mother's grave. Emma and I place a kiss on our hands and put it on their father's headstone.

Eduardo stands and walks over to Emma, offering her his hand. I feel Jameson behind me. He doesn't come forward, unsure of his position at this moment, but I want him to understand he belongs with me as long as he'll have me. I lean into his strong, hard frame, as he wraps his arms around me. Eli, Gus, and Philip begin to pack up the items for us to take them to the vehicles, so that we can make it back to the condo before it gets too late.

I extend my hand out to my sister like we've done to each other our whole lives. I take out the silver ring she had made for me for a birthday present. I begin to talk to my mom and start our final goodbyes.

"This ring saved my life, Mom. I was supposed to have died in that fire the night you passed away. In a way, I feel that a part of me did. It wasn't until I met someone that I can finally let go and surrender myself to being loved. I need to fully feel all the emotions I have kept suppressed for so long. We were forged in fire and came out stronger on the other end after all."

I bend down and grab the little spade the guys left for me while they packed everything away. I dig a hole into the ground where their gravestone rests. Under their names, the inscription reads: *'Forever forged in our hearts.'*

I place the ring into the hole, and Emma covers it with dirt. It rests between the two headstones of my parents. We hold hands, smiling at each other, and back away.

Mateo steps forward and bends down to my mother's grave, touching her name. "Whatever your reasons were, Mom, I just want you to know that I forgive you. I know that in your heart, you believed you were doing the right thing. Maybe if circumstances were different, you would have returned to being my mother, but that time was taken from us. All I can do is move on and heal. I have to forgive you to move on. Thank you for giving me my life, and I promise to do something with it to make you and my family proud, but most of all, I am going to live and love every day I have on this earth." He places a kiss on the stone and stands.

I smile at him through tear-stained eyes, and I don't have to look at Emma to know that she is doing the same thing.

Eduardo clears his throat. "I'd like to say something if I could."

Emma tenses, and Eduardo gives her hand a squeeze, reassuring her that it will be okay, like he does frequently.

"I just want you to know, Mr. and Mrs. Taylor, that I love your daughter. I have always loved her, and I am going to marry her. I forgive you for keeping us apart, but I hope you find peace in knowing that I would give my life to keep her safe and give up my own for hers."

Emma reaches up to Eduardo and kisses him.

"Marry me, Emma."

Emma pulls back to look up at him. "We are already engaged, Eduardo." She giggles, not understanding his words, but I know what he means.

The look in his eyes says he is done waiting.

"Marry me *now,* Emma."

It's not a question, even though he poses it as one. She looks at him, her head tilted. Assessing.

"When?" she asks.

"As soon as possible," he answers just as quickly.

She beams a full smile at him. "Yes, I'll marry you whenever you'd like me to."

He picks her up in one fluid motion and twirls her around. He places her back on the ground, kissing her. "Did you hear that, guys? We're getting married."

PART III

THE FUTURE

EPILOGUE

"NOTHING ELSE MATTERS" BY METALLICA
"DANCE MACABRE" BY GHOST

THE WEDDING

We are gathered in the church for Emma and Eduardo's wedding. He meant it when he said he wanted to get married right away. His manager at his gym, Helena, helped Emma organize everything. They both had similar tastes in music, so it wasn't hard to get contacts who could meet the requests of what I can only describe as a goth wedding. Eduardo didn't care what wedding he had as long as he was married to the love of his life. It's been a long time coming, and I can't deny him the opportunity to marry her right now. One thing our past has taught us is that life is short. Make the best of it while you can because, even though they were given a second chance, we know that is rare.

I look out to the crowd gathered here, and I think we did well. The band is the same one Eduardo used to replace the original band the night we were going to be sold off at Mr. Martinez's party. I love their style, and they eagerly agreed to the handsome fee Emma's soon-to-be husband offered them for the day.

I look in the mirror at my deep blood-red dress. It's gorgeous, but not as gorgeous as my sister's. I can't wait to see Eduardo's reaction to her as she walks down the aisle. Her friends made the trip up from Corpus to be here, and some are bridesmaids. Eduardo has Jameson, our brother, Gus, Eli, and Philip as his selected groomsmen. They are all in tuxedos, much like on the night of the party. The jacket has silk embroidered roses, and Eduardo is wearing a ridiculous top hat.

"Oh God, is that black eyeliner?" Emma laughs behind me. She looks nervous.

"Are you ready?" I ask her, and she smiles. She looks over to Ainsley, Val, and Piper who are also wearing blood-red dresses.

Liv comes up to her. "Hey, babe. How are you holding up?"

She shrugs. "Nervous, but excited." There is a twinkle in her eye that always leads to mischief. "I wish I had a drink."

I bring the champagne bottle over and pour us each a glass.

"Ah, my wonderful sister." She sings my praises.

I raise my glass to hers. "To amazing second chances."

She pouts. "Don't make me cry, Eves. It's too much black eyeliner."

We take our drinks and down the champagne. Liv puts hers down without a drop being taken from the glass. Emma raises an eyebrow, and Liv shrugs.

Emma laughs, tossing her head back. "I knew it." Her hands go flying up in the air for emphasis. She throws herself at Liv. "Love you, bestie."

Liv hugs her back. "Love you, Em."

Helena comes through the door at us. "It's almost time. Are you guys ready?"

We all line up in anticipation of the procession starting. She takes the bridesmaids and groomsmen and lines them up. We are ready to start when Helena, the promoted wedding planner, gives us the okay. I hear the band begin, and the song "Nothing Else Matters" by Metallica begins to play. Fucking perfection.

I'm paired up with Jameson, and Liv is paired up with our brother. They go out first, and we follow. The rest of the party starts down the aisle as we take our places by the makeshift altar. Eduardo waits patiently, but the nervous energy is palpable. He is ready to have his bride.

She walks down the aisle, escorted by our Uncle Andrés. She is utter perfection. If there was ever a more beautiful bride, I would call them a liar. She is in a white lace dress that bells out with a black lace bodice. There are black embroidered flowers on the bottom part of the dress. She has a black choker with diamond hearts and earrings to match. Her bouquet of roses is a deep red to match the bridesmaid's dresses. And her red-soled shoes.

As she walks to Eduardo, she sees tears in his eyes. He swipes them away, not caring if anyone sees him.

I steal a glance at Jameson, and he stares at me. I bite my lip, and he licks his lip in response. I can't wait to get him alone after the wedding. I've done nothing but wedding planning.

Eduardo removes his hat as Emma stands beside him, and our uncle gives her a kiss on the cheek before walking away to take his designated seat.

The officiant begins the wedding, and there isn't a dry eye in the place. As the ceremony concludes, Eduardo doesn't need to be told twice to kiss his bride. There is a roar of applause and whistles as he kisses her in the most inappropriate fashion in front of all that are gathered to celebrate this joyous day.

We walk out of the venue and into the planetarium where the reception will take place. Jameson and I are hand in hand, following the guests.

The night sky is illuminated with a big moon in the background. There are more lights lit along the walls of the room to offer more than the provided twinkling of the stars. There are also lights on each table. The band is set up on the stage, with a large dance floor in the middle. The cake is off in the distance, and the ghoulish character bride and groom are on top.

The band announces the bride and groom to the crowd, and there are cheers and whoops as Emma and Eduardo take their place for the first song as husband and wife.

The band breaks into the song by Emma's favorite band Ghost, "Dance Macabre." Eduardo holds her hand and leads her to the dance floor. He pulls her into his embrace, swings her out, and brings her back to him. She walks around him in a circle as he tracks her with his eyes in a suggestive move. She touches his cheek and, as if in a trance, brings her into him again and kisses her as they dance in one another's arms in a solid embrace.

We return to the table and see Mateo is talking to his grandfather who is in a wheelchair and is giving off pissy vibes at being wheeled around. I am trying to listen in on their conversation, but soon a lady walks in, and Mateo freezes mid-sentence. Ramón looks over at the two with amusement. He wheels himself over to the table as they stand there staring at one another.

I hit Jameson's shoulder. "Hey, who's that?"

He looks in the direction I am pointing, where Mateo is trying to talk to a woman who is trying her best to avoid him, then leaves him there talking mid-sentence. He calls after her, but she continues to walk off as he follows her out of the planetarium.

"Hm. That's interesting." Jameson laughs. "Yeah, that's Ramón's nurse from the agency that has been helping him get around."

"Why do I get the feeling that there is more to that story, Jameson?" I lift an eyebrow up to him in question.

He chuckles, bringing my chair closer to him. "Well, because with you guys, there always is?"

I go to protest, but my words are silenced with a kiss.

"Jameson, did you just shut me up with a kiss?" I ask jokingly.

He stands and brings me to my feet with him. He looks around. "Actually, I'd like to shut you up with my cock."

I laugh, then stop, rethinking that. "Let's go."

We take off to find a place where we can be alone, when we see Mateo and Ramón's nurse sneaking into a room of their own.

I look over to Jameson. "I think they have the same idea."

We walk into a hall and see a door open that leads to a room with books lining the walls on astronomy. The fireplace is lit for ambiance, creating a soft glow throughout the spacious interior. I take it all in, feeling the warmth as Jameson comes over to stand in front of me.

I look up at him, feeling the intensity of his stare. "So now that you have me here, Jameson, what will you do with me?" I rest my hand on his white dress shirt. His hard muscles flex under my hand involuntarily.

"I'm just glad that everything is all over." He exhales in relief. He brings me closer to him, and I look into his eyes, which are so full of love and adoration.

"Oh, Jameson," I reply. I grab the back of his neck, pulling him to me. "We've been over this." His lips hover over mine. "I have a feeling that this is just the beginning."

I can feel the smile ghost over his lips. He pulls me to him again and kisses me. He pulls back slightly, looking into my eyes. "Our new beginning."

THE END

THANK YOU FOR READING!!!

Did you enjoy reading *Forged Hearts, The complete series?* If you did, I would be grateful if you could please consider taking a second to leave a review on one, or all of your choices below. Reviews help to make me a better writer, and I appreciate your words and constructive criticism!

Love you all,

L. Renee Richard

ABOUT THE AUTHOR

L. Renee Richard is a Hispanic author who lives in rural New England with her family. She's a born and raised South Texan girl who implements BIPOC characters into her books imbued with her cherished Hispanic culture. She is an avid reader, complete with her never-ending TBR, and a romantic at heart who appreciates a strong female main character and a good book boyfriend in the books she reads or writes. She loves summers in New England, sitting on the beach with a book, driving with the windows down through rural roads on cool autumn nights, and iced matcha lattes. Her books promise angsty romance where the journey to a happily ever after isn't always easy, but it's worth the trip.

KEEP IN TOUCH WITH L. RENEE RICHARD

Follow me on my socials

Author page:
www.authorlreneerichard.com

Amazon:
http://www.amazon.com/author/lreneerichard

Facebook page:
https://www.facebook.com/Author-L-Renee-Richard-105887815914160

Instagram:
https://instagram.com/l.renee.richard?igshid=OGQ5ZDc2ODk2ZA==

TikTok:
TikTok @l.renee.richard

Join my hype team:
https://forms.gle/9cnsA4gSfbezY7a17

Sign up for my newsletter:
https://mailchi.mp/authorlreneerichard/signup